THE *Heart* OF RUTHERFORD

LIFE LESSONS NOVELS 1 – 3

BY MELANIE A. SMITH

WICKED DREAMS PUBLISHING

TABLE OF CONTENTS

NEVER *Date* A DOCTOR

CHAPTER 1

"So what's it going to take, Sasha?" Becca asks pointedly before taking another sip of coffee.

I shoot her a pointed grimace. "I'm not asking for fucking Henry Cavill," I grouse. "Is it really too much to want a good, steady guy who treats me well but also makes my toes curl and my lady bits swoon when I see him?"

She arches an eyebrow and thinks about that as she continues to drink her coffee. Way too slowly for the small break we're allotted. I tap my fingers impatiently next to my empty coffee cup. Finally, she finishes and sets hers on the peeling laminate tabletop.

"Yes," she says flatly, rising to rinse her cup. "Because the type of guy who curls *your* toes is going to know he's hot shit. And that doesn't exactly translate to boyfriend material."

"Oh? And what exactly is my *type*?" I rise from my chair, setting my coffee mug back in its usual spot without rinsing it. Lord knows I'm going to be back in here for another cup soon anyway.

"'Henry Cavill' says it all, my dear," she replies airily as she heads back into the main office. "Tall, dark, handsome, blue eyes, rockin' bod. *Your type.* You set your standards too damn high and you're stuck in a no-dating rut."

I frown deeply as I approach the intake station and grab the chart slotted into my cubby. I'm not exactly in a position to argue, as she's not wrong. But having it pointed out so bluntly is beyond annoying. Just because I hold out for my "type" doesn't mean I'm hopelessly stuck.

"It's called having standards," I respond drily. "I can define that if it's unclear."

"So are you ever going to tell me *why* that's a type you can't seem to break away from?" she teases, totally ignoring my not-so-subtle dig as she settles in at the nurses' station. Her eyes suddenly widen. "Oh god, that's not what your dad looks like, is it?"

My eyes flick up from the chart in my hands.

"Becca, that's disgusting." I gesture to my dark blond hair. "Besides, where do you think I got this?"

She shrugs and grins mischievously. "Good. Because daddy issues are a whole other ballgame. So who was it? First boyfriend? First lay? Both?" Her eyebrows waggle suggestively.

This time I slam the folder closed. "Christ, Becks, keep your voice down." My eyes dart around, hoping nobody else heard her.

"Oh, this must be good, you little prude, you," she says, greedily rubbing her hands together.

"I'm not a *prude*," I protest. "I just don't talk about my sex life at work. Or jump into bed with every guy I date." I shoot her a meaningful, if not teasing, stare.

"Maybe you should give it a try sometime. It's every bit as fun as it sounds," she retorts with a wink. "Fine, have it your way. Go to your ten a.m., but we're having drinks after work, and I *am* getting this story."

"Have it your way," I reply mockingly, "just so long as you're buying."

"I think I will have it my way, thank you very much," she replies airily. But then her eyes go wide as she looks over my shoulder.

I turn to see the chief of our unit headed at us, a stern frown on his grey-bearded face. He's always in a shit mood, and I know I need to get in to see my patient before I become his next target.

"Dr. MacDougall is all you, Becks," I whisper with a sly grin before shooting into exam room seven. I just catch her annoyed glare as I close the door behind me.

* * *

"I swear. I love my job, but if one more old man tries to feel me up while I'm doing an echo, I'm going to respond with violence." I take a huge gulp of the martini in front of me, knowing even that won't wash away the memory of his wrinkled paw squeezing my ass.

Becca shoots me a sympathetic look from across the small table we're perched at. It barely fits our drinks, and the place is packed, but I guess I should've realized that, as it's a Friday night. I just don't pay much attention to the days of the week anymore, unless it's a school night. The hazards of working at a cardiac unit that's open seven days a week while going to school to graduate from nurse to nurse-practitioner. My days have two classifications: non-school days that are just long and difficult, and school days which are so grueling they could be considered a form of torture. Christ, I'm such a masochist.

"Been there," Becca agrees. "But honestly, I wouldn't have even minded. It's been way too long since I've had *any* action."

I laugh incredulously. "I find that hard to believe."

She shrugs. "Oh, believe it. Even I go through dry spells. And you know what they say about desperate times ..." She looks around at the crowds wistfully before her eyes wander back to mine. "If only there were anyone here worth going after. But we have other business to get to anyway. Now. About Henry Cavill."

"What about him? Did you want to go see a movie after this?" I dodge jokingly.

One of Becca's perfectly shaped eyebrows lifts. I throw up my hands in defeat.

"Fine. But you're going to make fun of me."

"*Moi*? I would never." The evil glint in her eye belies her innocent tone. "Seriously, though, out with it. I'm on a mission here to get us both laid."

"Getting laid isn't really an issue," I reply with a shrug. At five-and-a-half feet, with blond hair and curves in all the right places, attracting male attention has never been a problem. The opposite, in fact, especially working in the medical profession. Though frankly I think just being female is enough, since I know most of the other nurses and MAs at work have to deal with the same crap. You'd think it was still 1950, not 2020, the way some of these old bastards behave. And in a facility that deals exclusively with heart problems, we pretty much get mostly elderly patients.

"So out with it," Becca prompts. "Maybe we can cleanse you of your need for Superman."

I stick my tongue out at her, and she laughs.

"Fine," I reply with a sigh. "But if I tell you, you have to promise not to laugh."

Becca presses her lips together in amusement and gestures for me to continue, twirling her dark brown hair around a finger while her equally dark brown eyes survey me. We've worked together at the cardiac unit for too many years — she was already a medical assistant when I started there during nursing school — and have been friends just as long, so she knows me better than almost anybody. But this … this, I've never told *anyone.*

I down the rest of my drink. What the hell. Here goes.

"When I was fourteen, I went to my first airshow sans parents," I begin. Becca grins widely. I don't have to explain the significance of that to her; she grew up in San Diego too, attending the annual airshow just the same as I always have. Ogling the hot guys on offer, in uniform and out. Going on your own meant the chance to flirt unimpeded by parental units.

"So, your Henry was a hunky sailor, huh?" she teases.

I shrug. "I don't know," I reply honestly. "He wasn't in uniform. We didn't even speak. My friends were pulling me toward the hangar, and I looked up and there he was. He was with a group of guys heading the other direction."

I close my eyes, bringing up the mental picture that hasn't faded in detail, despite it being ten years ago.

"He was older than me, maybe late teens? But he had dark-brown hair and the most beautiful, clear blue eyes I'd ever seen. Seriously, when we locked eyes, I froze in place. I couldn't move. He was so gorgeous. So fucking perfect. But mostly …" I open my eyes to see Becca staring, enraptured.

"What?" she prompts impatiently.

I scrunch up my nose. In for a penny …

"I felt *it,*" I admit on a sigh. "A tug in my chest. Like the world dropped away, and it was just us. Like the universe went quiet so I could hear the pounding of my heart. Feel the connection between us like it was a living thing." I lean back, lamenting my empty glass. "And then my friends pulled me away and I lost him in the crowd."

Becca sits up straight, her face dropping.

"That's it? You saw some guy during fleet week ten years ago who got your hormones going and you're spoiled for anyone who doesn't have dark hair and blue eyes? Fuck, Sash, that's nuts."

"And that's me, done for the night," I reply, rising from my seat.

She reaches out and grabs my hand, pulling me back as I retreat. "I'm sorry," she replies. "Please, stay. I'll even buy you another drink."

A small smile finds its way onto my lips, and I sink back into the chair.

"You're forgiven. But I swear I'm not crazy. I don't think I date guys who look like that because of him. I think that's just what I find attractive. But what I can't seem to find is something that moves me the way looking into his eyes did." I pause, trying to figure out how to explain it. I look back up, and Becca is staring at me curiously. "It was like ... seeing a stranger, but knowing everything about him was just there, waiting for me to know. And everything in me *wanted* that, wanted to know him. Like it would be the answer to everything." I can tell by the look on her face that she totally doesn't get where I'm coming from, so I just stop, shaking my head.

"I can't say I understand," she replies slowly. "But that's cool. I mean, I get wanting to really feel something with someone. But I guess I didn't realize you were such a fucking romantic."

I laugh at Becca's talent for keeping things from getting too serious. "I'm really not. It was just a thing that happened. But it's always stuck in my head. Like that's the way it should be. That's how I should feel when I meet the right guy."

"So that's why you've only had a handful of relationships that never lasted longer than a few months the whole time I've known you?"

"I don't know. I guess I always chalked that up to focusing on school, and my career. And, I mean, I'm only twenty-four. But I guess, yeah, I've never really felt that again. I'm not stupid, though, Becks. It's not like I don't give guys a chance. Even if there's not that initial spark. I try to stick around, waiting for it. But it never comes."

"Wow," Becca mouths.

"Have you ever felt that way?" I ask, suddenly wondering if something is wrong with me.

"I've been attracted to guys. Wanted to jump their bones. Well, actually jumped their bones," she allows. "But I can't say I've ever had my *universe go quiet*."

"Fuck you, Becca. Fuck you." Becca, thankfully, is extremely difficult to offend, and she just laughs in response.

"You wish," she jokes with a wink. "You know I don't swing that way."

"Me neither. But wouldn't that just solve both of our problems," I tease back with my own wink.

CHAPTER 2

The next morning I fill my coffee mug to the brim and stifle a yawn as I head into our mandated morning staff tag-up. Becca joins me as I pass the nurses' station, cradling her own giant cup of java.

"Someday," she sighs, "I'll have a job where I don't have to be in at six a.m. on a Saturday. I wonder what MacDougall wants, anyway."

"There's a new doc on the block," a cheery voice comes from behind us.

We both look back to see my supervisor, Julianna Magnusson, approaching, looking every inch the morning person she is, all bright-eyed with a pep in her step. Well, supervisor, mentor, and friend. None of us would make it without Jules. She's been a nurse practitioner at Rutherford Hospital for ten years and was a nurse here for six before that. She knows more than just about anyone at the hospital how things run across units. Which also makes her privy to the best gossip.

"Yeah? Any dirt?" Becca asks gleefully as Jules joins us.

Jules sweeps her burgundy hair into a ponytail with a quiet smile. "Only that he's coming from Cedars-Sinai in L.A., where he also apparently did his cardiac surgery training." Becca gives her a disappointed look and Jules laughs. "Sorry, babes, I bumped into Dr. MacDougall and that was all he had time to tell me. We're all about to find out anyway."

Becca gives an indifferent shrug, clearly having wanted to know before everyone else, and Jules and I share a look as we enter the staff meeting room. We seem to be the last in, aside from Dr. MacDougall and our new addition. Becca sniffs the air suspiciously.

"Oh god, what is it?" I ask. In a hospital, you never know what an odd smell is going to lead to.

Becca takes another deep sniff and her eyes go wide. "Donuts!" And she's off, dragging me across the room to where, behind a cluster of MAs, there are, in fact, two huge boxes of donuts.

"Damn, Becks, you're a freaking bloodhound," I tease as she grabs the nearest donut and stuffs it in her face.

"Oh my god, they're still warm," she groans around a mouthful of pastry.

"You're a nutjob," I say with a laugh.

"Good morning, everybody," Dr. MacDougall's voice booms from behind me.

I spin in place at his clear call to order. As the room quiets, my eyes fall on our chief … and a man I've never seen before standing next to him. It takes my brain about two seconds when a loud gasp of recognition escapes me. Everyone turns to look, including him, and I blush deeply. Thankfully, Dr. MacDougall clears his throat, bringing the attention back to the front of the room. As he starts his usual greeting speech, Becca leans in.

"What was that all about?" she whispers.

I turn toward her so she can see the shock on my face, and my hand finds hers, gripping it tightly.

"It's *him*," I hiss. Becca gives me a confused look, and I roll my eyes. "*Universe Guy*."

Becca gives me a skeptical look, her eyes turning back to the front. Taking in what I did. All six-feet-two-ish inches of the dark-haired, blue-eyed, and unquestionably sexy hunk of a well-built man in blue scrubs and a white lab coat standing next to Dr. MacDougall as he rambles about our round stats for the week.

"Are you sure?" she whispers back. "Maybe you just *think* it's Universe Guy because we were just talking about him."

With a lump in my throat, I chance another look at him. Thankfully, his eyes are roaming the crowd as Dr. MacDougall gives his usual boring speech that is now shifting toward a lecture on proper chart notes. The young man I remember was clean-shaven, and though this guy has a well-trimmed beard that defines his sharp jaw, otherwise it's the exact face I remember, just a bit older. Same broad shoulders. Same trim waist. Though he's filled out in the chest and arms, and I can practically see the muscles straining against the fabric of his shirt. But I've got the same butterflies in my stomach.

"I don't know. I'm pretty sure it's him," I mumble. As if he heard me, his eyes land on me. And the sound of Dr. MacDougall droning on muffles under the pounding of my heart in my ears. My insides tighten. And, for the second time in my life, the universe goes quiet. A surge of emotion pounds through me, even stronger than the one ten years ago. I've never reacted to anyone this way, and it's equal parts terrifying and thrilling, and I can't stop staring back into his baby blues.

But when his eyes snap away suddenly, the volume comes rushing back. And I notice that my heart is pounding and I'm breathing like I just ran sprints. I take a deep breath to steady myself, hoping nobody noticed my ridiculous reaction to him.

"… and so, finally, I'd like to introduce the newest addition to our team, specializing in cardiac surgery, Dr. Thompson. Though he was heavily recruited out of his residency with Cedars-Sinai, he chose to stay there — until now. We are extremely lucky to have him, so please join me in welcoming him to our team."

A smattering of applause rings around the room, and I clap my hands together with them, but I'm completely numb with shock.

Dr. Thompson puts a hand up in greeting, and the room once again falls silent.

"Thank you, everyone," he says. And my jaw drops at the unmistakably posh British accent. "I'm Dr. Caleb Thompson. As you've probably noticed, I'm not originally from Los Angeles." A few in the crowd, mostly females, titter at his comment. "I graduated from Cambridge seven years ago now, then moved to the States for my residency. While I enjoyed my time at Cedars-Sinai, I'm already very impressed with Rutherford Hospital, and I'm pleased to be working with you all. I will be making my rounds to get to know each of you throughout the day. But first, may I ask, who are my surgical nurses?" Jules' hand goes up, as do several others. "Excellent. Good to put faces to the names on my sheet." He holds a clipboard aloft with a smile that gets another few titters from the peanut gallery. But my heart is in my shoes.

He moved here seven years ago. He can't be Universe Guy. My eyes scan his face as he continues to talk about how he plans to integrate into established routines, consultations, and the like, but all I can think about is how much he looks like The Guy. I even had the same reaction. And then some. By the time he's done and we've all been dismissed, I'm dumbly zoning out in my own bubble of confusion.

I feel a tug on my elbow as Becca tries to get my attention.

"Hey, I have to start processing patients. You okay?" I finally look up to see the look of pity on her face. She's clearly also realized he can't possibly be the same guy from my story.

"Sure, yeah," I mumble. "Sorry. I just could've sworn it was him."

Becca gives a light shrug. "Probably better that it isn't," she says gently. "After all, what's the first rule of Nurses' Club?"

That gets a smile out of me. "Never talk about Nurses' Club?" I tease.

She wrinkles her nose and jiggles her head. "That just gets funnier every time I hear it," she replies wryly, then gives me an expectant look.

"I know, I know," I reply with a sigh. "Never date a doctor."

It's been drilled into me so many times. Not because it's against policy; it's not. But the relationship between doctors and their support staff is already difficult at best, and lives are literally on the line every day. Even in my time here, I see the wisdom of not complicating that further. Not that it matters. Even if he was Universe Guy, what chance would I have with a guy like that?

"That's right, boo," Becca says. "Chin up." She shoots a look at Dr. Thompson, who is deep in conversation with Jules. "If it helps, there are still donuts left."

A little chuckle escapes me, and it snaps me back to reality. What am I even doing thinking about this guy? He's not who I thought he was. He's now a doctor in our unit. Even if he was interested, it's *not* going to happen. And while I hadn't been planning on having one, I decide a donut sounds pretty damn good.

"It does help," I reply with a grateful smile. "Thanks, Becks. See you in a bit."

She gives me a wink and slips out the door. I grab the last glazed donut and follow suit, not even looking at Dr. Hottie on my way out. It's better that way, because I have a feeling being too close to him wouldn't go well for me.

But Jules apparently has other ideas.

"Sasha," she calls as I step over the threshold, "come meet Dr. Thompson."

I turn slowly on the spot to find Jules staring at me expectantly. Dr. Thompson is looking at me, a half-smile on his face as he studies me curiously. His eyes sweeping casually over me sends chills down my spine.

"Of course," I reply, clearing my throat and switching the donut to my left hand so I can extend my right as I step toward them. "It's a pleasure to meet you, Dr. Thompson."

His large, warm hand slips into mine, and my insides do their little clenching thing again. He may not be who I thought he was, but, as Becca teased me about on Friday, I have a type. And he's definitely it. I swallow hard and try not to let the nervous tension I feel affect my smile as I look up into his eyes. It doesn't work, and I push back against the well of want that is bubbling up inside of me.

"Sasha … Suvorin?" he guesses.

I clear my throat, willing back my body's reaction. "You're a quick study," I reply.

His answering laugh is warm and rich, and does nothing to help me forget how attractive he is. "I am a doctor. We pretty much just memorize things for a living." I'd like to respond, but for a moment all I can think is, *Damn, that accent is sexy as hell*. His hand lingers in mine for a little longer than is strictly necessary. Jules looks between us both, and I withdraw my hand self-consciously.

"I have some experience with that. I'm working toward my master's in nursing, and it's pretty much the same," I finally reply, finding myself again.

His eyebrows jump and a slow smile spreads across his lips. I can't help but stare, noting his bottom lip is fuller than the top. I watch him tuck it into his mouth, the hair under the center of his lip moving with it. It's undeniably sexy.

"Ah, yes, getting your MSN? That's lovely," he replies. And the way he says "lovely," I know I'm going to be repeating it to myself in his accent for the rest of the morning. "So I don't detect a Russian accent, despite the surname …"

I smile tolerantly. I get that a lot. To the extent of actual strangers full on speaking to me in Russian like I should understand. "My grandparents came here many years ago, and my parents preferred we speak English at home so I didn't have any trouble at school. I'm afraid I know about as much Russian as Jules here."

Jules smiles at me right as Dr. Franklin, one of our cardiologists, pops into the room. "Cal, my first consult is here. Join me?"

Dr. Thompson — or Cal, apparently — gives him a sharp nod.

"I expect I'll be seeing you both around," he says to Jules and me.

"Of course," Jules pipes chirpily.

"Yes, nice meeting you," I reply softly, but he's already headed out the door. Thank god. I finally relax, the weird pull he has on my hormones now absent.

Jules fans herself dramatically. "Is it hot in here or was it just him?" she gushes. "Whew! And he seems so *nice*. Definitely trouble with a capital T, that one."

My gut twinges unpleasantly, and I turn to toss the donut in the garbage, having completely lost my appetite.

"He seems okay," I say with a shrug.

Jules smirks at me knowingly. "Oh please, if eye contact was a sex act, you two would've just gotten to third base."

"He's too old for me," I protest. Or at least, I assume he is.

Jules snorts as she heads out the door, so I follow along. "He's about my age," she scoffs. "And I'm only ten years older than you. That's no biggie."

"Except he's a doctor, and —"

"Yeah, yeah, yeah, never date a doctor. I practically invented that rule, Sasha. And do you know why?"

I look up at her, since she's a good four inches taller than me, not sure if this is a trap. "Why?"

"Because I've dated enough doctors to know better."

"Precisely," I respond. "So it doesn't matter how old he is. It's not like either of us is going to date him."

Jules cackles. "No, Sasha, *I've* dated enough doctors to know better. That's part of the fun of having rules: breaking them to find out why they're rules in the first place."

I shoot her a concerned look as we approach the supply closet. "I'm not sure how I feel about someone responsible for so many people's lives on a daily basis having that kind of attitude," I tease. Well, mostly tease. Jules is usually one of the most cautious people I know, so I find this reversal oddly confusing.

She waves a hand at me as we start prepping our supplies for the day.

"You know I would never endanger a patient. I'm not talking about that. I'm talking about you," she replies seriously, maintaining firm but kind eye contact as she mechanically sorts syringes. "You're so serious, so focused. If someone catches your eye, don't write them off because of a rule that's not even really a rule. You never know. That's all I'm saying."

I raise an eyebrow. "I happen to like focusing on things that really matter," I reply archly. "Ever since I started volunteering at this hospital as a teenager, I've always known this is what I wanted to do. I like focusing on it." And not getting distracted by ridiculously hot doctors.

"I know, Sash," she says, handing me a stack of dressing gowns. "Just don't be so focused that you miss out on other opportunities that are part of the human experience." She winks at me, and I find myself a little aggravated. I may not be the most social person, but I've dated. I've gotten out. I mean, not exactly frequently these days, but she's talking like I'm eschewing men and I need to drop everything to go after this one because we made some flirty eye contact. She doesn't need to know about the other stuff, it would just encourage her.

So instead of arguing, I just shake my head and wheel the stocked cart away, intent on focusing on what I always focus on: my job.

It's not long before Becca catches up with me, as I'm cleaning instruments in the sterilization area.

"Hey, Dr. C is looking for you," she tells me.

I raise an eyebrow. Dr. Carson is my least favorite cardiologist on the unit. He's *extremely* particular about how his exam rooms are set up and shoves most of his work off on the nurses regularly. Not that that's terribly unusual, it's just extra annoying because of his attitude.

"Gee, well, I'll just jump right over then," I reply sarcastically, wrapping the scalpel in my hand in muslin before setting it in the sterilization tray. "You know. In a little while."

Becca leans back against the counter with a chuckle. "I thought you might say that." She taps a long fingernail on her arm thoughtfully. "So, Dr. Thompson might not be your Universe Guy, but he's still pretty cute, right?"

I roll my eyes. "If you and Jules think he's such hot stuff, you guys should go after him."

"Jules thinks he's hot?"

"What female in that room didn't?" I reply with a shrug. "He was hot even before he opened his mouth."

Becca sighs dreamily. "Yeah, that accent is pretty amazing." She shudders dramatically.

I wrap the last instrument and settle it in the tray, then slide the tray into the autoclave and switch it on. We both step back to let it do its thing.

"Look. I get it. He's my type. He's hot. He's British. But he's also a doctor, a coworker, and too old for me. I appreciate that you guys want me to find a guy, but I promise that I'm *happy* being single."

Becca looks past me, agape. On instinct, I turn around. And Dr. Caleb Thompson is standing in the doorway with a look on his face that says he heard everything. I internalize a heavy sigh. Yep. That's about right. That's pretty much how things go for me when it comes to men I might potentially be interested in.

"Is there something I can help you with, Dr. Thompson?" I ask as evenly as I can, but inside I'm dying. Becca skitters out of the room, just squeezing by him. The fucking traitor.

"I'm sorry, I — I didn't mean to interrupt anything, I'll just … I can come back later …" He's clearly horribly embarrassed, as he's stumbling over every other word.

Despite my best efforts, I feel the heat creep up my cheeks. "No, I'm sorry. We shouldn't have been —"

"It's okay, I really should … I can come back later." He turns, but I stop him with a hand on his arm.

"Please, can we just pretend like that never happened?" I shift nervously from foot to foot as his gaze meets mine. His clear blue eyes search mine for a moment, and my stomach flip-flops.

"I'm sorry, pretend what never happened?" he replies with a small smile.

Some of the tension in my shoulders lift at his obvious out.

"You needed something?" I prompt, but still pretty much just wanting this to be over with so I can go crawl in a hole and die.

"Yes, of course," he replies, finding himself again. "I wanted to acquaint myself with the supplies, since I needed a few things anyway. I have a catheter angiography this afternoon."

"Well, I'm happy to show you where everything is, but one of us will take care of all of that for you," I assure him.

"I'm perfectly happy to, especially at first. It'll be good for me to get to know where things are and how everything works, just in case."

Ugh. Seriously? As if his mere presence doesn't reduce me to an idiotic mess, he's also willing to do menial work that most doctors, especially surgeons, see as a waste of their time. They almost always expect the nurses to take care of everything that doesn't strictly require an M.D. I mean, I get it, there are more nurses per patient than doctors, but still. He couldn't just be smart and gorgeous, he had to be considerate too. And against my better judgment, I want to know more about him.

"In that case, I'll give you the grand tour," I reply. I can only hope focusing on explaining everything will help me stay coherent this close to him. So I proceed to show him everything in the room, including a brief description of the sterilization process we use, before suggesting we go to the standard supply closet.

"Yes, excellent, let's," he replies, tapping a finger to the side of his jaw. "But just one quick thing."

I pause, looking up at him expectantly. "Yes?"

"For the record … I'm only thirty-two," he says, as a blush creeps up his neck.

I suck my lips into my mouth to stop myself from smiling, and my stomach does another little flip-flop. Breathe, Sasha, just breathe. He ducks his head self-consciously.

"Duly noted, Dr. Thompson," I reply, looking away to hide my blush.

He looks up sheepishly. "After you, then, Nurse Suvorin," he replies with a stern tone and a mock-serious expression to match.

I'm usually a hard nut to crack, but that does it, and I can't help laughing. I gesture for him to follow as I continue his tour.

Not long after, we part ways, as he's off to another consultation, this time with Dr. MacDougall. And Becca is waiting at the nurses' station, obviously bursting to know what happened.

"You're dead, Dillon," I say. "How could you leave me like that?"

She pushes up on the balls of her feet and wrings her hands together. "I know, I'm sorry. I panicked. But it looks like you did just fine." She gives me a pleading look, inviting me to spill every detail.

"Only because he's such a gentleman," I insist. "But I'm still humiliated. God, I can't believe he *heard* that." I swipe a hand over my eyes, not wanting to go full meltdown in case he happens by again. "We need to seriously can it with the personal talk at work."

"Aw, man. Does that mean you're not going to tell me more?" Becca pouts.

"Later," I insist, watching as one of my least favorite medical assistants, Lacey Petersen, heads towards us. Becca catches sight of her and nods understandingly.

"Gotcha. Drinks after work?"

"Dinner. You can drink if you want, but I'm going to need to eat. I've got a packed schedule this afternoon and I have to study later."

"Fine, fine," she agrees. She waits a moment for Lacey to drop off some paperwork and walk away. "But come on, just give me *one* detail before you go."

I'm not normally one for gossip. But remembering the sparkle in his eyes when he was looking down at me in the sterilization room has me hard-pressed to keep from smiling. I inhale and close my eyes, letting myself sink into that moment. Allowing myself just a bit of hope before I squirrel it all away inside, never again to see the light of day.

"He wanted me to know, for the record, that he's thirty-two."

Becca squeals as quietly as she can manage. "He likes you," she whispers gleefully.

"I think he was just trying to make me feel better. You wanted a detail, now you've got one. Don't make a thing of it." I shoot her a firm look before returning to my rounds. But as soon as my back is turned, the façade melts, and I allow myself my own gleeful grin. Though I almost immediately chastise myself for it. *No, Sasha. Strictly off limits.* And I keep repeating it in my head every time my thoughts drift where they shouldn't that afternoon. Eventually I lose track of how many times.

CHAPTER 3

Between my remaining shifts that week, class on Tuesday and Thursday nights, and studying, by the end of the week I'm beyond exhausted and thankful that I have Friday and Saturday off to recuperate and catch up with homework.

It doesn't stop Becca from texting to make sure I'll be joining them all for happy hour after work on Friday. I ask her who "them all" is and she's strangely evasive. And I kind of suspect she's going to try to get me to go after Dr. Thompson again. So while I'd normally avoid hanging out with more than Becca and Jules, as crowds aren't my thing, the idea that Dr. Thompson might be there worms its way in, and I agree to show.

We crossed paths a few more times this week, though only fleetingly, but the heavy eye contact Jules pointed out at our first meeting continued in spades. And at some point I stopped being humiliated about what he'd overheard and started wondering if maybe he was embarrassed because he might be interested.

And I can't get the thought out of my head. Even though I know better. Even though I really don't have time to date right now. Even though I'm pretty sure every other single female medical assistant, nurse, and nurse-practitioner on the unit will probably be there, vying for his attention. So maybe I just get to know him. And hope like hell that I find out something that's a total turnoff.

I purposely don't even dress to impress, swapping out my loungewear for skinny jeans, a red, long-sleeved V-neck tee, and my favorite pair of black low-top Chuck's. I leave my shoulder-length blond hair to fall in its naturally straight way and, as usual, don't bother with makeup. I touch my face a lot and have learned the hard way that habit doesn't work well with anything but maybe a basic lip balm.

It takes me only fifteen minutes to get to the bar, which is unusual for six o'clock on a Friday. So when I show, not that many people have arrived yet.

I find Becca and Jules at a large booth with Lacey and two of the other MAs, Harper and Avery. As I suspected, the female contingent is already strong.

"Hey, babe," Becca greets me, scooting over to make room. Jules shoots me a smile from Becca's other side as I take a seat. Lacey merely gives me side-eye, while Harper and Avery each wave hello.

I wave back. "Hey, guys," I greet them as I slide in next to Becca.

The waiter comes over with another round of drinks and I order a diet soda. I'm definitely not looking to make an ass of myself tonight, so best to stay away from alcohol.

We all make small talk about the gossip of the week. It's not my favorite thing, but it's hospital standard, as it's a good diversion from the stress of the job. Or that's the usual defense for it, anyway. We're soon joined by Zoe and Ethan, two of the other nurses in our unit. I can see the distress on poor Ethan's face as he goes from looking like the cock ruling the hen house to overwhelmed by the estrogen in two minutes flat. You'd think he'd be used to it by now. I simply sit quietly, listening to the banter bouncing around the table and watching him look increasingly bored. So when I see him look past me, his face lighting up, I know what that must mean.

"Ladies, and Ethan, is there room for two more?"

I freeze in place at the unmistakable accent and turn to see Dr. Thompson and Dr. Franklin stopping at our table. Dr. Thompson's eyes meet mine for a second, and I nervously look away.

"Sure, we'll just need to pull up a chair on that side," Jules offers.

The nerves work at my stomach, and I feel a sudden need to flee. Thankfully, Zoe and Ethan had settled on the other side of the booth, so I'm able to step out quickly.

"I need to use the restroom," I mumble. "Be right back."

Becca shoots me a look that I ignore as I bolt down the hallway to the bathrooms. Once I'm done, I stand at the sink, splashing some cold water on my face. Even so, I can still feel the heat in my cheeks. *This is ridiculous, woman up, Sasha*, I think to myself. It's just a bunch of coworkers having drinks. So what if he's attractive? So what if just looking at him makes me want to melt into a puddle of goo? I'm not this easily shaken. I take a deep breath, look myself in the eye in the mirror, and gather my wits.

When I return to the table, Becca and Jules are still on one side, and Harper, Avery, and Lacey are at the back. And on the other side are Dr. Thompson, Zoe, and Ethan, with Dr. Thompson somehow seated at the back of his side next to Lacey. Dr. Franklin sits at a chair on the exposed side of the table, having left the seat I'd vacated open for me.

I slide back in, trying to suppress a frown as I watch Lacey already flirting with Dr. Thompson. She's flipping her dark hair over her shoulder when she lays a hand on his arm with a laugh as the waiter returns. And this time I opt for alcohol to take the edge off, swearing to myself that I won't go overboard.

I end up talking mostly to Dr. Franklin, who's actually a really nice guy. In his forties, with a wife and two adorable little girls, he tells me funny stories about them and also asks me how things are going with work and school. I do my best not to pay attention to the conversation happening in the opposite corner of the booth, but I'm not sure how successful I am. This evening is definitely not turning out how I thought it would.

As the place gets busier, and after both Dr. Franklin and Zoe head out to get home to their families, I realize it has been a while since the waiter has been around, and I'm impatient for another drink.

"I'm going to the bar, anyone need anything?" I ask. Becca, Ethan, and Dr. Thompson each ask for another beer, and I don't miss that Dr. Thompson barely stops talking to Lacey long enough to do so. I manage to contain my reaction until I step away, but once I do I let loose a huge eye roll. The wait at the bar is a welcome reprieve from forced socialization and watching Lacey sink her claws into the new man meat. I try not to let jealousy bubble up in me. He's not mine, what is there to be jealous of? When I'm finally able to place the order for the three beers and a mixer for me, I sink against the counter, deflated.

For about two seconds when I *feel* it. Dr. Thompson slides up next to me, leaning with his back against the counter.

"Thought you might need a hand," he offers, looking down at me with a smile. My insides flutter, but now it's tainted with the recent memory of him flirting with someone else.

So I give him a tight-lipped smile in return. "Thank you, but I've got it. Feel free to go back to your conversation."

He does the thing where he rolls his bottom lip into his mouth again, and I have to look away. Why does he have to be so sexy?

"To be completely honest," he says, turning around to face me, "I was glad to have an excuse to break away. Ms. Petersen seems pleasant enough, but I'd actually hoped I'd get to talk to you a bit more."

I look up at him skeptically. Lacey is gorgeous. Stick thin, with big boobs. Though to be fair, I suspect they might be fake. In any case, with her overdone makeup, tight clothes, and clear willingness to give it up, she's every man's fantasy.

He gives me a sly smile in response to my expression. "You don't like her," he teases.

I shrug, unwilling to outright admit it, and he laughs.

"That's okay, you don't have to own to it. The prettiest girls always dislike each other," he says matter-of-factly.

I feel my cheeks heat, both flattered that he thinks I'm pretty but irritated that he obviously thinks Lacey is too. Even though I know she is. God, this guy messes with my head.

Finally, the damn bartender hands over the drinks, and Dr. Thompson grabs all three beers, leaving me with only mine.

"Becca and Julianna are beautiful, and they're two of my best friends," I finally reply.

"Yes, they are," he agrees as we pick our way around the tables to get back to the booth. "But they don't hold a candle to you." He gives me a wink just as we arrive back at the table, then starts handing out the beers. He slides back into the booth next to Ethan, who happily scoots toward Lacey. Dr. Thompson pats the seat next to him. It only takes one look at Becca to see the glee on her face at his gesture. Obviously, she won't mind if I move seats.

Lacey, however, doesn't even try to hide how annoyed she is as I sit next to Dr. Thompson, and she immediately goes about totally ignoring Ethan in favor of Avery. The gesture really irritates me, because Ethan is an absolute sweetheart.

"Hey, Ethan," I say, leaning forward. "How'd that performance review go?" He'd been on vacation during our beginning-of-the-year performance evaluations, and I know he was nervous that he'd pissed MacDougall off. Er, more than usual. The man's honestly a ticking time bomb waiting for any one of us to displease him.

Dr. Thompson leans back into the booth, allowing Ethan to look over at me in relief. "Actually great, thanks for asking. I thought I was toast after misplacing that blood sample last month."

I wave a hand dismissively. "It happens to everyone. And MacDougall was just in an especially bad mood. But I'm glad it didn't affect your review."

Ethan huffs a laugh. "Yeah, me too. Not that it's going to mean I get a raise or anything."

Dr. Thompson arches an eyebrow. "Nurses don't get pay increases?" he asks sharply.

I shrug. "Not this year. Budget issues." I purse my lips together, keeping back a snarky response about them still being able to hire a new doctor. But it's not his fault, and I obviously don't need to point it out anyway, as he clearly looks troubled.

Jules looks over, having caught that part of our conversation, and shakes her head. "Please don't get me started," she grumbles. Jules rarely complains, and I know how she hates discussing hospital politics, so I immediately try to switch the topic.

"So how was your first week, Dr. Thompson?" I ask. Jules goes back to her conversation with Harper and Becca, and Avery chooses that moment to rope Ethan into her conversation with Lacey.

"All around, it went well," he replies, turning toward me. "I think I might actually start being useful soon, as I've learned quite a lot." He leans in and lowers his voice. "But please, call me Cal."

My heart skips a beat as I look up into his eyes.

"Are you always so informal with the nursing staff?" I tease slyly.

His lips curl at the corners in a half-smile. "Never, actually," he admits quietly.

"I find that hard to believe," I murmur. Though I recall he did refer to Lacey earlier as "Ms. Petersen."

"I guess you'll just have to get to know me, then." His gaze holds a challenge. One I can't decide if I should accept or not.

"Of course. I make it a point to be on good terms with all of the doctors in our unit." I give him back a look that says, *I can do this dance all night, buddy.* Even though I can't. And if I was forced to, I can't honestly say I wouldn't give in to his advances. Damn this man.

His mouth pulls into a full-on smile at that. "Even the ones who are your type?"

I wrinkle my nose, annoyed that he knows that. "That's not pretending like you never heard that," I point out, trying to keep from blushing. "But yes, even the ones who are my type. As you clearly also do with nurses." I nod toward Lacey, who is obviously watching us out of the corner of her eye.

"Mmm, except she's not my type," he replies in a low voice, without even turning toward her. His implication is obvious, and a part of me does a little happy dance. But the professional in me squirms.

"Probably for the best. Dating coworkers is messy, at best."

"Ah, but not against the rules." His eyes dance with mischief. "I checked."

"I doubt that was the wisest use of your time in your first week on the job."

He laughs and shakes his head. "You're a tough one, Ms. Suvorin."

With a satisfied smirk, I lean in and lower my voice. "Please, call me Sasha."

He laughs quietly. "That's ace," he says, leaning back into the booth once more. But the expression on his face is puzzled. I'm happy not to be easy prey for him. I'm still very much of two minds where he's concerned, so it's best if I keep him guessing. For now, at least. "I do have one question, though."

"What's that?"

"Have we met before?"

My eyes go wide and my heart pounds in my chest. "Why do you ask?" I counter, dodging his question. Could he actually be who I thought he was?

"Your reaction when you saw me in the conference room suggested recognition," he explains, and I deflate.

"You don't miss a trick," I admit. "Yes, I did think I knew you. But once you started talking I realized that you weren't who I'd thought you were."

He takes a sip of beer, thinking that over. "Who did you think I was?"

I take a drink of my own cocktail, deciding how to answer him. "Nobody important," I finally reply.

From across the table, I hear Becca scoff. I look up and quickly gather that she'd been listening to our whole conversation. She goes pink when she realizes she's been caught, a rarity as it takes a whole hell of a lot to embarrass her.

"I think your friend disagrees," Dr. Thompson says with an amused look.

"I just … choked on my beer," Becca squeaks unconvincingly.

"I think that's my cue to leave," I grumble, attempting to slide out of the booth. But Dr. Thompson catches me by the hand.

"So soon? You haven't even finished your drink," he says.

I look over to find Becca and Jules staring at me in a silent plea to stay. Between the three of them, I'm hard pressed to just bail. And with his hand on mine, his strong fingers sending warm sparks over my skin, it'd take a Herculean effort to resist.

"Fine," I allow, settling back in the booth. "I guess I can finish my drink. So long as we change the subject."

Dr. Thompson gives my hand a final squeeze before letting go. "Fair enough," he agrees.

This time I draw Becca and Jules into the conversation to keep it from going anywhere heavy or flirty. But for the rest of the evening, I can feel the warmth emanating from him as he sits mere inches away. I'm also wrapped in his scent, a mixture of soap and what I can only describe as "hospital." It's oddly appealing. And the thought of accidentally grazing hands again keeps me on edge until we all head home.

It's not until I've climbed in bed that I admit to myself I enjoyed the feeling.

CHAPTER 4

I spend the better part of the following week alternating between avoiding Dr. Thompson and hoping to see him. My indecisiveness is starting to wear on me, and I wish I could just forget about him already. But that's difficult to do when I don't know what exam room he'll pop out of or what corner he'll come around at any given moment. Though I'm definitely leaning toward forgetting. I mean, what kind of man is he to take a job and immediately start hitting on his coworkers?

At least, that's what I keep trying to convince myself. But it gets harder and harder as I see him around, interacting with people, even Lacey, and being nothing but professional. While simultaneously rocketing my hormones to high alert every time I see him. Unfortunately, the whole thing has me more distracted than I'd like, and I keep having to recapture screens on the echo I'm performing because of it. My patient is getting understandably twitchy too, and that doesn't bode well. This particular gentleman has made inappropriate comments in the past, so I'm loathe to take longer than necessary in case he gets any other ideas. I shake myself and refocus.

"How's it looking, sweetheart?" Mr. Bowen asks, craning to look at the screen just behind his line of vision.

I put my hand to his shoulder. "Just try to stay still, and I'll be done as soon as I can."

"Why don't you put that hand a little lower, darlin', and I promise *I'll* be done soon," he says with a leering grin.

Repulsed, I immediately remove the transducer I have pressed against his chest and set it down, stepping away.

"You need to refrain from inappropriate comments if I'm going to continue," I tell him sternly.

"Ah, come on, I was just joking," he replies with a frown. I raise an eyebrow expectantly. "All right, all right. I promise I won't say anything else." He gives me another smile that's no less creepy.

Reluctantly, I pick the transducer back up and move it to his ribs to take translateral images, which means I don't have to hover over him. At least, for a minute. But as soon as I go back to chest images, I feel a hand squeeze my backside — hard.

"Mr. Bowen," I snap, jumping back, my chest constricting at the unwanted contact.

He cackles. "What? I didn't say anything this time," he responds.

I set the wand back down and lock the computer.

"Please stay here. I'm going to get someone else to come finish your echocardiogram," I reply tightly. I leave as calmly as I can. But as soon as I close the door behind me, tears of anger flow down my cheeks. I round the corner to the nurses' station.

This time Lacey is manning it and she gives me a harsh look up and down as I wipe the moisture from my cheeks.

"Where is Julianna?" I ask shortly.

Lacey crosses her arms over her chest. "She's with a patient."

I sigh deeply. "Do we have a male nurse available to finish an echo?"

She shakes her head. "There's only one on duty at the moment, Mark, and he just started a stress test."

"Okay, please tell Julianna I need to speak with her as soon as you see her. And I need a man capable of performing an echo ASAP."

"You should probably just finish it yourself," she replies unkindly. "Whatever happened couldn't have been that bad."

I'm about to give her a piece of my mind when Dr. Thompson comes out of an exam room down the hall. I'm actually glad to see him, grateful for the buffer between me and the dumb bitch behind the counter who seems to think a patient sexually harassing me is no big deal.

"Please just have Mark deal with the patient in room twelve when he's done, okay? I don't care how long he has to wait," I insist, turning away from Dr. Thompson and trying to discreetly finish wiping my eyes.

"Mark has another patient right after that," she argues. "It'll throw off our whole afternoon."

"I'm free for a moment. What do you need?" Dr. Thompson asks as he gets to the counter. He hands Lacey the patient file in his hands.

I sniff and turn, but when he sees my face, his expression darkens.

"Ms. Petersen, is exam four still available?" he asks in a clipped tone.

"Yes, doctor." She looks nervously between us.

Dr. Thompson gestures for me to follow him into the room just down the hall from the nurses' station and closes the door behind me.

"Tell me what happened," he instructs tersely, fists clenched at his sides as he leans against the counter. His tension is palpable in the ticking of his jaw and the firmness with which he crosses his arms over his muscled chest.

Avoiding his gaze, I relay exactly what went down, word for word, with as little embellishment and emotion as possible. I leave out Lacey's borderline insubordination. I'm not the kind of person to throw someone else under the bus, even if she is. But when I finish, another wave of anger washes over me, and I start to cry again. Not for the first time, I hate that this is how I respond when I'm angry, and I furiously wipe at my eyes.

"I'm sorry," I tell him. "I'm just mad. He's made comments before, but he's never groped me. I'm just sick of these old men thinking they can get away with this shit." I look up at the ceiling and take a deep breath before I look back at him.

"Did you report his previous comments?" His voice is sterner than I've heard it yet, and I wonder if he's going to reprimand me for stopping the appointment like any of the other doctors would. But what I've seen of him so far gives me hope, so I decide to be honest.

I shake my head. "No. It's a daily occurrence around here. I've reported before, but nothing ever comes of it, so I just stopped."

He shakes his head angrily. "But you've been touched inappropriately before?"

I nod and he scrubs a hand over his beard, clearly agitated.

"How often?"

I shake my head again, not trusting myself to speak, or upset him further.

"Daily?" he presses.

I sniff and look at the wall. "Not that often. Once or twice a week, maybe."

I glance back at Dr. Thompson and he's staring down at the floor, the muscle in his jaw now ticking furiously.

"I'll take care of Mr. Bowen," he says lowly, with a chilling note of authority in his voice. "Please go document this — everything you've told me — and send it to Ms. Magnusson, myself, and Dr. MacDougall. Understood?"

My eyes widen at the instruction, and my stomach drops. This wasn't what I wanted. There's a reason we don't report these things more. Unless it's undisputable, which it almost never is, it nearly always blows up in the victim's face, whether that's management's intention or not.

"Hey," he says, softening his tone and taking a tentative step toward me to take my hand. "I promise, it'll be all right. I'm going to take care of this. But I need you to trust me and do as I ask, okay?"

The reassurance of his grip calms me considerably, and I have to fight the urge to wallow in that for too long. "Okay," I whisper.

"Take a minute to collect yourself. I'll come see you when I'm done."

"He's in room twelve," I offer.

Dr. Thompson nods and quickly leaves. I take a moment to do exactly as he suggested by washing my hands, splashing some water on my face, and having a quick drink. When I head back to the nurses' station, I'm considerably calmer as I take a seat at one of the computers to write down everything that happened. Lacey thankfully keeps her big fat fucking mouth shut while I work.

After I'm done, I start catching up on paperwork. About twenty minutes after he'd left me, I see Dr. Thompson heading back to the nurses' station with another chart in hand, and Mr. Bowen in tow, looking none too comfortable.

"Nurse Suvorin," Dr. Thompson says as they approach, handing me the chart. "Mr. Bowen has something he'd like to say."

Mr. Bowen dips his head down onto his double chin, looking like a child that's just been scolded.

"I'm sorry for my inappropriate comments and behavior. It will not happen again," he says robotically.

I dig deep to suppress a snort of disbelief, opting instead to tersely say, "I accept your apology."

Mr. Bowen looks up at Dr. Thompson, who nods. And I've never seen anyone scurry off the ward so fast.

"Wanker," Dr. Thompson mutters at Mr. Bowen's retreating back.

I can't help sharing an incredulous look with Lacey before we both burst into laughter. But as the laughter dies down, fear grips me at what I may have just started. Dr. Thompson must see it on my face.

"You should both know that I'm not accustomed to tolerating inappropriate behavior by patients toward any of the hospital staff. I'm going to see that this sort of thing is handled properly, and that you are all supported in putting a stop to anything before it can escalate." He pauses and looks at Lacey. "That's a bit of gossip I encourage you to spread around." He gives us both a calm wink before he heads down the hall, presumably back to his office.

Lacey half-stands to lean over the counter and watch him walk away.

"And he has a nice ass too," she mumbles as she sits back down. "There's got to be *something* wrong with him."

I smile vaguely as I return to my paperwork. She has no idea how much I wish I knew what that was. Because right now he's a little *too* appealing on just about every level. As I get back to my work, it occurs to me briefly that Becca is going to be crushed that she missed this. And that, at least, gets a little smile out of me.

* * *

When the shit hits the fan, it really hits the fan. By the next day, management is interviewing every single staff member about patient sexual harassment, with a hospital-wide memo clarifying their zero-tolerance policy and reporting process.

Becca was, as I predicted, ticked that she didn't get to see Dr. Thompson in action, but as we sit the next afternoon catching up on yet more paperwork, I give her the blow-by-blow quietly whenever we're alone at the desk.

"God, could he be any dreamier?" she sighs. "And you're sure you don't want this guy?"

I shoot her a glare. "Why? Thinking about going after him yourself?"

"Guilty," she replies with a grin. "But I don't care what you say. I know you're into him, so I'd never actually do it. Besides, I just heard there's a hot new orderly over in intensive care."

"Of course you did," I reply drily. "And you're right. I'm into him. Even though I really don't want to be." I'm surprised at how good it feels to actually admit it.

"Acceptance is the first step to hot, kinky sex, my dear," she teases.

I scrunch my nose up at her. "What makes you think it would be kinky?" I almost can't believe I'm asking her that question.

She drops her head and gives me a look. "Oh, girl, please, that body of his was made for something special," she says. "I'll bet you fifty bucks right now he's a beast in bed."

I shake my head and laugh. "No bet. It's not going there. I like him. I confess. But that doesn't mean I'm going to do anything about it. And we're going to stop talking about hot, kinky sex right now before one of us gets accused of sexual misconduct in the workplace."

"Yeah, yeah, yeah," she gripes. "Ruin all my fun, why don't you?"

"No fun allowed." We look up at the voice to see Jules approaching. It's the first time I've seen her since I sent the email. She comes around the corner and pulls me into a tight hug. "I'm so sorry about what happened."

I shrug her off. "Thanks, but it wasn't anything unusual. You know how it is. I'm just glad they're taking us seriously now."

"I think we all are," Jules agrees. "And we have you and Dr. Thompson to thank for that."

"It was pretty much just him. He insisted I send that email."

"He told me what happened. He really likes you, Sash. Like, *likes you*, likes you."

I wave a hand. "Doesn't —"

"Matter," Becca finishes with an eye roll. "Yeah, we know." She purses her lips and gives Jules a look. "I just got her to admit that she likes him too."

Jules holds up a hand and they high-five.

"You guys suck. What happened to the first rule of Nurses' Club?" I admonish them. "For shame."

I take a stack of folders I've completed inputting to the file room to put away, leaving them no doubt rolling their eyes at me as I leave.

* * *

If I thought admitting my feelings to myself would make anything easier, I was sorely mistaken. I have Sunday, Monday, and Tuesday off of work, so I use it to study ahead of a class test Tuesday night. Or, attempt to study, as it were. But I can't get Dr. Hottie off my mind. It seems unfair for him to be gorgeous, smart, sexy, and such a good person.

Unfortunately his recent behavior makes me reevaluate my previously negative opinion of his early flirtation. Because he's clearly got strong convictions, so maybe he doesn't just flirt with pretty girls. Maybe he really likes me. The thought simultaneously makes me want to never have to face him again and go to the hospital on my day off so I can get him alone. And do all the things I keep dreaming about doing with him.

Oh, the dreams. Those are another fun new thing since his heroics with Mr. Bowen and the hospital's enforcement — or lack thereof — of sexual harassment policies. Mostly featuring a much different set of events in exam room four.

For what feels like the thousandth time, I shake it off and refocus on the textbooks in front of me.

* * *

When I return to work on Wednesday, I'm feeling damn good. I crushed my test, had my best Dr. Thompson sex dream ever, and woke up with the realization that I've been an idiot. Dr. Thompson … Cal. He's amazing. What's wrong with me? Am I really going to let a non-rule stop me from giving it a go with what might be the perfect man? Not that I have complete say in it, but I'm going to find a way to tell him I've reconsidered my position on dating coworkers.

I imagine Becca will be gleefully chock-full of ideas on how to make that happen. Hopefully, it doesn't involve signs, or public declarations, or anything else embarrassing. I have to draw the line somewhere.

"Shhh, she's here. Close it, close it!"

I come upon the nurses' station to find Becca furiously stabbing the mouse, with Jules hovering over her shoulder.

"Close what?" I ask suspiciously.

"Nothing," Becca replies with an unconvincingly chipper smile. "How'd the test go?"

I decide to let it go. I'm sure I'll get it out of her eventually. "Great, actually. And I realized something this morning."

"Oh?" asks Jules. "What's that?"

"I'm crazy," I reply with a laugh that causes them to exchange worried glances. I snicker with satisfaction. "You were both right about Dr. Thompson … Cal. There's no reason not to give it a shot. Now I just need to figure out how to go about doing that. Who's ready to help?"

I'm grinning right up until the moment they share another glance, this one guilty. And my stomach drops.

"What is it?" I ask.

"You," Becca hisses at Jules. Jules presses her lips together and nods.

"Dr. Thompson had a visitor yesterday," Jules says.

"And?" I press tensely.

"It was a woman. She told us who she was and then identified herself as his …" Becca grimaces, "fiancée." She gestures for me to join her behind the desk. "Once we had her name, we found this."

I practically vault over the partition as she turns the monitor for me to see. Bile rises in the back of my throat as I take in the website on the screen. "Caleb and Rachel" is emblazoned at the top, and underneath it reads, "We're getting married June 20, 2020!"

He's getting married. A little more than four months from now.

My insides freeze, and I go numb.

"I'm so sorry, Sash," Becca whispers.

I shake my head, drawing back into myself. "Don't be. It's okay, really. This is the universe telling me I was right in the first place." I blink hard to keep tears from forming. "Seriously, I'm glad you found this out before I made a complete ass of myself."

The knowledge starts to sink in, and I look back at his flirtations with even more judgment than I had before. He's getting married. What right does he have to talk to other women like that? It's inexcusable.

My eyes flick back down to the screen, where under their wedding date announcement is a picture and "About the couple" section. She's stunning, almost as tall as he is, with dark hair that falls in perfectly styled chunky curls to her slim waist. She actually looks a lot like Lacey, despite his claims that Lacey wasn't his type. So maybe he meant "snarky bitch" wasn't his type.

Reading quickly through the text, I also learn she's a lawyer. Great. So he likes them supermodel gorgeous and genius smart. Turns out I really didn't ever have a shot with this guy anyway. My revulsion grows as I stare at the screen, so I force myself to pull away.

"If it makes you feel better, he didn't seem happy to see her," Jules says softly. "But they went into his office, so that's about all I know. I was with a patient when she left."

My gaze flicks to Becca. "They were in there for almost an hour," she admits. "She looked pretty happy when she left."

I close my eyes and grind my knuckles into my eyelids.

"Okay, stick a fork in me, I'm done," I declare. "From now on, he's just another doctor. Okay?"

"Maybe you should talk to him," Jules suggests.

A sharp laugh escapes me. "About what? I'd already basically told him nothing was ever going to happen between us, subtly though, as he never out-and-out even said he was interested. It was just a little flirting. What am I supposed to do, walk up to him and say, 'Hey, Dr. Thompson! So, turns out I kind of would like to date you after all and I was *just* about to tell you when I found out you're actually getting married. So yeah, what's up with that?'" I shake my head ruefully.

Becca and Jules are both staring past me wide-eyed.

"Oh fuck, he's behind me, isn't he?" I groan.

I turn, but it's not Cal who's behind me. It's Lacey. Like this couldn't get any fucking worse. It would've been better if it was him. Because Lacey's grinning at me like the cat who ate the canary. So not only will Cal hear about it, so will every other person in the unit. Scratch that, the hospital. Fuck, fuck, fuck. When will I learn to stop talking about this shit at work?

To my complete and utter horror, Lacey says not a word, simply dropping her coat and purse behind the desk, grabbing a set of files, and stalking off smugly. Becca, Jules, and I stand silently, watching her until she's gone.

"If you want to go home sick, we'll cover for you," Becca says as she watches Lacey disappear around the corner. She looks up at me apologetically.

"You guys couldn't warn me she was there sooner?" I snap, rubbing my temples.

"She came around the corner just as you were finishing," Jules explains. "It was obvious she was listening to the whole thing. I'm so sorry, Sasha."

"This is great," I say with a sarcastic laugh. "Just great. Whatever. I'm not going to hide. I'm going to do my goddamn job and not give a shit what anyone says. About anything."

Easier said than done. The rest of the day is peppered with knowing looks and snickers behind my back. But Cal is mysteriously missing, until I find out midday that he'd called out to take care of some personal business. Thank fuck.

Because gossipy, judgy nurses I can handle. But I don't know how I'm going to face him. Though I know it has to happen. And soon.

CHAPTER 5

Apparently, I don't have to face Cal as soon as I thought I would. He calls out for the rest of the week, so I end up dealing with the continued talk behind my back, which unfortunately doesn't really let up. It probably won't until everyone has a chance to see us interact and gets their delight at my embarrassment out of their system.

I have Sunday off, so I have lunch with my parents — something that doesn't happen as frequently as I'd like, given my commitments. I tell my mom about everything, and she suggests I strike first and call Cal.

Once I get back to my place, I decide that's not a half-bad idea, so I text Jules to see if I can get his cell number from the roster. She happily passes it on, and I hope I'm not committing some sort of work violation by using information provided for work-related issues to contact him about something personal.

I practice my spiel a few times before drumming up the courage to just call him and get it over with. But it rings through to voicemail. I don't know whether to be thankful or more worried that I now have to explain it all at once, with pretty much no preface.

Before I can panic too much, I hear the beep, and it's time to do my thing.

"Hi, Cal, it's Sasha. From the hospital. I'm actually calling you about something personal. I'm so sorry to do this, but I didn't want you to come in unaware tomorrow, or whenever you'll be back." I sigh. "I don't know how to tell you this, so I'm just going to say it. I came in on Wednesday morning having decided to let you know that I thought maybe dating coworkers wasn't such a bad idea after all. Well, dating you, as it were." *Idiot, idiot, idiot.* "I know that by itself is a huge assumption, because all you did was flirt a little. I wasn't trying to assume anything. I just … anyway. Turns out, you're getting married though, so yeah. It doesn't matter. There's just been a lot of office gossip since someone overheard me talking about it, and I wanted you to hear the story straight from me. I hope everything's okay on your end. Um … yeah. Bye then."

As soon as I hang up, I'm overwhelmed by the feeling that I just made another huge mistake. I literally crawl under my comforter and beat my fists into the mattress, feeling like a complete moron. At some point I decide what's done is done and get back to studying.

Jules starts texting asking how it went, and I just can't deal, so I shut off my phone completely. Even with it off, it's the toughest battle I've ever fought to concentrate on my homework. Around nine I quit pretending I'm getting anything done and surrender to the comforting blankness of sleep.

* * *

On Monday morning, I wake noting that there were no sex dreams. Thank god for that. But dread settles in the pit of my stomach as I get ready for work. I'm not even positive he'll be back today, but either way, I'm not looking forward to what the day has in store.

It doesn't occur to me until I pull into the parking lot at work that I never turned my phone back on. Once I do, there are a good half-dozen text messages from Jules, a couple from Becca, and a voicemail from Cal, timed after ten p.m. With my heart in my throat, I listen to the message.

"Sasha, it's me. I'm so sorry I missed your call. I can't … I don't want to do this over voicemail. Call me, please?"

That's it. I close my eyes against the tears I feel coming. No crying. I'll find him, let him have his say, then we'll all move on with our lives. Probably not without more gossip, whispers, and heckling, but if that's all it is, I can manage. So long as I haven't made it irrevocably awkward for us to work together, it'll all be okay.

Unsure of my ability to stay cool, I shoot him a text message. *Just got your message. I'm in the parking lot at the hospital. Can we meet somewhere and talk?*

The three dots come immediately, followed quickly by his reply.

I'm in my office. There's no place here to meet without eyes, so just come see me.

I think about that for a full minute before responding. *Will it get you in trouble?*

Again, the dots start as soon as my message is delivered, then the reply: *Let me worry about that.*

Since I'm a little early, I don't waste that advantage, as the sooner I go, the fewer people I'm likely to encounter.

And I'm not wrong, in fact, seeing nobody else in my unit until I'm safely at Cal's office door. I give a sharp knock.

"Come in."

With a shuddering breath, I slip inside and close the door behind me. He's standing at the windows, rubbing his temples as he looks out.

"Hey," I say, approaching cautiously.

His eyes are soft as he drops his hands and looks over at me. Though he looks stressed out to the max. I start to feel like an asshole for causing that … until I remember he's the one who was flirting while engaged to be married.

"Sasha," he breathes, gesturing for me to join him at the windows. He motions out to the sprawl of buildings, the first light of morning beginning to wash over them. "It's my first office with a view. Can't say I mind."

"Cal, I —"

He shakes his head, cutting me off. "I appreciate that you wanted to warn me, but Julianna had already called and explained," he says, shocking the shit out of me.

"She did what, now?" I ask incredulously.

He steps toward me, now inches away, putting his hands on my shoulders. "Don't be angry with her, she just wanted to help."

"If you already knew, why am I here?" I ask, annoyed, refusing to look up into his face, but unable to step away and break contact.

"So I can explain." His voice is laced with sorrow.

Now I can't help looking up. His face is drawn and tired, but he's every bit as handsome as always, and I dig deep not to let it overwhelm me.

"Explain what? I'm the one who needed to explain. I mean, it's between you and your fiancée whether flirting with other women is a big deal, but otherwise I was the one making assumptions and going someplace I never should have gone in the first place. But don't worry. I'm prepared to keep things strictly professional if you are. I love this job, even with all the crap that comes with it."

"She's not my fiancée," he says plainly, his hands falling back to his sides.

"Your wedding website and her calling you her fiancé would suggest otherwise," I reply slowly, not understanding his meaning.

Cal studies me carefully, then sucks his bottom lip into his mouth for a moment, causing me to look away again. But I'm still rooted to the spot.

"She's the reason I left Los Angeles," he finally admits. "We decided to call off the wedding and take some time apart. She's had a little trouble dealing with that."

"To the point where you just spent the last five days with her?"

He smiles dimly and shakes his head. "That's ... not exactly what I was doing."

"But you were in Los Angeles. And you saw her." I glare up at him accusingly.

"Yes," he admits with a sigh. "I was. And I did."

"And it's not over between you two."

"It would seem it's not going to be that easy," he allows. Suddenly his stress makes more sense, and I'm relieved it's not my doing. Well, not completely anyway.

"Well, I hope it works out how you want. And I hope that we can put this behind us and move forward as coworkers."

He stares down at me intently. "Is that what you want?"

I break eye contact for fear of ... I don't know what. Instead, I stare at the expanse of his chest. Not that that's much better, as it's a reminder of how gorgeous every damn part of him is with his blue scrubs straining over the muscles of his pecs. It takes me a moment to calm myself enough to reply.

"I don't want drama. And I don't want to get in the middle of a lover's spat. So yes, that's what I want."

"Sasha," he pleads. That one word nearly undoes me. Because in it I can hear the pain of whatever it is that he's going through, and his desire to make me understand. But I already have enough on my plate, and I just can't do this.

"Please don't," I reply, still refusing to look at him. "Last week when I … well, I expected wanting to date someone I work with might be complicated, even if you returned the sentiment. But not like this. This isn't … I've got a lot going on right now."

"As do I," he agrees. "So I respect your position."

"Good," I reply firmly. "So we're in agreement."

"Perhaps. Would you like to hear what I want?"

I close my eyes and give a slight shake of my head. "Will it change anything?" I open my eyes and look up at him. Mistake. He's painfully, heartbreakingly beautiful as he looks down longingly into my eyes.

"I guess I won't know until I've told you," he says simply. "But I don't want to overwhelm you. I can only imagine how the wolves have been treating you while I was away." He gives a faint smile.

"Fine. What you do want?"

His eyes light up at the question, and his heated gaze pins me to the spot. "A good many things. But just one that you need to know about." His hand reaches up, and he strokes a finger down my cheek. "Put simply: You. From the moment I saw you. Even though I knew it would be messy on many levels. Though I'm afraid I haven't behaved entirely honorably. And I do understand where you're coming from. But you should know that I'm not going to give up."

I squeeze my legs together to quell the shaking I feel starting in my knees. "You're awfully vocal about your feelings. I thought the English didn't do that?"

That gets a full-throated laugh from him. "No, we're not known for it, I suppose, are we?" he murmurs, continuing to cup my cheek in his hand. "I can't say I usually am. But then, this is an unusual time in my life."

He stares down at me, and I'm mesmerized. His eyes drift to my lips, and it causes heat to rise from my core, all the way up to my cheeks. And I'd be a liar if I said I didn't want to kiss him right now. I came in here so sure I was going to put him back in the "coworker" box. But now? I'm of two minds again. One wants him to take me on his desk, against the wall, anywhere. Now. The other wants to run and hide.

"So, has it changed anything?" he asks softly, stroking my bottom lip with his thumb.

And the next thing I say takes all of my strength to get out. "That depends. What's left between you and your fiancée?" I ask, hating myself for even wanting to know. For letting the part of me that wants him hope.

"Essentially? Paperwork. We own property together. Whatever was left between us was finished last week, though I'd known for some time that our 'time-out' would be permanent. And now that she can no longer pretend we have a romantic relationship, she's using legal matters to keep me in her snare. It'll be bumpy, but our relationship is, in fact, over." He lets me absorb that for a moment before continuing. "I've never dated a coworker, either, Sasha. This is new territory for me too, in more ways than one."

His explanation should comfort me. Just a few days ago I was so ready to take this chance. And with him looking down at me, clearly ready to kiss me at any moment ... my body sways into him at the thought and I hear his breath hitch.

Our eyes meet again, and he lowers his face to mine. Desire and panic war inside me as I feel the heat of his lips near mine, waiting for permission, and I'm forced to make a split-second decision.

I press a hand to his chest and look down, breaking the spell. And cursing myself at the same time.

"I need time to think about all of this. Let's give the gossip some time to die down, and I'll let you know."

But really, I wish I hadn't let him tell me what he wanted. It would be so much easier to pretend I didn't want him despite everything. Putting myself out there has never been my strong suit.

"All right then," he accedes, dropping his hand. "But don't take too long, or I'm going to have to resort to dodgy tactics to win you over."

I look up into his almost-too-casual smirk and give him a small smile in exchange.

"Come, I'll help you make your getaway," he says, slipping his hand in mine and walking me to the door. He pokes his head out and looks both ways down the hall. "Coast is clear." He reluctantly lets me go and I slip out the door.

I give him one last glance over my shoulder, trying to think about anything but how much I want him. I put as much distance between us as fast as I can, but even that doesn't help me forget how it felt to be so close to him … or that he wants me too.

* * *

We make it a point to have professional, civil conversation every time we cross paths, and within just a few days the gossip, looks, and snickers have died down considerably. But I still decide I should keep my distance, as I'm not sure I really want to start something with him while he's still working through things with his ex.

That is, until I remember how close we came to starting something in his office. The thought sneaks up on me and sends chills down my spine. Even though the rumor mill is always ready to pounce on any little thing, and just a week of being subjected to its machinations has me wondering what it would be like if they got hold of something substantially juicy enough to cause real excitement. I can't help dreading the idea, and it stops me from marching into his office and claiming that kiss.

But as if she could smell it in the air, Becca gets on my case Thursday afternoon to go out for drinks after work, since class was cancelled at the last minute. I told her earlier in the week that I'd talked to Cal and that we were keeping it professional but refused to go into any other details at work. Thankfully, she knows me pretty well, so she knows trying to force answers before I'm ready is a fruitless endeavor. But her patience has clearly worn thin. So naturally, her solution is to get me out of work and ply me with booze.

I only resist a little.

"Look, chica," she says, plunking a martini down in front of me once we've made it to the bar, "I've given you time. Now you've gotta tell me what's going on in that head of yours. The suspense is killing me."

"I don't know if I can, Becks," I reply, drinking deeply.

"Why not?"

"Because if I talk about it, it's real. And then I have to decide what to do."

"What are we deciding?" She takes a prim sip of her Manhattan.

I chuckle at her use of "we." Between that and the small amount of alcohol, I'm loose enough to just tell her. I'm going to have to eventually anyway. But really, it's mostly because I think I'm finally ready to talk. So I don't hold back, and even telling her what happened, I realize what the answer is. But it goes back to fear, in the end.

"Sooooo …" she breathes, and I can tell she's about to lay down some trademark Becca bluntness. "You want him. He wants you. Work bitches be talkin' shit, ex-fiancée be makin' trouble. That about sum it up?"

"Sasha be freakin' out," I add, pointing at myself.

Becca nods and laughs. "All right, all right, at least you can admit it to yourself," she says. "What's the worst case for each negative?"

I blow out a huge breath. "Well, say we date, and things go spectacularly wrong. You know our coworkers are going to make our lives hell for a while. And they'll never let us forget it. Work will become more or less permanently uncomfortable and awkward."

"Can't argue with that," she agrees.

"You're supposed to be making me feel better, not validate the things I'm freaking out over," I grouse.

She shrugs. "I call it like I see it. Keep going."

I pull a face and shake my head. "Oookay. His ex could continue to drag him through the mud, making him miserable and ruining him financially."

"Aight, that's where I'ma call bullshit. The man's a doctor, and they never got married. Girlfriend isn't entitled to his money, and the good lord knows he's going to keep making plenty of that."

"You have a point," I concede. She gestures for me to continue, but this is the worst one, for me at least. "And I'm freaking out because I've never felt this way about someone who might want me back in the same way. What if it doesn't work out? What if it's not what we thought it would be? What if he breaks my heart?"

"Ahhh, there it is, babe," she replies with a smile. "That right there. Yes, that's the worst case, and far outstrips dumbass coworkers and vindictive exes. But consider this: what if he *doesn't* break your heart? What happens then?"

I don't want to admit that she's right, even though I know she is. Because the odds aren't in my favor, and that always makes me uncomfortable. I'm not a risk taker, not by a long shot.

"You just think about that, and when your big sister Becca's worldly wisdom sinks in, you'll get there," she says with a wink, then takes a huge sip of her drink. "Mmm. I'm gonna need another one of these."

"You seem extra saucy tonight," I accuse her, happy to get off the topic of Cal. "What's going on with you?"

A huge grin breaks across her face. "I finally laid eyes on the new orderly and *dayum,* he's hotter than hot."

"Yeah? Have you talked to him? What's he like?"

"Pfff," she scoffs. "You don't just go up to a guy like that and start talking to him. I'm going to have to strategize on this one, babe. Just give me a little time, and he'll be at my mercy before you know it."

"Well, he must be scorching hot to put you in such a good mood."

"You have no idea. Total bad boy. Tattoos, leather, the works. Beyond yummy."

"He was wearing leather at the hospital?" I ask skeptically.

"He was leaving after his shift wearing a leather jacket," she explains with a lascivious grin that says he's every bit as hot as she's making him out to be.

"Well, I hope that works out for you."

She tilts her head and gives me a loving smile. "I hope things work out for both of us, boo." Thankfully, we get off the topic and onto other, more frivolous things. Which is better, since we both get a little tipsier than we probably should've on a work night.

But when I go to sleep that night, it's with a peace I haven't felt in a while. And I'm thankful for a good friend like Becca who, even when things are still difficult, can make you feel less alone in the middle of it all.

CHAPTER 6

Even though I'm pretty sure about what I'm going to do, the next day I tell Becca I want to sit on it, unable to bring myself to take the leap. But I can tell Becca is ready to march into Cal's office and take care of it for me. To sidestep her interference, I assure her I've got it handled.

I'm totally lying. I don't have it handled. I have to process one final exercise stress test that I had to take over for a tech who went home sick earlier, then I'm going home and hiding under a blanket until I have to be back in to work on Tuesday morning.

But two minutes into the test, everything flies out of my head as I watch the monitor.

"How are you feeling, Mrs. Sampson?" I ask, trying to keep the note of panic out of my voice.

She shoots me a dirty look but doesn't seem to be in pain. "I'm seventy-two and walking on a treadmill with a bunch of crap stuck to my chest. How do you think I feel?" she grouses.

I round the desk. "I'm just going to triple-check that everything's hooked up properly," I tell her. "Are you sure it doesn't hurt? Are you short of breath?"

She lifts her shirt and allows me to verify that everything is, in fact, set up correctly.

"Like I told Dr. Carson, it's just a little pain," she points to her sternum, "here."

I head back to the monitor to confirm what I'm seeing. "Okay, well, I think I need to take care of something on my end. I'm going to stop you for a minute and get someone to help me."

She nods, and I can tell she's starting to have trouble breathing. The blood pressure cuff is showing that her BP is rising steadily despite her slowing down. Not that I ever got her going that fast in the first place. So in addition to her readouts, I'm seriously concerned.

As the treadmill slows to a stop, I don't waste time. I pick up the phone and engage the hospital intercom. "Paging Dr. Swift to cardiac unit exam room fourteen," I call clearly, using the code for the closest doctor to come stat. And then I calmly replace the receiver and help Mrs. Sampson back onto the prep chair.

"Someone will be in shortly to help," I explain, retrieving an aspirin from the small, emergency stash in my pocket. "I need you to chew this. It's not going to taste good, but it's important, okay?"

Mrs. Sampson looks at me with her sharp eyes but does as I ask. "It's bad, isn't it?"

"I'm not sure," I lie. "But something wasn't quite right, so I'd rather be safe than sorry."

She huffs and goes about chewing the aspirin as I start gathering IV supplies. The door opens before I can get far, and Cal enters. Fuck.

"You must be Dr. Swift," Mrs. Sampson grumbles. Though her tone suggests she knows it was a code.

Cal smiles disarmingly, despite clearly picking up on the tension in the room. "He's occupied at the moment," Cal replies. "I'm Dr. Thompson. Nurse Suvorin?"

"We were conducting a diagnostic exercise stress test," I explain, gesturing for him to join me at the monitor, scrolling back to the first instance of abnormal data. He takes over quickly, scanning through, then meeting up with her present stats. He doesn't bother discussing it with me, so I know it's exactly what I thought it was. Her blood pressure is continuing to climb, so I know we need to act fast.

"Mrs. Sampson, I'm afraid there is some cause for concern. To be on the safe side, we're going to take full precautions and check you in," he tells her. "Once we've done some non-stress diagnostics we'll be able to determine the full extent of what we're looking at."

"Do what you gotta do," she replies with a sigh. "There goes bridge night."

Cal shoots me a look that's halfway between amused and concerned. "Let's start an IV with nitro, get her on oxygen, and set up a full twelve-lead EKG. Complete blood panel, expedited, and I want her in one of our monitoring rooms while we run the workup."

He pokes his head out of the room, and seemingly spots someone, opening the door and gesturing for them to enter. It's Zoe, and he immediately directs her to start the Hep-Lock and get blood, while he gestures for me to follow him out of the room.

We step a few paces away from the door so our voices won't carry.

"Don't stress her. It looks like a near complete blockage on top of arrythmia, and anything could send her into V-fib. Get me her full file immediately and have her call a family member who can make medical decisions for her if needs be. She'll need surgery as soon as possible. Stick close to her until I can get her into an OR for a stent."

"Of course," I say. "I'll go get started."

He gives me a curt nod. "Good catch, Sasha, you've probably saved her life."

I give him a thin smile in return. "We're not out of the woods yet, Cal."

He looks up at the door behind me and runs a hand through his thick, dark hair. It's the only sign of agitation I've ever seen him show in regard to a patient, and I try not to let it make me worry more than I already am. "No, we're not. I'll see you soon." And then he's off.

I head back into the room, opting to call the nurses' station rather than leave Zoe with partial instructions. After I've called to get a room ready, we work on getting her leads and drip set up, and I send Zoe off to get the mobile bed from whatever will be her room.

As soon as he's gone, Mrs. Sampson gives me a look. "I'm glad Dr. Swift was busy, that Dr. Thompson is pretty easy on the eyes."

I chuckle. "Well, I'm sorry to tell you that your blood pressure is on the high side at the moment, so if he's going to get your heart racing, we may have to get you another doctor," I tease. Well, sort of. Because I'm also kind of serious. I've gone through this enough to keep a decent poker face, and I'm pretty sure she has no clue how close to dying she is right now. And I'm sure as hell not going to tip her off until the danger has passed.

Zoe returns with the bed and a male orderly, and I leave them to get Mrs. Sampson moved and set up in her new room. A glance up at the clock tells me I'm over shift anyway.

I head back to the nurses' station and print off everything Cal will need and take it to his office. The door is open, so I enter timidly. He's sitting at his desk, staring at his screen with one hand over his mouth.

"I'm reviewing the data again. Is that her file?" he asks without looking up.

"It is," I agree, sliding it onto the desk in front of him.

"Thank you. I have her booked in to start within the hour."

"Good. I won't be back until Tuesday, but let me know how it goes."

That gets him to look up, a frown pulling at his mouth. "I'd like it if you stayed."

I press my lips together, unsure of how to respond to that. Surely he doesn't need moral support? I can only imagine he's done this dozens of times, if not more.

"Please?" he asks, dropping his hand to the desk. He really does look miserable, and it tugs at me, despite myself.

"Are you asking as the on-shift cardiac surgeon, or as something else?" I ask.

"I think you know the answer to that," he replies, leaning back in his chair and scrubbing both hands over his face. "I have a bad feeling about this one. Please, Sasha, stay. For me."

"Cal …" I start, but stop abruptly at the pleading look on his face. "I still haven't decided —"

"Bollocks," he interrupts.

My eyebrows fly up. "Excuse me?"

"You've decided, Sasha. But maybe I was wrong about which way."

All I can do is stare at him, confused, and borderline pissed off. "I'm so glad you know my mind better than I do," I reply sarcastically. "Next time I make a decision I'm not aware of, please do be sure to tell me about it." My anger rises as I think about the timing of this conversation. *Now? Really?*

He huffs an unamused laugh and shakes his head. "You decided all right, Sasha. Right around the time you started calling me 'Cal.'" He rises from his chair, closing his laptop and taking it and Mrs. Sampson's file with him. He stops in front of me, staring down at me, his blue eyes stormy. "I hope you decide to stay. I also hope you realize you've already decided about everything else. And that you don't change your mind."

And then he leaves me alone in his office. Completely fucked in the head. I wander numbly back to the nurses' station to find Becca dutifully working away.

"Becks?"

She looks up. "You look like you're about to vomit," she says bluntly. "What's wrong?"

"Have I been calling Dr. Thompson 'Cal'?"

She snorts. "Yes. You didn't realize?"

"No," I admit, sinking into a chair next to her. "No, I didn't."

Thankfully, Becca keeps her opinions to herself, allowing me to stew in my own thoughts.

Offhand, I can't remember when I started calling him by his first name, but they're both right. I have been. Though the more I think on it, the more I'm sure it was even before he confessed his feelings. Which is when it occurs to me that I'm fairly certain I started doing it when I confessed mine ... to myself. When I first let myself admit it out loud. And I didn't stop, even when my mind started to resist giving in again.

Being a nurse, I'm well trained in being careful with the language that I use. Words have power. They can keep someone calm. Or they can freak someone the fuck out when they're in a bad place. They can keep someone at a distance. Or they can bring them close. It's why I resisted when he suggested I call him by his first name. I was keeping him at a distance. But apparently my subconscious has been telling me this whole time that I shouldn't do that.

"Aren't you done with work?" Becca asks, breaking into my reverie.

I look up dully. "Yes."

She looks at me expectantly. "Well ... aren't you going to go home, then?"

I catch a laugh before it escapes me, and I end up making a garbled huffing noise. "No. No, I'm not."

That earns me a befuddled look, but I ignore it and work on catching up on the nearly endless pile of paperwork that is both a nurse's bane and pretty much what we spend most of our time doing. Things they tell you in nursing school but that you can never fully understand until you're stuck at a computer all the time. Apparently, sometimes even when you're not supposed to be working.

* * *

Only an hour later, I'm still not caught up, and am almost hungry enough to consider cafeteria food when Zoe approaches looking somber.

"Dr. Thompson wants to see you."

"Isn't he supposed to be in surgery?"

She shakes her head and frowns. And my heart drops. *No.* I fly out of my chair.

"Where is he?"

"Downstairs. Post-op in suite three."

I don't even bother with the elevator, walking briskly for the stairs and breathing through my nose while I try to keep calm. I don't fear the worst. Fear is for when you don't know what to expect. And there's only one reason he wouldn't be in surgery right now. Death is a rarity in our unit, but it happens.

I descend as quickly as I can, bursting into the operation theater corridor. Suite three is the first door on my right. I enter without hesitation, veering right into the post-op area. Only to find Cal sitting on the end of the bed, head in his hands, shaking slightly.

"Oh, Cal," I breathe, going to him and wrapping my arms around him.

His arms snake around my back, pulling me close as he buries his face in my shoulder. He stops shaking almost immediately, and I don't hear a peep from him for a full minute.

"They were prepping her for surgery," he says, his voice thick. "She had a massive heart attack despite the drugs, and there was nothing we could do." He looks up at me, his eyes red. "We did it all anyway. But she was just gone. What good am I if I can't even keep a patient from dying in my OR, when I knew exactly what was wrong?" He presses his forehead against my shoulder, diving back into his self-pity.

I remove the surgical cap still covering his hair and throw it on the bed behind him, then run my fingers through his dark hair. I grip it lightly and tilt his head back up. His eyes are red, and so sad it pains me to my core.

"I'm so sorry about what happened. But you're not God," I say firmly. "You don't get to decide who lives and who dies. Did you do everything you could?"

He nods. "Of course."

"Then that's all you can do."

He sniffs deeply. "Why are you better at this than I am?"

"You were already going through a rough time," I remind him. "This kind of thing always hits harder when that happens. I've been where you are. I've been there when patients have died and I was already in a vulnerable state. It's never easy, even under the best of circumstances. But that doesn't make it any more your fault."

"Thank you," he breathes. "You're right. I guess I just needed to hear that."

As he calms, I start to feel a little self-conscious that my fingers are still wrapped in his hair, as I'm wrapped in his arms. I look down, a little fearful as his eyes meet mine and his lips part. I stare at that full, bottom lip of his. And my emotions are running high enough right now too, that kissing that beautiful lip doesn't seem like such a bad idea.

He sucks it into his mouth before the thought can translate to action, and the tight pull at my insides finally causes me to press away. A woman just *died* mere feet away and here I am thinking about kissing him.

"Please don't do that."

He pulls back, looking puzzled.

"Your lip," I explain, pointing. "You pull it into your mouth. It … please don't do that."

He releases it with a dull shake of his head. "It's a recent habit. I apologize, I didn't realize it upset you."

"I'm not upset," I protest. But I don't want to say what I am. "Do you do it on purpose?"

He levels a tired look at me. "I do it to keep myself from kissing you, if you must know."

"How can you even be thinking about kissing at a time like this?" I admonish him. Hypocritically. Thinking about all the times he's done that in my presence.

"Weren't you?" he asks plainly. He shakes his head and stands up. "I'm sorry, I'm not myself at the moment." He goes to move around me, but I stop him with a hand on his chest.

"No, I'm sorry. You're right, I was. And I felt like a total jerk for it, then I made you feel like one. See? I suck at this too." I sigh and rub my eyes with my knuckles.

I feel his hands slide around my wrists, tugging them away from my eyes. He uses a hand to tip my chin up.

"I don't feel like a jerk," he corrects me. "I feel … mortal. This kind of thing always reminds me of how short life really is. How precious."

I close my eyes and nod my agreement with a sigh.

His hands drop from my face and I feel him take a step back. I open my eyes, looking at him quizzically.

"This may be an odd time to suggest this given that I just snotted all over your scrubs," he hedges. "But I think it might be best if we keep things professional in the workplace."

A lump forms in my throat at his words, and I withdraw.

"You're right. I'm sorry, I —"

He holds a hand up. "Let me finish, please, Sasha." With wide eyes and terror in my heart, I nod. "As I was saying, I think we should keep things professional in the workplace. But I want to see you outside of work. I want you to give this a shot. Give us a shot."

The grim but determined look on his face tugs at my heart. Because deep down, I want to give this a shot too. Despite knowing it's likely to blow spectacularly up in my face. Fuck it.

"Okay."

"Okay?" He looks incredulous.

"Okay," I repeat with a nod, much more calmly than I feel.

"Well, then. I suppose that's the last we'll speak of it here. I need to go break the news to Mrs. Sampson's daughter. But I'll call you tomorrow?"

I take a deep breath through my nose as my heart starts to hammer in my chest, thinking about what comes next.

"Sounds like a plan."

CHAPTER 7

My hands are shaking and I can't stop pacing. Even though it's five minutes before Cal said he'd be here, I'm ready and waiting. And a complete nervous wreck.

Between Friday evening's events, agreeing to go out with Cal, and talking to him yesterday to set up a brunch date for today — the earliest I'd agree to meet up — I've had plenty of time and opportunity to change my mind. And believe me, I have. About five thousand times. But I'm back to "go for it." Not that that's any less nerve-racking of a proposition.

I've changed outfits almost as many times as I've changed my mind, finally settling on a cream and gold long-sleeved Mohair-blend minidress with a pair of nude leggings underneath. The dress is silky soft and thick yet casual. It makes me feel confident. Well, usually. Right now I just feel vaguely nauseous.

I haven't even told Becca or Jules about the date. Just so they didn't get their hopes up in the event that it goes spectacularly badly. And, you know, so it doesn't hit the rumor mill sooner than it absolutely has to. It's not that I don't trust them, but the fewer people who know, the less likely that word will get out.

I'm saved from my internal torment by a knock on the door. I open it to see Cal in something besides scrubs and a lab coat for the first time. Wearing black slacks and a white button-front shirt with the sleeves rolled up to the elbow, he looks beyond gorgeous. It doesn't hurt that his top two buttons are undone, giving just the tiniest peek at his toned chest.

We both stand there, staring at each other for a moment, each clearly in shock. I realize it's the first time he's seen me out of scrubs too, or with my hair and makeup done, for that matter.

"Hey," I finally say.

"You look …" he trails off, clearly at a loss, and I laugh.

"You too."

That gets a smile from him, and he offers a bunch of flowers I didn't even notice he was holding. "These are for you," he says.

I suppress a laugh, determined not to tease him for the obvious statement. Instead I opt for, "Thank you. Would you like to come in while I put these in water?"

He gives me a knowing smirk. "Why do you think men bring beautiful women flowers?"

"I'll take that as a yes," I reply, stepping back to let him in while hiding my blush at his compliment.

After I lead him through to the kitchen and start putting the flowers in water, he wanders the small apartment, looking out the windows to the street below.

"I like your place, it's very cozy. Just one bedroom?" he asks.

I nod, putting the vase on the counter. "Yes. It's simple, but I like it. Have you found a place here yet?"

"I bought a house, also in the neighborhood, but on the other side of the freeway, closer to the hospital," he replies.

I can't help it, my jaw drops. "You've only been here a little over a month and you've already bought a house? How on earth did you manage that?"

Cal chuckles tolerantly, joining me back in the entryway. "I'd been planning this move for a while, Sasha," he explains patiently. "I closed on the house before I moved here."

"Of course you did," I reply, feeling silly. "I guess you're planning to stay a while then?"

He looks down at me, a small smile tugging at his mouth. "I think so," he murmurs. And for a moment I think he's going to kiss me. Butterflies start dancing in my stomach, but he doesn't come any closer. "Shall we?" He gestures to the door.

I'm simultaneously relieved and disappointed. I want to kiss him, but I think I'm going to need more time to prepare. Because if it's bad … well, I don't want to think about that. I just want to enjoy these moments where everything is still full of hope and possibility.

* * *

"That. Was. Amazing." I lean back in my chair and sigh with satisfaction, looking out the window at the clear blue skies and calm water of the marina. "And the view is phenomenal. How have I not been here before?"

"Everyone has their routines. I think sometimes when you're new to a city, you end up looking around more than if you'd lived there your whole life," Cal offers, watching me with an amused look on his face. "In any case, I'm glad you enjoyed it. I didn't think it was possible to have better Mexican food than in Los Angeles, but here we are."

I chuckle softly. "Welcome to San Diego," I tease. "I'd say we should walk off those carnitas chilaquiles, but it's a bit cold for that."

Cal's eyebrows shoot up. "If you think this is cold, you'd hate London."

"What makes you think I've never been?" I counter.

A slow smile spreads over his face. "Have you?" he challenges.

I laugh and lean in to rest my arms on the table, giving him a flirty look. "No," I concede, earning a chuckle from him. "But I've always wanted to go. Do you miss it?"

"Sometimes," he admits. "But not right now." He leans in too, returning the flirtation. "I have to admit I didn't have any brilliant plans as to what to do next. But I really don't want to take you home."

"So take me to yours," I reply without thinking about it. I flush at the implication, and race to explain. "I mean, I'd love to see where you live. Since you've seen my place. You can tell a lot about someone from their home."

He gives me a sly smile and pulls his bottom lip in. Butterflies erupt in my stomach and I point at his mouth.

"You're doing it again," I say quietly.

He cocks an eyebrow and lets his lip loose. "I know." He rises from his chair, extending a hand. "Let's go."

My heart picks up speed as I put my hand in his. After I've risen, he doesn't let go, pulling me close to his side, intertwining his fingers with mine. In fact, he barely lets go the whole way back to his place. The drive is silent and laced with sexual tension, and I'm already wondering what he expects. After all, it is only a first date. Even if I have mentally undressed him many times, I'm not really a have-sex-on-the-first-date kind of girl. But then, I've never been so attracted to someone.

When we pull up to his place, I'm floored. The house itself is set back from the street, with a façade of rough-looking earth-toned bricks. The yard is more like a garden, with beautifully trimmed hedges, flowers of all colors overflowing from the beds, and rows of cypress trees on either side, isolating the property from its neighbors. It's a far cry from my one-bedroom apartment and probably easily cost over a million dollars.

"Wow," I whisper.

"You like it?" he asks with a smile.

"It's stunning," I admit.

He gets out of the car, coming around and opening the door for me. "It was built in the 1920s. It's just as beautiful inside. Come," he says, offering his hand.

I allow him to walk me up the cobblestone pathway, under the brick arch that encloses the small porch, and up to the giant, dark wood door. As he goes to unlock the door, I allow myself to briefly imagine the bachelor pad inside. Since he works so much, I can't imagine it'd be all that furnished. But even so, if the outside is any indicator, it'll probably still be stunning.

But if I was shocked by the outside, I'm knocked over by the inside. Fully furnished and decorated, we enter into the lush, palatial interior that is somehow both warm and intimidating. Not unlike its owner. Cal gives me a brief tour of the main rooms before offering me a drink, which I decline as I'm still full from brunch, before we settle on one of the two, huge leather sofas in the living room.

"How on earth did you manage to accomplish all of this so fast, and with your work schedule?" I ask, sinking into the soft leather.

"I didn't. I paid someone else to do it," he replies with a grin.

I can't help the appalled look that crosses my face. Must be nice to have that kind of money.

"What?" he asks, suddenly self-conscious.

I shake my head, unwilling to spoil what has so far been a fantastic date. "Nothing. This place is … well, it's very you. I can see why you're so happy here." I cross my arms over myself, suddenly feeling very inadequate.

But Cal's having none of it. He tugs my arms away from my chest, gathering my hands in his and looking deeply into my eyes.

"This is all just stuff," he insists. "Well, stuff I've worked hard to get, I suppose. But at the end of the day, it's not what makes me happy."

"Fair enough. So what does make you happy?" I ask, curious.

He sinks into the couch next to me, running a hand lightly up and down my forearm. "Up until now? Work," he says plainly. "I love what I do. It's my main focus. What makes you happy, Sasha?"

"Work as well. I'd say school, but I'd be lying. It's a means to an end."

"To becoming an NP."

"Yes. But why did you say up until now?" I ask, looking up into his eyes, suddenly worried that Mrs. Sampson's death may have had more of an impact on him than I realized.

"Because now, being with you makes me happy," he admits, looking back at me.

"You barely know me," I point out. But as his hand comes to rest on my thigh, and he leans in, close enough that his breath is warm on my face, I realize how little that matters right now. From the moment I saw him, I've been drawn to him. And I realize that this was inevitable.

A smile tugs at his lips. "That doesn't make it any less true," he replies carefully. "It's rare for me. This," he gestures between us, "is rare."

I swallow hard, the proximity to him reminding me of how true that is. How he affects me in ways I can't control or explain. "It is," I agree softly.

He runs a hand through his hair, tucking his lip into his mouth and a wave of desire tingles through me.

"Are you going to kiss me or what?" I tease. "Because if you keep doing that thing with your —" I'm cut off by his mouth descending hungrily onto mine. His hands slides up my thigh, pulling me into him as his lips tease at mine, his tongue sliding across my lip. I open to him, moving my hands into his hair as the kiss intensifies.

I needn't have worried about it being bad. Sparks shoot through me as our tongues meld, as his hands grip and massage at my thighs and backside. I pull myself into him without thought, needing more. The world melts away for the second time since I first saw him, and all I know is the feel of his mouth on mine, the sexy texture of his rough beard on my face, the pounding of my heart.

When he ends the kiss, he leans his forehead to mine, and we're both breathing heavily.

"Bloody hell," he says on a sigh. "That was so much better than I'd ever imagined."

Unable to respond, I slide a hand down to rest on his chest, where I can feel his heart pounding every bit as hard as mine. His hand finds my chin, and he leans back, tilting my face up to look into his.

"Ever since that first day when I thought you knew me, it left me with the sense that I knew you too," he says, his eyes searching mine. "You feel … I can't even explain it …"

"Familiar," I whisper.

His eyes close for a moment and he nods. "Yes," he agrees.

"You may not have been who I thought, but that didn't change how much you affected me that day either," I admit.

"I know you said that whoever you thought I was was nobody important," he says carefully, "but I can't help feeling like that might not be entirely true."

I pull back a little, uncomfortable at his focusing on that part. "Does it matter?"

Cal scratches at his cheek. "I think it might. Something held you back all this time, and it wasn't the lame 'coworkers' excuse, no offense. I can't help feeling like that bloke might be part of it."

With a sigh, I consider whether he's right.

"In a way, maybe," I allow. "It was someone I came across in my early teens. It wasn't a big thing. It just … it was the first time I *felt* anything for someone, and it was *strong*. So strong I'd never felt like that again with anyone I'd dated, and eventually all of my relationships fizzled out because of it."

"Ah. I see. So you were worried that would happen to us?" he asks.

I look up at him, a little bit afraid to tell him the truth. But I've been holding back long enough. "No. Because I only just felt that again the day we met. I was worried that you wouldn't feel the same. Or maybe I was worried that you would." I huff a dry laugh, not really sure how to explain myself.

"I get it."

I look up in surprise. "Well, then I hope you can explain it to me, because I can't say I fully understand it myself."

He chuckles, leaning in to swipe my hair behind my shoulders, and cupping my jaw in his strong hand. His thumb traces over my cheek as he looks down at me, and it has me slightly dizzy with the desire to kiss him again.

"Giving yourself permission to fall for someone is hard. Well, terrifying, really," he amends. "But sometimes we have to let go of how we think things should go and just let them happen. It's the simplest and most difficult part of giving a relationship a go."

"How do you do it?" I ask. "I mean, especially since you just got out of a serious relationship. Doesn't this freak you out?"

"You'd think it would," he answers with a smile. "But I've never been less 'freaked out' by anything." As if to prove his point, his lips lower to mine again, this time much more gently. Though no less heated. As he kisses me, something in me shifts, and I'm almost overwhelmed with need. It's been so long since I've had any kind of physical connection with anyone, much less one this powerful. And I know I need to be careful.

After a minute, I press away.

"You are too much, Caleb Thompson," I tell him.

"And you are too sexy, Sasha Suvorin." He pulls me back to him, not allowing me to escape so easily again by wrapping his arms around me and half-dragging me into his lap. This time, his kiss is demanding, his hands roaming more freely. For a moment, I surrender, my own hands exploring the hard planes of his chest, the strength of his arms.

His mouth drops to my neck, his lips and tongue tracing a path that causes heat to flare between my thighs. My nails dig into his back and he moans against my ear.

We continue to make out like teenagers for a bit, until I feel like I might be approaching the point of no return. So I slow down, then stop, opening my eyes to look deeply into his as I settle into his lap, my thigh brushing his unmistakable erection. But that … that's a whole other level. And I'd best be sure I'm really ready for that. So I shift, making sure not to torture him if I don't plan on going there.

"I enjoyed that even more than I thought I would," I admit.

"As did I," he murmurs, giving me a half smile. "I wish I'd done it sooner."

A shiver rolls down my spine, despite myself. "Sooner than the first date? How's that even possible?"

Cal laughs. "This may be our first official date, but we've been dancing around each other for weeks, Sasha. And I'm not exactly known for my patience."

"Cal, that was amazing, but I'm sorry, I'm just not ready to —"

"Shhh," he interrupts. "I didn't mean I expect anything more from you." He strokes my cheek, looking tenderly into my eyes. "And I didn't intend to do anything at all in that respect today, really. But I can't help how much I want you. I'm not going anywhere, though, okay? You're worth waiting for."

I want to say I'm ready now. Or at least, parts of me do. And if he can get me that turned on with a few kisses and touches, I have to admit I'm dying to see what he can do with the rest of him. About as much as I'm dying to see the actual rest of him. The hard muscles of his body have been evident from touching him over his clothes, but it's just fueled my curiosity.

Unfortunately, my logical brain is screaming at me that there's no rush, and to get to know him more first. And I'm far too attuned to doing what it tells me.

"Good," I finally reply. "Because I'm not going anywhere either."

"Brilliant," he says. "And now that I've got you alone …" He leans in close to whisper in my ear. "I'm going to need the real dirt on everyone we work with."

That gets a huge laugh out of me. "You know I'm the least gossipy nurse in the unit, right?"

He grins and nuzzles into me. "Sure, with everyone else. But I still feel like I'm flying blind here. And you're the only one I really trust."

I pull back, a little more shocked than I probably should be at his revelation. I cup his face in my hands and place a gentle kiss on his lips. "Are you sure you can handle what I know?" I tease.

"Lay it on me, gorgeous," he replies, skimming his hands down my arms.

With an amused huff, I comply, and we spend the rest of the afternoon wrapped in each other's arms, discussing coworkers before he drops me back home so I can study. With one, final, sultry kiss on my doorstep, he leaves me to it. Alas, it turns out that it's really hard to focus on studying when all you want to think about is the amazing guy you're totally falling for.

CHAPTER 8

On Monday, pretending like there's nothing going on between Cal and I proves nearly impossible. It takes every ounce of my strength not to kiss him every time I see his gorgeous face. Which, as it happens, is way more often than I realized. We cross paths constantly at the nurses' station, in the halls coming and going from appointments, in the breakroom, you name it.

It's almost as difficult as not telling Becca or Jules what's going on. Which becomes exponentially more difficult when Cal approaches the nurses' station in the afternoon while I'm inputting exam results and hands me a patient file with a folded piece of paper on top.

"Note for you. I'll be in my office if you have any questions." I don't know how he does it, but it sounds perfectly clinical. Not wanting to betray myself, I give him a sharp nod and he walks away.

"What was that all about?" Becca asks, watching his ass as he walks away.

"I don't know, but you're going to get caught staring at the goods if you're not careful," I tease her.

She throws me a sharp look. "I could say the same to you," she replies sweetly.

I wrinkle my nose at her and pick up his note, being careful to read it at an angle that Becca can't see. And it's all I can do to contain my reaction to the three simple words written on the paper: *I need you.*

I take a few subtle breaths to calm my racing heart.

"Okay, I have questions. I'll be back," I say as lightly as possible, being careful to bring the note with me.

"Why do they do that?" Becca muses. "Couldn't they just stick around for thirty seconds and have a conversation? Ugh."

I shrug, trying not to crack. "Doctors say jump, we say —"

"Go fuck yourself?" Becca offers with an innocent smile.

"I'll be right back," I reply drily. "Try not to tell any of your superiors to go fuck themselves while I'm gone, won't you?"

"Can't make any promises."

I laugh and head down the hall. My nerves ratchet up with every step closer to Cal's office. When I knock, he immediately calls for me to come in.

I step inside, hovering at the threshold, unsure of whether closing the door is a good idea.

"Close the door, please," he says curtly, not looking up from the paperwork he's perusing. And I'm not sure if he's always looked this sexy, or if having experienced his skills firsthand I'm now more easily drawn in, but watching him work definitely does it for me. So I close the door. Against my better judgment, as my hormones override my good sense.

"Thank fuck," he breathes, hopping up and rounding the desk, pulling me roughly into his arms. I go up on my toes to meet his descending mouth, wrapping myself in him. In a frenzy of hands and lips, I take what I've been dying for all day: my Cal fix. God, I'm already so addicted to this man.

When our mouths finally break apart, I look up at him longingly. "Well, so much for keeping it out of the office. I don't know how we're going to do this every day," I admit.

"Me neither," he agrees. "It's been torture watching you sashay around all day with that gorgeous ass of yours."

That gets a grin out of me. "*My* gorgeous ass? You do know we all watch you when you walk away, right?"

"I do," he says, "but you're the only one I *want* looking." He places another gentle kiss on my lips. "I'll probably be here until at least seven, but can I see you tonight?"

"I really shouldn't, I have a quiz tomorrow night that I need to study for," I reply with a frown.

He groans and buries his face in my neck. "Bugger. So Wednesday, then?"

"I think I could make that work," I say with a sly grin.

"Probably best if we go someplace public and have a proper date. I don't trust myself alone with you."

"Me neither," I admit wryly. He gives me a mock offended look. "No, *me*. I don't trust me alone with you either."

Cal chuckles and kisses my cheek. "I was just kidding." He lets me go and retrieves a piece of paper from his desk. "Here's an alibi for you."

I take the paper from him and scan it. It's a simple report request. "How very thorough of you," I tease him. But when I look up to find him giving me the most sexy and suggestive grin I've ever seen, my mouth dries out.

"Oh, I'm very thorough," he says lowly, dipping his head to whisper in my ear. "In everything I do." And with a wink, he goes and reseats himself at his desk. "That'll be all, Nurse Suvorin."

On jelly legs, I return to the nurses' station. I manage to pull off presenting my alibi and going about my business for the rest of my shift. But all I can think about is Cal and how very much I'd like him to show me exactly how thorough he can be.

* * *

Unfortunately, Dr. Carson has a family emergency on Tuesday that forces him to take the rest of the week off. Which means Cal, being the newest and lowest on the totem pole, has to step up to cover for him. Which, in turn, means he's forced to cancel for Wednesday night.

I try not to be disappointed, I really do. But Cal is also almost completely unavailable the rest of the week, even for stolen moments in his office. On one hand, that's probably for the best. On the other hand, every fleeting look we share is laden with all the things we can't say — or do — to each other.

We have a few brief text message exchanges, but between his crazy schedule and my work and school schedules, they're barely above basic conversations. By the end of the week, the magic of our first date has started to wear off, and I'm feeling unsure and awkward.

As I'm sullenly sterilizing instruments at the end of the day on Friday, I'm doing my best to focus when I hear Dr. Franklin call out Cal's name in the hall outside the door. Apparently he was passing by, as they stop and chat idly for a moment, clearly not realizing, or perhaps caring, whether someone is in here. But then, why should they? And it definitely doesn't bother me. Just listening to Cal's voice is calming, as I've heard precious little of it all week. I wonder briefly if it's weird that his voice already has such an effect on me.

"So, stop me if this is inappropriate," I hear Dr. Franklin say. "But I know you're new to town, so I thought you might need someone to show you around. My wife's sister is on the management team for the Padres, and we're all going to their first training game tomorrow. Think you can get away? Tracey's a real stunner, and I think you'd hit it off. And thanks to her job, she's got connections at all the best restaurants and attractions in town."

I freeze in place, my heart taking off at a gallop in my chest. Cal hesitates long enough to make me doubt his response. What man wouldn't want to be set up with a beautiful woman who can get him VIP access to all of San Diego? And it's not like we've had any kind of discussion about being exclusive. It's far too early for that.

"That's kind of you, but I doubt I'd be able to get away," Cal replies.

His lack of turning down the actual setup doesn't make me feel good about his response.

"Well, you could always join us for dinner after," Dr. Franklin offers.

My jaw clenches, and I force myself to keep working. Anything but thinking about how I like Dr. Franklin a little less than I did a few minutes ago. Or about Cal's response.

"I appreciate that, but I'm actually seeing someone."

I freeze again. This time I put down the instrument I was wrapping, realizing it's probably best to stop handling sharp objects right now.

"Oh? Can't say I'm surprised, I guess. All the females in the office were on high alert the moment you started," Dr. Franklin jokes, and I hear a noise that sounds like he just slapped Cal on the back. I roll my eyes and continue about quietly putting everything away. "Well, the offer stands if you ever change your mind."

"Thanks, but I won't. This one's special," Cal replies. I can practically hear the smile in his voice, and it tugs on something inside of me. My annoyance melts into … is it longing?

"Suit yourself. Anyway, I'm off to wrap things up for the day," Dr. Franklin replies jovially. I hear footsteps head down the hallway. I tuck the unused muslin back in a drawer and head out into the hall.

Only to find Cal still standing there, looking down at a file in his hands. I watch him for a moment, seizing the chance to examine him without him knowing I'm there. He looks tired, his hair and clothes rumpled and worn. But he's still as ridiculously handsome as ever.

"Hey," I call softly, leaning against the doorframe.

His head snaps up, his eyebrows shooting to his hairline as our gazes connect. As he realizes I'd likely just heard every word.

"Eavesdropping?" he teases, sauntering toward me. He stops a respectable distance away, looking down at me with a smirk.

"I don't know what you're talking about," I reply coyly, looking back up at him. "I was just doing my job."

He chuckles and crosses his arms over his chest. "I see. So you didn't hear anything at all then, I suppose?"

"Oh, I heard plenty," I admit. "And I wouldn't blame you one bit if you wanted to date Tracey the stunner. Hell, if you don't, maybe I will. I do love baseball."

Cal shakes his head and looks down at me with amusement. "Do you really think I would want to date Tracey — or anyone else, for that matter — with you around? Apparently, you didn't listen to everything I said. Everything I've been saying." The intensity of his gaze burns through me, but I don't break eye contact.

"I've heard every word, actually," I murmur.

He leans forward, closing the small gap between us. His smell fills my senses, and my eyes drop to his lips as he tucks the bottom one into his mouth. Butterflies erupt in my stomach.

Until voices from around the corner snap us out of the trance we're in. We jump apart just as Zoe and Ethan appear. Zoe looks up.

"Oh, thank god you haven't gone home yet. We just finished inventory and we're missing a crash cart. Mind helping us find it so we can all get the hell out of here?" she asks me.

My eyes dart to Cal, who simply smiles innocently. "Of course," I reply. "Let's go." I walk away with them, Cal giving me a subtle wink as we proceed to walk in opposite directions.

* * *

I spend Saturday studying, while Cal spends it working. Finally, in the afternoon, he texts that he's going to finish at a reasonable hour and wants to pick me up to have dinner. Short notice? Sure. But I've thought about him too much to play games or pretend that I'm not dying to see him. So I tell him to come by when he's done.

Which was a great plan until, about forty-five minutes later, I have to stop reading a research paper on pathophysiology and run to the bathroom to throw up. And I don't stop throwing up for a while. Once it finally ceases, I meekly rinse my mouth and hands. I've just finished and am rubbing some feeling back into my sore knees when the doorbell rings.

I weakly make my way to the door, slumping against the cool wood. Great. Fever too.

"Cal?" I call through the door.

"It's me," he reassures me. "Everything okay?"

"Noooo," I groan. "I've got some sort of stomach bug. I'm so sorry."

"Sudden, uncontrollable vomiting?" he guesses.

"Yes. How did you know?"

"We had two other staff members go home with it today. Let me in."

"I'm not getting you sick," I protest.

"And I'm not leaving you alone like this."

"What if I don't give you a choice?" I croak.

"Then I'll go to the store, get supplies to take care of you, and sit on your doorstep until you give in," he insists.

I let out a dry chuckle but stop quickly as it shakes my now-volatile stomach. "You're crazy."

"Maybe. But I'm also a doctor. I deal with sick people every day. You're not getting rid of me that easily."

I open the door with an incredulous look to find him leaned against the frame, staring back at me with concern. "Oh please, you deal with old people with angina all day, not people who —"

My stomach heaves and I flee, leaving the open door and Cal behind me.

When I finally reemerge, I find Cal rifling through my fridge and cupboards, typing things into his phone. He looks up and quickly puts his phone in his pocket.

"What are you doing, Sasha? You should get in bed," he chastises me as he approaches.

I throw a hand up. "Stay away, I smell like vomit," I warn him.

He smirks down at me, then leans in and kisses my forehead gently.

"You're burning up. You need to rest."

"I'll be fine. You really don't have to do this," I insist. But my traitorous body swoons against the complete exhaustion of having just emptied my stomach several times over.

Without hesitation, Cal scoops me up and carries me to my room. Too weak to protest, I slump against his taut chest. Despite my feeling like death warmed up, being held by him is not unpleasant.

All too soon, he's gently placing me on the soft surface of my bed. I sink into the pillows, unable to fight it anymore. He leaves but returns a moment later with a large pot from the kitchen.

"Stay in bed," he instructs. "You can throw up into that if you need to. The worst of it should pass soon, then we can get some water into you. For now I've got a list of what you're missing, so I'll go to the corner store and come back as quickly as I can. Where are your keys?"

My illness-fogged brain can't make heads or tails of what he thinks I'm missing, but I gesture to the bag on the chair in the corner. "Keys are in my purse," I mumble, rolling onto my side and curling into a ball so I can hold my stomach. I try not to think about how horribly, embarrassingly bad I must look right now. Thankfully, he's gone before I can care too much. And before I start throwing up again.

He returns not twenty minutes later, and I hear him putting things away in the kitchen. While he does, I empty the pot in the bathroom and rinse it in the tub. That's as much as I have energy for, as it happens, so I slump back against the cool tile.

It's how Cal finds me a few minutes later, as I feel the pot gently tugged out of my hands. My eyes open. Apparently, I'd closed them.

I watch Cal set the pot on the counter. He stares down at me, half amused, half … I don't know, annoyed? Worried? It's hard to tell, and I don't feel well enough to care.

"I should shower," I say meekly. "I stink."

Cal shakes his head and slides his strong arms under me. And I'm still too out of it to stop him. He carries me back to the bed, puts me down, then retrieves the pot and sets it next to me.

"Rest. You can shower in the morning. I'm going to wash the hospital off of me. I'll be back."

My muddled brain tries to work out that he's going to be naked mere feet away while I lay here, helpless, but fatigue wins and I black out.

* * *

When I come to, it's dark, and my stomach protests immediately. It's not as urgent of a complaint, but I'm not sure I'm strong enough to get out of bed, so I throw up in the pot that's still next to me. Once I finish, I lean my head on the cool rim and groan.

A weight settles next to me on the bed and a warm hand rubs circles into my back.

I bolt upright to find Cal next to me in the dark.

"You're still here," I say, surprised.

"Of course I'm still here," he says sleepily. "Where else would I be?"

"At home? In your own bed?" I shake my head and sigh, taking in the white T-shirt and sweats he's wearing. "Where'd you get those clothes? And where were you sleeping?"

"Well, you're asking questions in full sentences, so you must be feeling better," he remarks drily. "I already told you, I'm going to take care of you, and I'm staying until you're well. I had a go-bag in my trunk with a change of clothes, and I was sleeping on the couch. Now lie down, and I'll clean this up." He reaches for the pot, but I stop him.

"I have to get up anyway," I grumble. I shuffle out of bed self-consciously, dragging the pot into the bathroom to clean it after I attend to my needs. As I do so, I note he's right. My head hurts, my mouth tastes disgusting, and my stomach is tender, but I think that was the last of it. In any case, nothing is spinning, and I don't feel like my insides are in a vice anymore.

I take a few minutes to brush my teeth, comb out my hair, and peel off the sweater I'd been wearing. By the time I'm done, I'm pretty confident I can ditch the pot, so I bring it into the kitchen and put it in the dishwasher. When I get back to the bedroom, I find Cal, still sitting on my bed in the dim light from the lamp on the nightstand, holding a glass of water.

He offers it as I walk toward him.

"Small sips," he instructs.

I take it with a frown. "Thanks. You didn't need to stay, though." I settle onto the bed and do as he told me, but even a few small sips is enough, and my stomach protests feebly. I set the glass down on the nightstand and turn back to him. "Really, I appreciate it, but you can go home now."

He reaches up and touches my face with the back of his hand. "You're still feverish, Sasha. I think the vomiting may have passed, but you're still weak, and you need rest and care."

"I'm a nurse, I'll manage," I reply stubbornly.

With his hand still at my cheek, he turns it so he's cupping my face. "I'm sure you could. But maybe I just want to take care of you."

Looking into his eyes, I see the sincerity. And it frankly terrifies me. Because I've taken care of myself for so long, and it's so part of my nature to take care of others, that the thought of letting someone take care of me is tough to swallow. No. Scratch that. The thought of him taking care of me, that I *want* him to take care of me, is what's alarming.

"Fine," I say with a sigh. "But only because I'm too weak to fight you."

Cal laughs. "I'll take it." He rises from the bed. "Get some more sleep. I'll be right out there, okay? Call out if you need anything."

He starts to back away, but I grab his hand. "You don't have to. I mean … you can sleep here if you want." I feel the heat creep up my neck.

He looks down at me, and a muscle ticks in his jaw as if he's trying to restrain himself from saying or doing the wrong thing. "Are you sure?"

I shrug, trying to seem more comfortable than I am. Because the thought of him sleeping in bed next to me ... but then, the wave of exhaustion that washed over me reminds me that I'm not exactly up for anything more than sleep anyway. "Yeah, I mean, it's just sleeping, right?"

"Okay," he agrees with a small smile.

I slide back down into my spot in the bed as he walks around and gets in on the other side. He looks like he's about to perch himself on the opposite edge, so I gesture for him to get closer. His smile widens and he slides behind me, spooning me with one arm draped carefully over my waist. I sink comfortably into his embrace, letting the sleepiness take over. Even in my sick and weary state, I don't miss how good it feels, how right, to be tucked into him.

"When did you know you wanted to be a doctor?" I ask sleepily.

A low chuckle vibrates through our joined bodies.

"What?" I protest.

"This is just not what I thought we'd be doing the first time I had you in bed at two in the morning," he replies. I rub my thumb over his hand, encouraging him to answer. "Okay. My mother died of heart disease when I was a teenager. The signs were there, but she didn't know to look for them. I wanted to make sure nobody ever had to lose their mother so unnecessarily again."

I swallow hard and look back at him. "I'm so sorry, Cal, I had no idea."

He props his head on his hand and smiles down at me. "Thank you. But it was a long time ago, and at least something good came of it."

My tired brain fights to form a thought just outside of my ability to grasp. A minute later, I suck in a sharp breath. "Is that why you were so upset about Mrs. Sampson?" I ask softly.

Cal rubs his thumb along the back of my hand. "Yes, I suppose it was, though even I didn't put that together until just now."

I shrug and give his hand a reassuring squeeze. "There are some things our conscious minds don't want to think about. I hope I didn't upset you by making the connection."

"It's hard for me to be upset when I'm close to you like this," he admits, looking down at me intently.

A wave of emotion washes through my exhausted body, and I close my eyes against the prick of tears. I take a deep breath and shove back the tide, unwilling to think too hard about the feelings his words evoked given my current, vulnerable state.

"I'm glad," I whisper. "Ready to sleep?"

He nods, so I reach out and turn off the lamp, plunging us back into darkness. I feel him bury his face in my hair, and his warm lips press a soft kiss to my neck, and it's the last thing I know.

CHAPTER 9

The whole next day, Cal attends to my every need as I feebly perform the basics of showering, eating, and hydrating between solid naps. Being weaker and more wiped out than I'd realized, I spend a good portion of the day sleeping.

In the evening, after Cal has served me homemade chicken soup that my stomach finally accepts, he gathers his things and heads home, needing to get himself ready for the workweek to come.

Once he's gone, and I'm floating back toward sleep once again, I find my thoughts difficult to control. And all I can think about is his tenderness, his gentle insistence on taking care of me, his strength. If I thought I was falling for him before, it was nothing compared to now. Today I was at my most vulnerable and Cal treated me with utter and complete respect and attention. It has not only deepened my respect for him, but it has also made me realize that he's not just everything I thought I wanted; he's also everything I didn't know I needed. A warm tear slips over my cheek as I drift off once more.

* * *

I'm tempted to take Monday off, but when I wake I feel strong enough. And I can't do nothing all day unless I'm as sick as I was yesterday. Since I'm not contagious anymore, I see no point in taking a day off anyway. Still, I don't push things too hard, leaning heavily on Becca and Jules to get through the day.

I don't see Cal until the afternoon, when I hand a patient off to him. The tenderness in his eyes nearly undoes me, but we manage to keep it professional. When he hands the patient back to me, he slips me a note. I can't read it until I'm back at the nurses' station later, though. When I do, I almost giggle like a schoolgirl but stop myself just in time.

Do you want to go out with me on Wednesday night (circle one)
Yes
No

Suppressing a grin, I circle "Yes" and fold the note. I grab a stack of papers from his cubby and let Becca know that I'll be right back. She's so busy she barely looks up, thank goodness. Cal isn't in his office, so I leave the papers on his chair, with the folded note right on top. As I return to the nurses' station, he walks by.

"The form you wanted filled out is on your chair," I inform him nonchalantly.

He raises an eyebrow and gets a glint in his eye but otherwise keeps a straight face. "Thank you," he replies simply. "I'll be in my office if anyone needs me."

I don't know if that's code for "meet me in my office," but Becca is now paying attention, watching his ass as he walks away. So I don't chance it, even though I wish I could see the look on his face when he reads the note.

Later that night, though, he texts me another kind of note. This one is a lot sexier. Well, not at first. At first it's just talking about plans for Wednesday. But then Cal jokes about the things he would have rather done Saturday night if I hadn't been sick, and it quickly devolves into what he would really want to do in bed with me at two in the morning.

I don't get as much sleep as I probably should, but I'm feeling fit as a fiddle on Tuesday. So much so that my thoughts are occupied with playing out all of the texted suggestions and other thoughts I've been having about Cal since his nurturing heroics this weekend. Needless to say, the workday is filled with all kinds of tension. I try my best not to stare at him because I'm still not ready to let the cat out of the bag, for so many reasons. I also have to work to ignore my phone during my evening classes, but we have another round of flirty texting while we each get ready for sleep.

By Wednesday, the waiting is pure, unadulterated torture. So when my shift is over, I tear out of there like a bat out of hell, intent on readying myself in the hour and a half or so I'll have until Cal picks me up for our date.

As I take a long, hot shower, I wonder idly if we'll even make it out of the apartment. The sexual tension is now thick, and if we don't do something about that soon, our secret won't keep much longer. At least, that's what I'm telling myself to justify my desperate need to have him naked stat. Funny how much things can change in such a short amount of time when you're being honest about what you want.

So when a knock comes at the door a good twenty minutes early, I'm both surprised and excited. But when I open the door, I get an even bigger surprise.

"Dad? What are you doing here?"

"Hi pumpkin, your mom wanted me to drop this off for you," he replies, holding up a bag. "She made Ptichye moloko cake, your favorite. We figured you could use a pick-me-up while you're studying." He eyes my fitted jeans and lacey white shirt. It's not exactly my usual study attire.

I step back to let him in. "That was sweet, thank you," I reply, suppressing a sigh.

He steps inside and sets the bag down on the tiny table just across from the door. "You're most welcome. How was your quiz?"

"It was fine. But I —" I'm interrupted by another knock. And this one must be Cal. Unless Becca decided to check on me too. "Just a sec, Dad." My father looks at me, a bit bewildered, but shrugs and wanders around the corner into the living room to make himself comfortable.

Opening the door does, in fact, reveal Cal, with an eager expression. And he looks fantastic in a pair of loose jeans and a V-neck white tee. It gives me my first glimpse of his well-muscled upper arms. They're every bit as amazing as I expected they'd be, and I'm momentarily stunned.

"Hello," he says, stepping forward to put those incredible arms around me.

I put a hand to his chest, intending to stop him, forgetting how distracting it is to touch him there. His questioning look snaps me back to reality. "My dad's here," I whisper.

"Okay. Then why don't you introduce me?" he whispers back.

"Are you sure?" I ask, still quietly but no longer whispering. "He just kind of showed up. I don't want to put you on the spot. He's going to ask who you are." I shift nervously from foot to foot. Knowing I'm basically asking Cal to define our relationship right this instant.

He grins at that. "I think I can handle it."

With a nervous huff, I gesture for him to follow me. We find my dad seated on the couch, flipping through one of my textbooks.

"Thinking about becoming a nurse practitioner, Dad?" I tease.

He looks up with a smirk, which quickly falls off his face when he sees Cal. "Ah, you have a visitor. I'm sorry, I didn't know this was a bad time," my dad says.

"It's fine," I assure him. "Dad, this is Caleb Thompson. Cal, this is my dad, Anatoly Suvorin."

Cal extends a hand, which my father accepts. "Mr. Suvorin, *rada poznakomitsya*."

"*Akh, vy govorite po-russki*," my father replies, clearly enthused.

They continue on in this manner for a few minutes with me looking between them, completely bewildered. Cal never mentioned that he spoke Russian. Though it does explain why he was so interested in my last name when we met.

After a few minutes of banter — and laughter, which made my jaw actually drop, as my dad is never so comfortable with strangers — they shake hands and my father starts to walk toward the door.

"Well, it was nice to see you, pumpkin, but I'd best be going." Still agog at what just happened, not that I'm entirely clear exactly what *did* happen, I see him to the door. "And I like your boyfriend. Seems like a good boy."

"You're only saying that because he speaks Russian," I grumble, not sure I'm entirely happy with what went down. And wondering if it was Cal who called himself my boyfriend, or if that was an assumption on my dad's part.

He pats me on the shoulder. "Any man who speaks Russian and asks my permission to take you on a date is in my good books," he replies with a smile. "We'll see you soon, *da*?" I smirk, as he hasn't used Russian expressions around me since I was little. I can tell he was pleased to be able to speak it again.

"Of course. Tell Mom thanks for the cake."

He gives me one last pat and smile and he's gone. I pick up the bag from the table and take it to the kitchen. Once the cake is in the fridge, I return to the living room, ready for an explanation.

Cal is sitting on the couch in the spot my dad vacated, socked feet up on the matched ottoman.

"I like your dad," he says, patting the cushion next to him.

"And he likes you," I reply, settling down next to him. "You never told me you speak Russian."

"It never came up. I lived there for a couple of years when I was young." He wriggles into the couch sinking back into the cushions. "This is ridiculously comfortable."

I can't help laughing. "Long day?"

"Ugh. The longest. There was the hottest nurse I couldn't stop running into all day. And when I wasn't drooling over her, I couldn't stop thinking about her. And there were some patients, a bunch of paperwork, and all that other crap," he says, waving a hand dismissively.

"I see. And this nurse, does she seem interested in you too? Because I might have to kick her ass."

He laughs and slings an arm around me, pulling me into his lap. "Hey, you," he murmurs, running his thumb across my lip.

"Hey yourself. Now what did you and my dad talk about?"

A mischievous grin spreads across his face. "Don't worry. I told him that we met at work, that I admire you greatly, and I would like to date you. He seemed pretty okay with that."

I stab a finger into his burly chest. "No, you *asked his permission* to date me."

He mock frowns. "Was I not supposed to do that?"

"I'm a grown woman. You don't need his permission."

Cal slides up on the couch. "I don't know how to say this without sounding like an asshole, but he's a Russian man. I needed to ask his permission to date you. I don't care if you're sixteen or sixty, it was the respectful thing to do."

"I thought you only needed to ask for permission to propose, not to date."

He shrugs. "Well, look at it this way: Better safe than sorry. Now. I'm starving. I'd planned to take you to this Italian place I found, but I'm knackered. Fancy ordering in? There's a killer diner down the street that delivers."

"I'm game. I know which one you're referring to, and it's one of my favorites. Know what you want?"

He nods and tells me what to order, and I call it in. Thankfully, they're speedy, and in only about twenty minutes we have a feast of burgers and fries spread out on the ottoman.

We chat about work as we eat, and my quiz, and all sorts of other random stuff. It's not lost on me that it feels like we've been dating far, far longer than we have. I'm usually not comfortable with people I don't know well and conversation is forced, but with Cal it just flows. And by the time we're done eating and have snuggled up on the couch to watch a movie, I'm feeling pretty good about my decision to be with him.

And when he looks down at me mid-movie, his eyes full of fire and mischief, I'm feeling *really* good about my decision. I pull his face down to mine, languishing in the feeling of him next to me as we slowly explore each other's mouths with our tongues and bodies with our hands. Like before, it heats up quickly.

Soon, Cal is pressing into me, laying me back on the couch and hovering over me. As our kisses turn feverish, I grind against him, looking for relief for the ache that has already started building. Though really it's been building for days, possibly weeks, so I shouldn't be surprised.

"You have no idea how much I've thought about doing exactly this all week long," he says into my lips.

I stroke my arms down his back. "Oh, I do. Because I've been thinking about the exact same thing, I promise you."

"Yeah? What exact thing are you thinking about right now?"

I pull my lips into my teeth and inhale sharply. "You touching me," I admit.

"Mmm," he mutters, sliding a hand between my legs and rubbing me through my jeans. "Like this?"

"Yes," I breathe. "But with less clothing."

He slides a hand between us and pops the button of my jeans, slowly lowering the zipper. And I've never realized it before, but it's just about one of the best sounds in the world. I lift my hips so he can peel them off, trembling with anticipation.

"I want you naked, Sasha," he says, pulling me up by my hands.

With a shudder, I lift off my shirt, then unhook my bra. He helps me pull it off, then stares as I lay back down. Totally nude, and totally at his mercy. The look on his face alone could make me come if I'm not careful.

"Fuck, you're beautiful."

"I want you so bad, Cal," I plead.

With a smile, he settles himself between my legs. "Patience, love." He leans in, kisses me lightly on the lips, then moves down to take one of my nipples in his mouth. As his mouth moves to service the other nipple, he drops his hand between my legs to find me wet and ready for him.

He groans into my breast at finding me so turned on and slips his fingers inside me, pumping slowly as he continues to work my nipple. I pull my knees up, urging him to go deeper, and writhing with desire.

When his head drops between my legs, and his tongue flicks against my clit, I'm pretty sure I've gone to heaven.

"Oh, yes, god, yes," I moan.

His tongue flattens against me in response, licking firmly along the hard nub, and one of my legs starts to shake. He stills it with his free hand, continuing his oral and manual assault, slowly pleasuring me.

"Fuck, Sasha, you make the most gorgeous noises," he groans. He removes his hand and licks all the way up my core. His hands press my knees apart, widening me and exposing me fully to his wicked, hot mouth. "Now keep your legs open." He looks up and waits for my acceptance. I can barely nod I'm so worked up.

And this time when he resumes, he holds nothing back. He slips in two fingers, mercilessly curling them and pumping into me as he sucks my clit into his mouth, rolling his tongue in circles as his mouth creates a pull that has me instantly hurtling toward ecstasy.

I don't even have time or the ability to warn him before I clench around him, and my vision explodes with bright, popping lights as the hedonistic pleasure vibrates through my entire body, my bones, out into my extremities in an orgasm so intense I'm rendered incoherent as my moans of "oh god" turn into one loud and unearthly cry.

As I sink back down, Cal covers me with his body, his lips hot on mine, his hands holding my face to his. Because apparently I can't even control my own neck at the moment. I wallow in the feeling of his tongue in my mouth, my mind blissfully blank and helpless against the effect of his touch.

"Sasha," he whispers against my ear.

"Mmmm," I mutter, lolling my head toward him.

His low chuckle meets my ears as I start to drift. "Never mind. Just sleep," he says lowly. The warm comfort of a blanket envelopes me, and his lips meet my neck. It's the last thing I feel before drifting off.

CHAPTER 10

The next thing I know, my phone alarm wakes me up on Thursday morning. And I'm still naked. On my couch. Alone. On the ottoman sits a note. *You were so comfortable and happy, I didn't want to move you to the bed. Which I will be joining you in again soon, just didn't think I should tonight. Miss you already. — Cal x.*

I cover my face with my hands, fully embarrassed. The man comes over, impresses my father, woos me with my favorite takeout, then cuddles me and gives me an amazing orgasm, and what do I do? I fall asleep. God, I feel so stupid.

Unfortunately, I don't have time to wallow, and I rush to get ready for work. My mortification starts to fade as my mind drifts to all the goodness of last night. Being close to him. Talking with him like we've known each other forever. His hands on me. Other parts of him on me. I stuff the last one down, knowing I'm going to have to have my game face on at work if we're going to keep this from our coworkers. And thinking about him doing the things he did … well, that's definitely not going to help. Nor will thinking about his promise to join me in bed. For more than just sleep. Which no longer scares me. In fact, if it doesn't happen soon, I may end up jumping him in his office.

But by the time I get to work, I've flipped back to insecure again. I cringe, shake my head, or facepalm every time I think about him leaving because I fell asleep. After our first sexual encounter. My self-conscious behavior is not lost on Becca.

"You look like I feel," she grumbles.

"Well, thanks," I say sarcastically. "What's got you so grouchy?"

"I just heard from one of the MAs over in intensive care that bad boy hottie has a girlfriend. So I've had better days. Looks like you might be in the same boat. That wouldn't, by any chance, have anything to do with Dr. Thompson, would it?"

I pull a face. "What makes you think it has anything to do with him? Maybe I'm just extra tired," I reply snarkily, lifting my traveling mug to demonstrate.

"Oh, I know you, my dear, and I will get it out of you. But right now coffee sounds like a very good idea. For everyone else's safety." And with that she slips away.

I spend the rest of the day trying to avoid her. But avoiding two people is immensely stressful, and by the time my shift is over I have no desire to go to class. But I do anyway. Because I'm paying for school myself. And fuck if I'm going to miss out on something I'm spending good money on.

* * *

But on Friday, I'm not so lucky, and Becca finally catches up with me midmorning.

"Don't think I haven't noticed you avoiding me," she says, sliding into the chair next to me in the breakroom, coffee in hand.

"Just been busy," I lie. "And my break's up, so I should get back to it." I start to rise, but Becca shakes her head.

"Oh, Sasha, you're a horrible liar. I saw you come in here two minutes ago. Sit that adorable ass back down."

I slink back into my chair with a sigh. "I'm sorry, you're right, I've been avoiding you."

"Well, duh," Becca says, rolling her eyes. "What I want to know is *why*. Did I say something to piss you off?"

"No," I protest. "I just … you know sometimes I kind of close ranks. This is one of those times."

Becca sighs, spinning her mug in circles. Finally, she looks up at me, with a wounded air about her. "You know you can talk to me about anything, right? Even if I do get a little cray-cray from time to time, I've got your back."

I reach over and squeeze her hand reassuringly. "I know. And when I'm ready to talk, you'll be the first person to know. I promise." But part of me wonders how much of this is her still pushing to know if this has anything to do with Cal. On the bright side, that means we've done a passable job of acting normally at work. It could also mean Becca wants to be privy to the gossip first, being as nosy as she is. But I'll choose to give her the benefit of the doubt. She has a big heart, and I know she's mostly looking out for me.

"Good. Now, I know you'll probably say no, but we're doing happy hour tonight. You're welcome to join. Or not. If this has anything to do with Dr. Thompson, he won't be there, I already asked him."

I press my lips together. No, he wouldn't be going, because he's already agreed to make me dinner at his place.

"Thanks, but I need to catch up on studying. Finals are week after next." That's not a lie. And I will be studying most of the weekend. Well, tomorrow at least, since Cal will be working anyway.

"Suit yourself," she says with a shrug, looking defeated. It's *exactly* how she looked yesterday, so it occurs to me that it probably has less to do with me and more to do with the bad boy orderly who apparently has a girlfriend. She must've been more into him than I realized. Like more into him than anyone she has been in a long time, because I can't remember the last time I've seen her so bummed out by something. It's definitely dulled her usual sparkle.

"Hey," I say, catching her eye. "How about we do lunch tomorrow instead? I can take a break."

She sighs. "That's sweet, but I switched shifts with Harper. Thanks, though."

"Okay. Well, I may be doing my thing, but you know I'm always here for you too, right?"

That gets a wan smile at least. "Thanks, boo."

It does little to reassure me, but I decide to leave her be. She'll snap out of it. She always does.

* * *

"Aren't you supposed to be cooking?" I tease Cal as he pins me against the island in his kitchen.

"Oh, I've got something cooking all right, it's just not food," he teases back, his lips closing over mine again.

I giggle through our kiss, loving every minute of this. The flirting, the kissing, the lighthearted and lusty part of dating someone. It's sublime.

"I love making you laugh," he murmurs. "You're always so serious at work."

"Mmm," I reply noncommittally. "Not much to laugh about there."

"I also like it when you sound like this ..." He slips a hand under my skirt, stroking me through my panties, eliciting a deep moan.

"Ohhh, if you keep doing that, we'll never finish making dinner," I say, sagging into him. Not that I really want him to stop. But he's catered to my pleasure long enough that I'm ready to take matters into my own hands. Literally. I reach down and stroke him through his jeans, for the first time getting a good feel of what promises to be an impressive cock.

"Oh fuck, Sasha, if you keep doing that, I'm going to end up taking you *on* the food, then where will we be?"

"In bed, with lettuce on my back, but still having great sex?" I tease.

"You cheeky little minx," he purrs, kissing me lightly on the nose. "And for the record, it's going to be better than great, you can bet on that."

"Promises, promises," I cluck.

He raises one eyebrow. And it's all the warning I get before he scoops me up, tosses me over his shoulder, and carries me to his bedroom like a caveman. I'd be lying if I said I didn't love it, but I squeal in surprise anyway, which is only rewarded with a low chuckle.

Once we're in his room, he tosses me on the bed, immediately climbing on top of me and claiming my lips with his while he grinds into me. When he releases my mouth, I'm gasping for air but still scrambling to pull his shirt off of him. I've been dreaming of this for weeks, and I need to see this man naked as soon as humanly possible.

But as he removes his shirt, I realize my wildest fantasies had nothing on reality. Lean and sculpted, every muscle in his shoulders, arms, chest, and abs are defined and popping, with smooth grooves between that are begging to be touched. I lean up, running my fingers over them, then repeating the motion with my tongue. He looks down at me, amused, as I worship his muscled body.

My kisses trail down to the waistband of his pants, my hands working quickly to unbutton and unzip them. He continues to watch me, now more alert and focused as I unfurl him from his boxers. All of him. And as hinted at, it's not inconsiderable. A low moan escapes me and I push him back onto the bed, ready to pleasure him. Not that it's going to be a sacrifice. Because damn the man is gorgeous.

I grab the base of his cock in my fist and look up at him. His hands are behind his head, his abs tensed in preparation for the sensations that are about to come. I give him a wicked grin and slowly unleash my tongue on the tip.

His face tenses with the effort it takes to keep watching. So I give him a show that's sure to send his eyes rolling back in his head as I lick down then back up his full length, swirling my tongue around and working his shaft with my hand. It does the trick, and he groans, his head tipping back and his eyes closing. But I'm only getting started.

I unleash on him, same as he did on me, sucking and pumping until he's making the most erogenous noises I've ever heard. His hands drop to the bedspread, gripping it tightly as he struggles to stay still under my provocation.

Abruptly, as if he can't take being the sole focus, he sits up, grabbing my hips and turning them so my backside is toward his head, but at such an angle where he can still watch me. And he slips a hand under my panties, feeling the wetness that's there. It causes me to lose focus as heat creeps up my cheeks while his finger flicks against my clit.

"I'm done playing," he announces, pulling my skirt and panties toward him in one, sharp tug. I roll over, allowing him to remove them completely before sitting back up and tugging off my own shirt and bra. He leans over to the nightstand, retrieving a condom from the drawer and handing it to me.

Heat shoots through me knowing I'm about to have him inside of me, finally, and I can't get the damn thing on him fast enough. Finally, I swing a leg over him, and he guides my hips into place.

Slowly, I sink onto him, letting myself expand around him inch by inch. He watches me with bated breath as I do, and it makes me so wet for him that it's barely a challenge to sink him to the hilt, despite his size. We both groan as soon as he's fully seated in me. I lean forward to kiss him, and the fullness shifts, causing me to shiver with desire.

Looking intently into his eyes, I give him the lightest of kisses before tilting my hips over him. And it feels beyond amazing. I slowly work up my speed, but the sensation proves to be so overwhelming, I start to swoon. He grabs me by the hips, steadying me so he can pump into me from below. The muscles of his abs and chest pull together with each thrust, and it turns me on so much I think I might orgasm on the spot.

As if sensing it, he sits up, hauls me over onto my back, and slides back in. Rearing back, with my hips in his lap, he pumps deeply, and an ache builds inside with tremendous force. But I can't contain it, and before I mean to, the orgasm takes me, I tighten around him, and he groans but keeps up his rhythm. As my muscles begin to relax, he withdraws, turning me on my side and laying down behind me.

For a moment, I think he's going to hold me, as one hand wraps under my head, holding my chest. But he uses his other hand to pull my hips back, then lift my leg. And I feel him slide into me again, this time from behind.

"Holy …" I cry out.

"Too much?" he asks gently.

I shake my head. "Just give me a second," I breathe.

He nods, dropping a kiss on my shoulder. He props my leg up on his hip, then reaches a hand below it, gently stroking my clit in circles. I feel a fresh wave of arousal rip through me, and he starts to move, slowly. The pressure recedes, and it's replaced with pure enjoyment.

"Oh, that's good," I say with a sigh. "Soooo good."

He picks up his speed, and I nod encouragingly. We go back and forth in the same manner until his speed is too much.

"Slower," I plead.

He backs down accordingly but switches to harder thrusts, and my body does not miss that change. I feel the ache immediately, and I gasp.

"Bad?" he checks.

"God, no. That feels — ohhh — that feels so good," I moan.

"You like it hard like that, Sasha?" he asks, thrusting hard and slow. The ache spreads, and all I can do is nod. "God, you feel amazing."

He keeps going, pounding slow and hard, but suddenly his breathing changes, and the hand on my chest grips my breast in a way that spins me teeteringly close to the edge. So when he speeds up, I can't help it, and I come hard as he pounds into me in a frenzy. I hear him groan his release softly into my ear, and it spikes my orgasm again, causing me to cry out as I'm thrown back to my peak.

Finally, I descend, shuddering blissfully around his abating erection. He doesn't pull out but instead sinks into me, wrapping his arm around my waist. I relax into him, and he holds me until our breathing has returned to normal.

"I'll be right back," he murmurs. And then he's pulled out, and pulled away, and the absence of him brings a coolness to my skin that would be welcoming if it didn't mean he'd gone.

Thankfully, he returns quickly, and I feel him slip into position, followed by a trail of kisses down my arm.

"You were right," I say.

I feel him shift, and I turn to look up at him, with his head now propped on his arm.

"About what?" he asks with a curious expression.

"That was way better than great."

His answering grin gives me flutters, and I can't help smiling back.

"I'm glad you enjoyed it," he remarks, dropping another kiss on my shoulder.

"Mmmm, you know what else I'd enjoy? Dinner."

He laughs heartily. "Demanding little thing, aren't you?"

I wriggle against him. "I was promised food."

"Yes, I suppose you were," he admits. But then his mouth drops to my neck, his pelvis tilting into my back as he kisses and rubs into me. "Though that was before I had a taste of you. I'm not sure I'm ready to let you escape."

And even though I'm completely spent, the feel of his hard body, soft lips, and sexy words has my core aching for him again and I groan out a response before I can stop myself. "You make a persuasive argument," I say, panting as his hands slide over me. My stomach chooses that moment to let out an almighty growl.

I feel his low chuckle against my neck, then, sadly, he pulls away. I look over to find him pulling his clothes back on, covering his gorgeous body. With a resigned sigh, I do the same.

* * *

A couple of hours later, I have no regrets as I sit with my legs in his lap on his couch. The "fry up," as he called it, was delicious and absolutely hit the spot. But between a tasty meal, a comfy sofa, and our antics from earlier, we're both happy to simply relax and spend the rest of the night talking, kissing, and touching with no particular agenda.

Eventually, Cal nuzzles against me, nodding toward the clock on the opposite wall. "It's getting late."

With a pout, I run a hand down his arm. "That's right, you have to go in tomorrow."

He pulls back, his blue eyes drinking me in in the low light. "Stay."

A small smile pulls at my lips. "Are you asking or telling?"

He smirks and shakes his head, leaning in to kiss me. It's another sweet, playful kiss, and as I melt into him, his strong arms wrap around me.

I thread my fingers through his hair. I'm practically high on him, and I couldn't leave if I wanted to. And since I've got a long weekend of studying ahead of me, I'll happily take as much of him as I can get.

Eventually he stops kissing me long enough to scoop me up, rising from the couch and carrying me off to bed where he throws me into the soft pillows. I squeal with laughter as I land and he plops down next to me.

He finds a shirt for me to wear to bed and we spend far longer than we should laying together and talking. It's comfortable and exciting all at once, and neither of us can seem to get enough of learning about the other, even as our eyes start to droop and yawns start coming more frequently. At some point we admit defeat, and as I fall asleep in his arms, I wish I hadn't resisted him all those weeks. Even though on some level I realize it's because of exactly this; that I knew how much I could feel for this man. That our chemistry both inside the bedroom and out would be like nothing I've ever felt. It both excites me and terrifies me in equal measure. I close my eyes and hope for the best.

CHAPTER 11

I'm supposed to be studying. I need to be studying. This degree is everything I've been working toward for the better part of ten years. But all I can think about is Cal. His eyes. His smile. His gorgeous body, and what it can do to me.

It didn't help that I woke up in his bed this morning, albeit alone as he'd already gone to work. But my hair, my clothes, my skin all still smelled like him. All the way home. Through breakfast. And now, I'm sitting here, wallowing in the scent of him on me, and the memories of last night.

I finally realize I'm going to need a shower and a fresh set of clothes if I'm going to have a real shot at getting anything done today. Unfortunately, that can't do much for what's going on in my head, but once it's done it does help enough for me to start making slow progress.

I inch through the morning, lunch, and part of the afternoon before I cave and pick up my phone to text him, only to find he's already texted me. *Miss you x.*

With a silly grin, I text him back. *Miss you too.*

All progress comes to a screeching halt as I continually check for a response. But it doesn't come. Eventually, I'm able to get back to it, but when I take a break for dinner, I find I'm decidedly pouting.

It makes me want to smack myself. *Really, Sasha? You're letting a guy distract you?* I chide myself. I'm about to have the cake my dad dropped off for dinner when the doorbell rings. I slam the fridge door shut, still grumpy.

Though I'm instantly less so when I open the door to find Cal, still in scrubs, standing on the doorstep. Which ironically annoys me, as I'd just finished beating myself up for letting him sidetrack me.

"Hey," he greets me, looking a little confused at the less-than-thrilled expression on my face. "I texted you that I was coming over. Did you not get it?"

I furrow my brow. "No, I didn't," I reply, stepping back to let him in and pulling my phone out of my pocket. As I go to unlock it, I realize it's on silent. Which is why I didn't see his first text, and now there's another asking if I want to grab some dinner. "Sorry." I give a shrug.

"Everything okay?" he asks, stepping into me and lifting my chin up. He runs his thumb over my cheek and, staring up into his baby blue eyes, I find it impossible to be cross with him. Besides, it's not his fault that he's apparently like crack to me.

"Didn't get much done today," I admit.

He raises an eyebrow. "Me neither."

That gets a small smile out of me. "I guess I could use some dinner. What'd you have in mind?"

He smiles so wide it crinkles the corners of his eyes, and I melt just a little. "There's a great sushi bar between yours and mine."

Happy that it's not the usual after-work hangout, I nod. "I'm game. Let me just grab my purse."

I get my things and he leads me out and down to his car. We chat idly about his day on the short drive, and I start to relax again for the first time today. Once we've gotten to the restaurant, I find I'm ravenous, and the food does wonders to lift my mood, to the point where the tension has completely drained away and we're back to our normal, comfortable banter.

That is until — as I'm playfully feeding Cal a spicy tuna roll, the last of our meal — Becca and Harper walk in. All four of us freeze, even Cal who is clearly now too stunned even to chew. It's obvious from the looks on their faces that they saw me feeding him. Becca reacts first, and when her expression closes, I know she's furious. I'd led her to believe something bad had happened between Cal and me, and I can see the betrayal in her dark brown eyes. Cal looks between us for a moment, finally finding himself as he quickly chews and swallows and wipes his face with a napkin.

"Ladies," he greets them, as casually as if this happens every day and that our obvious display of affection was in no way strange. "Nice to see you. Would you like to join us?"

I start losing the battle against the heat of embarrassment and guilt creeping up my neck as Harper also looks between Becca and me, then Cal and I, as if completely unsure how to act.

"Thanks, but we don't want to interrupt your date," Becca replies pointedly.

"It's really no trouble," Cal insists, in no way refuting her supposition that this is a date. I mean, of course it is, but he's now basically confirmed it, and Harper looks like she can barely suppress her glee. Hello, rumor mill.

Becca presses her lips together, looking like she's about to explode.

"That's kind of you, but it looks like you're finishing up," Harper interjects, looking askance at Becca. "It'll probably take us a while to figure out what we want anyway, right, Becca? I wasn't even sure I wanted to come here, since I've never had sushi before. But I insisted on treating Becca for picking up my shift today so I could go with my family to see my grandma in hospice." Harper abruptly stops, realizing she's rambling, and smiles nervously.

"Well, I do hope your grandmother is comfortable and being well looked after," Cal replies kindly, though even he's starting to succumb to the awkwardness of this encounter. He shoots me a look, pleading for me to say something.

I clear my throat. "Yes, I hope she's doing okay," I amend, throwing a sympathetic look toward Harper before shifting my gaze to Becca. "Why don't we talk for a minute and give Harper a chance to go look at the menu?"

A sudden sweet and completely dangerous smile breaks over Becca's face. "Yes, let's," she says, venomously cheerful.

Cal squeezes my hand and I look over at him. Pity is written all over his face, as he clearly senses what's about to go down. "I'll be in the car," he murmurs softly before sliding out of the booth and giving Becca a wary smile. "Enjoy your evening."

Becca just shoots him a look as he leaves, folding her arms over her chest. Since she's obviously not going to sit down, I stand up and approach carefully.

"Hey," I say lamely.

"So. How long has this been going on?" she asks sharply.

"Okay, so, we're doing this," I reply with a sigh. "It's been about a week. I'm sorry, Becca, I just wanted to keep it to myself until … I don't know, until I knew where it was going."

She barks a sharp laugh. "So instead you made me think something awful had happened between you two? Right. Just be honest, Sasha, what you really mean is that you wanted to keep it from me because you don't trust me."

"It's not about that," I insist. "You know me, Becks, I'm just a private person. Taking this step was huge for me. I just needed some time."

"Well, you guys looked pretty cozy," she grumbles. I breathe an inward sigh of relief as I feel her anger starting to dissipate. And lo and behold, she turns the puppy dog eyes on. Now I brace myself for the oncoming guilt trip. "Were you ever going to tell me?"

I shift uncomfortably. "I hadn't thought that far ahead," I admit. "Probably? It's just been nice to be in this little bubble of it being only me and him." I shrug, not sure I can fully explain it. Becca is so different, always telling me everything, usually in far more detail than is necessary.

She just stares at me for a minute, the hurt written all over her face. Her mouth opens and closes a couple of times before she shakes her head. "You probably shouldn't keep him waiting," she finally says, averting her eyes.

My heart sinks into my stomach at the thought of leaving things like this with her. Because even though she's not mad anymore, I know she's still disappointed and that things won't be right with her until she's come to terms with it enough to forgive me. Unfortunately, I'm not very good at explaining myself to others. It just doesn't come naturally. And I know it's going to make getting over this bump in our friendship difficult.

"Becca, I'm sorry, I don't know what else to say," I reply honestly. "I hope you don't stay mad at me forever. Our friendship means a lot to me."

Normally a huge softie, my words don't have any effect on her; if anything, she looks even sadder. "If that were true you would've told me. And you definitely wouldn't have lied to me." She sighs, and a leaden weight settles on my heart. "I'll see you around, Sasha." She turns and heads to the counter to meet back up with Harper.

I stand there for a few moments, gathering the will to leave. I stare after her, hoping for her to turn around with forgiveness in her eyes. But she doesn't.

Eventually, I turn and walk out. I don't even register I've found my way back to the car until I'm sliding into it. Cal looks over at me nervously, his dark hair tousled from running his hands through it. Thankfully, he doesn't say anything, doesn't ask what happened, and definitely doesn't throw me a pity party. He simply takes my hand and drives back to my place.

When he parks in front of my building, I sit there numbly for a moment, unsure of whether I want to be alone to process all of this or invite him upstairs and distract myself from the sting of Becca's reaction.

"So I take it that was Becca finding out about us," he says lightly after several minutes of silence. "And that she wasn't terribly thrilled you hadn't told her."

I nod morosely, examining my hands in my lap. "I kind of … let her believe something bad had happened between us last week," I admit. "So she has good reason to be upset."

"Ah. I see." He stares out the window for a moment. "And I hate to add to things, but I fear this means we've reached a tipping point."

I huff a laugh through my nose. "Meaning?"

He turns to look at me. "Meaning, we can continue seeing one another, knowing our coworkers are all likely to soon know that that's exactly what's happening," he replies, "or if you'd intended to keep this a secret and now that it's not would rather put an end to things …" He looks at me meaningfully. He knows how much that thought scared me.

It sinks in that he's giving me an out. If I'm really not okay continuing a relationship with our coworkers being all up in our business, I can walk away.

I quickly weigh the options in my mind. Staying together will mean constant gossip, interference, and tension at work. Possibly indefinitely. Even thinking about the drama makes me want to run and hide. But ending things … that thought sends a sharp pain through my gut. Neither option is sunshine and roses. And the idea of giving him up now … I look up at him, tears swimming in my eyes.

"I don't want to end things."

The relief on his face is obvious, and he reaches over to brush a tear from my cheek. He then unclips his seatbelt and gets out, coming around to open my door. He helps me out, then leads me up to my apartment.

As soon as I let us in, he pulls me into his arms. His thumbs stroke my cheeks, his strong hands holding my face. I look up into his eyes, which are now a stormy blue-grey, and I see a swirl of emotion too complex to read. His thick brows are pinched together, his mouth turned down as his eyes search mine. A thumb slides across my lip. He leans in and brushes his mouth over mine tentatively.

I close my eyes and let the tears slip over my cheeks, not caring anymore whether I cry in front of him. Between Becca's disappointment and realizing that Cal and I are truly at a crossroads, the emotion is just too much. I've never handled my feelings well, always pushing them down. But these … well, they're not staying down. I push my lips into his, needing the connection. Needing to forget everything else.

He seems hesitant at first, his lips keeping light contact. But I need more if I'm going to wipe all of this from my mind. I grab his bottom lip with my teeth and wrap my arms around his neck. I push my tongue into his mouth, needing to taste him. Finally, he relents, and he presses me into the wall next to the door, his whole body responding to my invitation.

His hands slip under my shirt, sliding up my back and undoing the clasp of my bra as his hips pin me to the wall. I lift my arms, begging him silently to undress me. With a growl, he pushes off my lips and tears off my shirt and bra together, exposing my breasts to the cool air. His mouth dips down, mercilessly pulling at each nipple in turn. The heat begins to rise in my core, blessedly taking away any thought but him from my mind.

I pull at his shirt until it's joined mine on the floor, running my hands over the muscles of his chest and stomach. My hands slip to his hips, working his scrub bottoms and boxers down until they fall to the floor. He steps out of them impatiently, grabbing at the waistband of my jeans and pulling me into the bedroom behind us.

He pushes me backward onto the bed, climbing quickly after me and tugging off my bottoms. I roll over and scoot to the head of the bed, retrieving a condom from the nightstand. When I turn back, he's sat on the end of the bed on his haunches, staring at me with so much raw passion on his face I can barely stand it. I toss him the condom, which he deftly catches, then I turn around so I'm facing away, and look back at him pointedly, silently saying, *"Take me."* His muscles tense and his cock twitches, growing so hard it makes me beyond ready for him. I turn my head toward the headboard again. I can't handle his intensity any more than I can handle my own right now.

His hand runs over my backside, dipping between my thighs. His fingers slide over my wet core, and he sucks in a sharp breath. I hear the foil packet rip and then a moment later, the hard tip of his cock nudges between my legs.

My hips tilt back reflexively, begging him for it. I need this. I need him. The realization breaks the dam of emotion, and tears slip out of my eyes as he pushes into me. But it doesn't diminish how good he feels buried inside. I tilt forward then push back, starting a rhythm that he quickly picks up. He grabs my hips, reinforcing each thrust.

Tears continue to leak silently from my eyes as we both pant quietly into the pleasure. The loudest sound in the room is the sound of his hips slapping into my backside, flesh meeting flesh: the sound of us. Together as one as we experience the basest of pleasures, as he rides me through this mess of feelings swirling inside of me. The dull ache of my orgasm building begins, and I spasm around him. He wordlessly takes note, slamming harder on each thrust until little gasps escape me every time his cock fills me, with every inch I climb up the peak until I need to bury my face in the bedspread as I cry out my orgasm.

Suddenly, he pushes forward until his knees are at my sides, lowering my hips into his lap so he can go deeper, harder, faster. He takes me like an animal, pounding furiously. As the sheer force and speed of his thrusts register, I'm thrown back over the edge into an oblivion so deep and wide that I lose all sense. He's fucking me so hard that it's starting to hurt, but in a way that only adds to the pleasure. He keeps going, and so does my climax, taking me so deeply, so completely that I'm shaking with the gratification spreading through every cell of my body as he masters me completely.

Finally, unable to hold myself up, my arms collapse underneath me and I sink into the pillow. Only then does he slow and stop, backing off so I can sink fully down to the mattress.

He rolls me gently over, and I'm not surprised to find him covered in sweat. What I am surprised to see is his huge, hard cock still fully at attention. Unsure if I can take anymore, but unable to speak, I simply shake my head.

He leans forward, his expression veiled, and gives me a light kiss. One that he trails down my body, until his mouth covers my pussy, his tongue oh-so-gently flattened against the throbbing, slightly sore surface. He licks up my core, flicking the tip of his tongue across my clit. I moan quietly in approval. So he does it again, and again, until I can't tell if it's because of his tongue or if it's my own arousal spread all over.

It's then that he climbs over me, one hand gently cupping my face, the other positioning his cock to enter me. But he waits, tip at my entrance, for me to give permission. And with one nod, he slides slowly in, filling my aching core. It straddles the border of pleasure and pain, but as his mouth finds mine, his body covering me completely, I surrender and let him take what he wants. His head drops next to mine, his breathing labored in my ear.

"Stay with me." He says it so quietly I almost don't hear him.

I press my hands to the sides of his face, lifting his head so I can look at him.

"I'm with you," I whisper.

"Completely?"

"Completely," I agree as tears flow afresh out of the corners of my eyes.

With his forehead pressed to mine, his hips tilt rapidly and I feel the orgasm take him in the tightness of his shoulders, the gasping of his breath. And then he stills, sinking down onto me, his head tucked into the crook of my neck. I wrap my legs around him, holding him with my arms until his breathing evens out and his heart rate returns to normal.

Once it does, he climbs off of me, offering me a hand. I take it, unsure of what he intends to do. He leads me into the bathroom, where he turns on the shower and discards the condom. He helps me into the tub enclosure, then joins me, pulling the curtain closed.

Wordlessly, he rinses off under the hot stream of water. I twist my hair up and use the clip on the tub ledge to hold it in place so I can step closer to him and get clean. He's still strangely so quiet, though, through the entire shower and after as we dry off.

"I'm afraid I don't have a change of clothes with me," he admits as I strip the damp comforter off the bed and replace it with a clean, dry blanket.

I throw him a vague smile over my shoulder. "Well, if you want to stay I can throw your scrubs in the wash."

He grabs my wrist, gently tugging me into his arms. "Of course I want to stay."

I smile up at him lightly. "Then I'll go put them in." I press out of his arms but feel a swell of emotion as I turn away. *God, what is wrong with me?*

Shaking myself a little, I retrieve his clothes from the hall, as well as my own, and toss it all into the washing machine.

When I get back to the bedroom, Cal is under the covers, one arm slung behind his head to prop him up. In a word, he's stunning. But I realize all this emotion is because I've chosen him. Which was fine when we were in our bubble. Consciously remaking that choice when I know how hard things are going to be at work because of it is a completely different ballgame. And it's not the drama I'm more scared of, it's how much I already care for him that I'd even make that decision in the first place.

I sit down on the bed next to him, facing him. "Do you think this is going too fast?"

He frowns deeply, drawing himself upright so he's sitting opposite me. "That's a loaded question if I've ever heard one."

I shrug. "You seemed pretty worried that the thing with Becca and Harper would make me change my mind about us."

"I was. I am."

"Even though I've told you twice since then that I'm still in this?"

He gives me a half-hearted smile. "It's easy to do now, as the shit's only starting to hit the fan. Them finding out is just the beginning."

"Yes," I agree. "But it doesn't seem weird to you that we've only been seeing each other for two weeks and we're both ..." I trail off, realizing it might not be fair to lump his feelings with mine. Because maybe I'm misinterpreting things.

"Really into each other?" he offers with a sideways smile, running his hand along my thigh.

I snort. "That's the mild version, but yes, that's basically where I was going with that."

He reaches up and his fingers now trail down my jaw. "I don't know. One day at a time, love. And this was a particularly intense one."

I take a deep breath, realizing how truly exhausted I am. "Fair enough." I slide down into the bed and Cal slips behind me, wrapping me in his arms. It doesn't take long for me to fall into a blissfully deep and dreamless sleep, despite my worry.

.

CHAPTER 12

When we wake on Sunday, Cal convinces me to let him spend the day with me, despite my need to study. But he thoughtfully accounted for that, agreeing to reward me for my accomplishments with food and *other things*, said with a wink. There's no way on earth I could say no to that. Besides, it's his only day off, and if that's how he wants to spend it, who am I to stop him?

I surprisingly manage to get quite a bit done. The simplicity of the day and the sheer decadence of having Cal wait on me helps me keep my mind off of anything that might worry me. That can all wait.

But as Cal goes to return to his own home and bed for the night so he can get ready for his workweek, I'm reluctant to let him, knowing reality is about to come crashing back in.

I even dream about it. Well, they're borderline nightmares. Even unconscious, my mind flips through all the horrible possibilities that await.

So when I wake up on Monday morning at my normal ungodly hour, I'm even more reluctant than usual to leave the warmth of bed. But I've always been one to put on my big-girl panties and take what's coming. It's the fastest way to get it over with.

When I get to work, I attempt to approach the nurses' station from the opposite direction, hoping to just drop my things off without Becca noticing.

"Morning meeting has been moved back fifteen minutes," she says without turning around. I jump about a foot in the air, not having expected her to notice me, much less say something.

"Okay, thanks," I mumble, glad for the extra time to go refill my travel mug. But before I can get far, Becca actually turns toward me.

"For the record, I'm not going to tell anybody. Not even Jules. Since you obviously don't trust me, I just wanted you to know."

My insides twinge with guilt. "Becks —"

"Don't call me that," she snaps.

And I can't help it, that really pisses me off. "Oh, no. *You* don't," I demand. "I screwed up. I'm sorry, okay? Either forgive me so we can move on, or don't. I can't make you. But just remember that you're not a fucking saint either, Becca, and I've put up with a lot of shit from you over the years. Because that's what friends do." I grip my mug tightly and stomp off to the break room more immaturely than I'd usually allow myself to. I swear, sometimes we're more like sisters than friends the way we get after each other. That thought just makes me even sadder and angrier with the whole situation.

My mood isn't helped when Harper, Avery, and Lacey enter the room, giggling among themselves. They stop once they spot me, give each other looks, and giggle some more. Just great. So Becca learns to keep her trap shut, but Harper's gone and mouthed off already. Awesome.

I shake my head and, without a word to any of them, stalk out of the room. I have a feeling I'm going to be making a lot of dramatic exits today.

I spot Jules talking to Becca at the nurses' station and instinctively move toward them. But I stop myself short, knowing I won't be welcomed by Becca. Unfortunately, Jules spots me before I can change course. Her pitying look tells me she's already heard the news. Well, fuck. This might be a new gossip record. Not even ten minutes into first shift.

"So who'd you hear it from?" I ask blandly as I finish my approach.

Jules looks down the hall both ways before answering. "That part doesn't matter," she says in hushed tones. "What matters is *what* I heard. Were you really awkwardly force-feeding Dr. Thompson in public?"

"Excuse me?" I ask, my eyebrows jumping to my hairline.

Jules looks sheepish. "I didn't think so."

"Spill, Jules."

She takes a deep breath to ready herself but is stopped short as Dr. MacDougall rushes around the corner, heading to the staff meeting room.

"Later," she promises, reaching out to squeeze my hand as others start trickling past toward the morning meeting.

Jules walks with me, not even noticing Becca hasn't joined us. She's going to be all over both of us once she figures out what else is going on. She fancies herself something of a mother figure toward us, so I know that once she finds out, she's not going to let our little tiff go.

The staff meeting is nearly unbearable. Cal comes in after it has already started, and all the looks of amusement I've been getting shift to empathetic looks being thrown his way, and I'm dying to know what else the rumor mill is saying. And strangely, he doesn't look at me once. After the meeting has ended, I realize I'm also getting the talk-behind-your-back treatment from almost the entire staff.

But I don't have time to dwell, as my first appointment has already technically started and I'm late. So I push through it all and focus on work.

By the afternoon I still haven't caught back up with Jules. Unfortunately, as I'm rushing between appointments, I encounter Lacey manning the nurses' station.

"You look like you're ready to go home," she says with fake pity in her voice. Something about it bothers me, in a different way than all the gossip clearly being passed just outside of my hearing.

I breathe in through my nose, determined not to let her get to me. "Nope, I'm great, but thanks." I go back to grabbing the file for the patient I'm supposed to see next.

Her fake tone of concern takes on a distinct edge of mockery. "Are you sure? Because if I went on a date with someone who was telling everyone he only did it out of pity, I'd be pretty upset."

I freeze, looking up from the file in my hand. And I can't help it, I burst into laughter. "*That's* what everyone is saying? Really?" I laugh so hard I have to clutch my stomach and wipe a tear from the corner of my eye. I don't think for one second that Cal said anything of the sort, and that actually warms my heart toward him. Because I can trust him. I know I can. That's why it's so funny, because it couldn't be further from anything that would ever come out of his mouth.

Lacey crosses her arms over her chest, clearly unhappy with my reaction.

"Yes," she snips. "And it's not exactly hard to believe. I mean, why else would a guy like that go out with someone like you?"

Realization dawns on me as I read between the lines. But I can't outright accuse her of starting, or at the very least helping along, that rumor. I simply give her a dangerous smile.

"I guess that would be hard for *someone like you* to understand," I reply smugly. And then I walk away. Once I've gotten around the corner, I chuckle softly to myself and make a mental note to find Cal and clue him in, if he doesn't already know. Strangely, I feel relieved. Because if that's the worst thing they're saying, this might be easier than I thought.

Unfortunately, I don't end up catching up with either Jules or Cal before end of shift, and I can't find either of them anywhere when it's time to head home. Though I'm not particularly worried. After Lacey's revelation, the looks became a whole lot easier to deal with knowing that once people realized it was all a lie, I'd get the last laugh, and in the end it would probably make them back the hell off. All in all, there are worse things that could've happened.

I'm at home eating leftovers and studying when the doorbell rings around eight. I open the door to find Cal.

"Do you ever take your phone off silent?" he teases, leaning in for a kiss.

"I don't know, is this another pity date?" I tease back.

He stops short of my lips, giving me a questioning look. "Pardon?"

"You haven't heard," I realize aloud. I figured when I hadn't caught up with him, he'd probably hear it from someone else eventually. But I guess not. I gesture for him to come in and close the door behind him. Once we've settled on the couch, I tell him what Lacey said. Before I can get any further, he jumps in, clearly upset.

"That's *absurd*," he scoffs in a clipped tone. "Who on earth would ever look at you and think I'd only date you out of pity?

Honestly." He's so irked, he's continually shaking his head and making disgusted sounds. "You don't think that, do you?" Suddenly, he's holding my hands earnestly, looking worried.

"Of course not," I reassure him. "In fact, I laughed at her. It's ridiculous."

He visibly relaxes. "Good. Because if anything, you took pity on me by agreeing to go on our first date."

"I disagree. But even if that were true, that would make you the best pity fuck I've ever had," I joke, trailing my fingers down his chest and looking up at him from under my eyelashes.

He raises an eyebrow, unimpressed. "Do you really need the qualifier?"

I laugh and smack him lightly on the chest. "I'd say no, but apparently your ego is already big enough."

"You have no idea," he murmurs before planting a light kiss on my lips. "Have you eaten?"

I nod. "Just. I have more if you'd like me to make you a plate."

"You mean a plate of the food I cooked yesterday?" he teases.

I wrinkle my nose at him. "As a matter of fact, yes," I reply haughtily.

"Sure, that sounds good," he agrees. "I'm just going to ..." He sinks back into the cushions and closes his eyes. Clearly, it's been a long day. I'm not usually the type of woman to wait on a man, but he did pretty much cater to my every need yesterday, so it's the least I can do.

So I not only heat him up some food, I also rub his feet while he eats, watching him hork the meal down with gusto.

"Boy, you really were hungry." I press my lips together to hide my smile, but he gives me a look, clearly getting that I'm making fun of him.

"I hardly ate, I was so slammed today. Apparently, so much so that I missed all the gossip. But don't worry, I'll handle *that* particular issue tomorrow."

"Oh?" I ask, raising an eyebrow. "How exactly are you going to do that?"

Cal sets his plate aside with a wide grin. "Let's just say I've been trying not to seem overly interested in you so we didn't draw attention to ourselves. I think it's high time that stopped." I give him a skeptical look, still not sure exactly what he means to do, but all he does is laugh and pat the cushion next to him. "Shall we cuddle and watch a movie until I have to go home?"

I snort. "What are you, a fifteen-year-old girl?" I stare at him for a moment, trying to decide how to suggest an alternative. But he's a guy, so I just go for it. I stand up, remove my top, and settle on his lap. "I had a different sort of entertainment in mind."

"Fuck, Sasha," he groans, skimming his hands over my back. "I think I've died and gone to heaven." His mouth covers mine, and he wastes no time finishing undressing me. And while I don't get any more studying done for the rest of the night, I can't exactly say I mind.

* * *

Even though I pressed, Cal still wouldn't tell me what he was going to do. So when I arrive at work the next morning, it's with a nervous sort of energy, not knowing when or how his plan will be enacted. And while Becca doesn't say a word to me, she does acknowledge me with a nod. I'll take it, as at least it's not impolite or snarky.

Jules pops around the corner, and it's the first opportunity I've had to stop her since yesterday morning.

"Hey," I greet her.

"Hey, babes," she casually tosses at both Becca and I. Becca gives her a small wave without even looking up, and Jules raises an eyebrow as she hangs up her jacket.

I shake my head slightly, warning her not to ask right now. "So thanks for trying to give me the heads up, but I pretty much got the message through the rumor mill yesterday anyway," I tell her.

"Ah. Yeah, sorry about that. Yesterday was nuts," she apologizes.

I wave a hand dismissively. "For all of us, don't worry."

"What I'd like to know is, why you didn't tell me you two went out?" she says pointedly, crossing her arms over her chest and giving me a mock-stern look.

I chance a glance at Becca, who is pretending to focus on her computer screen. "We just needed some time to ourselves first," I explain. "You know, just to see if it went anywhere."

Jules makes a noise in the back of her throat. "Oh please, anyone who has seen you two together could've told you it was going somewhere fast. At least now the eye-fucking can stop. Publicly, anyway."

"You're not mad at me for keeping it from you?" I ask, trying not to sound as if I'm making a point to someone else who is still pretending not to pay attention. But I'm also extremely glad she clearly didn't believe the rumors for a minute. It gives me hope that maybe there are others who didn't either. Not that it really matters, I guess.

Jules, for her part, considers my question for a minute. "Well, you know me, I still want to hear the juicy details. But maybe one day after work. It'd probably be too weird to talk about it here. In any case, I'm not offended. You're a private person, Sasha, we all know that. I just want you to be happy."

Truly moved by her words, I step forward and hug her. She's surprised for a moment, but quickly hugs me back. "Thanks, Jules," I murmur.

"Of course," she replies. "Now let's get our gorgeous selves into the staff meeting and ignore the gossip-mongers who clearly don't know their ass from a hole in the ground." She starts dragging me down the hall, but a few paces in notices Becca not following. "Hey, grumpy pants. Your gorgeous self was included in that statement. Now stop acting like you weren't listening to every word, pull the stick out of your butt, and let's go."

I stifle a laugh, not wanting to piss off Becca more than she already is based on the look on her face. But she begrudgingly rises, stepping to Jules' other side and going with us to the meeting. Albeit silently, but I'll take it. And I'm suddenly filled with hope. Hope that Jules can warm Becca up to forgiving me. Hope that whatever Cal plans to do will get people to leave us alone. And hope that Cal … well, that he's everything I think he is. That's the scariest of all, because I'm already falling for him. Hard.

When we get to the meeting, Cal's already there. That's surprising, given that he's almost always late. He's leaning against the far wall, talking to Dr. Carson. I swear the man should be a scrubs model. Cal, of course, not Dr. Carson. The way the material pulls across his pecs and skims his hard abs, giving just enough of a hint as to what's underneath is beyond distracting.

As if he senses me ogling him, he looks up and a huge grin breaks across his face. He excuses himself and comes toward me.

"Hey," he greets me, looking down at me with a smile. He's closer to me than he usually is at work but keeping enough distance to not cross any lines.

"Hey," I reply, dreamily staring up at him. It's hard not to when he turns that smile on me. It makes me understand the phrase "weak in the knees" just a little better every time.

He leans in, putting his mouth by my ear. His soapy-hospital smell envelops me, reminding me of waking up covered in his scent. "I missed sleeping next to you, beautiful."

He straightens up, his gaze locking on mine again, and I've never wanted to kiss him more. His face tells the same story, with his eyes darting to my lips, his teeth grabbing his bottom lip and pulling it into his mouth. A smile creeps across my face as I realize that this was his plan. Simple, effective. Because as Jules pointed out, anyone paying attention could see how much we want each other. Though she was wrong about the eye-fucking stopping at work. If anything, it might be worse now, because I know exactly what actually fucking him is like.

We're interrupted by a booming Dr. MacDougall calling our attention to the front. I don't miss that Cal and I are the first ones to do so. It takes everyone else a moment to tear their eyes from us and focus on our chief. I hear Cal chuckle lowly beside me, clearly pleased that his plan seems to have worked.

* * *

"Your little demonstration this morning backfired."

I look up to find Harper leaning over the counter of the nurses' station. I give her a steely glare.

"I'm sorry, are you referring to something having to do with our jobs? Because if not, I'm not interested," I reply icily. I'm still pissed at her for starting the rumors, even if I'm not entirely sure of how much of the story concocted was her or Lacey.

Harper slinks around the counter, crouching next to me and whispering. "Look, I'm sorry I told Lacey and Avery about seeing

110

you two at the sushi place. But that's all I did, I swear. I'm sure you know Lacey hates you. And that she's been after Dr. Thompson since he started here. Which is why what you two did this morning was a bad idea." She looks around nervously, clearly terrified that someone is going to catch her ratting out her friend to the enemy.

Against my better judgment, I'm curious what she means. "Why was it a bad idea?"

Harper shakes her head. "I think she had really convinced herself he couldn't actually be interested in you, and still, look at the story she came up with to try to get you to stay away from him. Now that she knows he *is* interested ..." She looks around again and drops her voice even lower. "I've never seen her this angry or this fixated on someone. She won't shut up about you. She's been saying the nastiest things all day. I think she's going to try to get back at you, or break you guys up or something."

I shudder with disgust. "How can you even be friends with someone like that?" I hiss back.

Harper shakes her head. "I don't know. She's not always like this. But after this ..." She looks up at me desperately. "I'm really sorry. Just watch your back, okay?"

I shake my head, utterly sickened by the drama. "Fine. Thank you for the warning."

With a nod, she sneaks away, quickly disappearing down the hallway.

I sit at the desk, staring at the monitor blankly, completely unable to focus on what I was doing. I check Cal's schedule and see that he'll have a break after his current appointment, so I go and leave a note on his desk to page me at the nurses' station when he's free. Thankfully, I don't have to wait long, and not ten minutes later I'm headed into his office.

"Hey," I greet him, closing the door quietly behind me. "I'm sorry, I know this isn't the best way to do this, but I have class tonight and I needed to talk to you."

He rises from his chair, skirting around his desk to meet me. "Are you okay?" he asks, his voice laced with concern and alarm.

"I'm fine," I assure him, laying a hand on his arm. "But you need to know what Harper told me." I relay everything to him, and the creases in his forehead deepen.

"Well, that's disturbing, but I'm afraid there's not much to be done for it," he murmurs.

"I agree, but I thought you should know," I reply. "And also … I had to ask: Harper said Lacey has been after you. Has she done anything that I should know about?"

His eyes meet mine, and they're suddenly flat and unamused. "Do you tell me every time a man flirts with you?"

I jut my chin out. "No, but this is different and you know it."

He shakes his head and sighs. "She has heavily hinted that she would like to see me outside of work. I'm always polite in return, never rising to her bait, and quickly getting things back in line if she wanders toward anything less than appropriate for coworkers. But yes, she's clearly interested."

"I saw you talking to her at the pub that time. If a man displayed that kind of focus toward me, I'd think he was interested in me," I point out.

He throws his hands up. "Americans. You're polite, you take care to pay attention to the words coming out of their mouths, and they think you just want to get them in bed," he says heatedly.

"Shhh, keep your voice down," I caution. "She's young, Cal. And extremely immature, if you hadn't noticed. If she likes you, she's going to take *any* attention you give her as encouragement."

"Isn't she about your age?" he asks shrewdly.

"Yes, I'm only a few years older than her," I allow, still seething. "But age doesn't dictate maturity. And that was *so* not my only point."

"Fine. You're right. Is that what you want to hear?" he snaps.

My eyebrows shoot up. "Well, I didn't think of this as an argument I was trying to win," I retort. "But yes, I'm glad to hear you agree with me." I stare at him for a moment, finally registering how agitated he is. "You really don't like explaining yourself or answering to someone, do you?"

He folds his arms over his massive chest defensively. Bingo. There's the surgeon's ego. Finally. I was starting to wonder.

I take a deep breath and step into him, running my hands over his arms, up to his shoulders before resting them on his traps.

"I trust you, Cal, that's not what this is about. But if you're not careful, she could ruin your career," I explain. "Just one accusation, one time where you're alone with nobody to prove what happened."

He lets out a breath and drops his arms, pulling me to him. "You're right. Of course, you're right," he agrees, kissing my forehead. "I'm sorry."

I can't help grinning into his chest. "Say it again," I tease.

He tilts my chin up to look me in the eyes and gives me a gentle kiss. "I'm sorry. You're right. You're a goddess, my Lada, my Venus, my Aphrodite. I bow before you, your humble servant, yours to command." A smile tugs at his lips and his eyes twinkle.

"That's more like it," I reply imperiously. "You may kiss me now, servant."

With a chuckle, he obliges, his lips meeting mine in a slow, sensual, yet mostly chaste kiss. When he's done, he leans his forehead against mine.

"To be continued," he promises. "Now get out of here before I'm forced to fully worship every inch of you."

"Promises, promises," I mutter as I pull away.

He laughs and shakes his head as he returns to his desk. I slip out of his office quietly, returning to the nurses' station. And though I felt the need to warn Cal, I can't help feeling like he's not the one who needs to worry the most.

CHAPTER 13

The rest of the week creeps by, eerily uneventful. It's not until Friday morning, when I'm supposed to be off work, that I get a call from Dr. MacDougall asking me to come to the hospital and see him in his office. Grimly determined, I head in, prepared to face whatever bullshit Lacey has concocted to warrant this. Because really, what else could it be?

But when I enter his office, Lacey isn't there. Instead, an older woman with a severe gray bun and an equally severe black suit sits off to the side of the room.

"Dr. MacDougall," I greet him formally.

"Ms. Suvorin, please have a seat," he replies just as formally. "I'm afraid we have something rather serious to discuss."

Even though I knew something like this would happen eventually, my heart still pounds in my chest as I perch on the edge of the black plastic chair in front of his desk. I glance to my left at the other woman.

"That's Mrs. Knowles, she's from administration and will be assisting with our, er, discussion today," Dr. MacDougall grumbles. He folds his hands together on the desk, looking sternly at me. "Now. You won't have known this, but pain medication has been going missing from the stores for some weeks now. We've implemented measures to determine the cause, to no avail."

"What about the cameras? And the logs?" I ask carefully. Though I know how easy it would be to "lose" pills or other forms of narcotics in a way that would escape notice. So many of us have access, and some level of pain management is necessary for most of our procedures.

"Yes, well," he hems and haws, "unfortunately, those weren't able to direct us to the culprit." He shifts uncomfortably. "But that's neither here nor there."

"I'm sorry, why am I here?" I ask bluntly.

"Because someone witnessed you stealing narcotics."

I almost laugh, but I stop myself just in time. Really? This is all she's got. Next, I *almost* accuse Lacey of "witnessing" this. But then, she's not completely stupid, so in all likelihood she convinced someone else to report it.

"I categorically deny that accusation," I reply firmly, meeting Dr. MacDougall's and Mrs. Knowles' eyes each in turn. "I have never stolen *anything* from this hospital, much less narcotics. That is a very serious claim."

"Indeed," Mrs. Knowles agrees. "Which is why I will be escorting you directly for an in-house drug test. If it is as you say, then you have nothing to worry about." She rises from her chair.

I happily stand. "Lead the way," I reply confidently.

She tilts her head and examines me for a moment, then with a small shrug exits the room. I follow her through the unit, into the main hospital, then through to the labs. She asks for a female technician who then escorts me into a large restroom, where she instructs me in how the test will be conducted. And that she will be staying to ensure there is no tampering with the sample.

With a resigned sigh, I comply, knowing it's the fastest, and only, way to clear myself.

Afterward, Mrs. Knowles brings me to administration and seats me in a waiting area where a guard stands, informing me that the results can take up to four hours. I want to ask why I can't go home and wait for the results. But now that they've told me they think I've been stealing drugs, I'd imagine they think I'm a risk for cleaning them out and making a run for it. The whole thing is beyond infuriating.

After a half hour of flipping through magazines, I pull my cellphone out, but the guard stops me.

"You can't use your phone," he instructs me harshly. I give him an incredulous look and barely bite back a snappy comment about needing to call my buyers so they know my stash has been cut off. But lord, if it isn't tempting. It's all ludicrous.

A little over three very long hours later, Mrs. Knowles returns, grim-faced. She gestures for me to follow her and takes me into her office. The guard follows, and my stomach drops.

She seats herself behind a giant gray metal desk and gestures for me to sit. She slides a piece of paper across the desk.

"Your sample was positive for hydrocodone," she says flatly. "I'm afraid we have no choice but to terminate your employment, effective immediately. Hospital administration will determine what kind of charges will be brought against you, so please keep in mind that your behavior going forward could vastly affect the outcome of such a case."

She shakes her head dimly, but I'm still in too much shock to fully register what's happening.

"I'm sorry, you said my test was *positive*? For hydrocodone?" I ask incredulously.

"That's what I said."

"That's not possible," I reply as panic starts to well in my chest. "I've never even taken hydrocodone. And it's not something we treat our patients with in our unit anyway. How could I possibly be positive for something I've never taken and don't come into contact with on a daily basis?"

"Whether you admit it or not, hydrocodone is available to the cardiac unit, and it has been going missing. I'm afraid even if you aren't willing to admit to stealing it, your positive result alone is basis for termination. Along with a witness to your theft, I'm afraid the evidence is rather conclusive. I'm sorry, Ms. Suvorin." She slides another form across the desk. "These are your termination papers. You will be paid for hours worked to date, though the hospital will be pressing charges and any litigation may require monetary damages when judgment is passed down. You will be required to stay at least one hundred yards from hospital property at all times. You are not permitted to contact any of the hospital's staff. If you are found in violation of these terms until any potential charges are settled, it could dramatically increase penalties. Do you understand what I've explained to you?"

"I ... no ... I *don't* understand," I whisper, tears starting to fall. My mind is spinning, but it latches on to one phrase. "Are you telling me I can't contact any of my coworkers? Both of my best friends work here. My ... I'm dating someone who works here."

Mrs. Knowles shakes her head sadly. "I'm afraid if you attempt to contact them that will count against you."

"But …" My insides clench, and I feel like I'm going to vomit. "But what if they contact me? Do I have to ignore them until I can prove this is all a mistake?"

Her expression tightens, and I can tell she thinks I'm lying. That I'm just a user trying to elicit sympathy.

"We cannot legally require that nobody from this hospital contacts you. But I would strongly advise you to stay away from anyone associated with Rutherford Hospital until all legal matters have been settled."

I look up at her through hazy vision as tears continue to spill out unbidden. "How long could that take?"

She rises. "In all likelihood, it will probably be a few months. I suggest if you value your career, you use the time to prove that you can turn things around. They'll almost certainly offer you rehab within the next weeks in order to expunge this from your record. I seriously recommend you consider that option."

I shake my head, tears flying. "What good is rehab to someone who has never taken anything stronger than ibuprofen?" The words are useless, but I can't help it, and I didn't say them for her anyway. I'm just dumbfounded by this turn of events.

The guard towers over me expectantly. Not wanting to make things worse, I comply, rising unsteadily and letting him lead me out of the building. I don't even think about how humiliating it is for him to watch me until I've driven off the property. But as soon as I have, I pull over and let the tears out. I cry for what feels like hours, until I'm delirious and dehydrated. And then I do the only thing I can think to do. I call my mom and cry some more.

It was the smartest thing I could do. She doesn't doubt my veracity for a minute and points out that if Lacey really is behind this, she would've anticipated that they'd drug test me. And that she must have figured out a way to tamper with that. The possibility seems outlandish; tampering with lab tests results is a serious offense. Almost worse than stealing drugs. But there's enough truth to her words that I decide to immediately take her next piece of advice and go obtain my own drug test at an independent lab. Thankfully, I know all of them in the area, since we often refer patients to labs nearer to their homes or workplaces.

I make a pitstop at a gas station and buy a humongous bottle of water. The time for blubbering is over. It's time to start proving I was set up. If that's even possible. But I'm sure as hell going to do my best to try.

* * *

Even though I'm able to get in at another rapid-test facility, given the hours wasted at the hospital, my results from the independent lab won't be available until Monday. So I head home.

I sit in my living room, completely unable to focus on anything, my nerves compelling me to pace. I pick up my phone what feels like a thousand times, but I know I can't text Cal. And it's driving me insane. Especially thinking about Dr. MacDougall announcing to everyone that I was fired for stealing narcotics and that nobody is to contact me. Or at least, that's how it goes in my head. Though we've had people fired for exactly that once or twice before, and it's usually done much more discreetly. Still, when it happens, news travels fast, and even without an announcement Jules, Becca, and Cal probably already know by now.

My mother had invited me to come stay with her and Dad until this blows over, but if I can't contact any of my friends, I want to be here in case they try to contact me. And when a knock comes at the door shortly after six, I'm glad I did. I open the door to see Becca, her cheeks streaked with dried tears.

She launches herself at me in the fiercest hug she's ever given me.

"Oh, Sasha," she breathes. "Are you okay?"

I squeeze her back, battling with the tears threatening at the back of my eyes. I blink them away and clear my throat. "I've had better days. Tell me what happened today."

I let go and step back so she can come in. Being very familiar with my place, she heads into the living room and plops dramatically on the couch.

"First," she hedges, wringing her hands, "I need to apologize. Being mad at you for holding back your news about you and Cal was just petty and … and in the grand scheme of things, so, so stupid. I'm so sorry, Sasha. Can you forgive me?"

I scoot closer to her on the couch, putting a hand on her knee. "I already have. Now please, I'm dying here, what happened after I was escorted out of the hospital?"

"None of the higher-ups said anything," she says, answering the unasked part of my question. "It was all whispers and rumors, as usual. But the gist was all the same: You were accused of stealing drugs. They tested you and it came back positive, so you were fired."

I shake my head, willing the whole thing to be a dream. But I'm awake. And this is happening.

"Did you know I can't contact anyone? And they told me it would be better if I didn't talk to any of you if you contact me. Fair warning," I tell her.

"Will you get in trouble if I'm here?" she asks with wide eyes.

"How can I get in more trouble than being fired for drugs I didn't steal or take yet somehow tested positive for?" I growl, rubbing at my eyes. "I'm sorry, I'm not mad at you. This is just crazy."

"So you really did test positive? How the hell did that happen?" she asks.

"You have no idea how much I appreciate the implication that you don't think I actually took drugs," I reply.

"Holy shit, Sasha, of course I know you didn't. Anyone who knows you wouldn't believe you did."

I blink hard, again fighting tears. "Do you think Cal does?"

Becca shakes her head. "I don't know, hon."

I look up at the ceiling and sniff deeply.

"I went to another lab to get an independent test, but the results won't be back until Monday. This is going to be the weekend from hell," I grumble.

"Well, good on you. Do you have any idea why the test would've come back positive?"

A sarcastic laugh rips out of me. "Are you kidding? Don't you know who started those ridiculous rumors about Cal only dating me out of pity?"

Becca gives me a look. "What does that have to do with this?" she asks, clearly confused.

I lay a hand on her knee. "Oh, sweet, innocent, Becca," I joke drily. "Let me tell you a tale that a little birdie named Harper whispered in my ear." And I tell her about Lacey's jealousy, Harper's warning, Cal's response, and even go back to their interaction at the pub as evidence that Lacey is bitter, immature, *and* delusional. Clearly a more dangerous combination than even I realized.

"Wow," Becca whispers when I'm done. "But even if that's true, how would she mess with your test?"

"I don't know," I admit. "My plan went as far as proving that I'm not on drugs. I'll submit that to hospital administrators on Monday along with a statement about my interactions with Lacey and Harper, and my suspicions, and we'll go from there, I guess."

Becca shakes her head. "Lacey's played this well. If you write all this down, you're gonna make yourself sound like a serious crackhead," she points out.

"God, I hadn't even thought about it that way," I admit. "But you're probably right. What else can I do, though?"

"You leave that to me," Becca says with a determined expression. "Besides, you've got finals on Tuesday. Focus on that, okay?"

I scrub my hands over my face. "I'm not going to be able to focus on anything until I know where Cal stands on all of this."

Becca rolls her eyes and pulls out her phone. "Fine. Give me his number," she demands. I look at her like she's sprouted another head. "What? You can't call him, but I can. Gimme." She gestures impatiently. And I'm just desperate enough to hear his voice that I cave.

As it rings, she looks at me and mouths, *Will he answer?* Just as I'm about to reply that as long as he's not in surgery he always does in case it's an emergency, he picks up.

"Dr. Thompson," he answers curtly. And I could cry for hearing his voice, both from relief and longing.

"Hi, Dr. Thompson, this is Becca Dillon. I'm sorry to do this to you, but I'm calling on behalf of Sasha. As you probably know, she's not permitted to contact you, but I think you two really need to talk." Becca's tone is firm and businesslike, and I want to kiss her.

Cal is silent on the other end for so long that a worried lump starts to form in my throat. I hear a door close, and I picture him in his office. It only makes me remember being in there with him, and the memories crush my already fractured heart at the thought that it may never happen again.

"I appreciate your concern for your friend, Ms. Dillon, but as a doctor at Rutherford Hospital, I'm afraid I'm not allowed to contact nurses who have been fired for provable drug use, especially while matters have not yet been settled, legally speaking."

I've never heard him speak that harshly, not even to patients. His tone, his words, it all smashes the bits of my heart into even tinier pieces.

"Huh," Becca grunts. "That's a cute party line. But we're not just talking about any nurse here. We're talking about Sasha. The woman you're dating. The one who is sitting here looking like you just murdered her puppy."

My eyes grow wide and I shake my head violently.

"She's there with you? I'm on speakerphone?" he asks sharply.

"She sure is, and you sure are," Becca responds flatly.

"Ms. Dillon, I'm afraid I can't continue this discussion at the moment as I'm *at work*," he replies pointedly.

"I see," Becca replies slowly. "So does that mean you'll be prepared to finish this discussion when you're *not* at work?"

There's another long pause. "I'll see that that's the case when I'm done here. I trust you are where I think you are?" he replies.

"If you think I'm at Sasha's apartment, then yes," she agrees.

"One more thing, Ms. Dillon."

"Yes, Dr. Thompson?" she replies with an airy, mocking tone.

"It is best if we all *officially* keep our distance until matters are settled. Do I make myself clear?"

"Crystal. I'll take myself, my devastated and *wrongly accused* best friend, and our *unofficial* business out of your hair now."

She hangs up before he has a chance to say anything else, and I can tell it's because he royally pissed her off and she doesn't want to make things worse.

"It's a good thing he's so goddamn hot, because right now I don't know what else you see in him," she snips.

I shake my head slowly, not even really hearing her. My mind is working on parsing what he said.

"What if he's just protecting me?" I hazard.

Becca scoffs. "Girl, did you listen to a word he just said? That man is protecting *himself*. He's a damn doctor. I should've known he would. They don't know anything but their jobs. I'm surprised he'd even risk agreeing to come here. If I were you, I'd get the one-up and kick him to the curb before he can do it to you. I guess we found out why we have that rule, Sash. Never date a doctor. Apparently, they only look out for themselves."

"You're wrong about him," I protest. "You'll see." But given everything that's happened, I can't even say I'm right.

Becca leans in, catching my eye and putting a soothing hand on my shoulder. "I get it. You need to hope right now. And I don't want to see you get hurt, but that man has 'hurt' written all over his gorgeous self. Just be prepared, okay?"

"Okay," I agree.

"Good. I'm gonna scoot on out of here and start working on taking down that bitch, Lacey. And so I'm not around to kill your man when he gets here. I'd say call me if you need to, but …"

"Yeah. Thanks anyway. I'll probably be studying the rest of the weekend, like you said. There's not going to be anything else to do."

"Chin up, boo. We're going to clear your name, I promise," she says, rising. I stand with her, and she wraps me in a hug.

As I see her out, I'm glad that this has at least brought us back together. Especially because it seems like things with Cal are going to be precarious, at best.

In anticipation of a painful conversation, I continue my pacing, too stressed to eat, watch TV, or focus on anything in particular. It feels like a lifetime before I hear the doorbell.

And when I open the door, he's leaned against the frame with one arm, looking haggard. He doesn't attempt to come in, kiss me, or even smile at me.

"Hi," I say softly, tentatively.

"I take it Ms. Dillon isn't actually here any longer?"

I shake my head. "No, she's not. Do you want to come in?"

He sighs heavily and nods, running a hand over his beard. "Probably best to do this in private."

The knots in my stomach tighten, and I have to breathe to keep from freaking out. I follow him into the living room, where he settles on the opposite end of the couch from me.

He gestures to the bandage on my inner elbow. "They did a blood test?" he asks, clearly curious.

"Not at Rutherford. After … after they let me go, I had my own independent testing done, on every bodily fluid they use. I'll get the rapid results on Monday," I explain.

"I presume you're attempting to prove you aren't, in fact, using drugs, then?" he asks.

My throat constricts and I shake my head sadly. "Did you really think I was?"

He scrubs his hands over his beard again, then through his hair. "I don't know what to think about anything anymore."

Ouch. I decide I'll come back to that one later. "Did you mean what you said? That you can't be in contact with me while this is unresolved?"

His hands settle over his mouth as he stares down, seemingly contemplating his answer. Finally, he drops his hands, blows out a breath, then lowers his chin. "Yes," he replies, refusing to look at me.

"They said it could take months," I reply. I hear the weakness, the longing in my voice, and it just makes this so much harder.

"While there's a possibility that this could affect my career, I can't take that chance. I hope you understand."

"You mean while there's a possibility that I'm an addict, you can't take the chance on me."

He looks at me blankly. "Something like that, yes," he admits.

His words are like a punch to the gut. "God, Becca was right about you. They were all right about you. I should've never agreed to go out with you." The words tumble out, but it's too late to regret them. It's how I feel about what he said. About the selfishness of his words. "Never mind what *I'm* going through right now, I'm just a druggie. It's *your* career that's important. God, I'm so stupid."

"I don't blame you for being angry with me," he admits, finally looking up at me. "I'm angry with me. But it's a chance I can't take."

"Believing me? Trusting me? You can't take that chance? Well, I guess at least this shows me exactly where I stand with you."

"I wish I could just believe you, but I've never seen a drug test lie before. Though if somehow you are telling the truth, this could all blow over before —"

"*If* I'm telling the truth?" I snap. "Are you serious right now? God, I *am* stupid. And blind. Even if this blows over soon, there's no taking this back, Cal. And if it takes longer, well, you're still a selfish asshole who thinks I'm a liar and a user because some *test* told you that. Never mind what I say." I stand up, unable to take anymore. "Please leave."

He looks up at me pleadingly. "Please, Sasha," he says, his voice finally breaking. But it's not going to break me. I remain standing, refusing to back down. "I want to believe you. Really, I do. But … I just can't afford to. I wish you knew how sorry I am."

I glare at him furiously. "Seriously, feel free to take your pity party elsewhere," I seethe. "You clearly don't give a shit about what this is doing to me or the words coming out of my mouth. It's all about you. I see that now."

He rises, getting in my face. "I do care about you. That's why this is so difficult. Don't you see that?"

"No, Cal. All I see is you, not believing me and doing what's best for your career." I march out of the living room and open the door. "Please, just go."

He moves slowly into the foyer, his face a mix of emotions. I clench my jaw and jut out my chin, stubbornly refusing to cry. With one last pleading look, he goes. And as soon as I close the door behind him, I slide down to the floor and let it all out.

CHAPTER 14

"What do you mean, results won't be available until tomorrow?" I ask tightly into the phone. "I specifically requested rapid results on the urine sample." I listen impatiently to the woman on the phone apologize and insist that it wasn't checked on the submission, but that results for all the tests will be available by close of business tomorrow. In the grand scheme of things, another day isn't going to change much, but it's just another disappointment.

When the call is over, I chuck my phone onto the couch and rub my temples fiercely. And then I do what I've spent the last two days doing and bury myself in studying. Because if I can't control the shitstorm that is this drug test debacle, I'm sure as hell going to ace my finals.

* * *

I finally get the call Tuesday afternoon that the results are in. I drop by to pick up physical copies, then ask them to send the results electronically to Mrs. Knowles' office. I take pictures of the paperwork with my phone and email them to her myself too, letting her know that she'll be receiving them directly from the lab as well, and that I would appreciate her reviewing the results and explaining why, just hours after Rutherford's tests, another, more complete round of lab tests shows not a trace of any kind of drug in my system.

I head to campus, finally feeling like I might be getting some traction. I'm a bit early, but I spend the remainder of the afternoon in the library, doing some last-minute review.

When I head to class, I'm confident that I'm about to nail my tests. Then just one more quarter and I'm a qualified nurse practitioner. At least that's something.

But as soon as Professor Chaffin sees me, he scurries over before I can take my usual seat.

"Ms. Suvorin," he says, a note of panic in his voice, "what are you doing here?"

My heart sinks. "What do you mean?"

"I take it you haven't checked your university email this week?"

"I guess not," I reply, realizing I haven't. "Why?"

I can see him starting to sweat behind his giant, thick glasses. "I'm sorry, Ms. Suvorin, but the hospital contacted us regarding your termination. Due to the nature of the circumstances, you've been removed from the program."

My jaw drops in shock. "You've got to be kidding me," I reply. "When?"

"Yesterday. I'm sorry, but as I'm sure you know, the reasons for your, er, termination were also a violation of the student code of conduct, so they were ethically bound to notify us."

I close my eyes and take a deep breath. "I literally have test results right here," I rummage in my bag and produce the papers, "proving that their 'reasons' were incorrect."

His lips thin and he takes the papers from me. Clearly, they filled him in on *exactly* why I was fired, which frankly seems like a breach of privacy to me, as he quickly peruses them before declaring, "I see what you mean. Unfortunately, this is something you'll have to take up with the dean's office. It's out of my hands."

I want to stomp my foot, punch a wall, anything to blow off the steam building in me. I snatch the papers back from him and leave without another word. Nothing that comes out of my mouth right now is going to be good.

I go home. And wait. With literally nothing to do. No work, no school. For the rest of the week I alternate between crying and throwing things, hearing from nobody. Not even the hospital, despite repeated attempts at contacting them to follow up on the paperwork I submitted. So clearly they have no plans to un-fire me.

On Friday I finally decide to take my parents up on their offer and spend two days wallowing in my childhood bedroom, watching TV, and eating comfort food.

Come Monday morning, my mother drags me out of bed.

"Up," she insists, yanking the pink comforter I picked out in eighth grade off of me.

"Why?" I groan.

My mother crosses her arms over her slim chest. "You've done enough waiting. Now we do."

I open my eyes and sit up, curious. "Do what?"

"I'm taking you to a lawyer. If the hospital won't respond to you, you need to do something to clear your name. Even if you decide not to keep working there."

I frown at her, my mind working slowly on her words. She makes me realize that I've let the negative momentum of my pity party take over, and it pisses me off enough to get me out of bed.

"You're right. Thanks, Mom."

With a satisfied nod, she leaves me to get showered and ready.

When I come out for breakfast a bit later, Dad's already gone to work. Mom waits patiently for me to eat, then we're off.

* * *

Monday afternoon finds me back at my apartment. And while the lawyer did advise that I continue to not contact my friends and Cal, they seemed confident that this was an open-and-shut case. They'll write an official letter to hospital administration today and follow up with a phone call tomorrow. At worst, they will have to meet with the hospital attorneys to see if there was anything holding them up from clearing me. At best, it will scare them into responding to my original request for an explanation regarding the discrepancy between the two tests. Which hopefully will lead to them admitting they wrongfully terminated me.

And while the continued wait is near maddening, at least this time it's with some hope.

I'm not disappointed when, midday Tuesday, the lawyer calls me. Turns out the hospital has been investigating my original test this whole time and has asked for another business day to wrap up their findings. Based on their language, I suspect they know why but can't tell me.

So I wait. Some more. I finally decide to wander to the diner down the street for lunch on Wednesday, just to get out of the house. The pleasant March afternoon does wonders for me, and on my way back to my apartment, my cellphone rings.

"Hello?"

"Ms. Suvorin, this is Edward Nolan, Mr. Gomez's legal aide."

"Yes, of course," I say, freezing in place with nerves.

"I'm calling to let you know that we've come to a resolution with Rutherford Hospital administration. They have rescinded your termination and you will be back in rotation starting this coming Monday, with full pay for the hours you were denied. We've also contacted the dean's office at your school to let them know, and hospital administration should be following up with them as we speak. They should be contacting you soon to schedule makeup exams ahead of the next quarter starting in just over a week."

"That's great, but did they say why my original drug test came up positive?"

"Unfortunately, they were not able to elaborate on what caused the issue." He clears his throat. "But we've been assured that the matter was fully investigated and appropriate measures have been taken to avoid such problems in the future. Now, as advised, we wouldn't recommend pursuing any additional damages in this case, but if your feelings on the matter have changed, please do let us know before you start back at work, otherwise doing so will signal acceptance of their terms."

"I understand," I reply. "Does that mean I can call my friends that are coworkers now?"

"It does."

"Thank you," I breathe in relief.

"It's been my pleasure to assist, Ms. Suvorin. Do you have any further questions at this time?"

"No. I appreciate your help very much."

"All right then, take care, and do let us know if you need anything else."

I end the call, still frozen. It takes a minute to sink in. I'm cleared. I can go back to work. I can go back to school. I can call my friends. Unfortunately, both Becca and Jules are working today, so I doubt I'll get ahold of them immediately. But my fingers are already flying, texting them both with the news.

Admins admitted the test was wrong. I'll be back Monday!

And then I practically skip home, on cloud nine. Until I realize that doesn't change anything between Cal and me, and I come crashing back to earth. So when school calls to reschedule my exams for next Tuesday evening, it at least gives me an excuse to go back to doing one of the things I do best — studying. Even though I pretty much know the material backward and forward at this point.

I hear from both Becca and Jules that evening, and we schedule a happy hour meetup for tomorrow. They pick a bar a couple blocks away from our usual, making me wonder.

I don't spend too much thought on it until Thursday evening as I get ready, slipping into something a little nicer than the sweats and tees I've been wallowing, er, living, in since the shit hit the fan.

And when I show up at the noisy dive they've chosen, I can tell by the looks on their faces that they've got something juicy to share. Becca is practically vibrating out of her chair. Until she spots me, that is, then she vaults to her feet and throws herself at me.

"Oh, I'm so glad to see you," she gushes. She squeezes hard and rocks me back and forth until I'm laughing.

"Oof," I tease. "I can tell."

She pushes away and sticks her tongue out at me. Jules approaches less violently and gives me a gentle hug.

"It's been awful at work without you," she whispers in my ear. She pulls back, gesturing to the third seat at their table. "We saved a chair for you. It wasn't easy." She sounds like she's teasing, but looking around at the bustling tables and the raucous crowd around the pool tables, I'm thinking she's also kind of serious.

"Why's it so busy in here on a Thursday?" I ask as I take a seat.

"Spring break," Becca explains, taking a sip of her drink.

"Ah. To that end, I get to take make my finals up next Tuesday."

"That's great," Jules says warmly, reaching out and squeezing my hand.

"So, spill. What's going on? Why'd we meet here instead of the usual?"

Jules shoots a look at Becca.

"We didn't want to take a chance that anyone we work with would be here. There have been rumors about what happened with your drug test," Becca explains. "When they reinstated you yesterday, someone in the lab was fired. You do the math."

"They tampered with my test?" I ask incredulously.

Jules shrugs. "Those are the rumors. But you know, grain of salt. Well, boulder of salt when it comes to Rutherford. Who knows what really happened? It could've been something as simple as mislabeling or entry error. But either way they clearly felt they had to fire the person responsible."

My stomach sinks a little thinking an unintentional error might have led to someone being fired because of me. But then … "No. No, Jules. This had to have something to do with Lacey." The certainty forms in my gut.

Becca nods in agreement. "I think so too, even if Jules wants to give people the benefit of the doubt. But I have a small piece of good news on that front. Harper has agreed to try to get the truth out of Lacey. If she finds out Lacey had something to do with faking your drug test, she's going to turn her in."

I scoff. "Lacey's not completely stupid. She's not just going to admit to something like that."

Jules shrugs. "It's our best shot without doing something sketchy."

I shake my head. "Whatever. I'm back at work. They're not about to throw any more accusations at me lightly. And Lacey's plan worked. I'm not seeing Cal anymore. She can have him as far as I'm concerned."

"What?" Jules gasps. "Why?"

I smack myself in the forehead. "Crap, I forgot I haven't been able to talk to you guys," I say with a sigh. I tell them all about my last conversation with Cal. Becca is, predictably, furious.

"See," she insists. "Never date a doctor. That guy is bad news, Sasha. I'm so sorry."

Jules just looks bewildered. "He never seemed like such a jerk," she muses. "I mean, I can understand him wanting to protect his career, but not believing you? That's just bullshit."

"Exactly," I agree. "He obviously didn't know me at all. Or really care to. I guess I was just a piece of ass to him." I shake my head, my gut twisting at the thought. It didn't feel like that. It felt like we connected on just about every level. I've never been fooled quite this badly before, and it hurts.

"I don't know about that," Becca says, surprising me. But then she continues. "He's probably just not capable of thinking too much about anybody but himself." There she is. Though she kind of has a point.

"You're probably right. He's just a selfish *twat*," I reply, with a British accent on "twat." I flag down a waiter and order a drink. "Now, let's get our drink on and celebrate my coming back to work. And finding a way to stick it to Lacey. One way or another. Maybe her ending up with Cal would be a fitting punishment after all."

Jules gives me side-eye, clearly concerned at my vindictive switch. But I don't care. I may have been the type to rise above it all before, but this time the bitch has gone too far.

CHAPTER 15

My studies over the next couple of days are interrupted by alternating thoughts of rubbing my innocence in Cal's face and getting back at Lacey. I know it's not productive, and I know I should just forget them both, but it stings. I mean, how could you not want to get back at people who have humiliated you? Lacey at work, and Cal … the words "in love" pop into my head, but I immediately choke on the thought. Love? No, I don't think I love Cal. Or … maybe I do, and that's why this hurts so much. The thought makes me sick to my stomach, so I stuff it down into the dark, deep places in my mind not to be examined too closely.

I'm thankfully distracted by Jules texting to ask if I want to meet for brunch tomorrow. I'm glad for an excuse to go back to the place Cal introduced me to, tainted with memories though it is. Because let's face it, the food was phenomenal. And I probably do need to get out of the house. Besides, Jules will be a much more calming influence than Becca would be. So I agree.

The next day, I know I've made the right choice as soon as the first bite of carnitas chilaquiles hits my tongue. I moan in pleasure and Jules laughs.

"That good, huh?" she teases, throwing her auburn hair over her shoulder.

I nod and gesture with my fork at her plate, since she got the same dish on my advice. She takes the hint and scoops up a bite of her own. And soon, she's moaning in delight too.

"Oh my god, you weren't kidding," she says, laughing around the mouthful of food.

"I don't kid about food," I say mock-seriously, then we both laugh.

"Well, if Cal introduced you to this place, at least one good thing came out of your relationship, right?" She continues to shovel down her food unapologetically.

I grimace and set my fork down. "Ugh. Can we not talk about it?"

Jules purses her lips. "Sorry." Her voice is muffled from her meal, and it makes me smile.

I shrug lightly. "Let's talk about me going back to work tomorrow. What's the temperature? Do people still think I'm a druggie? Or am I the poor nurse who was almost screwed over by the hospital?" My eyes go wide. "Does anyone even suspect Lacey has anything to do with it?"

With a laugh and a shake of the head, Jules sets her fork down and wipes her mouth with her cloth napkin. "Slow down, Sasha," she replies calmly. "No, they don't think you're a druggie. And I wouldn't say they think you were screwed over, but they are pretty suspicious about the whole thing. Nobody seems to have made any connection to Lacey, but then, why would they? I think they just think it was someone in the labs trying to cover their tracks for stealing the drugs."

I pick my fork back up and play with the food, eating a small bite and chewing thoughtfully. "I guess that makes sense. I pretty much figured Lacey wouldn't let it get back to her if she could help it. And there's almost zero chance she'll spill anything to Harper. Even if she did, I doubt there's any proof."

Jules eyes me suspiciously. "You're trying to figure out another way to take her down, aren't you?"

I drop my fork again and this time push my plate away. It says a lot about how agitated I am that I've just lost my appetite. "How could I not?" I seethe.

"Sasha," Jules says with a warning in her voice. "You don't know anything either." I go to protest, but she holds up a hand. "I agree, it's suspicious. But you have to work together. Start practicing your game face and *be patient*. If she really has done what you think she has, she'll slip up again, and she *will* eventually get herself in trouble. It's karma, babe. It'll come back to bite her in the ass."

I frown deeply, finding that line of thought completely unsatisfying. "I'm just going to help karma do its job," I persist. "You know, so I can be there to witness it biting her in her annoyingly perfect ass."

Jules' eyes drift over my shoulder and her facial expression freezes.

"What?" I ask, moving to turn around.

"Don't," she hisses, grabbing my hand. "Speaking of Lacey's annoyingly perfect ass. I think she just sat down on the other side of the restaurant. And … oh, god …" Her mouth drops in horror.

"What?" I whisper insistently.

"I think she's with Cal."

Before I can stop myself, my head whips around. And she's right. Cal is sitting at a table across the restaurant, looking delicious in a white and gray rugby shirt and jeans, his hair freshly washed, smiling lightly at the woman sitting across from him. She has long, dark hair, just like Lacey, but something's not quite right … it's not Lacey, but she looks familiar. And she's got a ring on her left hand. On *that* finger.

"That's not Lacey," I say in a low, flat voice. "That's his fiancée."

"Don't you mean ex-fiancée?"

I close my eyes against the tears forming. "It would appear not."

The terror of the realization must show on my face, because Jules glances at a group of people next to us who are getting ready to leave, reaches into her purse, and throws a wad of bills on the table. As soon as they rise, Jules pulls me up with her, and drags me out the door, camouflaging us with their numbers.

Once we're outdoors, the panic really hits me, and I double over, clutching my knees and gasping for breath.

Jules rubs my back gently and eases me back a few feet to take a seat on a nearby bench. "Just breathe," she coaches.

I nod, focusing on calming myself down.

"Take your time," she says soothingly. "They hadn't even ordered yet, and they didn't see us. You're going to be okay."

It's all the things we're coached to say to people who are having a panic attack. And because I know that, this time it sets me off just a little more, and I can't fight the tears back anymore.

"It's not okay," I gasp. "I really was just a blip on his radar. A distraction until he decided whether he really wanted to get back with her. Oh god, Jules, I'm such an idiot."

"You're not an idiot," she insists. I shoot her a sharp look. "Well, then we're all idiots. You're not the first girl this has happened to, Sasha. But I know that doesn't make it suck any less."

"No," I agree. "No, it doesn't. Can you just … take me home, please?"

Jules gives me one last pitying look and then nods. "Okay. Let's get you home."

* * *

Becca is already going full tilt when I start back to work on Monday.

"I have a plan," she greets me gleefully.

I stare at her with dead eyes. "If it has anything to do with Lacey, just forget it. I'm done with all the drama. I just want to go back to my life."

"What happened?" she asks, pouting and clearly disappointed.

I shake my head, not ready to talk to her about seeing Cal and his fiancée back together. Or spending all night sick to my stomach from crying and agonizing over seeing them. Saying I'm done with drama is an understatement. I just want to sink back into the familiarity of work and school and forget that anything else exists. Possibly even Becca if she won't let me be.

"Come on, Sash, I'm here for you, you know that," she says softly, trying to look a little less manic.

"I can't. Go ask Jules if you really want to know," I reply flatly. And with that I take my travel mug to get a refill. But I purposely go off-unit to a different machine, hoping to slip into the morning meeting via the back door once it's already started to avoid dealing with anyone or being noticed.

It was a great plan until I hear my name being called down the hall as I head for the meeting room. I look back to see Cal gaining swiftly on me.

"Sasha, wait," he calls, seeing that I'm not slowing down.

135

I dart for the door, but he's too quick for me, grabbing me by the wrist while I'm still a good ten steps away, spinning me around to face him.

"Let go of me," I growl in a low voice.

Alarmed at my response, he does just that, stepping back in surprise.

"You're back," he says obviously.

"Astute observation, *doctor*," I reply mockingly. "Now, if you don't mind, I need to get to the morning meeting."

"I do mind. We need to talk."

"We have nothing to talk about."

"I disagree."

"Hm. I think your *fiancée* might agree with me," I reply pointedly, glaring at him.

"Excuse me?"

I narrow my eyes and shake my head in disbelief. "You heard me. Your fiancée. Rachel? You know, the woman wearing your ring that you were having brunch with yesterday."

His lips press into a thin line. "You saw us?"

My stomach turns and I make a low sound of disgust in the back of my throat. "Yes, I did. Now, if you don't mind, Dr. Thompson, I'd rather not give the vultures something new to taunt me with."

At the use of his formal title, he looks like I slapped him in the face. With grim satisfaction, I use his shock to my advantage and close the distance between me and the door, slipping inside without looking back. Thankfully, only a couple of people near the door notice, and I blend in. Cal never comes to the meeting. As disappointed as I am with the whole thing, I realize it's probably for the best.

* * *

The week is awkward and uncomfortable, to say the least, but thankfully I sail through my make-up finals and start the next quarter without a hitch. Cal avoids me, and Becca and Jules keep things light and perfunctory, letting me find my rhythm without anything extra. Back on plan, I bury myself in work and school, numbly surrendering to the demands of a packed schedule.

I ask Becca out for drinks on Saturday, but she declines, mysteriously citing "other plans." She's lucky I'm not her, or I'd be digging for details at the least, and stalking her for answers at the worst. But frankly, I'm fine having a few drinks by myself at home.

The rest of the weekend is blissfully boring, but by the time it's over and I decide I've had too much time to think, I'm ready to go back to work on Monday. Ready to take my mind off of all of this.

What I wasn't ready for was walking into chaos. Seemingly every nurse, medical assistant, orderly, and other employee on the unit is crowded into the hallway leading to the nurses' station. I press through the throng, wondering what the hell is happening. I look around for Jules, only to remember that she's off today. Instead, I find Becca, Harper, and Avery whispering angrily to each other behind the nurses' station counter.

I put a hand on Becca's shoulder. "What's going on?" I ask quietly. "What the hell is everyone doing out here?"

Becca turns to look at me, and it's then that I see the panic in her eyes.

"They just took Dr. Thompson away. I'm so sorry, Sasha, I didn't mean for this to happen," she replies, tears welling in her eyes.

"What?" I screech. "Back up. You didn't mean for *what* to happen? Who took him where?" I glance between her and Harper, and they both look guilty as hell.

Becca glances at the crowd behind us that's already starting to dissipate. So whatever happened to Cal must have happened right before I showed up.

"Hospital administration and security showed up about ten minutes ago and escorted Dr. Thompson out of his office," she says in a low voice. "The why … let's wait until everyone goes back to their stations, okay?"

I shake my head violently. "Tell me now, Becca. By the time they're gone we'll have to go to the morning meeting, then we'll be too busy to talk about it."

She hesitates just long enough that Sarah Marcus, our usual second shift nurse practitioner, comes tearing around the corner, looking less than pleased to be here so early as she shrugs out of her jacket and tosses her purse behind the counter.

"Morning meeting has been cancelled. Dr. Franklin has been called in to cover for Dr. Thompson. Get me the schedule for the day immediately," she commands.

Becca quickly grabs the clipboard she'd already prepared and hands it over without a word.

Sarah takes it with a grim nod. "I'll be in the break room guzzling the whole damn pot of coffee. I'll be back to go over this."

As she stalks away, the last of the stragglers take it as their cue that the spectacle is over and wander back to what they should be doing.

I whirl back on Becca, noting that both Harper and Avery have also slipped away.

"Spill it. Now."

"Fine," she agrees, pulling me to the back corner of the station. "Harper and I had a plan to get Lacey to confess on Saturday when we all went out for drinks after work. But it kind of backfired."

I hold up a hand. "*That* was your 'other plans'?" I demand.

"Yes," she admits with a sigh. "And if you had come it would've —"

"Stopped you from doing something incredibly stupid?" I interject. "What does that have to do with Cal?"

"He overheard us and he wanted to help," she responds, shifting uncomfortably.

"He *what*?" I say through gritted teeth. "Why on earth would he do that?"

Her expression shifts from guilt to tolerant pity. "Oh, Sasha, isn't it obvious?" she whispers.

I arch an eyebrow, determined not to rise to that bait. "Whatever. What did he do?"

She shrugs. "He just hung out with us. We all had a few. She was definitely laying it on thick, trying to get his attention. So he gave it to her. Everyone else eventually went home, and we left them there together."

My jaw drops in shock. Alcohol. Flirting. And Cal, who obviously sees women as his playthings. My stomach starts to churn thinking about what probably happened next.

"Don't worry, he didn't do anything with her," she assures me.

"How on earth could you possibly know that?" I snip, rubbing my temples. I internally scold myself for even caring. It doesn't matter. It's over between us, right? Then why does the thought upset me so much?

She puts her hands on her hips and looks at me smugly. "Because he texted me after he took her home. She admitted to him that she was the one stealing drugs. Well, her and her partner in crime in the lab, and that they were the ones who set you up to take the fall."

"How on earth did he get her to tell him all that?" I muse out loud.

Becca's eyebrows fly up. "You've seen him, right?"

I roll my eyes. "Whatever, I guess I don't really want to know anyway. So how did it go wrong? Why did they take Cal?"

She spreads her hands and shakes her head. "I don't know. But obviously Lacey's fighting back. I shouldn't have involved him."

I lean into the wall next to us. "He's a big boy. He can take care of himself. Better him in trouble than you."

Becca frowns. "Is that really how you feel? I'm just a medical assistant, Sash. I'm not that important, and I don't make a ton of money. I'm sure I could find some other job if Lacey came up with some bullshit to get me fired. But she could ruin him."

I huff a short, unamused laugh. "I warned him that she could. You didn't force him to do anything, Becks. This is on him." I look up and catch her eye. "And you are important, you know. You do a lot around here. You know we all appreciate you."

"Thanks. But honestly, I'm starting to see things from his point of view, and how precarious his career really is. He put a lot on the line by going after Lacey's confession, Sasha. Maybe think about what that means."

"Maybe I don't care what it means. He didn't believe I wasn't a fucking drug addict," I seethe. "There's no point in thinking about things because there's no going back from that."

Becca's chocolate-brown eyes look pleadingly into mine. "He's only human. And I can tell he loves you. Why else would he do this? Risk himself like this?" I go to protest, but she literally puts her hand on my mouth. "And don't even tell me you don't care. You do, Sasha. You're not a cold-hearted bitch. I know you want to be because he hurt you, but deep down you're just not."

Footsteps warn us of someone approaching, so Becca slides into her seat behind the counter without letting me respond. Not that I'm sure I could if I wanted to. Her words have more truth in them than I'm comfortable with. Because deep down, I know I'm reacting this way out of hurt. And though I'm not sure forgiveness is in the cards, I do care about Cal. I say a silent prayer that he makes it out of this unscathed. So I can go back to ignoring him in peace.

* * *

That afternoon, the rumor mill hands down that Lacey's been fired and walked out by security. Becca breathes a sigh of relief, presuming that means Cal is in the clear. But we don't see or hear from him the rest of the workday, so it's hard to say. His absence is unsettling. I chalk it up to not knowing exactly what's going on and get back to work.

Focusing is nearly impossible, though, and I end up having to reenter the same patient chart so many times I practically could've memorized it by the time I get it right. Clearly, my head isn't in it.

Getting off work isn't much relief either, and I'm distracted the whole drive home. When I make it to my assigned parking spot, I thank the universe for getting me home in one piece, as I remember little of the actual drive. I sit there for a moment, staring at the steering wheel, realizing I've been lying to myself about how much this has all upset me. But it's hard to put my finger on exactly why.

Shaking myself, I drag my ass out of the car and upstairs to my apartment.

I round the hall corner to my apartment and almost drop my keys in shock.

Cal, who is sitting on the floor with his back against my door, rises and dusts off his jeans.

"We need to talk."

I freeze in place. "I'm not ready to." The words sound choked and forced.

He crosses the distance between us, looking down seriously into my eyes. My insides twist and turn, part eating me alive with misery, part wanting to throw myself into his arms. My throat constricts when I recognize the desire, disgusted with myself for being so weak.

"Ready or not, it's time I told you the truth."

CHAPTER 16

"Fine. Probably best to do this in private," I retort spitefully.

He shakes his head and huffs a breath out but says nothing. I push past him and unlock my door, holding it open behind me so he can enter. He closes the door behind him and follows me into the living room. I sink onto one end of the couch, crossing my arms over my chest defensively. I can feel the resistance inside me, even though part of me wants to hear what he has to say. I can only assume it's my instinct to protect myself, but I'm already confused and he hasn't even started.

He settles onto the other end, giving me as much space as he can.

"I need to start with the day you were fired," he says, scrubbing both hands over his beard. I gesture for him to continue. "Rachel contacted me that day. She wanted to meet as soon as possible to finalize things. She wants to get married."

My whole body cringes. "You mean you got back together with her before you even came over here and ended things with me? That's … I can't even …"

Cal looks up at me, confused for a moment before realization dawns on his face. "God, no, Sasha," he says in disgust. "She's marrying *someone else*."

He stares at me while that sinks in. He's not back together with her. He's not marrying her. She's engaged to another man.

"Oh my god," I gasp.

"Yeah," he agrees drily, wringing his fingers together. "Turns out she'd been cheating on me for a long time, but her parents were pressuring her to seal the deal with me. It explains a lot of her behavior, actually, but I have to admit it, uh, it didn't put me in a very trusting frame of mind for our conversation." He looks down into his hands, blinking hard like he's trying not to cry.

And it hits me. That's why he didn't believe me. A woman he'd loved for years had just told him their relationship was basically a lie. How could I, a woman he'd known only weeks, possibly expect his full and complete trust? Even without the bombshell she dropped on him, framing it in context of the shortness of our relationship makes me understand the events of that day just a little better, and I realize I probably overreacted. And I feel my confusion start to fade.

"I'm so sorry she hurt you."

He looks up at me, his blue eyes rimmed with red. "She didn't hurt me, Sasha. Not really. It was a shock, sure. But I'm upset because I let it get under my skin, and then I pushed you away because of it. You have no idea how sorry I am."

"So you two had brunch —"

"To finalize things. It's all done, and I never have to see her again. Thank bloody fucking Christ," he grumbles. "But as soon as I left you here that day, I wanted to kick myself. I know you wouldn't do drugs, Sasha. God, I'm such a fucking idiot." He shakes his head, looking back into his hands.

"Thank you," I breathe. "For saying you know I wouldn't do drugs. Not for saying you're an idiot. Though, you know, you kind of were." He smirks in response, and I give him a tentative smile in return. "So what happened with Lacey? Becca told me you got a confession out of her."

"Ah, yes, that. She was drunk and trying to impress me, and it was surprisingly easy to coax her into telling me everything. I documented it all and took it to hospital administration. Naturally, they called Ms. Petersen in and levied the accusations against her. It was rather late in the day, though, so they weren't going to have conclusive drug test results on which to base a decision until today. She chose to attempt to further stall her termination by muddying the waters." I look at him, confused, so he adds, "She accused me of coming onto her in my office and saying if she didn't sleep with me, I'd make sure she was fired."

"*No,*" I gasp. "God, she's exactly as much of a scheming bitch as I thought she was."

"See, that's the thing," Cal replies. "You'd warned me about exactly that. So I had cameras installed in my office, as it's really the only place I'm ever alone. It didn't take long for her story to come apart after she learned that, even though it did rather add to the spectacle of it all."

"You listened to me," I say, touched that he actually took my advice.

"Of course I did. And I'm glad I could finally put a stop to her schemes. Now everyone will know what really happened and who's to blame. And hopefully anyone who still had doubts about you will feel as bad about it as I did."

"Is that why you felt like you had to help Becca and Harper get a confession out of Lacey? Because you felt bad for not believing me?"

He gives me a wry smile. "No. I did that because I love you."

My breath catches in my throat and my eyes go wide. "You … love me?"

Cal lets out a short, breathy laugh and his eyes glisten. "I do, actually. Damn, it feels good to finally tell you that." He slides toward me on the couch, and my stomach tightens with nerves. "From the moment I met you, I felt like I already knew you. Like we were meant to be. But I didn't want to say that and scare you off. And you reminded me of someone too, you know."

I stare at him as he settles next to me, completely unable to tear my gaze away. "You never mentioned that."

"I know," he admits. "Because it's stupid, really. My brother was going to school here, and I was visiting him on holiday. We went to the big airshow they have here every year and I saw this girl. Just glimpsed her through the crowd. She was the most beautiful creature I'd ever seen. She looked just like you — she had your same hair color, same height, same everything," he reaches out and tugs a dark blonde lock. "Then she was just gone. But I swear, that moment has stayed with me for years. And you didn't just remind me of her, but also of the feeling I had that day. And though that was ages ago, you could say I was already set to fall for you."

"Ten," I whisper as the tears start to fall. An ugly sob rips out of me, knowing I was right all along. Cal *is* Universe Guy. And I'd written him off so thoroughly and stubbornly that I didn't recognize my confusion and discomfort for what it was: the sadness of losing him. Because he's clearly meant for me. And I realize I already knew that on some level. And that I love him too.

"Ten what?" he asks, reaching up to wipe my tears.

"Ten years. It was ten years ago. Just outside the hangar. You were walking away from it with three other guys and wearing a blue shirt. I remember because it matched your eyes. Though you didn't have a beard then."

Cal's hand drops and he pales.

"You're not … there's no way …" he stutters, looking at me in disbelief. "That couldn't have possibly been you, Sasha. The odds —"

"Fuck the odds, Cal. That was me. And that's why I recognized you on your first day too."

"I was the one you had strong feelings for as a teenager?" he asks, astounded. "I thought you must've been referring to a first boyfriend or something."

"I *was* talking about you. I just didn't know it yet."

He shakes his head, still staring at me in disbelief. His hand finds mine, and he brings my fingers to his lips. "Please forgive me for being such an insufferable ass. I'm so sorry, Sasha. Even before I came here today I knew you were it for me. But now … fuck. This is just … it's incredible."

I close my eyes and take a deep breath. Breathing in the pain, the heartbreak, my stubborn, willful insistence on closing him out because he hurt me. Then I breathe out with forgiveness, love, and acceptance that you can only be hurt so deeply by those you love. And that the real lesson here isn't to never date a doctor; it's to let love in, no matter how much it scares you that you could be hurt. Because it's worth it.

"I forgive you." I open my eyes, free of tears for once, and entwine my fingers through his. "And I love you too."

His eyes shine back at me with everything I feel in this moment. He leans toward me, gently pressing his forehead to mine. I breathe deeply of his scent, allowing myself to sink into the moment as I wrap my hands around his neck.

Cal's hand gently strokes my cheek. "Say it again," he teases.

A grin breaks across my face. "I love you too."

His hands close on my face, tilting my mouth up as his lips claim mine. And I'm home.

BAD BOYS *Don't* MAKE GOOD BOYFRIENDS

CHAPTER 1

"Monday morning can eat a buffet of dicks," I groan, slumping my head onto the cool desktop.

"You would know about eating a buffet of dicks." I look up when I hear the voice of Julianna Magnusson, friend, supervisor, tormentor …

"With all due respect, fuck off, Jules," I grumble, rubbing my forehead as she passes by with a loaded medical supply cart and a shit-eating grin.

"Oh, come on, it's not *that* bad." My best friend, Sasha Suvorin, who is sitting next to me, rubs my back gently with one hand while she finishes pulling patient charts with the other.

"Easy for you to say when you probably spent all weekend having orgas—" Sasha claps her hand over my mouth.

"Obviously, I need to remind you that we are *at work*," she hisses.

That's my darling Sasha. Always such a prude. Like people don't know that she and Dr. Hottie are getting it on at every opportunity. The nurse and the doctor. Such a cliché.

And since I'm feeling extra salty this morning, I lick her hand. She pulls it away with a grimace.

"Gross, Becca. Gross."

"Dude, I grew up with four brothers. Licking someone's hand doesn't even show up on the list of the grossest shit I've done."

"I'd be willing to bet that list has more stuff on it from your dating life than from growing up with brothers," she replies with a smirk.

I grin widely, never one to waste an opportunity to shock my oh-so-proper BFF.

"I said 'gross,' not 'kinky.' That's a *whole* other list." I give her a wink and she rolls her eyes, pushing her dark blond ponytail back behind her shoulders.

"And that's my cue to head to the morning meeting," she replies, rising from the nurses' station desk.

I chuckle softly as I follow her. It's fun watching her squirm, so I never explain to her that none of my dating-related lists are actually all that long. Hers are just that short. Okay, well, maybe mine are a *little* long.

As we walk into the room, she lights up at the sight of her man across the room. And I have to remind myself her lists are probably not as short as they used to be. And mine aren't getting any longer.

He gives her a look that leaves nothing to the imagination. Well, to my imagination. Damn, this dry spell is killing me.

It takes all my strength to focus on the meeting. The chief of our unit, Dr. MacDougall — or Dr. MacBoring, as I like to call him — does his best impression of Charlie Brown's parents at the front of the room, and it's all I can do to stay awake.

"Make sure your chart notes properly reflect …" *blah, blah, blah*, "and make sure you read the revised policy documentation on …" *Snore*.

Why do I bother attending, you ask? Besides it being mandatory, even for medical assistants, as soon as it's over, it's open season for the latest gossip and the only time of the day where all the nurses and MAs are in one place.

As the meeting breaks up, I'm not disappointed when Avery Carter, a fellow MA, tugs at my wrist.

"I heard something you might be interested in," she says in a low voice.

I narrow my eyes, knowing Avery is rarely one to give up a juicy piece of gossip without expecting something in return.

"Yeah?"

"Oh, yeah. About that new orderly over in intensive care who you've been crushing on."

My eyebrows shoot up. "Who says I'm crushing on him? Dude's taken. I don't mess with guys with girlfriends."

Avery scoffs. "I prefer women and *I'm* crushing on him. The guy is hot as hell."

I shrug, feigning indifference. Even though she's not wrong. I spent the better part of last month uncharacteristically bummed when I found out the dude was taken. Because *da-yum*. "Hot as hell" doesn't even begin to cover it.

But then I remembered that it's always the best-looking guys who are the worst in bed. They've never had to work for pussy a day in their lives. You'd think with how much they get, they'd be better between the sheets. But why work on pleasing a woman when she's so eager to please you? No, I'm better off staying away from him. Besides, he screams "bad boy," and everybody knows that bad boys don't make good boyfriends.

Not that I'm exactly looking for a boyfriend. Four horny older brothers with loose lips and seemingly little respect for women have shown me exactly what's going on in a man's brain. And it isn't pretty.

"Sure, he's nice to look at. But I honestly don't care enough to cough up whatever you think you're going to get from me for you to spill the beans."

This is a game we play a lot. One that I usually win.

"Nina told us he's single," Harper Hughes, another MA, pipes up as she joins us.

Avery shoots her a dirty look, at which Harper just shrugs.

"He broke up with his girlfriend?" I ask.

"No, Nina was talking to Cindy, who was the one who said he had a girlfriend in the first place. Turns out she made that up to keep the vultures away," Harper explains. Avery throws her hands up and walks away. Harper chuckles. "She wanted you to cover her shift this Sunday."

"Well, that wasn't going to happen," I reply drily. "Does that mean Cindy struck out?"

Harper grins. "Big time. He wouldn't even talk to her about anything nonwork related. Apparently, it was hilarious. Almost makes me wish I worked in intensive care so I could've watched. Almost."

I huff a short laugh. Most people don't want to work in intensive care or emergency. The cardiac unit here at Rutherford

Hospital may have its challenges, but it's not nearly as demanding or stressful. It takes a special kind of person to deal with all that craziness.

Besides, one of the things I enjoy the most about my job is being able to leisurely talk with patients as I prep them for the nurses and doctors. Since we see mostly elderly patients who love nothing more than a good chat, I have all kinds of fun with the old coots. Most of them have been across multiple units for various health issues and have loads of good stories. They're fantastic sources of gossip and entertainment.

"So what do you want for this?" I ask curiously.

Harper blushes. "Nothing. Figured I owed you for … well, you know. All the trouble I caused with Sasha and all."

I give her a look. "Then you should be doing Sasha favors, not me." Not that I super mind.

"I would if she'd let me, but you know her." Harper shrugs.

"Yeah, she's pretty self-sufficient, that one," I agree. "Anyway, thanks. If for nothing else than putting Avery in her place for a minute."

"Anytime," Harper assures me with a smile as we head our separate ways.

As I go about my morning duties, my mind wanders more than usual. Dude is single. But apparently rejected Cindy, who is really pretty. Tall, thin, big blue eyes, corn silk blond hair, and a quiet, waifish quality about her that I think most guys dig. Nothing like my thick, curvy hips that are barely contained by our standard-issue hospital scrubs, the unruly dark brown curls that I keep coiled in a bun at the nape of my neck, and an attitude the size of California. I'm the J. Lo to her Taylor Swift. But maybe it had nothing to do with looks. Maybe dude's too good for everyone? Guys that hot usually think they are.

I'm still thinking about it that afternoon when Sasha finds me back at the nurses' station.

"You okay?" she asks. I look up to find her staring at me with a furrowed brow, hands on hips.

"Why wouldn't I be?"

"Because you typed the letter 'u' about six hundred times," she replies, pointing at the screen.

"I totally meant to do that," I reply with mock indignation. "It's a passive-aggressive rebuttal to MacDougall's incessant chart notes lecture."

Sasha smirks as she settles into the workstation next to me.

"Yeah, okay. Who is he?"

I heave a sigh, not even wanting to pretend I don't know what she's talking about.

"Vincent DeMarco," I admit.

"Who?" she asks, brows scrunched together.

"The hot orderly," I explain.

"Ah. He has a name."

I give her a look. "Of course he has a name. But apparently what he doesn't have is a girlfriend."

"And that's a bad thing?" she asks, looking confused.

"No. I'd just put him in the 'has a girlfriend' box in my head," I reply.

"So are you going to go for it then?" she asks. That would sound casual to someone who didn't know her, but I can hear the undertone of excitement. I shoot her a dirty look.

"Why bother? Been there, done that." Her mouth drops open, and I hold up a hand. "Before you can take that the wrong way, I haven't done *him*. But I've been with enough guys like him to know it's just not worth it."

"I don't understand. You were super into the guy before you thought he had a girlfriend," she objects.

"Yeah, that was before I remembered that guys that hot are all talk. It's all, 'Ooh, baby, I'm gonna do things to you you've never even dreamed of before' and 'Damn, girl, I could hit that all night.' Then five minutes later, a little rubbing, and they've come in their pants before you even got to see them naked, much less get off yourself. Nah, not worth it."

Sasha looks nervously down both directions of the hall we're on, checking to see if anyone heard my little diatribe.

"That was ... wow."

I shrug. "Just the truth. He'll remain good eye candy. I'll find someone else to have fun with. No biggie."

"If you say so, I just ..." Sasha chews on her lower lip nervously.

"What?" I prompt.

She sighs heavily. "I just wish you could have what I have. I know you're not really looking for a relationship or anything, but neither was I. And it's … I mean, I feel like an idiot gushing, but I want that for you too."

I lay a hand over hers. "You want me to be happy," I say, reaffirming the message I know she's trying to send. She nods. "I appreciate that. I *am* happy. Do you remember that time in the sterilization room you lectured me about being happily single? Well, that's where I'm at. I like my life the way it is."

Sasha sucks her lips into her mouth in a way that I know means she has something to say she thinks I won't like. I give her my best "just say it" look and patiently wait for her to spit it out.

"I thought I did too. That's all. I don't mean to belittle what you said. I just … I didn't know I could be *this* happy."

I shake my head and give her a dim smile, trying not to be annoyed. "I'm glad you're happy, Sash. You know I am. Maybe I'll have that someday. Maybe I won't. But I'm cool. I can get my oxytocin rush with some random guy, or a vibrator, or whatever, in the meantime. It's cool. Really."

"Do you really believe that? Because when you say something is 'cool' twice, it's probably not. Just sayin'." She rises and grabs a stack of patient files. "I'll be back."

I stare after her, trying not to be annoyed. I kind of have to admit to myself that she might have a point. Maybe I do want that on some level. But I really don't want all the other bullshit that comes with it. Because you have to kiss a lot of fucking frogs to find a man worth keeping around.

CHAPTER 2

"Tell me again why we're doing Friday night happy hour *here*?" Jules asks loudly over the music.

"Because there's more to San Diego night life than hoity-toity bars that cater to hospital staff and college students. And after this week, I need to *dance*," I explain loudly, adjusting my black crop top and shaking my shoulders to the beat. It's just a bar with deejay night and a tiny place to shake your thang, but it'll do.

Sasha shoots a nervous glance at Jules, who simply raises her hands in defeat. At least she knows it's pointless to argue with me. With a grin, I grab Sasha by the hands and pull her onto the dance floor behind us.

"Dance like you don't have a man," I shout to her, working my body to the music.

Sasha glances over my shoulder and points at the door. "How about like our coworkers aren't watching?" she shouts back.

I twist my hips and swing around to see Harper and Avery enter. Harper is still in scrubs but, like me, Avery has changed into more casual clothes.

I spin back around and shrug, continuing to let loose while Sasha nervously shuffles from one foot to the other in a horrible imitation of dancing.

"Why do you care so much? C'mon, girl," I grab her hands in mine and make her shimmy along with me. Soon, she's laughing and actually dancing. The girls join us, with even Jules finding her way onto the dance floor and bobbing her head to the music. I shake my head and laugh, pulling at Jules to get her moving.

"I'm too old for this," she shouts while laughing, her gorgeous dark-red hair swinging around her tall, lean frame.

"You're thirty-four, not ninety-four," I say back with a laugh. Just because she's one of our most experienced nurse practitioners doesn't mean she's too old to party. In fact, it means she probably needs to more than any of us. I put my hands over my head and bump her with a hip, causing her hips to sway away from me. Catching on, she sways back and bumps me in time to the music. "That's right, you got this."

She grins at my encouragement. "Old dog," she says, pointing at herself.

"New trick," I tease back, pointing at myself with a wink. "Now we just need to get down and dirty with some boys. Hey, Sash!" I grab Sasha and turn her toward me.

"What?" she shouts.

"Tell your man to get his fine ass over here and bring some of our male coworkers with him. Time to get scandalous up in here."

"I already took care of that," Harper pipes up, pointing toward the tables.

I turn around to see so many bodies in scrubs crowded around the tables we'd been at that it takes me a minute to catch all the faces. Dr. Thompson — Cal — is already making his way over to Sasha with a grin on that fine face of his, while Dr. Franklin stands at the tables making small talk with Zoe and Ethan, two of the cardiac unit nurses. A third cardiac unit nurse — Mark — hangs at the table next to them with two other guys and a girl. The girl I recognize as Nina, the MA from intensive care that Harper is friends with, but I can't see either of the guys that well as they're both on the far side of the crowd. But my gut tells me Harper is up to something.

I pull on Harper's arm until my mouth is at her ear. "What did you do?" I demand.

She shoots me a guilty look. "I just … invited some people I thought you might want to get to know," she responds lamely.

"A setup? Seriously? This isn't fucking high school, Harper."

She blushes bright red. "Sorry," she says, then leans in so only I can hear her. "I actually like his friend. I thought if you and Vincent hit it off, I could get Mason on his own."

I pull back, unable to keep from laughing. "Oh my god, this *is* high school." I wipe a few tears of laughter from my eyes. It's what I get for being a twenty-six-year-old surrounded by a bunch of newbie MAs in their late teens and early twenties. "Don't you worry about a thing, baby girl, I got you."

I fall back into the beat, circling around Harper so I can casually observe the guys. Their backs are still to us, but it looks like everyone is on their first rounds of drinks.

"I'm thirsty," I declare, grabbing Harper and Jules and dragging them back toward the tables. Avery follows behind.

Cal and Sasha are at the table with all cardiac unit peeps and Jules joins them, so I drag Harper and Avery over to the table with Mark, Nina, and the others.

"Hey, guys," Nina says, flipping her long dark hair over her shoulder. "We got a couple pitchers of beer. You're welcome to share."

"Thanks," Harper responds. "You remember Avery and Becca?"

"Of course," Nina chirps. "Avery, Becca, these are my friends Mason and Vincent."

"Nice to meet you guys," I pipe back. Avery echoes my sentiment and the guys mumble the same back. Before I end up staring at Vincent, I turn to give Mark a nod. "'Sup, dude."

A giant smile crinkles the corner of his blue eyes. Tall and stocky, his light brown hair is disheveled and his cheeks are red. And judging by the almost-empty pint glass in front of him, I can guess why.

"Becccccaaaaa," he says, much more loosely than usual, pulling me under his arm and giving me a squeeze. He points down at me with his other hand. "This is my homegirl, Becca, guys. She's awesome."

I slip out of his grip, not missing Nina furrowing her brow and taking a slightly possessive step toward Mark. *Interesting.*

"Heh. Thanks," I reply. "Clearly you've got a head start on me, though, so I'd better catch up." I pull three glasses and pour out, handing one each to Harper and Avery. I take a deep drink, checking out Mason as I do. He's probably in his early twenties, average height, with dirty blond hair and brown eyes. Decently muscular. All around a good-looking guy. He and Harper actually kind of have the same coloring and averageness. But then, I have heard that people tend to be attracted to people who look like them.

My eyes flick to Vincent, who is looking out over the crowd. It occurs to me that we have similarities too. Dark hair, dark eyes, thick. He's clearly muscled under the russet-colored T-shirt straining over his chest and upper arms. Damn, those arms with their bulging muscles and tattoos creeping out from under the sleeves. And while I consider myself pretty, this guy is off-the-charts gorgeous with his cut cheekbones, sharp jaw, and perfect olive-toned skin. My girlie bits start to tingle, and I internally bitch-slap myself back to the moment.

"So, Mason, what do you do at the hospital?" I ask, shifting my eyes back to him.

"I'm an MA in emergency," he says shortly. "You?"

"MA in cardiac," I reply just as shortly. "Same as my gorgeous friend, Harper, here." I turn to her and wink, and she pales, looking mortified. I take another sip of beer to hide my smile.

I look up at Vincent to find him staring back at me with an amused look on his face. I stare back, delicately raising an eyebrow. Normally, that'd make guys look away. Not this guy.

"You're new, right?" I ask him. "How are you liking Rutherford so far?"

He shrugs. "It's cool." And his bad-boy image is somewhat belied by his smooth, honeyed voice. Though it makes him that much more attractive, and I want to make him talk more so I can keep that voice in my head for fantasies later.

"He's been a godsend," Nina interjects. "He's one of the only orderlies who actually does what you ask, when you ask."

A light pink tinge graces Vincent's perfect cheekbones. Avery scoots closer to Vincent and says something in his ear. Vincent laughs. Like, really laughs, and I instinctively glare at Avery. Not that she's paying any attention to me. Or that I should care. I've written the guy off, after all. It's probably just the slight competition that always exists between Avery and me. We definitely have a love-hate thing going on. She can be fun, but she can also be a bitch.

I distract myself by chatting with Mark and Nina, leaving Harper free to talk to Mason, which she does, albeit self-consciously. I feel Mark and Nina out a little to see if Mark is into her too and am not surprised to discover that he is. But it doesn't seem like they've done anything about it yet.

"Okay, enough talking," I declare once I figure that out. "I want to see butts on the dance floor." I grab Mark and Nina's hands, shoving them together and toward the dance floor. I suppress my glee when, with a shrug, Mark offers his hand to Nina and she takes it.

I point at Mason and Harper. "You two next," I direct.

Mason shoots Harper an amused look. "Is she always this bossy?"

"Damn straight," I answer for her. "Dance now, thank me later."

Harper gives me a look somewhere between cautiously happy and mortified. I pull her toward me. "He likes you. I can tell. Just do it, girl," I murmur in her ear.

With a deep breath, she pulls a totally willing Mason by the hand. I clap softly as they walk away before realizing I'm now left at a table with Vincent and Avery, who are clearly enjoying their private conversation. And hell if I'm going to encourage them to start bumping and grinding in front of me.

Without a word, I head over to the other table to find that Cal and Sasha have also started dancing, as have Ethan and Jules. A couple of people have hung back to drink and chat, but I'd rather dance than talk. And while I don't have a partner, I don't need one.

I find a spot among my peeps and just go for it. Sasha finds me quickly, pulling away from Cal so we can all loosely dance together. She's sweet, but I feel bad for interrupting them, so I slink away back to the tables, only to find Vincent by himself.

"Where's Avery?" I ask, pouring myself another pint.

"Phone," he replies shortly, taking a drink of his own beer.

I presume that means she had to make or take a phone call, but I have to laugh at his brevity.

"Dude, shut up, you talk too much," I joke.

He raises a brow at me and I snicker.

"Harper and Avery are friends, right?" he asks, apropos of nothing. Damn, his voice is so sexy it actually makes me shudder.

I set my glass down. "Ooh, a full sentence," I tease. "Yeah. Like, best friends. Why?"

Vincent shrugs. "They're just really different."

"Oh, you mean, since Harper is nice, you thought Avery would be cool?"

Now *I* get his full laugh.

"Something like that."

"Yeah, that's not how girls work, bro," I joke. "She bothering you?"

"Nothing I can't handle."

I snort. "I'm sure you can."

Just then, Mason and Harper reappear. Harper asks me if I need to use the ladies' room, but I decline, so she heads off on her own. Mason and Vincent talk between themselves in low voices, I presume about us girls. I drink my beer, staring out at the crowd, wishing I was dancing.

When Harper returns she tells us that she ran into Avery, who was on her way out. Can't say I'm sad she couldn't stay. Harper darts a look at the guys, clearly reticent to draw Mason's attention back to her.

I set my glass down and dust off my hands dramatically. "Hey, Vincent." The guys stop talking and he looks over at me with a questioning expression. "I need someone to dance with." I step back from the table and extend my hand in invitation.

He continues to stare at me for a moment before glancing back at Mason, who gives him an encouraging look.

"Yeah, okay," he finally replies, rising to follow me. But he doesn't take my hand.

When we start dancing, he doesn't touch me, either. At least we're giving Mason and Harper space. But geez. And he seems really stiff and uncomfortable, though he's clearly got rhythm and, I suspect, some good moves by the sexy roll of his hips and his shoulders as he tries to contain his participation to the smallest movements possible.

I scan the dance floor, noting there are plenty of other single girls, and guys for that matter.

"If you want to find someone else to dance with, it's cool. I just wanted to give Harper and Mason some time alone," I explain.

"You like playing matchmaker, don't you?"

I shrug. "I don't make matches. But I'm happy to give people who I think like each other a little shove in the right direction," I clarify.

"Pretty sure they'd figure it out on their own," he returns with a challenging look.

I smile tolerantly. "Maybe. Maybe not. The first leap is the hardest. Not everyone is brave enough to take the chance. So I help them. You gotta go after what you want sometimes, even if it's scary. Even if you need help to do it."

He shrugs. "I guess."

I laugh and shake my head. "Whatever. Are you gonna actually dance with me or what?"

"I *am* dancing with you."

"No, you're moving ever so slightly from left to right near me," I shoot back. "Have you never really danced with a woman? Or maybe you're just scared to."

"Do you ever not say what's on your mind?" he retorts with an annoyed huff.

I grin, kind of happy that I've gotten under his skin. It feels like good payback for the weeks I spent lusting after him. Not that that was his fault, but still.

"Nope," I reply matter-of-factly. I scan the crowd again, looking for Sasha and Jules. I note that Jules is back at the tables, and spot Sasha and Cal across the floor near Mark and Nina, who are looking awfully cozy. "I'm gonna go dance with my friends."

Vincent levels a look at me and crosses his arms over his chest but doesn't say anything. I shake my head and huff a laugh, giving him a wave before I turn to make my way through the crowd.

That is, until I feel a large hand close around my wrist. Suddenly, I'm spun around and pulled against Vincent's massive chest. It takes my breath away, literally, as our bodies collide.

I look up into his eyes, warm and rich like melted dark chocolate, and for once I'm speechless.

He doesn't say a word. He wraps his arm around my back, pulling our hips together, his leading mine to the rhythm. It's innocent enough, our fronts melded as he gives in to the music, pulling my body with his to the beat. Just as I thought, he's no beginner at this, and his body works against mine expertly, playing out the sensuality of the song in our movement. But always staying maddeningly just this side of down and dirty.

Still, I let him lead, pushing down the yearning for more. I've already convinced myself not to go there and, despite my starved hormones begging for more, I don't want to encourage him to do something that would make that decision even more difficult to stick to.

But when the song switches to something slower and undeniably hotter, his body automatically switches too. He turns me around, sinking to meld to my body from behind, following my rhythm as I instinctively twist to the beat. His hands find my hips, resting gently as I lean back into him, freeing my mind and body to find my flow. The warm strength he exudes wraps around me as I move, heightening all of my senses.

So when his hands move to the exposed skin of my shoulders, sliding lightly down my arms, every hair on my body stands to attention, warmth shooting across my skin under his touch. Still, I don't overthink it, instead allowing the sensation to add to my oneness with the experience. I lean my head back onto his shoulder as his fingers lace with mine, as our bodies move as one together. Rarely have I danced with someone who could move like him, who fit perfectly behind me, who could keep me totally in the moment.

It makes me wonder, if he can dance like this, make me feel like this with clothes on … *No*. Not going there. Don't need a man who thinks he's all that. Don't need to be dating a coworker. Yep. That's my story, and I'm sticking to it.

So when the song ends, I'm relieved to leave the blissful cocoon that had been dancing with him. Because the curiosity it stirred is just trouble. Vincent DeMarco is just trouble.

"Hey, I need to use the ladies," I tell him, unable to look him in the eye.

He shrugs indifferently, following me as far as the tables, where he goes back to his seat as I head to the restrooms.

I take the opportunity to clean up and take a few deep breaths to control whatever reaction I'd been having to dancing with Vincent. When I return, it's fully locked down.

We all chat for a while and have more to drink. Eventually people start heading home — well, people from the big kids table, anyway. Though I say that like Sasha isn't two years younger than me. But since she's dating a guy nearly ten years older than her and kind of acts like an old lady, if the shoe fits …

She goes home with Cal, and only Ethan is left, so he joins our table. But that once again unbalances the guy-girl ratio, in the other direction this time. Mark and Nina go back to dancing, as do Mason and Harper. And I'm glad to see them all hitting it off.

When Ethan asks me to dance, I don't miss Vincent's complete lack of reaction. Good. I don't have to worry about him getting the wrong idea. To underscore that, I accept, and Ethan and I hit the dance floor.

And I almost immediately regret it. Don't get me wrong, Ethan's a sweetheart, but he's the epitome of the goofy white guy with no rhythm. So instead of enjoying dancing with him for his skills, I instead opt for some over-the-top hilarity, busting out some seriously antiquated dance moves, and we find our groove that way. At some point I start actually having fun. And after a while I'm laughing my ass off at Ethan's attempted moonwalk when Harper taps me on the shoulder.

"Hey, I'm heading out with Mason and Vincent, okay?" she says in my ear.

I give her a questioning look. "Vincent?"

"They came here together. Mason's going to take us both home. Do you need a ride, or are you good?"

My eyes flick up to the tables, where Mason and Vincent stand, clearly waiting for Harper. Vincent's hands are tucked in his jean's pockets and his eyes are floating lazily around the bar, not fixed on anything in particular, his boredom completely evident.

"I'm good," I assure her, my eyes snapping back to hers. "Make sure he drops Vincent off first." I give her a wink.

Harper blushes and nods. "Thanks for everything, Becks."

I give her a quick kiss on the cheek. "I got you, boo. Now go get that cutie pie alone and do everything I would do."

Her look of horror makes me laugh.

"Okay, fine, do *some of* what I would do," I correct.

She bites into her bottom lip and scrunches her nose, clearly self-conscious about her reaction. "That I can do," she promises. "Bye."

I push her away and go back to Ethan. As I do, Vincent's glance lands on me. But I don't turn back around. I'd rather go to sleep alone tonight than chase after a man who has to be coerced into even dancing with me. Even if it was a hell of a dance.

CHAPTER 3

"We've got a full schedule today, and Avery is out on personal business. I need you two to cover her check-ins, and I'll get one of our orderlies to handle running laundry and biohazardous waste disposal until she's back. They can do supplies too if you can't keep up." Jules puts her hands on her hips. "That means there isn't time to shoot the breeze. Not with patients. Not with each other. Not with the nurses. Understood?"

Harper and I exchange a glance.

"Sir, yes, sir," I bark, snapping to attention and saluting. Harper stifles a laugh and Jules rolls her eyes.

"Split up her charts and get to it then," Jules grumbles. "And maybe someday we'll get enough budget to staff so that we're not in dire straits when we're down a single MA." She stalks off without another word, clearly once again displeased with hospital administration. She usually handles stress much better than this, so I can only assume there's something else going on that I don't know about.

In any case, Harper and I immediately set to distributing files. Though we're attempting to sort them so we can physically manage to get them all done, I see one I must have.

I hold up the file marked "Cormac Quinlan Murphy."

"Oh, please, can you take my two o'clock so I can do this one? I love old Irish dudes. They remind me of my Grandpa Dillon," I beg.

"Ha. Sure, why not?" Harper agrees. "Remind me to kill Avery if whatever she's out for isn't really, really serious."

"Only if I don't kill her first," I agree.

We part ways to divide and conquer. The day speeds by, as it always does when we're effectively overbooked. But I'm still looking forward to my Irish grandpa patient when I head into the waiting room, chart in hand.

"Cormac Murphy?" I call expectantly.

To my surprise, a younger man whom I'd pegged as waiting for a relative rises.

"You're Cormac Murphy?" I ask, shocked.

He runs a hand nervously over the stubble on his face.

"That I am," he agrees. "But I go by Quin."

The accent. Oh, the accent. And the way his dark brown hair falls into his cognac-colored eyes … this guy's a total hottie, and he can't be more than thirty.

I clear my throat, getting ahold of myself. "Hi Quin, I'm Becca. Follow me, and we'll get you started," I say, gesturing for him to follow. I get his weight and height, then lead him into exam room five.

I gesture to a chair and take a seat on the rolling stool, setting my tablet up on the desktop. I verify his identity before proceeding, confirming that he's only twenty-eight. Yeesh. That's a good thirty to forty years younger than our average patient. I'm not sure what to think about that. I don't usually have to worry about being attracted to our patients, given their age. But this … oh boy.

"So what brings you in today?" I ask, determined to focus with my fingers poised over my traveling keyboard.

He rubs his chest self-consciously. "I'd had a weird, dull pain in the chest for a while. Then last week I got a really sharp pain and some tingling in my arm. I went in to see my physician, who said my blood pressure is high, but he wanted to make sure that it wasn't something worse. Just as a precaution," Quin explains.

It's hard to focus on his words, given his accent and the adorableness that is him. But I push through and document it all, asking him a few more clarifying questions, what medications he's on, and so forth.

"Okay, I'm going to take your blood pressure now," I say on a breath. I grab the cuff, wrapping it around his bicep and focus on inflating it and listening for the blood flow points. His eyes watch me curiously, making it even harder to concentrate. "Yep, you're a little high." I undo the cuff.

"Forgive me, but aren't you a little bit beautiful to be a nurse?" he asks.

I look at him, eyebrows raised.

"Oh my god," he says, turning red. "Young. I meant *young* to be a nurse."

I burst out laughing. "I'm a medical assistant," I reply. "Though I'm twenty-six, so not too young, or beautiful for that matter, to be a nurse."

"I'm so sorry," he says, putting a hand over his face. "I feel like a complete fool. Is there any way we can pretend that I never said that?"

"It's okay," I assure him. "It happens. It's no big deal."

I finish entering some notes and close the tablet.

"I hope I didn't make you uncomfortable. I imagine you get hit on all the time," he says.

"Well, I do," I admit. "But it's a bit different coming from an attractive guy my age rather than the usual patient, who could easily be my grandfather."

The look of hope on his face is priceless.

"Dr. Carson will be in momentarily," I say, turning toward the door.

"It was nice to meet you, Becca," he replies with a grin.

"You too, but I'll be back when the doctor is done with you," I respond. And I can't help giving him a little wink as I leave. Even though I know I shouldn't. But fuck it. That guy is hot. And he called me beautiful.

So I'm not sorry to have to go back a little more than half an hour later. Dr. Carson has ordered the usual echo and stress tests, so I grab the necessary paperwork as I head back in.

After I've provided him the forms and scheduled his appointment, I'm about to walk him out when he rises and stops in front of the closed door.

"Would you want to get coffee with me sometime?" he asks tentatively.

I look up, realizing he's quite a bit taller than me. And that while it's not the most professional thing to do, I honestly don't want to say no.

"I'd like that," I reply.

"Excellent," he says with a grin. He fishes a card out of his pocket. "Here's my cell number. Give me a call, we'll set something up soon."

I take it, sliding it into my shirt pocket. "I'll do that."

* * *

"Are you nuts? You can't date a patient," Sasha hisses at me from her usual late afternoon position at the workstation next to mine.

"Says who? There's not a rule," I reply. "I checked."

"God, you sound just like Cal," she says.

"And look how that worked out," I point out.

She gives me a stern look. "This is different."

"How, exactly?"

She opens and closes her mouth a few times, clearly unable to come up with a reply.

"Yeah, that's what I thought. I'm going to consider this a perk that balances out a lot of the bullshit I have to deal with getting hit on by skeevy old dudes."

"Fine, it's your reputation, your job. Do what you want."

"I always do," I retort with a wink.

"Not always," she parries back.

"What's that supposed to mean?"

She snorts. "You did a complete one-eighty on the hot orderly. You were all about him for weeks, then suddenly you're over it. Then you guys dance-fucked at our little after-work thing last Friday, but now you're acting like nothing happened."

"Did you just say '*dance-fucked*'? And while at work?" I ask, letting out a laugh of disbelief. "That might be the best thing I've ever heard you say, Sash. Say it again."

She glares at me and wrinkles her nose. "Don't be a pain in the ass," she snips.

"Oh, I live to be a pain in the ass," I tease. "But I'm acting like nothing happened because nothing did happen. We danced, which, by the way, I literally had to talk him into doing. I was dead right about him. He knows how hot he is, and he's totally weird and antisocial to boot. Not. Interested."

Sasha looks like she wants to argue with me, then thinks better of it. "Fine. So what about this Quin guy?"

With a grin, I proceed to tell her everything, trying to get her as excited about this as I am. But Sasha's a tough nut, and I'm unable to convince her that going out with Quin is a good thing. Guess I'll just have to prove her wrong.

* * *

"Irish coffee? Really?"

"What?" I ask indignantly. "We're in an Irish bar. Why's that weird?"

Quin laughs and shrugs. "Suit yourself. I guess I didn't imagine booze when I asked you out for coffee. Especially not on a Thursday night."

"Then you shouldn't have brought me to a bar," I reply with a grin.

"Fair enough, lass. I do love this place, though. About as close as you'll get to a real Irish pub stateside."

"When did you move here?" I ask.

He grips his actual cup of coffee in both hands. "Nigh on three years now."

"Is it too personal to ask why you left?" One of the few times I'll hedge my questions is on a first date. Who says I can't be polite?

"Not at all," he assures me with a smile. "It was a job opportunity. The right job at the right time."

"Do you miss Ireland?"

"Ach, no. I'm in love with California. It's beautiful here. And getting more beautiful by the minute," he replies with a wink.

"So what does a cybersecurity data engineer do, exactly?" I muse out loud.

Quin laughs heartily. "Do you really want to know? Because I'm afraid it bores most people."

"The Cliff's Notes version then?" I suggest, taking a sip of the deliciously intoxicating coffee.

"I purposely try to find ways to attack my company's website, software, that sort of thing. To see what someone trying to do damage could get away with. Then I fix the things I find."

"Well, you made that sound very simple and unboring," I commend him.

"Oh, good," he replies. "So do you have designs on being a nurse, or do you plan to stay just a medical assistant?"

"Is there something wrong with being a medical assistant?" I ask archly.

His ears tinge red. "No, not as such. Just wondering what your career advancement plans are."

"I love my job. Well, as much as anyone can love a job," I reply with a shrug. It's a nonanswer, really, but it was kind of an insulting question. Though I try not to dwell on his implication, choosing instead to move on. We start talking about music, movies, and anything else to find common ground, which there's enough of, thankfully.

By the end of the evening I've decided that he's nice enough but despite being enjoyable to look at, I'm not super attracted to him. And I definitely don't see it going anywhere after the career advancement comment. Don't like me the way I am? Next.

But it might not be a total loss. As we walk out later that evening, he sees me to my car. "Can I see you again?" he asks, standing a polite distance away.

I step toward him, placing a hand on his chest and looking up at him. "That depends," I reply. Though him asking tells me he's not very good at reading between the lines and body language. But he might be good for ending this damn dry spell.

"On?" he asks, his breathing picking up.

I grip the front of his shirt and go up on my toes, pressing my mouth to his. It's … nice. Not spectacular, but not bad either. I pull back and he grins at me.

"I'm free Saturday night," I say.

"Grand," he replies with a grin. "Talk later?"

I nod, unlocking my car. "'Night, Quin."

"'Night, Becca."

I drive home with the radio blasting as usual. It keeps me from thinking too hard about anything. When I lie down to sleep that night, I'd like to say I'm thinking about Quin. But I'm just not. Life would be so much easier if I were.

CHAPTER 4

Avery finally returns to work on Friday. Apparently, a close cousin of hers died unexpectedly. So, you know, valid excuse. But it means there's now enough downtime that things are on the boring side. At least I have time to fill Sasha in on my so-so date. She's even less enthused after hearing his comments about my "career plans," or lack thereof, in his opinion anyway. Can't say I disagree. Still, might not be a total loss. But that aside, the day drags on, seemingly never-ending.

That is, until that afternoon, when the mechanical doors between the cardiac unit and the rest of the hospital open to Vincent, navigating a patient in a wheelchair.

He stops at the nurses' station counter, plopping down a clipboard.

"Transfer," he grunts.

"Loquacious as usual, Mr. DeMarco," I comment drily, taking the clipboard.

"You know my last name," he replies with an uncharacteristic smile.

I shrug nonchalantly, rising to take over. "Rumor mill," I grunt back in the same tone he'd used to start, then greet the fairly out-of-it elderly woman in the chair quietly before starting to wheel her toward an in-patient observation room where she'll await surgery. Vincent heads back down the hall, punching the button to open the doors.

"Enchanting as usual, *Ms. Dillon*," he says with a wink. "See you at happy hour."

"Wait, what?"

But he's already gone.

As soon as I've settled the patient and gotten a nurse in to hook up her Hep-Lock, I hunt down Harper. I find her in the supply room, restocking the shelves.

"Harper, why did Vincent just drop off a patient and say, 'See you at happy hour'?" I demand.

She looks up, clearly confused. "We're still doing happy hour after work, aren't we?" she asks.

"Sure, of course, it's Friday. But why is Vincent coming?" I persist.

Harper shrugs. "Why wouldn't he? Mason will be there. They're best friends, after all."

"So he's just part of our group now?"

"I mean … things are going really well with Mason and me. So, yeah, I think he is. He's actually a really chill guy, Becks, you just need to give him time to get past the quiet and standoffish phase."

"You've been hanging out with him," I gasp accusatorily.

"A little," she admits, blushing. "I hung out at Mason's last night and he was there."

A catlike grin splits across my face. "Yeah? And what happened after he left?"

Harper blushes furiously, and I do a little happy dance on the spot.

"Get it, girl," I squeal.

"Shhhhh," Harper whispers. "I'm trying not to broadcast it until, well, there's something to broadcast. He hasn't exactly asked me to be his girlfriend or anything."

"Well, lock that shit down, because you know news like that isn't going to stay quiet for long," I respond. "Not that I'm going to tell anyone." She looks at me disbelievingly. "Seriously. Cross my heart." And I actually cross my heart.

She gives me another look. I put my hands on my hips and give her a look back.

"Okay, fine, I believe you," she finally says, cracking up.

"Good. Now. How was it?" I demand.

As if she's making up to me for adding to our group without warning, she gives me every last juicy detail. I soak it up like a desert in the rain. Lord knows I'm experiencing a drought.

So I'm considerably less pissed at her when I show up for happy hour that evening, changed into jeans and a blue knit cap-sleeve crop top, my curls loose and flowing for once. I have to keep it tied back so much it gives me a headache, and we're not dancing this time, only drinking, so no need to wear it up.

I ended up stuck at work longer than I'd planned, so everyone is there already, even Cal, who almost always works later than anyone in the unit. It's all the usual suspects minus Zoe, who just went on vacation with her partner to the Maldives. Lucky ducky. And of course, Vincent and Mason are there, as well as Mark and Nina. Mark has always been spotty on showing, but it seems now he and Nina are a thing, they're both going to be regulars too.

I try to suppress my frown as everyone greets me. I'm happy for them, but it seems like everyone in our group is pairing off. No pressure.

Since I'm last in, I end up in a chair just off the booth they're in, not particularly included in any of it. And even though Vincent is too far to talk to me, I somehow get the sense he's purposely avoiding even looking at me. Which is fine, because all I really want to do is drink. Jules, who sits next to me, finally brings me into the conversation, but then backs off as she senses I'm feeling grumpier than usual.

I watch Sasha and Cal whispering together as I drink my second Manhattan. My "I'm happy for them" mantra starts to falter a little as I realize how much I miss my best friend. We used to meet up for drinks after work outside of our usual weekly happy hour, but that hasn't been happening lately. On top of my massive involuntary dating hiatus — one I won't consider broken until I see some action — and I realize suddenly why I'm so grumpy.

"Hey, Jules," I say, nudging her in the side. "I'm going to go get some air. Be back."

"You okay?" she asks softly.

I nod. "Yeah, I'm cool. Just a long week."

"You should go home then, rest up. You're on again tomorrow, so you're going to need it."

I roll my eyes. Like I needed the reminder. "Thanks, but I'm going to need more to drink to be relaxed enough to go to sleep tonight. I'll be back. Promise."

As I rise to leave, I notice Vincent watching me. I don't bother giving him a second glance, instead continuing on my way and heading for the side entrance that's hardly ever used. It leads to a wide alley with a couple of outdoor tables that I'm sure are full on the weekends, but not so much on weeknights. Especially since there's a huge dumpster just a little farther down the alley.

I sink into one of the chairs, stretching my short legs out onto another. I twist in place, trying to relieve some of the tension in my limbs and back. Working in a hospital is hard on the body, and some days I feel it more than others. Today is one of those days.

"You shouldn't be out here after dark on your own."

I look behind me to see Vincent coming out of the side entrance, and I roll my eyes. What the hell is he doing out here? He can't be weird and aloof somewhere else? He closes the door behind him and sinks into a chair on the other side of the table I'm sitting at.

"I'm a big girl. I can handle it."

Vincent levels an impatient look at me. "All the same, I think I'll stick around if that's cool with you."

So now he gives a shit? This guy needs to make up his mind.

But I just shrug indifferently. "Suit yourself." I twist again, trying to crack my back.

"Rough day?" he asks.

"Rough month."

"I feel you. Come here." He stands, gesturing for me to join him.

I rise, and he gathers me in his arms.

"What are you doing?" I ask, pulling back. First he can't even touch me enough to dance with me, now he wants to hold me? Confusing much?

"Just shut up and trust me," he grumbles. "Stay loose."

Against my better judgment, I relax in his arms. He balls his fists together behind my back and pulls sharply toward himself. An immense crack echoes through the alley and a sense of relief washes through my body.

"Holy fucking shit, that was amazing," I groan as the ache seeps out of my back. I look up at him. "Thank you."

He drops his arms and takes a step back. "No problem." He shoves his hands in the pockets of his jeans self-consciously but doesn't back away further or sit back down.

"What else do you have in your bag of tricks?" I tease.

He smirks. "What else hurts?"

I bark a sharp laugh. "Nothing that you can help me with."

"You sure about that?" he asks.

"Pretty sure," I reply, looking up at him firmly and crossing my arms over my chest. I can't decide if I'm laying down a challenge or simply stating fact.

He steps back toward me, leaning in. "I think you might be surprised."

I raise an eyebrow. "And I think guys like you are all talk." Hmmm. Definitely a challenge.

That gets a derisive laugh out of him. "You don't know anything about me."

"I know that you're all over the fucking map. You're moody and withdrawn. I know that I really don't want to be attracted to you."

"But you are."

I throw my hands up. "Yes. Happy?"

"Not really."

I blanch at his words, not sure if he means that he's not happy that I'm attracted to him or that he's not happy in general.

"And why's that?"

"Because I already knew that."

"Pfff," I scoff.

"If it makes you feel better, it's not just you. You don't take shit and you speak your mind. Gotta say, as much as I don't want to, I find that pretty fucking hot."

I give him a skeptical look, fighting a blush from his compliment-slash … insult? "How do you know I don't take shit?" I ask back, a challenge in my tone.

He smirks. "You just made my point," he replies with a chuckle.

"Okay, fine," I allow. "What else do you think you know?"

His brow furrows and he steps toward me. While his eyes sweep over my face, I question whether I'm imagining the tension that's sprung up between us.

"You sure you want me to answer that?" he finally asks.

I swallow hard. "Yes?" I want to kick myself when it comes out sounding like a question, but he has me all kinds of nervous.

And I'm completely thrown off when suddenly, he grabs my hand, pulling me down the alleyway and around the corner to the back of the bar before I can so much as react.

He shoves me up against the wall, his face inches from mine, his eyes full of fire. It freezes me in place.

"I think I know what you really need right now," he grinds out as if the words are being tortured out of him. "And I'm going to fucking give it to you."

In a flash, his mouth descends on mine, his teeth suckling at my lip as he presses his body against me. I don't know if it's the surprise of it all or because it's so fucking good that I don't resist. It's the spectacular kiss I'd been looking for from Quin last night. No. It's a kiss that pretty much trumps every kiss, possibly ever. Filled with hunger, desire. And he's right: It's what I want from him, what I need right now. But where the fuck did this come from? How did he even know? And why is he giving it to me? Better question: Why am I letting him?

His hand reaches between my legs, stroking me through my jeans … and I stop caring why. My arms wrap around his neck, my tongue pressing against his lips. He opens to me, and we explore each other's mouths with a ferocity and urgency that would usually have me tearing off a man's clothes in a less public place. Clearly, he feels the same, as his fingers undo the button on my jeans, unzipping them enough to slip his hand down, under my panties, to the wetness that has bloomed between my thighs.

I don't stop him. I'm not sure I could if I wanted to. Not that I want to, even though this came out of nowhere. Even though this makes no sense. Even though this is everything I thought I didn't want. My body is screaming for release, screaming for his touch, and that's all that matters in this moment.

He moans into my mouth as his fingers find their slippery target. My moan follows his as he circles it with his thumb before slipping his fingers inside me.

He wastes no time, working me hard, his mouth pulling at mine until, in what feels like moments, I'm coming apart, choking back the groans of pleasure from the much-needed orgasm that flows through me. I slump my forehead against his shoulder, letting him support me as the pleasure takes over.

When my muscles start to relax, he withdraws, flicking my sensitive nub on the way and sending one last surge through me. I slump against the wall as he gives me a final, gentle kiss before withdrawing completely.

"Okay, maybe you know a thing or two. Anything else you know that you want to share?" I tease, looking up at him.

"That that's all I've got for you."

He turns away, allowing me to right my clothing. And my head. For whatever reason, he decided to jump me just then. But that's it. I'd be upset if I'd expected anything in the first place. But I didn't — exactly the opposite — so I don't question him further. Why would I? He's right. I had already decided I don't want anything from him. Though somehow he knew exactly what I needed anyway. And gave it to me. Damn, did he give it to me. One minute he can't stand to touch me, the next he's making me orgasm in two minutes flat. This guy is seriously confusing. Probably best that it starts and ends on a good note.

I lay a hand on his arm, and he turns his head to look at me. "Well, if nothing else, that was pretty damn memorable. Definitely the hottest thing I've ever done. Or, had done to me, as it were."

He gives me a smirk. "Surprised?"

"Completely," I admit freely. "Thank you."

He considers me for a moment with his dark gaze. "You're welcome," he finally replies slowly, reaching out and tugging at a crazy curl. "You should wear your hair down more."

I blink up at him, again astounded by the puzzle that is Vincent DeMarco. When I don't respond, he pulls me along back to the side entrance.

"I have to go," he says.

"Seriously? You're just going to give me an orgasm and bail? What am I going to tell everyone?"

"I really don't care what you tell them."

"So I can tell them you finger-fucked me in the alley then decided to take off?"

He grins widely. "Are you really going to tell them that?"

"Hell, no," I scoff. I can't begin to explain what just happened to myself, much less to other people.

He lets out a short laugh. "Bye, Becca."

And then he walks away without waiting for a response.

"Well, that was the weirdest fucking thing that's ever happened to me," I mutter under my breath as I watch him round the corner and disappear.

When I go back in, everyone is still chatting and drinking, clearly oblivious to what just happened. But why would they be anything but?

"Feeling better?" Jules asks as I slide back into my chair.

"Much, thanks," I say, trying to keep my expression neutral.

"Where's Vincent? He said he was going to sit outside with you," Harper asks.

"He decided to go home," I say as casually as I can.

"Scared him off, huh?" Avery quips.

I spread my hands out and smile. "Guess so."

I notice Sasha, who is on Jules' other side, give me a funny look and my smile falters. I shake my head as lightly as I can and she relents. But I know she's perceptive and more tuned into me than I often give her credit for. And I'm going to have some explaining to do later.

For now, I have another drink, considerably more relaxed than I was. Though way, way more confused.

CHAPTER 5

"I'm not telling you at work, Sasha, so stop asking."

"Holy shit. Hell has officially frozen over." Sasha leans back in her chair.

"Brunch. Tomorrow. Then I'll be able to tell you about my second date with Quin at the same time," I promise. And maybe that'll give me time to figure out what the hell happened. Scratch that. I don't think there's any figuring out Vincent, or his motivations. Either way, she's going to think I'm such a slut.

Why does that thought make me laugh?

"What's so funny?" she asks suspiciously.

"I'll tell you tomorrow," I say with a chuckle. "But I'm glad we're getting together. I miss you. Is that weird since I see you every day?"

"No, I miss you too," she assures me. "Sorry I've been so …"

"Orgasmic?" I tease.

"You're incorrigible."

"And you love me."

Sasha rolls her eyes but still smiles. "Yeah, yeah, yeah."

I go back to inputting patient data, unable to keep from smiling. Vincent is a fucking orgasm miracle worker. I can't remember ever feeling so relaxed for so long after one. And here I thought he hated me.

I should be pleasantly surprised, but the more I think about it, the more I just don't get it. So I try not to think about it. No sense spoiling my good mood.

"Well, whatever happened, you look pretty damn happy," Sasha remarks after a few minutes.

I look up to find her staring at me.

"Sure am," I reply with a wink.

"And you still won't tell me why?"

"Damn, girl. I've never seen you so curious. Keep asking. I'm really enjoying this," I tease her. It's quite the reversal. Sasha is so reserved, I'm usually the one trying to drag stuff out of her. Guess now she gets to see what that's like.

"Fuck you."

Hmm. Guess she doesn't like getting a taste of her own medicine. I blow her a kiss and return to work with a cackle. She'll live. Though I can't wait to see her reaction tomorrow. I swear sometimes that I do a lot of the things I do just to see how Sasha will react later. Well, maybe not quite, but it's still a huge perk. She's just so easy to shock. And apparently so eager to be.

Here's hoping my date with Quin tonight goes better than I expect, so I can really shock the shit out of her tomorrow. Though the closer it gets, the less I find myself looking forward to it. I've dated around, but something about being with Vincent yesterday has me shook. Don't get me wrong, I heard the boy, loud and clear. That was all. And I don't want more from him.

Who am I kidding? Of course I want more fantastic orgasms. Just without the side of WTF. But now that I've been reminded what real attraction feels like, going out with Quin seems like settling. Or maybe I'm just expecting too much? I don't know. I really have to stop all this thinking bullshit.

* * *

"Wow, you look beautiful," Quin says as I meet him in front of my building.

I spin, the light skirt of my little black dress flaring dramatically. "Why, thank you. You look quite handsome yourself," I reply, eyeing his fitted black slacks and light blue button-front shirt. He definitely cleans up well.

"Your chariot awaits," he says, gesturing to the car behind him.

With a chuckle, I approach, and he opens the door, helping me into the passenger seat before going around and climbing in the driver's side.

"Where are we going?" I ask curiously.

He flashes a grin. "You'll see. It's not far."

"Oooh, a surprise. I love surprises."

"Good, because I'm full of them," he replies with a wink as he pulls into traffic.

"Is that so?" I ask teasingly.

"You'll see," he says with a self-assured grin. "You really do look lovely tonight."

"Thanks, you clean up pretty good too," I reply.

"Your hair is … something. Do you ever straighten it?" he asks.

I raise an eyebrow. "I love my hair. It's as crazy as I am."

He huffs out a breath somewhere between a laugh and a scoff. Strike one of the evening. Still, I decide not to pull at that thread and let the conversation move swiftly on.

We make small talk on the way, and a few minutes later we pull up to the restaurant. And I realize I spoke too soon. It's an oyster bar. And I might be the only person in San Diego who doesn't eat seafood. The mere smell makes me sick to my stomach. But mostly … I'm pretty sure I mentioned that over coffee earlier this week.

"Just wait, they have the most amazing food," he gushes as he parks the car.

"I hate to be a party pooper, but I don't actually eat seafood," I say plainly, not bringing up that I almost certainly already mentioned this.

He waves a hand dismissively. "I'm sure they have other things on the menu. I've been dying to eat here all week." He gets out and I sit for another moment, contemplating being *that bitch*. But fuck it. I can survive one meal, right?

Wrong. As soon as we walk in, the smell of fish hits me like a brick wall of vomit waiting to happen. I lay a hand firmly on Quin's forearm.

"I really can't do this," I insist. "The smell —"

"No, really? It can't be that bad," he says, cutting me off with a disappointed look.

"It is. There's a great Italian restaurant just across the street, though," I suggest, trying to breathe as little as possible. Strike two. The fact that he's not immediately turning around and walking out is starting to piss me off.

"Ach, I'm not a big fan of Italian. Maybe we can find someplace else to eat around here."

I huff a laugh. "Dude, we're in the middle of *Little Italy*. We're literally surrounded by Italian restaurants." I manage to control myself enough not to ask who the fuck doesn't like Italian food. "We can drive somewhere else if you want, I just need to get out of here. Now."

He stares at me for a minute. A minute too long. I turn on my heel and exit the restaurant, gulping down the fresh evening air once I'm outside.

Quin approaches from behind me, grumbling and starting back toward the car. "Well, no need to be dramatic. Let's go then."

Oh. No. He. Didn't.

Strike. Fucking. Three.

You do not tell a half Puerto Rican, half Irish-Italian woman that she's being dramatic. That's three cultures of fiery women who will tear you to shreds.

It's on.

I cross my arms over my chest.

"How big is your dick?" I call after him.

Quin stops and turns back, his eyes wide, his mouth hanging open. "Excuse me?"

"How. Big. Is. Your. Dick?" I repeat slowly. "Is it as big as your *cojones*? Because you've got some pretty big fucking ones to talk to me like that."

He crosses the small distance between us. "Lord, woman, we're in public, keep your fecking voice down," he whispers angrily.

"I think I won't," I reply back at normal volume. "And I'd ask you to apologize for being a world-class prick, but that's not going to change the fact that you are. Or that I'm so done. Bye now."

"Yeah, and you're a classless whore," Quin calls after me.

I shake my head and laugh at the irony. Sorry, dude, if you're yelling after someone that they're a classless whore, you're pretty much describing yourself.

As I walk away, I realize that the restaurant next door to the seafood place is a fucking dessert restaurant. Now we're talking.

I open the door angrily, only to get inside and find it's not just a dessert restaurant, it's a *build your own dessert* restaurant. My fury evaporates when I realize that thanks to that asshole, I might have just found heaven. Who even knew this was a thing? But as tempting as that option sounds, they also have chocolate crêpes on the menu. So that's pretty much happening.

I get my food and sit at a table outside, people-watching while I eat. The crêpes are ridiculous. A delicate chocolate pastry wrapped around chunks of brownie and fudge, with chocolate whipped cream on top. This night didn't turn out so bad after all.

I'm downing a glass of water to cut the richness when I hear my name. I look up to see Vincent, across the street, coming out of the Italian restaurant with a plastic bag in hand. He waits a moment until there's a break in traffic, then jogs across the street. Time seems to slow as I watch him come toward me. It's like a fucking episode of *Baywatch*. Except with leather and tattoos.

"Hey," he says, stopping at the table.

"Hey," I reply. "Fancy meeting you here."

He shrugs. "Just grabbing some takeout."

I gesture to the seat next to me. "You're welcome to join me. I'm drowning my sorrows."

"I have just the thing for that." He sets his bag down and shrugs out of his black leather jacket, much to my dismay, and puts it on the back of the chair before sitting down. Though the clear view of his huge biceps doesn't hurt much either.

He digs through the bag and produces a foil-wrapped package. He opens it to reveal a humongous piece of garlic bread sliced neatly into slivers.

"Really?" I ask with a laugh. "How does that help?"

"All sorrows are less with bread," he replies cryptically.

"Ooookay," I say, reluctantly taking a piece. "Not sure how this'll go with chocolate crêpes, but what the heck, why not?"

Vincent smirks at me. "It's a line from *Don Quixote*," he explains. "And everything goes with garlic bread."

I give him a skeptical look, holding back a remark about his unexpected reading habits. So I just roll my eyes and take a bite. It's delicious. And while it totally clashes with the flavor of the crêpes, can't say I mind.

"Could you be any more Italian-American?" I joke.

"Am I wrong?" he returns with another smirk.

I narrow my eyes at him. "Not about the bread."

He doesn't take the bait. Instead, he pulls out a takeout container and starts in on the biggest hunk of lasagna I've ever seen.

"So you live around here?" I ask, going back to my crêpes.

"Yup," he says around a mouthful.

"What, no wild Saturday night plans?"

He shakes his head. "My best friend is busy fucking your best friend. Takeout and Netflix were my only plans for the night."

"Harper isn't my best friend," I correct him. I wonder quietly about his use of "were."

"Okay, fine, your friend," he allows. "You look nice. Why are you all dressed up?"

I eye him as I take the last bite of my food. I chew slowly. I'm not afraid to tell him, I just want to make him wait for it. But unfortunately he seems totally unperturbed. As usual, I guess.

"I had a date," I finally respond.

He laughs. "Well, that must've gone really well," he says sarcastically.

I stare at him for a minute. And I realize this guy is way more on my level than Quin. At least, when he's not being confusing as fuck. But really. We have similar jobs. He actually seems to pay far more attention to my words and signals than Quin ever did, despite having talked way more with Quin. And Vincent likes my hair. And Italian food, though, duh. Even more important, neither of us is looking for a relationship. And he gave me one of the best orgasms of my life. Maybe he's not the stuck-up, selfish jerk I'd pegged him to be. A complete enigma, yes. But perhaps I can salvage what's left of this evening.

"Worse than the first, for sure," I reply.

His eyebrows raise. "Wow, a second date. And he blew it? His loss."

"What makes you think he blew it?"

"Because I have eyeballs."

"Cute. I'm more than just a body, you know."

He drops his fork and looks up at me. "I know that, Becca. I wish I didn't." He closes up his food container and packs it back into the bag. "I should go."

"Why do you always bail like that?" I ask bluntly.

"I like to keep things simple."

I laugh. "Then you shouldn't have finger-fucked me in a dark alley," I point out.

He blows out a breath and drops back into his seat reflexively. "What do you want from me?" he asks quietly into his hands.

"I just want to know who the fuck you are," I snap. "I mean, there was 'cold and aloof' Vincent who wouldn't even dance with me. Then there was 'smoking hot' Vincent who made grinding magic on the dance floor. Then there was 'whatever' Vincent who ignored me the rest of the night after that. Then 'friendly' Vincent who wanted to see me at happy hour. Then 'sweet' Vincent who complimented my hair and fixed my back. Then 'off the charts sexy' Vincent who gave me the best fucking orgasm I've ever had completely out of nowhere. Then 'that's it, I've got to go' Vincent who just disappeared like it was nothing. Then there was 'casual and chatty' Vincent. And now we're back to 'disappearing act' Vincent. Which of these dudes are you, really? No. Never mind. That's not what I really want to know. What I really want to know is *why*? Why get me off when most of the time you don't seem to want to have anything to do with me and, by your own admission, you're not looking for this to be anything?"

He huffs a dry laugh. "That's not what you really want to know," is his only response. Then he leans back in his chair with an arrogant smile.

"Seriously? Fine. What do I really want to know?" I ask, folding my arms over my chest and leveling an icy glare at him.

His grin widens and he leans forward on his elbows, looking at me with a glint in his dark, beautiful eyes. "You want to know if I'll do it again."

My throat constricts. And so do other parts of me. He's not wrong. The bastard does have me pretty hot and bothered, on just about every level. Damn him.

"Dude, you're the one who wanted to keep things simple. If we can do it without the multiple personalities, I might be up for that. Because I like to keep things simple too. Otherwise, no thanks."

I rise, tossing my napkin onto my plate, totally disgusted with the whole night. Fucking men. Can't a girl just get a good lay without all the drama?

"Where are you going?"

"Home. To get myself off. Everything else is too much fucking trouble."

* * *

"You *didn't*," Sasha gasps.

"Damn fucking straight I did. I left that confusing motherfucker there with his mouth hanging open like the idiot he is," I reply vehemently. "Now, tell me something to restore my faith that not all men are clueless morons. How are you and Cal?"

Sasha snorts. "Oh, please, you know better than anyone that even he can be as clueless as the rest of them," she reminds me. "But he's good. We're good."

"That's it? 'We're good'? No juicy details for your bestest big sis?" I tease.

"You know I don't talk about that stuff," she says, turning bright red. "Besides, I don't want to rub it in your face."

"Mmm, I could use to have some things rubbed in my face," I say with a sigh. It gets exactly the reaction I expected, as Sasha pulls a face.

"Eww."

"Oh, come on, you know you like it when he does. Admit it, girl."

Sasha turns full-on crimson and I let out an evil cackle.

"I'm just messing with you, boo," I assure her. "Unclench. I won't make you admit you like it." I give her a wink that says, *But we both know you do*. Because I know her. Otherwise she wouldn't have blushed so hard.

"Not to change the subject ..." Sasha says.

"But to totally change the subject ..." I mimic.

"Yes, to totally change the subject," she admits with a laugh. "What's up with Jules? She's been totally MIA lately."

"End of the fiscal year," I remind her.

"Oh. Shit."

April is Rutherford Hospital's fiscal year-end. Which means Jules, being on the board as head nurse practitioner of the cardiac unit, spends most of her time arguing for more budget. Something she is equally passionate about and loathes. Because it never ends well.

"Maybe we can do something nice for her. Take her to a spa or something next weekend," I suggest.

"Funny, I was thinking we could do something nice for *you*," Sasha admits with a small smile. "You've been so all over the place, Jules suggested clubbing a couple weeks back, but I hadn't been able to circle back around with her to make plans."

"You guys want to go clubbing with me?" I ask, completely shocked. It's one of my favorite things, but my two best friends in the world aren't so into that scene. Harper will go with me occasionally, but now that she's preoccupied it hasn't happened in a long time. Which is also why I haven't gotten any real action in so long, because it's my main go-to to relieve the sexual tension. All sexiness, no messy relationship aftermath.

"If you want. Yes, that was the plan."

"Awww, you guys are so sweet. You know I'm not about to say no to that."

"Good," she says folding her hand over mine. "It's a girl date."

CHAPTER 6

"We missed you at happy hour," Jules says as we're standing in line at the club. She looks phenomenal in a fitted yet still somehow conservative black dress that wraps fully around her slender neck, completely covering those beautifully shaped boobies of hers, then hugging her tall, thin frame to just below the knee. Her matched black heels put her over six feet, totally towering over me and Sasha. Though as good as she looks, I can see the exhaustion in her face.

"Yeah, I just needed a break from … that group," I say awkwardly. Since it's the first time I've seen Jules with just us girls for more than a few weeks, I realize she has no clue what's been going on.

Sasha shoots me a pointed look.

"All right, all right. Since we'll probably be waiting a while …"

I purposely "ran late" to avoid this conversation. But I might as well get it over with. Well, the short version anyway. So I take a deep breath in, then let it all spill out in one quick diatribe. I tell her everything. About Vincent, Quin … more Vincent. And by the time I'm done talking I'm even more over it than I already was.

"But we all look sexy as fuck. So let's just have some fun, okay?" I finish, letting out a huge breath.

The line shifts forward, and we move with it. Jules is silent and Sasha plays with her skirt next to me. I look her up and down, once again admiring the clingy, silvery fabric of her strapless dress. Her hair is even up, with little dark blond wisps framing her made-up face. She almost never dresses up, and she really does look good. Mind, not as good as I do in my curve-hugging maroon halter mini dress. But still.

"I … damn. I'm sorry, Becca," Jules finally says. "What can I do?"

"Thanks. But I'm good. Really. This is huge, you guys coming out with me like this. I miss you both so much. So let's just get in there, do our thing, and have a blast."

She nods. "Roger that."

"How about you?" I nudge. "I know this isn't the best time of year. Need some help finding a little stress release in there?" I give her a knowing smile. Jules is so all about her job that I've never even known her to date, much less hook up in a club. But it's worth a shot.

"Oh, please, I'm sure everyone in there is at least ten years younger than me," she scoffs.

I laugh. "So? Plenty of young'uns likes them a cougar," I tease.

Jules wrinkles her nose and Sasha actually laughs.

"Thanks, but we'll leave that sort of 'stress release' to you," she responds drily.

I shrug just as we reach the entrance. "Suit yourself. But I'm still gonna get you drunk, happy, and dancing, girl," I promise.

"Now *that* I can handle," Jules replies with a giggle.

I lead her by the hand and, as soon as we're inside, the first thing we do is get drinks at the bar and sip them at a standing table, scoping out the dance floor. There are certainly plenty of hotties in the crowd, but one particular guy catches my eye immediately. With dark hair and big muscles, he looks a lot like Vincent, though not nearly as gorgeous. Still, could be fun.

I tap Sasha's shoulder and point the guy out. She rolls her eyes and gestures for me to lead the way, tugging at Jules to join us. Not to seem too eager, I start us at the opposite end of the floor. I dance with my girls, letting the music do its work and unwind the tension in my limbs.

I slowly work us across the room as the songs shift. But I lose track of the dude at some point. Oh, well. Sweaty and thirsty, at the next shift between songs, I haul Sasha and Jules back to the bar so we can get another drink and regroup.

"So what'd your man think of you coming out with us?" I ask Sasha loudly in her ear.

She rolls her eyes and yells back, "He told me if I came home horny to feel free to wake him up."

Jules laughs, but I give Sasha a worried look. "You guys aren't already living together, are you?" I shout back.

She shakes her head violently. "No. He said he'd come over if I was. He's at his own place. Yeesh. We're definitely not there yet."

Relieved that my best friend isn't already at the cohabiting stage, which leads to the marriage stage, I down the rest of my drink. Not long later, I spot the guy again, and he's much closer this time. I gesture for them to follow, and we slink up close to him and his friends, dancing seductively with each other. Both Jules and Sasha seem to be enjoying themselves. We clearly all needed this. And I'm glad they're both here so they have each other, and I won't feel bad when I make my next move.

I turn around so my back is against Sasha's front, and I make eye contact with my target. He's tall. Much taller than Vincent. And he's not as good-looking as I thought he was from afar. Definitely a Monet. But I have just enough alcohol buzzing through my veins to not give a shit. So when he slides up, I give him a sultry look and let him gather me into his arms.

Monet spins me around so he's basically dry humping my ass, and I'm not exactly feeling anything that would impress me. I look up to see Sasha and Jules tolerating dancing with his friends. It makes me chuckle, and I hope at least Jules leans into it a little. Girlfriend could use a good roll in the hay with a younger man.

But then I notice the guy dancing with Sasha getting a little handsy. Reflexively, I pull her toward me protectively, stepping out of Monet's embrace. Sasha signals that she's okay, and Jules pulls in tighter. But Monet must not have liked me stepping away, because he persistently steps back up behind me, this time running his hands down my sides.

A shiver runs down my spine. I can't deny that being touched like that feels damn good. So I turn back around, and I don't resist when Monet bends down and tells me his name, which I forget practically instantly. I tell him my chosen fake club-hookup name, and mere moments later, we're making out. There's nothing special about it, though he's still more skilled than Quin. Not so skilled as Vincent. I crush that thought as soon as it crops up.

Or, I try to. Unfortunately I have to admit to myself that despite the initial thrill of being touched so sensually, kissing this guy feels like kissing a wall. Zero chemistry. Nothing like the sparks that I felt with Vincent. The fire. The toe-curling need to take it further. My stomach turns when I realize that if it weren't for Vincent, I'd be going home with this guy tonight and probably having a pretty good time. The motherfucker has ruined me.

I'm so angry, I press away, making an excuse about needing to use the ladies room. Sasha and Jules follow, and we tumble into the large, multi-stall room, sweaty and panting. Once the door closes, things are quiet enough for me to think. And quiet enough for them to ask questions.

"You okay?" Jules asks softly as we wait for our turns.

"Yeah, I'm fine," I say shortly.

"You don't sound fine," Sasha points out.

That gets a laugh out of me. "Yeah, okay, I'm not so fine right now. But I will be. I just don't want to dance with that guy anymore, that's all."

Jules and Sasha exchange a look. Thankfully, a stall opens up, giving me a moment to do my business and collect myself.

When we leave the ladies room, we go back to our initial drink and dance mode, sticking with each other the rest of the night. It's fun, really. Much needed blowing off of steam. But not everything I was hoping it would be. No thanks to Vincent fucking DeMarco.

* * *

I spend the rest of the weekend contemplating this new reality where a man who drives me crazy is, ironically, the only one I can think of when I want to be driven crazy. Sexually, that is. It's pretty frustrating. It's interrupting my usual flow of dating around, having fun, then going on my way. But now?

Now I want a guy who sends me over the edge with one hungry look. A guy who I don't want to figure out but need to. I want Vincent. The maddening motherfucker.

* * *

"Exam three is ready for you. Vitals are entered, blood is drawn, and he's got his stool sample collection kit and instructions." I hand Sasha the folder in my hand.

"What's he here for?" She asks.

"He's got hypertension two with new symptoms. Tinnitus-like ringing in the ears and blood in his stool, thus the sample."

She frowns, looking through his history. "Did you go over his meds? He doesn't have antiplatelets listed, which those are both potential side effects of."

"I … did not go over that with him. Sorry," I reply with a grimace.

Sasha looks up with concern in her eyes. "You've been really off your game the last two days. You want to talk about it?"

"Later," I promise. "You should get in there. He's a crotchety old fucker."

She gives me a vague smile. "Right. Well, if you weren't my best friend I'd remind you not to talk about patients like that. But since you are, I'll point out I have class tonight. I'm free tomorrow, though."

"Tomorrow night, then," I assure her, plastering on a convincing smile.

"Okay." She reaches out and squeezes my shoulder.

I try harder to pretend like my head is in the game.

It works until Harper finds me that afternoon.

"Hey," she greets me, looking just as chipper as regular orgasms will make a girl.

I shake my head at my inner dialogue. I have got to do something before this bitterness eats me alive.

"Hey, girl, what's shakin'?"

"I wanted to invite you to a party this weekend. At Mason's place."

A host of thoughts and emotions flip through my mind. It must make me look like a fucking idiot, because Harper waves a hand in front of my face.

"Hello? You still in there?"

I shake myself, snapping my eyes back to hers. "Absolutely. Sorry. A party sounds like exactly what I need, thanks. Just let me know when and where, and I'll be there."

CHAPTER 7

When I met up with Sasha on Wednesday night, I didn't breathe a word of what I had planned, because I knew she wouldn't approve. So here I am, at ten o'clock on Saturday night, headed to the party solo. With Sasha good and distracted by her man. If my plan fails, she needn't be any wiser. And I won't need to embarrass myself any more than necessary.

Because if Vincent is here, I'm going after what I want. And if he's not, I'm going to do what I have to do to move on.

Job one was to dress for success. If the hot pink mini halter dress I'm wearing doesn't do the trick, I don't know what will. My hair is on-point, carefully styled so my curls look glamorously messy. Most people don't get how much fucking work that is, but it's worth it. I look hot. Which will help with job two: Make him beg for it.

Here goes nothing.

I step out of the car and make my way up the walkway to the house Mason apparently shares with a few other guys. As I knock, I can hear music, and people, but none of it sounds out of control. Hopefully, this won't be boring.

When nobody answers after a minute, I try the handle. It opens immediately. The small entryway holds a few people I don't recognize who don't even look up as I walk in. There's a kitchen to my right with a bunch of dudes tapping a keg. With a roll of the eyes, I keep going, hoping this isn't some college-level kegger. Just down the hall, the space opens to a large living room where music plays and people holding drinks talk in small groups all over the room.

"Becks," I hear just as I spot Harper with a small group of girls. She rushes over and hugs me. "I'm so glad you're here. Come meet some of Mason's college buddies."

"Um, sure, yeah, okay," I agree, allowing her to pull me along. She brings me over to the group she was in, and I notice Avery for the first time. "Hey, girl." I give her the nod, which she returns.

Harper introduces me to three other girls so quickly I know I'll never remember their names. Wendy? Natalie? Julie? I don't know. Doesn't really matter anyway, I'll probably never see them again.

They continue chatting about where they get their nails done or some shit like that, and I totally zone out, my eyes scanning the room for signs of Vincent. But nothing. I don't see Mason either.

"Where's your man?" I ask, tugging at Harper's elbow.

"He and some of the guys went to get more booze. They'll be back soon," she explains.

"Isn't there a keg in the kitchen? Or did I miss something?"

She laughs. "Yeah, but apparently they killed the last of the hard alcohol, so they went to get more," she says with a shrug.

"Ah. Well. I think I'll stick to beer tonight anyway. Be back." I don't want to get too hammered. At least, not yet.

She nods, and I slip away from the group. I make it into the kitchen to find a few guys still hovering around the keg.

"What have we got, boys?" I ask coyly, slinking up next to the tallest. He's pretty hot too, with dark brown hair, green eyes, and a swimmer's bod.

He grins down at me, revealing a dimple on his left cheek. Hello, Plan B.

"Natty Ice," he replies. "Want some?"

I pluck a red cup from the stack on the counter. "Don't mind if I do," I reply, dispensing some of the cheap beer into the side of the cup. I still end up with a shit ton of foam. I take a gulp before extending my hand. "I'm Becca."

"I'm Sebastian. But you can call me Seb," he replies, taking my hand and squeezing.

"Nice to meet you, Seb," I reply. "How do you know Mason?"

"I don't. I'm here with Jay —" he points to the blond guy leaning against the sink "— who went to school with him."

I nod at Jay, saluting him with my cup before taking another drink. I hear the front door open and a chorus of voices ring down the hall.

BAD BOYS DON'T MAKE GOOD BOYFRIENDS

"We come bearing liquor," Mason's voice booms before the man himself appears in the already-crowded kitchen, forcing me to take a step closer to Seb. Who doesn't seem to mind at all based on the dimpled smile he shoots me as our hands brush together.

Mason sets down several bottles of cheap vodka just as Vincent appears in the doorway holding two Black Label bottles.

"Well, looks like someone splurged on the good stuff," I say, taking another sip of beer. Vincent's eyes meet mine before they flick to Seb standing next to me. But he doesn't say a word. He simply sets the bottles down, gets himself a glass from the cupboard, opens the bottle, and proceeds to pour himself a good three fingers of scotch before silently heading to the living room.

I smile secretly to myself. He seemed irritated. Hopefully by me, because getting under his skin is the first step.

I shoot the shit with Seb for a while, solidifying my options for later. Turns out he's a little younger than me, but he seems cool. He lifeguards for a gym chain. So I was right about the bod. That's definitely promising. But as he and the guys start talking about basketball, I quickly lose interest and head back into the living room.

Someone has turned the music up, and couples now litter the couches, some making out, some clearly on their way to making out. Great. I hope this isn't going to be one of *those* parties. Although … maybe I should hope for that, since all of my designs are along those lines anyway. But I don't want it to devolve into that before I've had time to make my play.

At least, that's my thinking until I spot Vincent seated in an armchair in the corner. With motherfucking Avery on his lap.

And when she leans down to kiss him, something inside me breaks. Which makes me realize, it's so much worse than I thought. Because if it was just about sex, I'd be angry. But I'm not. I'm *hurt*. And that forces me to admit to myself that I want Vincent for more than just sex.

I don't even bother dissecting when that happened. The question is, what do I do now? My instinct is to march over there and bitch-slap Avery right off his lap. My second thought is to go get Seb and dry fuck him on the couch in retaliation. But my third thought wins.

I head back to the kitchen and pour myself a huge glass of scotch, downing it in one go.

"Whoa, slow down there," Seb says, coming over to ease me off the bottle as I start to pour another.

Abandoning the alcohol, I go on my toes and press my lips to his, desperate to erase Vincent from my mind. He pushes me away gently.

"Hey, I think you're great but …" He stares at me awkwardly.

Nonononono. This is not happening.

Just then Vincent appears in the kitchen doorway again, his eyes landing on Seb with his hands holding my upper arms, our faces inches apart. He grabs the whole bottle of scotch and disappears with it without a word.

And in an instant, I'm furiously ripping away from Seb and following after Vincent.

"I wasn't done with that," I call angrily after him.

I burst into the living room, but he's nowhere to be seen. Except Avery is, seated in the armchair she'd been straddling him in. Kissing him in.

I'm standing in front of her before I even knew my feet were taking me there.

"Why'd you do it, bitch?"

Avery stands up to face me. "Do what?" Oh, she sounds innocent. But the small, triumphant smile on her face says otherwise.

"You kissed him. You went after him even though you knew —" I choke on the words for a moment. "You knew how much I liked him. All those weeks when we thought he had a girlfriend. You knew because you were the first one to try to bribe me with the truth."

Avery folds her arms over her chest, looking beyond smug. And it's all I can do not to punch her.

"Guess he'd rather go for someone a little less crazy," she replies, her gaze shifting over my shoulder.

I glance back to find everyone watching. *Everyone.* Including him.

I turn back to her, my eyes searching hers for the friend I once thought I knew better. But Lacey, the maniacal bitch who once fucked with Sasha's life, was too close to Avery for too long. And I see more of Lacey in her now that her mask is off.

I sigh heavily and her smirk deepens.

I shake my head. "You shouldn't have fucked with me, Avery. Just remember what happened to Lacey." I back up slowly, refusing to turn my back to her. And for once, she has enough sense to look nervous.

I shoot daggers at Vincent as I walk by him. Maybe I knew him even less than I thought if he'd actually go for someone like her. Seb hovers in the hall just outside of the living room, clearly having witnessed the whole thing.

"Hey," he says, gently catching my arm. "Come with me?"

I look up into his emerald eyes and nod, letting him lead me out the door.

We settle on the porch, an awkward silence hanging between us.

Seb turns to me. "I don't know exactly what was going on back there, but I hope you're okay."

I huff a laugh. "I'll be all right. But thanks."

"I bet you will be. You seem pretty tough," he says. "I also wanted to let you know that I wasn't … when I said I came here with Jay. I meant *with* him." He looks at me meaningfully and it clicks.

"Oh my god," I gasp. I look back at the house, then lean in. "They don't know?"

He shakes his head, and I lay my hand over his.

"I won't say a word. Thank you for telling me, though."

"I figured you'd already had a rough enough night. I didn't want you to think I'd rejected you too."

"Well, you kind of did," I point out. "But at least for good reason. And hey, if you ever need a beard, I've totally got you."

Seb laughs. "I appreciate that, but I think it would *really* drive your boyfriend over the edge if you pretended to be with me, even if it was to keep my cover."

I blanch at his words. "He is most definitely not my boyfriend. Did you miss all of that in there?"

He looks at me knowingly. "I think I got the gist. You like him. Your friend made a move on him anyway. Did you miss how he was looking at you? Because I didn't."

He rises, extending a hand. I take it, letting him pull me up.

"He was looking at me?" I ask. And I hate how vulnerable it sounds.

"Yes. When he wasn't looking at me like he wanted to rip my head off for being near you. Trust me, whatever happened with that girl in there, he wasn't looking at her the way he looks at you."

"Nothing happened." Vincent's voice cuts sharply through our tête-à-tête.

I look back to see him hovering on the doorstep. As he moves toward us, Seb gives me a smile and slips around him, heading back into the house.

Vincent approaches, hands in pockets. "She kissed me. Apparently you saw that. Guess you didn't see me stopping her."

"Why was she on your lap in the first place? I thought you didn't even like her. At least that's what you —"

Vincent puts a finger on my lips.

"God, woman, do you ever stop talking?"

He pulls his hand away only to replace it with his mouth. There's none of the animalistic hunger of our first kiss. This is soft, yearning. As he sinks against me, wrapping his arms behind my back, pulling me into him, I return it and then some. I wind my fingers into his dark, luscious hair, pressing my body against his. He's right. I'm done talking. I'm done thinking. I'm done caring about who said or did what. I need him. I need this.

His hands dip to my backside, gently cupping me. He breaks the kiss and gives me that fiery look of his. "You're killing me with this dress."

I lick my lips and look up at him. "Then let's go somewhere you can take it off me."

I feel his cock twitch in his pants and he sucks in a breath, smoldering down at me.

"I don't know if that's such a good idea."

I pull away, my hands flying to my hips. "Excuse me?"

"I just mean …" He scrubs a hand through his hair. "God, I'm fucking this all up."

"Damn straight you are," I say, all sass. "You can't just drive-by-orgasm me, kiss me like you're tryin'a light a fire, then expect me to turn it all off on a dime." I go to push him sharply in the chest, but his hands close over my wrists before I can make contact. I gasp as he tugs me against him.

His eyes darken, his mouth set in a firm line as he glares at me. One of his hands slips to my neck, his palm flat against my throat.

"I don't expect anything. And you shouldn't either."

Despite his words, his lips crash into mine, his hand slipping to the back of my neck to pull me in. The animal is back, and the urgency of his mouth on mine wipes all thought from my mind.

His hand snakes back around to the front of my neck as his mouth leaves mine. He tips my head up, using his tongue and teeth to tease my throat. I bow into him, more turned on than I can ever remember being.

I slip a hand down his back, over his ass, then between us to the hardness straining against his jeans.

"Please," I beg into his ear as he sucks at my shoulder.

He tears his mouth away in a flash and grabs my hand, pulling me urgently behind him into the house.

A few curious pairs of eyes follow us as we enter, then hook a sharp left down a hallway I haven't been in yet. Another turn at the end of the hall and we descend a short set of stairs into a sunken den. Vincent closes and locks the door at the top of the stairs behind us, plunging us into near darkness.

His mouth finds mine again, and the hunger is back. He pushes me to a sofa in the center of the room, toppling me onto the soft surface. I gasp and open my eyes. My sight has adjusted to the small bit of moonlight coming through a window in the corner. It highlights just enough of Vincent's face to see the desire written there.

He drops to his knees, placing himself between my legs. His hands skim up my thighs, pushing my dress up to my waist, exposing my thin, flesh-colored thong. He slides a finger under it, dipping between my folds, sucking in a breath at what he finds. His strong hands slide behind my bottom, pulling until I'm forced to lie back on the couch, my legs parted as he sinks his head between them.

With the hand he had between my legs, he pulls my thong to the side as his mouth opens to taste me. I throw my head back the instant I realize what he's about to do.

"Fuck, yes," I groan. So much for making him beg. But hell if I care right now.

And when his tongue masterfully parts me, sliding mercilessly over every sensitive spot, I forget everything but the low ache building between my legs as he works. I was so wrong about him, about his skills, his priorities. Because based on the slow, pleasurable torment he's unleashing, the man is the exact opposite of all talk. It's the last thought I have before an orgasm takes me.

As I come down from the high, he raises himself over me, gathering my curls back from my face, kissing the side of my neck.

"That was fucking amazing," I moan into his ear. I feel him smile against my neck before he places a gentle kiss there. "But god, I can't wait to fuck you."

He pulls back to look at me, his expression inscrutable.

I run a finger down his cheek, deciding I'd rather not do this on the couch owned by a houseful of dudes. Who knows what's gone on here? And frankly, I'd like to take my time with the gorgeous man straddling me right now anyway.

"Do you want to come back to my place?" I ask in a sultry voice.

He closes his eyes and presses my whole hand to his cheek before turning to place a kiss on my palm.

"I —"

Whatever Vincent was about to say is cut off by a loud banging on the door.

"Vincent? Becca? You in there?" Harper calls through the door. She sounds panicked. Panicked enough that Vincent jumps up. I follow, hastily fixing my dress as we scramble to the door.

Vincent unlocks it and throws it open to a worried-looking Harper. And behind her stands a police officer.

CHAPTER 8

"Need to see some ID," the officer barks shortly.

Without a word, Vincent fishes his wallet out of his back pocket, retrieves his ID, and hands it over as I scramble for the zippered pocket on the side of my dress to get mine.

"What's this about, officer?" Vincent asks calmly.

With my ID in hand, I look up at the cop, whose eyes are now flicking between Vincent's license and his face. After a few more seconds of examining it, he hands it back over, gesturing for mine. I give it to him nervously.

He's silent as his eyes do the same dance between the piece of plastic in his hand and me. Once he seems satisfied, he hands it back.

"Neighbors reported underage drinking," he finally tells Vincent. His gaze searches the room behind us, then back to Harper. "That everyone, ma'am?"

Harper nods vigorously, shooting us an apologetic look. The officer retreats back down the hall, and Vincent follows Harper, who follows the cop. So I'm not left with much choice.

As we walk, I see the officer tap on partially open doors, quickly scanning each room. When we reenter the main area, another officer is talking to Mason just off the entryway. The officer looks up to see his partner and finishes up with Mason, gesturing for the other cop to follow him. They both leave the house and the few people left are completely silent. The music has been turned off as well, and the whole place is eerily quiet.

Mason shoots a worried glance at Vincent.

"You okay, man?" he asks. "I wanted to warn you, since … you know. But I couldn't."

Vincent shoots him a death glare. "I'm *fine*," he snips tersely.

I give Harper a questioning look, and she just shrugs her shoulders.

"So what the hell was that all about?" I ask Mason, referring to the cops showing up.

Mason is still giving Vincent a concerned look, but his eyes move to me after a moment.

"The seventeen-year-old next door thought it would be a good idea to come over here after his parents were in bed and sneak some alcohol. I caught the kid drinking a beer in the kitchen and made him go home. Guess his parents found out anyway and called the cops."

I gasp. "Holy shit! You didn't get in trouble, did you?" I ask.

"Nah, they went and talked to the kid, and he finally admitted we didn't give him the booze, he just took it," Mason assures me. "But ya know, they still checked everyone's IDs anyway. Pretty much scared them all off. Guess the party's over."

As if to prove his point, the last few people left in the living room give him a wave and head out.

"You guys are welcome to stay, hang out, crash here or whatever if you don't wanna drive home," Mason offers, winding his arm around Harper's waist.

Harper looks at Vincent, then me, with a barely suppressed grin. Apparently, I'm not the only one who wants me to get laid tonight.

"Thanks, man, but I think I'm gonna head home," Vincent replies.

I can't help the incredulous look I give him. Really? He's not even going to talk to me first? I did just ask him to come to my place before the cops pretty much shat all over my plans to get some. Er, some more.

"Okay, man, I'll see you Monday," Mason replies, holding up a fist. They bump fists as Harper and I share a look. Boys are so fucking clueless.

"Well, I don't want to be a third wheel, so I guess I'll be going too," I say, trying not to let the sarcasm drip out of my voice as Vincent actually starts heading for the door. Damn.

"Hey, Vincent, you should walk Becca to her car," Harper pipes up. "You know, because it's late."

He turns back and gives me a questioning look.

"No need, I'm right out front," I say coolly, folding my arms over my chest. He wants to pull the hit-it-then-quit-it disappearing act again? Fine. Fool me once, shame on you. Fool me twice … well, fuck that shit.

"Suit yourself," he grunts, then leaves. Double damn. No, he didn't.

"Cool, well, thanks for coming. Sorry for the cops and stuff," Mason says to me. Seriously. Clueless.

"Yeah, no worries, dude," I assure him. "See you guys Monday."

"I'll walk you to the door," Harper mutters, slipping out of Mason's grip.

Mason looks like he's finally getting the clue that something just went down, because he turns and heads into the living room, looking puzzled but giving us plenty of space.

"I can't believe Vincent actually just left without you. Didn't you guys just …" Harper whispers questioningly when we get to the door.

I shake my head. "We didn't fuck, if that's what you're asking. Not that we were in there having a heart-to-heart or some shit either," I grumble.

"So what happened?" she presses.

I give her a skeptical look. Sure, I told Sasha about our first sexual encounter at the bar, but I didn't tell Harper. Don't get me wrong, she and I have had a lot of fun together, but neither of us can keep our mouths shut. And we work with the dude. I really don't want to deal with all that if I don't have to.

"Fine, don't tell me, then," she says with an exasperated sigh.

"I want to, I just … I guess I don't really know what happened. But he's all over the damn place, so I'm just going to go home and just try to forget about him," I admit.

She shakes her head and pulls me in for a hug. "I'm going to earn your trust back. I promise, okay?"

I squeeze her back with a laugh. "You do that, boo. But I'm still not telling."

She huffs a little laugh and presses me away. "See you Monday?"

"Unless I win the lottery," I joke. And with a smile, I slip out the front door.

Only to find Vincent on the other end of the wide front porch.

I cross my arms over my chest. "I said I can walk myself to my own damn car," I say.

He looks back at me. "I know you can. But you also asked if I wanted to go home with you."

"And you said you were going home. You know. Your home. Not mine," I point out.

He shrugs, turning toward me fully as I join him at the edge of the porch.

"Maybe I changed my mind," he replies.

I snort. There's a shocker. "Well, maybe I've changed mine too," I return.

He raises an eyebrow and runs a hand down my bare arm, eliciting traitor shivers down my spine. "You sure about that?" he asks lowly.

"Maybe I'll change it back if you tell me why Mason was worried about you and the cops," I reply.

Vincent's hand drops back to his side and he scowls. "There are things you don't want to know about me."

"You mean there are things you don't want me to know about you."

He shakes his head. "Same difference."

"No, there's a big difference," I disagree.

"It doesn't matter. Let's just go back to your place," he insists, stepping closer and looking down into my eyes with an intense gaze that, despite myself, sends heat ripping through me.

"Oh, *now* you want to fuck me?"

"Isn't that what you wanted?" he asks, confused.

"Yes. But I don't *just* want to fuck you, you dumbass," I grind out. "Don't ask me why, but for some insane reason I want more than that. Wanted more than that. Starting with the story on you and the cops. But now? You're being all weird again, and I'm starting to lose my patience with this bullshit."

"I've been pretty up front with you, Becca," he replies calmly. "I'm not looking for a girlfriend. But I like you. And I'm sick of trying not to fuck you."

"Well, that's romantic," I reply sarcastically.

He laughs. "If you want romance, you're really barking up the wrong tree," he says. His eyes still glittering with laughter, he looks down at me again. "But if you're looking for someone to worship every inch of your gorgeous fucking body, I can definitely help you with that."

My breath catches in my throat. Goddamn him. He drives me fucking crazy. But that's just it. I'm into this guy on so much more than a physical level. Don't get me wrong: I'm not the girl who thinks she can change a man. But damn do I want to understand him.

And he's wrong about the romance. Dancing with me like our bodies were made to fit together? Sitting with me in a dark alley so I'm not alone? Fixing my back after a stressful week? Giving me orgasms with no expectation of getting them back? He's not acting like a guy who isn't thinking about what would make me happy. Even if he keeps saying he's not. He's a pile of contradictions.

But he's also unfortunately done things to my body I'll never forget. Twice. Is that why I'm so into this guy?

I have to admit that the answer to that is, *Maybe*. Or maybe it's my ego; maybe I just want to conquer him. Either way, I for sure don't want him for just a good fuck, though at this point he's proven he would be. I'm just as stupid and stubborn as he is. We're either perfect for each other or we're sexual napalm, about to explode all over downtown San Diego.

"I have to think about it," I finally reply.

"Really?" he asks, his brows pulled together.

"Really," I reply, hands planted firmly on my hips.

He stares down at me, and I wonder if he's about to try to get me in bed anyway. I stare back up at him stubbornly. But inside, I'm quaking. I hope he doesn't see because I'm not sure I could resist. Or maybe I hope he does. Goddamn, I'm driving *myself* crazy.

"Okay," he says, taking a step back. "I'll walk you to your car."

I'm simultaneously relieved and disappointed. So what do I do? I start walking. He slips his large hand around mine and walks me the short distance to where I'm parked.

I reclaim my hand to take my car key out of my zipper pocket. When I look back up, I barely have time to brace myself as his face lowers to mine, his mouth closing gently over my lips in a soft, innocent kiss that makes me want to throw his fine ass in the car and drag him home for something much less innocent.

Thankfully, he pulls back after just a moment, saving me from myself.

"See you around, Becca," he says, stepping back and giving a small wave. I watch as he wanders off down the road. But before he can turn around and catch me, I get in the damn car to go home and go to sleep. Alone. Again.

But I can't be mad at him. It's my own damn fault this time.

CHAPTER 9

"I'm proud of you," Sasha says, carrying the salad bowl from the kitchen and putting it on her dining room table.

"I can't decide if I'm proud of me too or if I need to get my head examined," I mutter as I fill my plate.

She chuckles and settles into the seat across from me. "Well, he isn't exactly the kind of guy I'd have hoped you'd fall for, but it had to happen sometime," she replies.

"I'm not *falling for him*," I scoff, stabbing a tomato angrily. "And what's wrong with him?"

I hear a spluttering cough coming from the living room, and I roll my eyes.

"Is peanut gallery over there going to be here the whole time, or what?" I ask, shooting a dirty look toward where Sasha's boyfriend is sitting.

"Sorry," she says with a shrug. "Like I said earlier, he's only here for the next few days while his place is being fumigated. But I've got to be honest, I'm kind of with him on this one. Are you sure you want to start something with this guy knowing it's never going to be what you really want?"

"Fine, have a point then," I say dramatically. "Of course I'm not sure. Thus the girl talk. Well … girl and Cal."

"Consider me one of the girls," he calls in his beautiful, deep British-accented voice.

Knowing he can't see me, I give a dramatic shiver for Sasha's benefit, and she laughs.

"Good thing Vincent doesn't have an accent like that, or we'd be having a very different conversation right now," I whisper to her before taking another bite.

"You have *no* idea," Sasha whispers back. "The dirty talk?" She shakes a hand up and down and rolls her eyes back in her head, demonstrating how hot it is.

"You're killing me," I groan. But I'm happy for her. She almost never talks about this kind of stuff, so he must be doing something right. Doing her right. A lot.

Cal appears behind Sasha. All more than six feet of his tanned, muscled, and stupidly hot self. Wearing a fitted T-shirt. Damn. He leans down and kisses her chastely on the side of her neck.

"I couldn't quite hear whatever you girls were just talking about, but my ears were burning," he teases as he straightens up.

I eye him openly as I continue to eat.

"I'd like to think my cooking is amazing, but I'm pretty sure that's not why you're drooling," Sasha says drily.

I snap my eyes back to hers with an innocent smile and a shrug.

"He should dress like that at work," I suggest, waggling my eyebrows.

Cal smirks as he heads into the kitchen to refill his coffee cup.

"Like I don't know you all are staring at me already. No need to make *that* worse," he says crisply.

I have to laugh. "Drat! I've been caught," I joke.

"You're not exactly subtle about it, my dear," Sasha points out.

"Well, we can't all date a Dr. Hottie. So sue me if I like to appreciate the goods."

Cal rolls his eyes as he takes a seat at the table between us.

"Maybe not, but please for the love of all that's good, don't settle," he replies, blowing on the hot liquid in his cup. "There's nothing less attractive than a woman who doesn't know her worth."

My eyebrows pull together. "I don't know if I should be flattered or insulted by that," I say honestly.

"My apologies," he says in his oh-so-British way. "Let me rephrase. You have a lot to offer, and you deserve better than the way he's been behaving. That's all."

"Oh," I say. "Well … thanks?" I give Sasha a bewildered look.

"I have to agree," she states. "But, unfortunately, you're already really into him. Do you think he's capable of more?"

I shake my head vehemently. "Nuh-uh. Not gonna go there. Whether he is or not, you know I don't play the 'fix him' game," I insist.

"Well, then, I think you have your answer," she says simply with a sorrowful look.

I sigh and finish my food. I both love and hate having friends who make me admit what's best for me. Because she's right, this is a recipe for bad. I'm not going to try to change him. He just wants sex and, strangely, for once I don't. So despite his *many* other attractive qualities, the fundamentals don't add up.

"I hope you guys are looking for a third wheel," I tell them both. "Because I'm going to need help staying out of trouble."

Sasha gives Cal a look, to which he nods.

"We've got your back, babe," she says firmly, laying a hand over mine and squeezing.

"You take Monday, Wednesday, and Friday," Cal says to Sasha. "I'll watch her on Tuesday and Thursday while you're in class."

I give him a look. "You don't have to fucking *babysit* me," I say with a sneer. "Oh, wait. Except on Friday. Happy hour. I *cannot* go to that, and I'm going to need someone to make sure I don't do anything stupid. So actually, yeah, there might be some babysitting required."

We all bust up laughing. Always better to laugh than cry, I say.

* * *

"I don't know why I let you make me watch this crap," Sasha groans, sinking into the couch.

"Mel Brooks is a fucking god," I reply defensively. "How can you not like *Young Frankenstein*?"

She shrugs and yawns.

"Oh, you did not just yawn while Dr. Frankenstein is meeting Frau Blücher," I chastise her.

Sasha delves deeper into the cushions, pulling a blanket over her as she lazily watches the screen. "Sorry, long week," she says on another yawn, then frowns deeply. "What's with the horses?"

I glance between her and the movie. "Damn, this comedy gold is lost on you, boo," I say, shaking my head. "Just go to sleep already." I sigh and lean back into the couch, pulling my knees up to my chest.

It's not long before Sasha is snoring softly beside me, so I lose myself in the movie, even though I've watched it about a thousand times and could probably act it out verbatim. But I guess that's why it's so comforting.

I've just finished watching the movie and am debating whether to move on to *Spaceballs* or just go to bed when there's a soft knock on the door. My brows pull together, knowing it's not Cal. Sasha and I were going to have a sleepover tonight to keep me strong, and I doubt he'd want to get all up in that. And lord knows Harper is probably all up in Mason right now. Or, you know, the other way around.

I slip silently off the couch and tiptoe toward the door. A glance out the peephole shows me a shock of dark hair and a leather jacket that instantly raises my hackles. I slip the chain off and open the door, my indignation purposely on full display.

"Vincent," I hiss, and his dark eyes snap up to meet mine. "What the fuck are you doing here?"

He runs a hand through his hair, his eyes tired. But he still looks like sex and sin. Bastard.

"I need to talk to you," he says, sounding as tired as he looks.

I slip out the front door, letting it rest against the frame behind me and folding my arms over my chest as I glare up at him. "Well, I don't need to talk to you," I whisper-hiss. "How do you even know where I live?"

"Harper," he says with a shrug, his voice low. "And why are we whispering?"

I roll my eyes. "Sasha's asleep on my couch," I reply, jerking my head back toward the inside of the apartment. "And I'm going to fucking kill Harper."

"Don't — I snatched your info off her phone when she wasn't paying attention. She really needs to use a passcode," he says. "So can we go inside and talk, or what? I'd really rather not do this out here."

I raise my eyebrows. "I'm sorry, was I talking to myself a second ago? I've got nothing to say to you," I reiterate.

He raises an eyebrow in return. "What happened to thinking about it?" he asks.

"Oh, I thought about it," I assure him. "Not interested."

A smirk settles on his gorgeous lips. "Yeah, well, as much as I doubt that that's really true, I've been doing some thinking too," he says.

I scoff a laugh. "I hope you didn't hurt yourself," I reply.

"Mmm, see, that right there," he says, taking a step toward me with a glint in his eye that's half smolder, half warning. "You wouldn't be angry if you didn't feel anything."

He stops inches shy of me, and I instinctively pull away. But my back hits the doorframe. And there's nowhere to go as he stares intently down at me.

"I didn't say I didn't feel anything. I said I'm not interested in doing anything about it," I insist. But my voice sounds small and unsure. I try to tell myself it's just the physical effect being so close to him has on me. But staring up into his eyes has a way of stripping me bare. The rawness in his gaze is impossible to hide from.

"Not even if I'm willing to meet you halfway?" he asks softly, his breath hot on my face.

In spite of myself, I'm intrigued. "I thought you weren't looking for a girlfriend?"

A half smile pulls at his lips. "I'm not. And I don't know ..." He looks up at the ceiling. "I'm not promising anything." His eyes flick back down to mine. "But when you walked away last Saturday, it didn't take me long to admit to myself that I didn't just want to fuck you either."

His admission takes the breath right out of me, and all I can do is blink up at him stupidly for a minute. No sassy comeback. No challenging questions. I'm struck dumb.

"What, exactly, are you proposing?" I finally manage to ask.

His broad shoulders lift gently. "I'll answer your questions, if I can. You decide if you still want to take it to the next level," he says simply.

"And what about you? Do you get to ask me questions to decide if that's what you want too?" I shoot back.

Vincent's eyes go hard, and I suck in a breath.

"I said I'm not looking for a girlfriend. Not that I didn't want one."

I stare up at him, totally baffled. Well, that's confusing as fuck. It takes my brain a minute to unravel that and realize … maybe he actually does want me in the same way. But … can't? And now I have a *million* questions.

"Okay," I agree abruptly. "I get to ask you questions. As long as you're going to answer them honestly."

"If I can," he repeats.

My eyes narrow. "Is that douchebag for, 'I'm going to do whatever it takes to get in your pants'?" I ask skeptically.

Vincent tips his head back and laughs. "If that was my plan, wouldn't I have done that last Saturday?" he asks.

"You really think you could've?" I challenge him, tightening my arms over my chest as I glare up at him resolutely.

He smirks down at me. "I think we both know the answer to that," he says with a slow shake of his head. "Look, we can take sex off the table completely if it makes you feel better."

"Why the hell would that make me feel better?" I reply. "I want to fuck you, dipshit — I just want you to let me in a little first."

"So, is that a yes?" he asks with a small smile.

"It's not a no," I say with a sigh, still not sure if all this is worth it.

I feel a burst of air on my back and spin around to see the door now wide open, with Sasha standing behind me looking tired and cranky.

"I see we have company," she says pointedly, her eyes meeting mine before turning a hostile glare on Vincent.

"I was just stopping by to say hi to Becca," Vincent replies. "But it's late, and I should let you guys get back to … whatever it was you were doing."

"Say hi?" Sasha scoffs, in total protector mode. "If you just wanted to say hi you wouldn't have showed up this late on a Friday night." Her unspoken implication hangs in the air.

I turn back to Vincent with a smirk. "Girl's got a point," I agree.

"I swear, all I wanted to do was talk," he replies, holding up his hands.

Sasha grabs me by the arm, pulling me back inside with a roll of her eyes. "That's what they all say," she grumbles.

"Wait," he says, throwing up a hand to keep her from closing the door. "What do you say, Becca? Give me a chance?"

Sasha looks at me questioningly.

"He wants to answer my questions," I explain to her. "See if I still want to go out with him after that."

Sasha's eyes narrow as she takes Vincent in.

"You need to ask at least twenty-four hours in advance. And it has to be during daylight hours, *in public*," she insists.

"Boy, your mom is really strict," Vincent jokes with a sparkle in his eye, causing Sasha to shoot him a death glare. "Fine. Becca, can I please take you to lunch on Sunday, *in public*, so we can talk?"

Sasha looks at me impatiently, and I sense she wants me to tell him to fuck off. Which I'm not going to do. But it also seems, shall we say, imprudent to just cave.

I tap a finger to my chin in an obviously theatrical demonstration of thought.

"Hmmm, I just don't know," I murmur. "How about I check my social calendar and let you know tomorrow?"

A knowing smile pulls at Vincent's mouth. "You do that," he says with a chuckle. "Goodnight, ladies." And with a wink, he leaves. Sasha can't close the door fast enough.

"I swear, I'm asleep for a minute and you —"

"Nuhnununuh," I protest, interrupting her. "You were asleep for a couple hours, boo, and you're not putting this one on me. I didn't ask him to come over here. My mind was made *up*."

"And now?" she presses, settling back onto the couch and pulling the blanket over her.

I shrug. "Couldn't hurt to see what he has to say."

She huffs a sarcastic laugh. "Oh, yes, it could. That one has trouble written all over him."

"And you think his friends aren't saying that about me?" I point out.

Sasha laughs. "Fair enough."

I pick up a throw pillow and whack her with it. "Well, damn, girl, you weren't supposed to agree with me," I tease.

"The truth hurts," she jokes back, pulling the pillow from behind her and fighting back. We go at each other playfully for a few minutes before she freezes and drops her pillow.

"What?" I ask, worried at the stricken look on her face.

"Oh my god, this is exactly what guys think girls do at sleepovers," she says in horror, looking down at the pillows in our laps.

I burst out laughing. "Careful, or I'm gonna ask your fine-ass man to come over here and take a video of us doing it," I tease.

She pulls a grossed-out face. "Oh, gross, Becks, too far," she protests.

I cackle with delight. "Sasha, my darling bestie," I say with a sigh. "You know I live to take it too far."

"Yes, I do know," she says, pulling a face. "I'd warn you to keep a lid on that on Sunday, but I know I'd be wasting my breath."

I pull my head back. "We'll see. If you didn't notice, I haven't agreed to anything yet."

"*Yet*," she stresses. "But let's be honest. You're going for it. You don't know how to *not* go for it, Becca."

I chew on my lip. "Yeah, you're right about that," I agree. "Am I crazy?"

"Absolutely," she says with a smile. "But it's one of my favorite things about you. You've talked me out of my comfort zone more times than I can count. And it was almost always a good thing."

"It's *always* a good thing," I correct her. "Even when shit goes bad. Because that's life, boo. We gotta take our lumps and learn from them."

"Well, for what it's worth, I hope Vincent's not a lump," Sasha offers.

I give her a distracted smile. "Me too, babe. Me too."

CHAPTER 10

"I have to admit, I'm a little surprised you didn't pick the Italian restaurant."

Vincent shrugs as he sits across the secluded booth in the tiny, hole-in-the-wall taco place he picked in the heart of downtown.

"It's so close to my place that I already eat there too much anyway," he replies before taking a bite of the last of his carne asada fries. "And I like the food here."

I set my napkin down, my plate now completely empty of the amazing chicken burrito that had sat there a few minutes ago.

"Well, that was the best burrito I've ever had," I admit. "How'd you find this place?" I reach for my water glass.

He wipes his mouth with a napkin, sets it down, then points at the north wall.

"Do you know what's a block away?" he asks cryptically.

Mystified, I shake my head.

"It's the San Diego County Jail, Becca. I got out of jail one night, and I was hungry. That's how I found this place."

It's hard to render me speechless, but the man seems to have a talent for it. I sit there in silence, while he patiently stares back at me with his dark, soulful eyes. For someone who doesn't talk much, his eyes sure say a lot. Right now they're begging me to say something, but I don't know where to even start with that.

And suddenly it hits me.

"That's what Mason meant about the cops. That's why you thought I'd decide I wasn't interested after all," I say, comprehension settling over me.

"Yes," he admits, leaning back with a sigh.

"So what'd you do?" I ask as casually as I can.

He smirks at me, his hand ruffling his dark hair. "I didn't do anything."

I roll my eyes. "Fine. What were you arrested for doing?"

He leans forward onto his arms. "My boss at the time accused me of stealing equipment from him."

"Is that why you work at the hospital now?"

Vincent blinks. "That was about ten steps ahead of the conversation I pictured happening in my head," he replies.

I laugh. "Sorry, my brain jumps around sometimes," I respond with a shrug.

He blows out a breath. "It's cool. But yeah. The stuff he accused me of stealing was magically found in my truck, so the charges stuck. Luckily, I didn't have to do any more time, just got slapped with a fine and a hefty parole since he got all his shit back and it was a first offense. My parole officer got me a job at the hospital. Good thing, since it's not exactly easy to find work with a record."

"You'd seriously never been arrested before?" I ask curiously.

He laughs. "That's what you want to know?"

I shrug.

He shakes his head.

"Yeah, I'd been arrested before. But not for anything serious. Underage drinking, criminal mischief, that sort of thing, years ago when I was just a kid, though that was back in Queens. Grand larceny is a whole other level."

"Wow," I murmur, tracing my finger over the design in the tablecloth.

"So any of this freaking you out?" he asks.

My eyes flick back up to meet his. "Do you want it to?" I challenge.

His answering smile knocks me on my ass. "No," he admits. "No, I don't."

"Is that why you can't have a girlfriend? Because you're on parole?" I ask, hoping I don't sound stupid. As blasé as I've been about my dating life, I've never dated someone who has been on parole, or even in jail, for that matter. Though one of my older brothers has been arrested a few times for things similar to Vincent's youthful indiscretions — except as an adult.

"Something like that," he replies slowly.

"How much longer?"

"Six months."

I pull nervously at my napkin, tearing it into pieces.

"That's not so bad," I reply.

"Not by itself. But it's just the beginning. Things aren't going to be easy, even after that," he responds.

I look up into his eyes. "I'm sorry," I tell him honestly. "Is there any way to appeal? To prove you didn't do it and clear the record?"

He shrugs. "Maybe, but that would take a lawyer I don't have money for, among other things."

"So, what, you just planned on never having a girlfriend because your life is too complicated? On just having casual sex for the rest of your life?" I ask.

He laughs. "I hadn't planned on anything." He pauses, his eyes darkening. "Especially not you."

That gets a small smile out of me. "I hadn't planned on you either. I've never exactly been the girlfriend type, anyway. So maybe we just keep talking, see how things go," I suggest as carefully and casually as I can. Not wanting to admit that this guy makes me feel things that defy logic.

Vincent appraises me silently while rubbing his cheek.

"I've never been great at taking things slow," he finally says.

"Me neither," I admit with a grin. "But then, it's been a really long time since I've wanted to take things anywhere. So maybe that's worth not fucking up."

His eyes cloud over as he studies my face. "I agree, but that's kind of the problem," he replies slowly.

I tilt my head and raise an eyebrow. "How's that?"

He looks down into his hands, the first self-conscious thing I think I've ever seen him do.

"Because my life is already fucked up. And I'm afraid bringing you into it is just going to end in disappointment," he replies honestly. His eyes drift slowly up to meet mine. "But I can't stop thinking about you."

I close my eyes at his words, a surge of heat rushing into my cheeks, my chest, and … other places.

I open my eyes once the sensation has passed. "I'm a big girl, I think I can handle it," I assure him. "And it's not exactly like I'm all sunshine and roses. I think you're getting into just as much shit as I am."

It's meant as a joke but also as a warning. I don't really know how to do relationships. Sure, my parents have been together forever, but they fight as much as they fuck. Which is a lot. Not really what I want out of life. But what *do* I want? I don't really know. Right now … him. And that's about as far as I've thought. I want Vincent DeMarco. All of him.

Sasha's going to kill me.

"What about work? You don't think it'll be weird?" he asks.

I snort. "Well, first of all, it's not like it's anybody's business anyway. Second, Mason and Harper seem to be handling it just fine. So even if people do find out, it's not the end of the world," I reply. Though I'm not exactly looking forward to the rumor mill knowing my business.

"So, we're doing this?" he asks softly.

I shrug. "Looks like. Strap in, it's going to be a hell of a ride."

A smile cuts across his handsome face and he rises, extending his hand. I take it, and we leave the restaurant, walking around downtown for a while.

We window shop, make small talk, and try out the whole getting-to-know-each-other thing. Did I mention all while holding hands? The sweetness and simplicity of it is mind-bogglingly emotional for me. It's *intimate*, and scary for me in a way casual sex isn't. Ironic, really — normalcy is terrifying to me. It almost makes me laugh that he thinks he's the one with the baggage. This guy has no idea what he's gotten himself into.

When he walks me back to my car later that afternoon, we step into our first awkward moment since lunch. He stares at me, clearly unsure whether he should make a move.

But this time, I know what to do. I've been fighting against my usual way of doing things all afternoon, but not now. With a grin, I step into him, going on my toes to press my lips to his.

He hesitates for only a moment before wrapping his arms around me and pulling me into him, opening his mouth against mine, running his tongue along my lip.

A shudder rolls through me, and I lace my fingers into his hair, deepening the kiss by meeting his tongue with mine. Knowing what he can do with that amazing fucking tongue makes keeping control incredibly difficult.

But after a minute, I pull back, determined to play by the rules. He looks down at me, desire clear in his eyes.

"That's not going to help me take things slow," he says in a husky voice.

"I'm sorry, did you not want me to kiss you? Because next time I —"

I'm cut off when his mouth descends on mine hungrily, his body pressing me into the side of my car. His hot mouth consumes mine, his hands skating down my neck, shoulders, and sides. The light touch of his fingers is a stark contrast to the heavy insistence of his lips, his tongue, and the whole thing has me melting into him, humming with need.

When he finally breaks away, I'm so worked up that "going slow" isn't even in my vocabulary anymore.

"I'll see you on Wednesday?" he asks, smirking down at me.

I look up at him, still trying to control my breathing. He looks so fucking smug, I realize he just did that on purpose. Got me all worked up on purpose.

"Did you just revenge turn me on?" I demand.

A look of pure and complete innocence settles over his face. It looks totally out of place on him. He may have the most gorgeous face in God's creation, but he's as far from angelic as it gets.

"I have no idea what you're talking about," he replies, fooling nobody.

"You're playing with fire," I warn him, ignoring his denial.

The smile drops off of his face, and he places his hands on my cheeks. "I know," he says softly, kissing my lips gently, chastely. "Wednesday." He drops his hands and waits for my agreement. The quiet smolder in his eyes makes my insides clench.

I swallow hard and nod. We're both playing with fire. And fuck if I don't want to burn with him.

* * *

Wednesday night is spent in a similar fashion, going out to dinner after work and wandering around yet another part of San Diego I'm not very familiar with. We end up in a small bar with a live band. It means I get to dance with him, but since the music is upbeat, it's not the suggestive, sensual kind I'd like it to be.

Still, his strong body moving against me is never a bad thing. And the more time we spend together, the more we find we're alike. It's funny, really, since outwardly we have such different personalities, and he was raised on the East Coast, an only child of a single father. A far cry from vying for attention with four older brothers and two questionably sane parents. And lord knows I'm a Cali girl, through and through.

But we like so many of the same things, have similar outlooks on life, and then there's the whole deep, intense physical attraction. That part's only getting stronger by the minute. Though it still feels like he's holding back on some level.

When we part that night with another epically delicious and frustrating make-out session at my car with a promise to see each other at the usual team happy hour on Friday, I start to question exactly how slow I'm really capable of going.

CHAPTER 11

"So, am I actually going to get to spend time with you this evening, or is Vincent going to be stealing your attention again?" Sasha asks impatiently on Friday afternoon as we input patient file data.

"He'll be there, but Jules is finally done with all that budget shit and is going to join us. So while we're at the bar, I'll be all about my girls, I promise," I assure her.

She heaves a big sigh. "I'm starting to understand how you must've felt when Cal and I started dating," she replies drily.

I bat my eyelashes at her. "Nah, that's different. I had other friends to hang out with," I reply with a wink. Though I'm kind of lying. I did notice, and it did sting a little to lose my best friend, especially since I didn't know that's what she was doing at the time. But water under the bridge, and I'm not going to make her feel bad about disappearing or hiding it from me.

"Hey, I have other friends," she protests.

I smirk at her. "Besides Jules?"

She shoots me a dirty look but can't refute the truth of it. I give her a big smile back.

"Fine, you and Jules are my only friends. Happy?" she asks with a pout.

"Meh," I reply flippantly. *I'd be a lot happier if I was getting a piece of Vincent's fine ass right now*, I think to myself.

Sasha gives me a look like she knows what I'm not saying.

"So you've been uncharacteristically quiet about the whole Vincent thing," Sasha points out. "Everything going okay?"

I shrug. "We're taking it slow," I admit, trying not to show how impatient I am with even the idea of it.

Sasha barks a laugh. "Well, that's a first," she says.

I look at her, ready to play it down, but something inside me breaks.

"It's toooooortuuuuure," I whine. "I just want to jump his damn bones. But I don't want to scare him off either. Gahhhh, Sasha, I don't know what to dooooo." I slump my head forward onto the desk dramatically.

Sasha rubs my back in gentle circles. "Okay, I have to ask. Why would jumping his bones scare him off?" she asks quietly.

I force myself upright and give her an exhausted look. "Because I like him, Sasha," I admit. "I *really* like him. Like … want to crawl-inside-him-and-let-my-universe-go-quiet kind of like him."

Her eyes widen. "Okay, not exactly how I'd used that phrase, but … holy shit, Becks," she breathes. "That's … wow. Yeah, I could see how that would scare him off."

I frown, letting my brow dip exaggeratedly. "Would you stop agreeing with me already? It's fucking annoying," I snipe, half-joking.

"Sorry," she replies with a shrug. "But maybe it's better if he knows how you feel. Because if he can't handle that now, I don't think that's going to change with time. You guys are either on the same page, or you're not."

"That's a little more truth than I can handle right now," I grumble.

"Well thank fuck that I can give that back to you for once," Sasha teases.

I shoot her a dirty look. "Is that really what I'm like?"

"God, yes," she agrees emphatically. "Irritating, isn't it?" She smiles beatifically, and I have to laugh.

"Honestly? Yes. Very. God bless you for putting up with me."

She lays a hand over mine. "All joking aside, you're an awesome friend, Becca, and as hard as it is to hear the truth sometimes, I know I can always count on you for it. And if Vincent doesn't see how amazing you are and jump all over that, then he's an idiot who doesn't deserve you."

My eyes fill with tears, and I throw my arms around my best friend.

"Thanks, boo, that's exactly what I needed to hear right now."

She squeezes me back reassuringly.

"Good. Now get back to work so we can finish up and get our drink on," she commands, pulling away.

I give her a look. "Boy, I'm really starting to rub off on you, aren't I?" I tease.

She gives me a wink. "You wish."

I can't help but burst out laughing. "Okay, who are you, and what have you done with my best friend?" I ask between gales of laughter. Then I shake my hands. "No, no, no. Never mind. I take it back. I like this Sasha. She's *extra*."

She grins but blushes a little, so I know my Sasha is still in there. Though I also can't help noticing how fucking happy she looks. How free. And damn if that isn't how being in love should make you feel. The thought would bring me back down to earth if I wasn't so happy for her. So I focus on that.

* * *

"You did *not* tell MacDougall to go fuck himself in front of the entire budget committee," Sasha shrieks while laughing at Jules's confession.

"Well, I didn't use those exact words," Jules admits. "But pretty close." She grins.

"Oh my god, once that gets around, you're going to be hero-worshipped," I tell her. Sasha and I exchange glances before throwing ourselves down toward Jules's side of the table in *Wayne's World*-esque supplication as we start chanting, "We're not worthy!"

Harper, who is on the other side of the booth, laughs uproariously, causing her to choke on the sip of beer she'd taken. I stop my adoration to clap her on the back.

"Easy there, tiger," I tease her.

She waves a hand and sniffs deeply, indicating that she's fine.

"So, Avery still too chicken to show her face?" I ask Harper, changing the subject.

She nods as she finishes wiping her nose. "She doesn't even talk to me anymore. I found out she's still hanging out with Lacey and read her the riot act. She won't so much as look at me now."

Sasha stiffens next to me. "No big loss if she's hanging out with Lacey," Sasha says frostily.

And that's as mean as my bestie ever gets. Because that bitch Lacey almost fucked up Sasha's career, her nurse practitioner degree, and her relationship with Cal.

Thankfully, we're saved any more awkwardness by the arrival of Ethan and Mark, who slide into the booth on Jules's side.

We exchange greetings, and I note that Mark is alone.

"Hey, where's Nina?" I ask him.

He exchanges an awkward look with Ethan.

"Yeah, uh, Nina and I aren't seeing each other anymore," he admits.

"Oh, bummer, I'm sorry to hear that," I reply.

He shrugs. "It's cool, but thanks." And that's all he says on the subject.

I shoot Harper a look. She leans in and talks lowly, so only I can hear.

"Don't worry, Mason and Vincent are still coming," she assures me.

But I don't feel all that assured, suddenly reminded of the awkwardness that can come of dating, then breaking up with, a coworker. Yeesh.

"Have you thought about how it would be? If you and Mason broke up?" I ask quietly.

Harper leans back in her seat, contemplating that.

"Of course. All I can do is hope that if and when it happens that we can be adults about it," she replies softly with a shrug.

"Yeah," I murmur. "But to have to run into that person all the time …" I shudder lightly but am saved thinking about it anymore as Mason and Vincent arrive, with Cal just behind them.

Sandwiched between Harper and Sasha, I can only watch as Jules, Ethan, and Mark shuffle out to let Cal sit next to Sasha, squishing me closer to Harper. As I scoot over, I notice Mason is sitting next to her, with Vincent on his other side. I look at Harper, silently wondering why he didn't sit next to me. She gives me an apologetic look back like she knows exactly what I'm thinking and shrugs.

General casual greetings are thrown around the table again. And I don't miss that Vincent barely glances at me. As Mason launches into a story about why they're late, something involving an old guy with Alzheimer's and far more old-man nudity than I wanted to hear about, Sasha leans into me.

"Everything okay with you and Vincent? Why's he sitting over there?"

I roll my eyes and shrug, not making eye contact and trying not to be pissed about it.

"Fine, as far as I know. And I don't know. He's a grown man, he can sit where he wants," I mutter back, taking a deep drink of the cocktail in front of me.

"Then why are you downing that thing like it's liquid patience?" she whispers back pointedly.

This time I look her in the eye, giving her my best irritated glare. She presses her lips together, wisely keeping her trap shut. Cal draws her attention back to him, thankfully, saving her from me.

Because it takes me exactly the time to finish my drink to realize I'm not annoyed. I'm furious. The man has had his head between my damn thighs, and he's sitting over there like we're just coworkers who barely know each other. It wouldn't bother me if he hadn't been the one to come to me, wanting to give this a shot. If I hadn't opened up to him this past week like I can't remember doing with a guy in … I don't know, probably ever.

As soon as Mason is done with his story, though, Mark jumps in.

"That's nothing," he scoffs. "Hey, Becks, you remember when you were prepping that old lady for her screening tests and she ran buck-ass naked through the halls?"

"How the hell could I forget that?" I reply. I bring my hands up to my chest, mimicking the flapping of her huge, sagging breasts as she ran and imitating her raspy soprano. "'If you can't catch me, you can't make me!'"

Everybody bursts out laughing as we continue to recount Mark and I trying to corral her into one of the exam rooms but failing miserably because of the double-entrance setups in all of our rooms.

By the time we're done, everyone is screaming with laughter. Well, not so much Vincent. He's more trying to look anywhere but at me, but I can tell he's chuckling to himself. Mark, who is sitting across from him, is openly wiping tears of laughter from his eyes, and I can't help but be struck by the difference between the two.

Mark has always been interested, and I've never gone there. But he's such a fun, great guy. Why can't I be into someone like that? Someone who isn't afraid to tell people how awesome he thinks I am, like he did the night I officially met Vincent. Someone who will tell stories and laugh with me. Someone who, oh, I don't know, hasn't been to jail and is now pretending like we barely know each other.

My laughter dies when that thought settles in. I withdraw as conversation around the table continues, though every single other person at the table *except* Vincent addresses me directly multiple times. By the end of the night I've got myself pretty worked up.

So when everyone decides to go home, I latch myself onto Jules hoping we can walk each other out so I don't have to deal with it. I don't look at or for Vincent as we leave. I'm just tipsy enough to start a fight but too tired to go there.

She squeezes my arm reassuringly, without me even having to explain. As soon as we're out in the evening air, she leans in.

"I thought you and Vincent were going out now?" she asks quietly and casually.

"Huh," I half laugh, half huff. "Yeah, I thought so too. Not that you would have known it by the way he was acting tonight."

Jules wraps an arm around my shoulders as we find our way into the parking lot. "Maybe he just doesn't want everyone to know yet?" she offers.

I shake my head. "I don't even want to talk about it."

Her hazel eyes look down at me knowingly. "Well, I'm always here. And you're stuck with me a little longer, because I can smell the alcohol on you and I'm driving you home."

I squeeze her around the middle, only because I'm that damn much shorter than her. "Thanks, big sis."

And I know I've had too much to drink when I get in her car and snuggle down into the seat, suddenly mentally, emotionally, and physically done.

I manage to stay awake long enough to get home and climb into bed, though still fully dressed, when my phone pings with a text. A glance tells me it's the last person I want to hear from right now.

Can I come over?

With a snort, I tap out a quick response.

Fuck no.

And, well pleased with myself, I turn off my phone and pass out.

CHAPTER 12

Thankfully, for once, I have Saturday off, so I sleep in and enjoy some much-needed time lying around the house in sweats while watching TV and eating ice cream.

I'm not moping, you're moping.

Okay, maybe I'm moping a little bit.

Vincent wants to pretend like I don't exist in front of people we know? Fine. I'll pretend like he doesn't exist, period. That doesn't mean I have to be happy about it.

And he doesn't make it easy either, with so many texts asking what's going on that I finally just turn off my damn phone. Unfortunately, he's clearly as stubborn as I am, because when someone knocks on my door after dinner, I just know in my gut that it's him.

Because it's what I would do if someone was ignoring me.

I don't even get up from the couch.

"Fuck off, Vincent," I call to the door.

"Not until you tell me why," he demands back.

That gets me on my feet and wrenching the door open.

"Are you fucking kidding me?" I snap at him, hands firmly on my hips.

My icy demeanor slips as I take him in, his tanned, muscled arms crossed over his broad chest, which is barely contained by the Rage Against the Machine T-shirt he's wearing. His dark eyes are filled with fire, and I hate him for looking so goddamn good while I'm angry at him.

"I'm not fucking kidding you," he snaps back.

I cross my arms over my chest, mirroring his aggressive posture. "Well, then, I'd be happy to enlighten you," I reply, letting my voice absolutely drip with sarcasm. "You acted like you barely even knew me, like I hardly existed, in front of all our friends last night. I'm not interested in talking to someone who is *that* ashamed to be going out with me. So I think we're done here."

I make to swing the door closed, but he throws up a hand to stop it. With a solid shove, he pushes into the apartment, closing the door behind him. I'm so surprised by the move, and he looks so menacing as he advances on me with wrath written all over his face, that I take a step back.

"I *acted* that way because *you* were the one who said our relationship was none of their business," he says dangerously quietly. "If you think I'm ashamed of you, you obviously haven't been paying attention." He stops in front of me, hands clenched into fists at his sides.

I open my mouth to shoot back when I realize … I *did* say that.

"Well, you didn't have to not talk to me at all," I insist. "You could've just acted normal. You didn't say a damn word to me or even look at me all fucking night. You think people didn't notice?"

His brows draw together. "That *is* how I act normally," he points out. "Who the fuck noticed?"

"Um, I …" I stutter, flabbergasted. Because I realize he's right. That is how he used to act around me when we didn't really know each other. How he usually acts with everyone unless they engage him directly. "Jules noticed. But … yeah, that may have been because she knows we're going out." I feel a blush creeping up my neck, realizing I may have overreacted. Again.

"So it's none of their business, but you're telling people?" he asks, shaking his head. "Look. I'm a pretty private person, so I was happy to not make it a big thing. If you want to tell your friends, whatever, but you can't have it both ways. Just don't give me the silent treatment because you changed your mind and didn't fill me in."

I look up at him sheepishly, totally deflated. "That's fair," I admit.

He pulls his head back, a confused look on his face. "Really?" he asks. "I mean, I know it's fair, but you're not going to fight me on it more?"

I scoff a laugh. "Do you want me to?"

He gives me an incredulous look.

"Yeah, didn't think so," I tease. "Yes, I told Sasha and Jules. I know I said it's not our coworkers' business, but it really hurt when I thought you didn't want people to know. That that's why you were ignoring me."

His face softens, and he steps into me. "If I'd known that, I would've handled it differently," he murmurs, looking deeply into my eyes. "I hope you know that."

I bite into my bottom lip, the tension totally gone. Well, the angry tension anyway. The sexual tension? That's always there. And now that I'm not angry anymore ...

"Yeah? What would you have done?" I ask in a teasing tone.

A smile pulls at his lips and his hands slide around my backside, pulling me into him. His face drops to my neck, nuzzling into me.

"I would've sat next to you, put my arm around you," his murmurs in my ear send tingles down my spine, "thought about all the things I was going to do to you after I got you alone." His lips slide across my earlobe, and my core tightens as my breath speeds up.

"Show me," I breathe.

He pulls back so he can look into my eyes. "Really?"

Unable to speak under the intensity of his gaze, I nod.

I don't even have time to revel in the anticipation before his mouth is on mine, his tongue insistently pushing past my lips as his hands lift me into his strong arms.

I wrap my legs around his waist, my hands tight around his neck as our tongues slide together in a hard, hot dance that says things are about to start going very not slow anymore.

Between heated kisses that send me spinning, I manage to navigate him to the bedroom. I get a moment to breathe as he drops me on the bed, tearing his shirt off as soon as I've hit the mattress.

And holy. Fucking. Shit. Sculpted, tanned, and tattooed, his torso is the definition of perfection. The thick, muscled arms I've seen plenty of times lead into the most defined set of shoulders I've ever seen. And it never even occurred to me that collarbones could be so erotic. But somehow his are, sharp and dipping into a hollow in the middle of his chest that frames his pecs perfectly. The man is walking sex.

Just like the dark trail of hair that walks to the top of his jeans that he's now rapidly unzipping and pulling down. I watch, mesmerized as his dick springs free, hard and ready, and perfectly sized.

And I can't help myself. I pounce, closing my lips around him and using my hands on his ass to push his shaft deep into my mouth. He gathers my curls in his hands, holding them behind me while he groans into the pleasure.

I slip a hand around to hold the base of his cock while I work so I can look up at him, so I can watch him enjoy this like he's watched me twice before.

His eyes, deep pools of inky darkness, glower down at me so sexily it takes my damn breath away. I keep working him with my hand until he sucks in his own sharp breath, tipping his head back.

I half want to make him come like this, but there will be time for that later. Right now, I need to ride this gorgeous creature until he's screaming my name. Until I get a reaction out of this stoic man. *My man.*

The thought sends a surge through me. A possessive passion I've never felt before.

I rise to my knees, pulling him onto the bed and pushing his chest until he falls backward on the mattress. I finish tugging his jeans and boxers off, then quickly strip off my T-shirt and sweats.

He stares at me, resting a hand behind his head, then playing with one of my nipples with his other hand.

I dip down to lick up his length, then crawl up his body until our mouths meet again. Both of his hands move to cup my face as I settle over him, straddling him.

Thankfully, we've already had *the talk,* so I know he's safe, and lord knows I've been on the pill since I was old enough to sneak off to Planned Parenthood on my own.

So it's with no hesitation that I slip a hand between us, positioning him exactly where I want him. But just to torture him, I rub his tip over me, teasing us both with it.

His head tilts back again, and he sucks in another breath.

"You like that?" I tease, licking my lips in anticipation.

His head tilts back toward me, his eyes flying open.

And with a merciless swing of his hips, he buries himself inside me, causing me to gasp and brace my hands on his chest as he fills me.

"You like that?" he asks back huskily.

I narrow my eyes at him, pushing myself upright. And with a twist of my hips, I pay him back in full. His cock shifts inside me, and we're both rendered speechless again. But as much shit as I talk, there's a time when there is no need for words. And right now, all I need to say I can say with my body.

My hips talk for me, moving over him, back and forth, until I'm soaking wet and writhing with pleasure. His hands find my nipples as I gyrate, pinching and pulling, working me as I work over him. I feel the pleasure start to build, and I hadn't realized how much I missed it. An ache spreads like fire not only through my core but through every part of my body. His warms hands trail over my skin like he knows exactly where I need touching.

One slides over the sensitive skin of my side, slipping down to lightly encourage my hips, while he settles the thumb of his other hand between us so that my clit rubs over it with every thrust. It's a move that, without consciously thinking about it, makes me go faster. So I stroke over his digit in an increasing frenzy until, before I can stop it, my orgasm crashes through and over me, and I tighten around him.

As my hips slow, he holds them in his strong hands, continuing to tilt them himself while he flexes into me, rubbing me deep inside. Not for his own pleasure but to keep mine going.

When the wave recedes, I slump forward as he rises to meet me. Our mouths join lazily while his hands push my now-sweaty curls from my face.

With a gentle motion, he holds and rolls me under him, slipping out of my still-pulsating core. The absence gives me a moment to relax before he has me on my back, rearing up to position himself at my entrance once more.

Still panting, I look up at him, every perfect inch of his glowing skin a complete turn on. But his face. His gorgeous, intense expression, his beautiful mouth pulled into a tight bow in concentration, it just undoes me in a way I can't even explain.

So when he slides back in, I'm already a goner, totally lost to this. To him.

I close my eyes, unable to handle watching him take me. I wanted to make him mine. But I didn't consider how much I wanted to be his.

"Becca," he murmurs.

I open my eyes and look up at him.

When our gazes lock, the corner of his lips pulls up in a smile, his hand reaching to cup my face. When his thumb slides over my lip, I open my mouth to him, take it in, suck it, and clench my legs around him until he's buried completely in me.

His small smile turns into a full grin, and he raises an eyebrow. He removes his now-wet thumb and uses it to work my clit. I gasp and lose my hold of his hips, which he takes as his cue to continue pumping into me.

Like some kind of torture, his strokes seem almost lazy, and his thumb rotates slowly. He watches me carefully until I'm squirming with the need for more.

And then he gives it to me. But only a little at a time. When I feel the beginnings of another orgasm, my breath hitches. Clearly, it's the cue he was waiting for.

He drops down, his mouth meeting mine as our bodies fully merge. His strong arms lock around me, carefully balancing his weight so he can both run his tongue over every part of my upper body and tilt his hips into me at a dizzying pace. Since he's laid over me, every thrust slides him over my clit, setting my orgasm off as if it were a speeding freight train.

Like a ton of bricks, it hits, white-hot pleasure licking through every vein, every inch, every pore of my body. Without thought, I hold onto him for dear life, not sure how I can withstand the level of pleasure coursing through me. A wave of dizziness washes over me as it peaks, and I groan with the strain of keeping myself together. Or at least it feels like that — like if I don't try, I'll come apart at the seams.

Through it all, I can feel him still gaining speed, pounding into my tightened core until his own orgasm takes him. On his final push, I feel the muscles of his back clench as he groans my name into my neck.

His release is my release, and I finally cascade down from my peak, the descent no less pleasurable as I feel his still-hard cock pulsing in my quivering pussy. It adds to the eroticism of our spent, entwined bodies, as we both gasp for breath in the wake of the intensity of the experience.

After my breathing has returned to normal, I'm still lying under him, wrapped in his scent, relishing the feel of his skin when something shifts.

I giggle, pressing a hand to his chest. "As much as I want to stay like this forever, we need to get up or we're going to ruin the bedspread," I tell him.

With a smile and a light kiss on my nose, we pull a quick maneuver to avoid the mess.

When I've cleaned up in the bathroom, I walk back into the bedroom to find him still completely naked, the bedspread thrown back.

"Goddamn, you're fine," I murmur as I approach.

He sits up, readily accepting me into his arms as I slide into the bed next to him.

"And you're a fucking goddess," he tells me, stroking my cheek with his thumb.

"Mmm, you sure know how to make a girl feel special," I hum under his touch.

"Yeah, well, I had to prove I *could*," he teases. "You know, after apparently coming off like a total dickhead."

I look up at him. "Hey, water under the bridge," I assure him. "As long as we can do that again. Soon."

"Demanding little thing, aren't you?" he teases.

I smack his chest indignantly. "Hey, I'm not little," I gripe.

"If you say so," he says with a grin.

I shoot him some stink eye. But I leave it there. I'm too spent to admit it, but I have a theory that my personality is so big to make up for being so short. But I don't like being called little, even if I know I am. In any case, right now, I just want to lie here, touching this gorgeous man and pretending like the rollercoaster that has been our relationship wasn't a thing. And that this bliss, right now, is all that matters. In a way, it is.

"It's not my fault," I reply. "It's my mom's."

"Yeah? She as beautiful as you are?" he asks, rubbing his thumb softly over my arm.

I trace a hand lightly up his abs. "Have you always been such a charmer?"

He giggles and swats my hand away. *Ticklish.* Interesting.

"Just stating facts," he replies.

"Mmm. Yes, well. I do look a lot like her. Except lighter. She's full Puerto Rican, and my dad is Irish-Italian."

"Well, that explains a lot," he says drily.

I smack him hard on the chest and look up to find him smirking down at me.

"Stuff it, guido," I snipe at him.

He laughs unreservedly at my insult. "Guido? I find that funny coming from a girl who's also part Italian," he teases.

I shrug. "I have four batshit-crazy older brothers. If I learned anything growing up, it's how not to take shit from muscleheads."

"Damn, four? Should I be worried?" Though he seems anything but, still tracing a hand lazily over my arm and side.

"Not in the least," I assure him. "I'm sure you guys will get along swimmingly. You'll probably be a hero in their eyes for putting up with their pain-in-the-ass little sister."

I feel his body stiffen a fraction. "You want me to meet your family?"

I shift away and prop myself up on an elbow so I can look at him. "I was just talking," I say, trying to sound as casual as I can. Not wanting to admit that I'm dying to see how he'd manage against the insanity of basically me times six. Lord knows that's the true test of whether he's a keeper.

He lifts a hand up and traces a finger down my cheek. "I didn't mean it like that. I'd love to meet them sometime," he says softly.

And I swear, my heart fucking melts. But I rein it in.

"What about you? What's your family like?" I ask.

He shrugs and pulls himself up so he's leaning against the headboard.

"My mom left when I was seven. My dad's a construction worker. And a total pussy. We never really got along. Can't say I was sad to leave New York," he responds, clearly uncomfortable.

"Really? That's a pretty big change. There wasn't anything else to stay for?" I ask, purposely avoiding the can of worms that he just cracked open. Because as much as I want to know why his mom left, why he doesn't get along with his dad, I also don't want to make him talk about something that clearly bothers him.

"There are always reasons to stay. But I had to leave," he responds, looking at me intently. "Can't say I'm mad about it right now." He gets a predatory glint in his eye and laces his fingers with mine.

Gently, he tugs me close, his lips softly caressing mine. And as he slides his hard body against me, even though I'm pretty sure he just distracted me out of asking more questions, can't say I'm mad about it either.

CHAPTER 13

"Boy, when you end a drought, you don't go by half measures," Sasha mutters, continuing to enter patient data despite the deep blush she still has from hearing about the rest of my weekend which was, naturally, spent naked.

I let out a happy sigh. "What can I say? The man is … damn, Sash, I don't even have words."

She chuckles. "There's a first."

"I'm so happy right now, I don't even care that you just insulted me," I reply airily, gathering an armful of files.

"Oh, good. Then you won't mind running the hazmat drop for me after you're done with those," Sasha replies with a big, cheery smile.

I wrinkle my nose at her. It's everyone's least favorite chore around here. Not because the collection itself is difficult. But the guy who runs the disposal unit is a total creep.

"Come on," she coaxes, sensing my hesitation. "You'll have to walk right by intensive care."

"Oh, I'll do it. But only because you're basically in charge right now and you know I can't say no," I reply.

She gives me a knowing look. "Yeah. Okay. Whatever you've got to tell yourself, Becks." She gives me a sly wink and turns back to her monitor.

I huff and roll my eyes, but the files are getting heavy, so I just stomp off to take care of them. Once that's done, I do the rounds, empty all the hazmat bins, and load them up to take them to the disposal unit across the hospital.

As I push the cart through the network of hallways connecting each unit, I shake my head at Sasha's silly appeal to my hormones. The odds of seeing Vincent are practically nil.

And, as expected, I make it to the drop-off having seen only a few other hospital staff along the way.

I tolerate Creepy Kyle's lecherous stare as I unload, thankful that one of the first things Cal did when he started at Rutherford was to get administration to take sexual harassment around here seriously. So even though, when I walk away with my empty cart, I still feel like I need to take a shower, at least I didn't have to throw any punches due to wandering hands.

Oh, yeah, it's happened. The women working in this hospital have long been wary of the dangers of bending over, but sometimes it has to happen.

Thankfully, it's not like he could admit why he got punched without getting himself in trouble. But still. Working in a hospital should be classified as a contact sport. And that's even before anything having to do with patients.

As I'm about to round the corner to the hall between intensive care and cardiac, I hear a feminine laugh. One I know. Avery.

Lo and behold, as soon as I make the turn, I see her, clearly flirting — with *Mason*. My past issues with Harper aside, there's no way in hell I'm going to let this bitch flirt with my friend's man.

"So do you just pretend to prefer women so you can hit on the guys your friends are with?" I ask in the nastiest tone I can manage as I approach. Avery turns, clearly surprised. "Oh, wait, my bad. Your *former* friends."

I shoot a look at Mason, wondering why he's even talking to this bitch. He doesn't look the least bit guilty, so I guess he's just clueless. Boys.

I stop my cart and fold my arms over my chest, arching an eyebrow.

"We were just talking," Avery scoffs. "Not that it's any of *your* business."

"Bitch, please," I scoff. "Flipping that greasy hair, using that fake, 'Oh, you're *so* interesting,' laugh. Stop embarrassing yourself."

Avery turns red, and Mason glances helplessly between us.

"I should really get back to work …" Mason shuffles back a couple of steps. "But hey, you and Vincent are meeting us for dinner tonight, right?"

My lips tighten. Vincent had gotten me to agree to it. Since my friends knew, he wanted his best friend to know too. And though I was reluctant to bring Harper in on the current state of our relationship, Avery is the absolute last person I'd want to know.

And by the triumphant, catlike grin on her face, she's perfectly aware of the juicy bit of gossip that just landed in her lap.

Motherfucker.

"Yes, we'll see you later," I reply tersely, giving him a pointed glare.

He looks confused but retreats quickly, disappearing down the hall toward emergency.

Avery folds her arms over her chest, mimicking my posture. But looking a whole fuckload smugger.

"So you managed to trick pretty boy into going out with you, huh? Guess we'll see how long *that* lasts," she says meaningfully. And I can just tell the bitch plans to make another play for him.

"Why don't you run along and go find someone who *isn't* taken to fuck?" I suggest archly. "You know, instead of playing with fire."

"Oh, please, I have no intention of fucking Mason," she scoffs. "Vincent, on the other hand — now, he is entirely fuckable."

"Oh, he definitely is," I assure her. "More than you'll ever know."

"We'll see about that," she murmurs, holding my glare. "But right now there are some people I should talk to." The evil glint in her eye as her smile turns nasty tells me she's about to go do exactly what I knew she would the moment the words tumbled out of Mason's mouth.

"You do you, girl. But don't say I didn't warn you," I reply quietly. I park the cart against the wall and breeze past her through the doors to intensive care.

At the very least, I need to warn Vincent that by the end of shift the whole hospital is going to know we're together.

* * *

"I'm going to fucking kill Mason." Vincent's jaw ticks against the tightness with which he's clenching it.

"He doesn't deserve to die for being stupid," I reply levelly. "Avery, on the other hand …" My own jaw feels like it's about to fall off. But all we can do is glower. The small, quiet corner we found to talk has no guarantee of privacy.

"You don't get it," he spits, uncharacteristically venomously. "For you, this is just gossip. People knowing more than you want them to. For me …" He trails off, shaking his head resolutely.

I frown, unsure why this would get him in so much trouble. "It's not against policy," I assure him, though he must already know that since so many of our coworkers are dating one another. "So it's not like we're going to get fired. Is it really a problem for," I drop my voice to a whisper, "your parole?" I find it hard to believe it would be, but then, what do I know about being on parole?

He gives me a hard stare. "It's …" he shakes his head. "It's complicated. But yes, it's a problem. Not that there's anything we can do about it now." He shoves his hands in his pockets and looks away, still shaking his head at regular intervals like he's having some sort of debate with himself. I get the strong sense that there's something else he's not telling me.

"That's not true. We can end this, now, then it was just rumors. This doesn't need to be … I don't think either of us needs more drama," I say flatly. "So if that's what we need to do, that's what we need to do."

When his eyes find mine again, I can see the hurt.

"Is that what you want?" he asks, his voice thick and low.

"Fuck, no. And I sure as hell don't want to let that bitch win."

He blanches at that. "So you'd keep dating me just to spite her?"

I roll my eyes and throw my hands up. "No, dumbass," I chastise him in a low, angry voice. "I'd keep dating you because I want to date you. Spiting her would just be a bonus."

That gets a quiet chuckle out of him.

"You know, you're pretty fucking cute when you're mad," he murmurs.

"I know," I reply without a hint of modesty, crossing my arms over my chest. "So what do you want, Vincent?"

His dark brows pinch together, his perfect features contorted in worry. "I just want to live my life without worrying about all the bullshit from my past."

I tilt my head at his words, now sure there's more to this story than he's telling me. The sag of his shoulders, the air about him, it all seems … like more than just the parole thing.

"Is your old boss still screwing with you or something?" I ask.

His brows jump in surprise. "Why would you think that?"

I shrug. "I dunno. From his perspective, maybe you got off too light? I just … I feel like there's something else going on here. Something you're not sharing."

I can practically feel his guard go up. Bingo. My intuition never fails me.

He stares at me silently for a minute. I let him. Uncomfortable silence is the bringer of truth, after all.

"I'm sure there are things you haven't shared with me," he finally replies.

"Oh, nuh-uh. You're not going to make this about me," I protest. "There *is* something you're not sharing. And that's fine, but don't play it off like it's no big deal, or like I'm imagining things."

He worries at his bottom lip. "Okay, fine, you're not imagining things," he finally allows. "But now really isn't the time or place."

I fight the urge to take him by the hands. Instead, I pour everything I'm feeling into my expression, hoping he'll understand. "I'm not asking you to spill your guts," I clarify. "I'm just trying to figure out if whatever's going on is going to stop this." I gesture between us. "Because, like it or not, now's the time to figure that out."

He slumps back against the wall behind him. "I can't think as fast as you, Becca. I'm going to need some time."

I look at my watch. "Well, we're supposed to have dinner with your friends in a few hours. So I suggest you get on that."

And I'm such a mixed-up ball of emotions, I don't even have the patience to wait for his response. Instead, I head back to cardiac. Back to ground zero.

As soon as I walk in the doors, I get knowing looks. Damn, that bitch works fast.

I approach the nurses' station to Sasha shaking her head. "This is my fault," she says.

"I see you've already heard," I reply drily.

"Everyone's heard," she responds.

"So how is this your fault?" I ask.

"Well, obviously something happened while you were doing the drop-off. If I hadn't asked you to go —"

I wave a hand, cutting her off. "Let's not play that game. It is what it is. People were bound to find out eventually."

"Then why do you look so pissed off?" Sasha points out.

With a sigh, I slump into the chair next to her and quietly relay my conversation with Vincent.

"Sweet baby Jesus, Becca, I swear you deal with more drama in a day than I can tolerate in a month," Sasha grumbles.

I shrug. "Most of the time I enjoy it," I admit.

"Except when it's about you," she says perceptively.

"Well, yeah, who wants people messin' in their business?" I reply. "I swear Avery's taken some serious bitch lessons from Lacey."

Sasha's eyes tighten. "Let's hope she's not that bad," she says firmly.

"Hey," I say, catching her eye. She looks at me warily. "Avery can't hurt me, okay? I'm a big girl. I can take whatever she wants to try to throw my way. Don't worry."

Sasha folds her hand over mine. "I know. But I'm a born worrier, Becks. Just … be careful, okay?"

I put my other hand on top of our hand pile and pat her gently. "I will," I lie.

But Sasha doesn't need to know I'm lying. Or that I plan to find a way to put Avery in her place. Oh, I'll choose my opportunity wisely. But I'll go for it, even if it costs me. Though not if it costs anyone I care about. I may have no regard for the consequences for me, but damned if I'm going to let Avery hurt my people. And right now, it would seem she's already hurting Vincent and trying to hurt Harper. Game. On.

* * *

We end up going to dinner with Harper and Mason, though Vincent still hasn't said a word about the status of our relationship. Needless to say it ends up being pretty tense and awkward. And that's even without me saying anything to Harper about Avery's advances toward Mason. That can wait until the dust settles.

As Vincent silently walks me to my car after, I decide I'm not going to ask for his decision. Not tonight. I don't chase boys. He wants to be with me, he needs to choose that.

I stop at my car door, turning to face him.

"Thanks for walking me out. I'll see you around," I say, trying not to let it sound angry or sarcastic.

He huffs a sarcastic laugh. "You'll see me around? Why does that sound like a 'fuck off'?"

I glare up at him. "What am I supposed to say? You're the one still figuring things out. It's a 'fuck off' if you want it to be one," I say plainly. "But I'm not going to sit around pining after you, hoping you pick me, if that's what you were expecting."

"I wasn't expecting any of this," he shouts, throwing his arms out widely, then running a hand through his hair in agitation. "Fuck, Becca. I'm sorry. I wish I knew what to do right now. What to say."

I shake my head. "If you don't know what to say, that says all I need to know," I reply.

He juts his chin out, his eyes burning into mine. "You don't understand," he responds. "I'm not good at this."

I cock my head to the side. "Good at what, exactly?" I ask.

He steps forward, placing his hands on my arms, looking down at me. "Talking about my feelings," he murmurs. His thumb brushes over my lips. "But I can't lose you."

I close my eyes, my lips pressing against his thumb. "That's all I needed to hear." I open my eyes to find him staring at me.

"Really?" he asks.

"Yes, what did you think I was asking for, a proposal?" I snap. "I just had to know that you're still in this."

"I'm so fucking in this," he breathes, and his mouth drops to mine. His kiss is hungry, desperate, and so overwhelming it makes me dizzy.

I break away to take a breath, to calm my racing heart, but he presses me against the car and grabs my face, bringing it back to his. His intensity is off the charts, and within minutes, we're both so worked up we can barely breathe.

"Take me home," I demand.

He stares down at me. "I was thinking I might just fuck you right here."

My breath catches in my throat. "The last thing we need is for you to get arrested for public indecency," I point out, despite the dampness between my legs agreeing it would very much like him to take me right now.

He buries his face in my neck. "Dammit, you're right," he agrees.

"Then let's go, for fuck's sake," I groan in frustration.

With a chuckle, he pulls back, letting me get in the car.

"I'll follow you," he assures me with a light peck on my lips, then closes the door.

I have to take a few deep breaths as I watch him walk away. I'm practically shaking with desire. And if I get into an accident on the way home, that will delay getting that gorgeous man naked.

So I drive very, very carefully.

CHAPTER 14

"He picked you," Harper gushes. "That's so romantic, Becca."

"Let's not make it a big thing," I hedge, rolling my eyes. Even though I secretly agree, and kind of loathe myself for it. "We're just going to give it a shot. Despite the drama."

"Yeah, but you know Rutherford. Someone else will do something and be the new gossip du jour. The attention won't be on you two for very long," she replies.

I pick at the fries on my plate. "I hope not," I admit. "And I have to be honest, I've kind of lost my taste for gossip, so that can't happen soon enough."

Harper puts down the soda she had halfway to her lips, looking beyond stunned.

"You've … lost the will to gossip?" she asks in a dramatic whisper, a hand fluttering to her chest. "Are you feeling okay? Should we get you back to the hospital?"

"Ha. Ha. Ha," I snip. "Look, that's not why I asked you to dinner tonight. I need to tell you what else happened with Avery on Monday."

Harper picks her soda back up. "It's okay, Mason told me."

I shoot her a skeptical look. "Oh, yeah? What, exactly, did he tell you?"

"That she was hitting on him. Which apparently he didn't get until you came along." She rolls her eyes. "Boys."

I let out a laugh. "Well, I'm glad he told you, anyway. I don't know what I'm going to do about her, but she's gotta be stopped."

Harper shrugs. "I'm honestly not that worried about it. The more attention you give her, the more power she has over you."

"That's surprisingly mature of you. Aren't you worried she's going to keep coming after your man?" I ask.

She laughs. "Becca, he didn't even get that that's what she was doing. I'm *so* not worried about it," she replies. "Are you, really? Because I've seen how Vincent is around you. He's totally smitten. I don't think you have anything to worry about. I mean, she took a shot before, right? And he didn't bite."

A memory from last night of Vincent's teeth on my neck surfaces, and I smile. But Harper can be even more of a prude than Sasha, and the good lord knows we're not as close, so I don't say anything.

"You're right," I agree. "I guess I just have a hard time letting that shit go."

"I'm a big believer in karma," Harper says. "And Avery's got lots of it coming her way, don't you worry. And if we're really lucky, we'll get to watch." She grins, and it's almost evil. But I know she's a little too well-meaning to really want to hurt someone. Though intentions aside, we're all capable of hurting people.

"Well, I don't trust her, but I guess I don't have to be the one to dish out her just desserts," I finally agree. "But damn, it's going to be hard to just not do anything. Girl's gone after both our men *and* participated in that whole Lacey-Sasha madness."

Harper's features pinch together. "Yes, but so did I," she reminds me with sadness in her voice.

I point a finger at her. "You did, but you regret it. You've apologized, and now you're showing us that we can trust you again," I correct her.

She beams at me. "Yeah?" she asks hopefully.

"Yeah," I reply with a wink. A comfortable silence falls for a minute, while we regard each other. And the thought that we're finally getting back to where we were improves my mood considerably. "Now. The next important question: What should we have for dessert?" I pluck the dessert menu from the caddy at the back of the booth and lay it out between us.

"Oh, that's easy: The answer to all important questions is chocolate," she teases, pointing at the chocolate fudge brownie pie a la mode, the only chocolate option on the page.

"Well, I certainly can't argue with that," I reply with a laugh.

We order our dessert and spend the rest of the evening on less stressful topics. By the end of the night, I'm thinking Harper is right. Life's short, and I've got the guy. I need to let it go. Avery can fuck off for all I care. Though I do still hope that when karma comes for her, I *do* actually get to see it.

* * *

The rest of the week goes by in the usual bustle of patients, admin duties, and, unfortunately, still dealing with gossip and looks, as nothing juicier has come up.

But Friday happy hour is the complete opposite of last week. Vincent makes sure to sit next to me, holding my hand and otherwise making it obvious that we're a couple. If I'm being honest with myself, it makes me nervous. Especially when I see how happy Sasha is watching us acting all couple-y. She even makes me promise that we'll go on a double date soon. Yeesh.

But going home with Vincent afterward wipes it all from my mind, as usual. I may have reservations about the whole being-in-a-real-relationship thing, but we have no issues on the sex front. In fact, it's where things flow the best. Where we just fit. But still in a much deeper, more meaningful way than I'm used to. Though when we're together, absorbed in each other, I find it much easier to let it be what it is and not think too hard about it. In short, it's still my favorite thing, even in the context of a relationship. I guess I shouldn't be that surprised.

We even double date with Harper and Mason again on Saturday night, which I *don't* tell Sasha as I'd hemmed and hawed about doing that with her and Cal. But that's different — Sasha is practically like family to me. And I'm not quite ready to go there with Vincent. Not until we get to know each other better.

Sunday is half spent having sex, half getting to know more about each other, though in a pretty casual way. Like, what were our favorite TV shows growing up. Which bones we've broken. Places we've worked. That kind of crap. All good stuff, but still light enough not to be too scary, too deep, too … commitment-y. If that's a word.

Still, I can't remember the last time I dated the same guy for two weeks. It's definitely been a minute. Which, I know, is all kinds of messed up in and of itself. In any case, this guy has been different from the start. Because I've been into him for more than three months, so he was already a record for me. Well, not counting Jimmy Dugan in fifth grade. I was into that dude the whole school year until he saw my bra strap at our elementary school graduation and made fun of me. As if wearing a training bra wasn't already awkward enough. He's also the first boy I had an actual fistfight with, because even then I didn't take shit from anybody. Though I think the odds of that happening with Vincent are pretty low.

Thankfully, on Monday morning, one of the PAs from maternity becomes the instant star of the gossip circuit when it gets out that he was arrested for hiring a prostitute. Whom he had sex with *at the hospital*. Hospital workers have hard jobs, so we love nothing more than some good, stress-relieving gossip. But it's so much more exciting when something happens on premises. Maybe because it's so much more real? I don't know. Either way, it's a hot topic, and Vincent and I finally get relief from scrutiny.

I'm practically giddy waiting for him to come over after work, having felt a lightness all day at being out of the spotlight.

So when I answer the door to find him showered and changed into his usual jeans and tee, I practically jump him.

"Well, I'm glad you waited until we were alone," he jokes as he enters the apartment. "I think we've all learned a little lesson about getting busy at work today." The grin on his face is infectious, so I give him a teasing pinch as I smile back.

"Someone's feeling peppy," I tease him.

He shrugs, trying to appear nonchalant and totally failing. "I can't say I love working at the hospital, but I have a new appreciation for working there and *not* being the juicy gossip of the moment."

I tug him into the living room, crashing onto the couch. "God, you're telling me. I got so much done today. Plus, there was the sunshine and birds chirping and all of that again," I joke.

He settles in next to me, slinging an arm around my shoulder.

"So, do they ever go back to old gossip?" he asks curiously.

I shake my head. "Nah, there will always be something new and more exciting for them to latch onto now," I assure him. "I think things are back to normal for good."

"Good," he says with a sigh of relief. "I like normal."

"Hey, before I forget," I say. "Sasha asked if we wanted to get dinner with her and Cal on Wednesday. You know, so they can get to know you."

I look up at him, trying to hide how nervous even asking that question makes me. And when he shifts uncomfortably, I can't help the knots in my stomach that suddenly squeeze tightly.

"I, uh ..." he mumbles. "I can't do Wednesday. I ... I check in with my parole officer on Wednesdays."

I raise an eyebrow at the tension that has seized him. "Okay," I reply. "You don't have to be embarrassed about that."

"I know. It's just ... not something I really want them to know," he responds.

"Don't worry, I'm not going to tell them anything you don't want me to," I assure him. "Sasha may be one of my best friends, but you're important to me too. And I mean, if you don't want to go out with them at all, that's ... I mean, that's okay."

I kind of choke on the words, because it's really not okay. At least, not if we really have hope of this working. Because I can't even imagine Sasha not liking someone I'm with. It's part of why I'm so nervous about them getting to know each other. Probably even more so than him meeting my actual family, whom I only see every once in a while when my mom nags me to visit.

"Hey," he says, folding his hand over mine. "It's not that. Just ... another time, okay?"

I look up into his eyes and nod.

"Okay," I reply softly.

"I'm sorry, I didn't mean to bring down the mood," he apologizes, pushing a stray curl behind my ear.

"You were just being honest," I reply with a shrug. "It's all good."

"Hmmm," he hums. "I think I know how to make it better."

I raise an eyebrow. "Yeah? How's that?"

A wicked grin spreads across his gorgeous face as he topples me back onto the couch.

"Just you lie back, relax, and I'll show you," he promises, kissing me lightly on the lips before moving his mouth down my body.

I dimly register that he's distracting me with sex. Right before I remember that I don't give a damn why, as long as he keeps his amazing hands on me and uses that talented tongue of his. Which is exactly what he proceeds to do, and everything else melts away.

* * *

My week continues to be epic until Thursday afternoon, when I walk into the break room for more coffee only to find Avery there.

"Oh, Becca, I'm so glad we ran into each other," she says in a sweet voice that somehow has a sharp edge to it.

Not one to be deterred from a necessary caffeine fix, I ignore her in favor of the coffee machine.

"Well, I thought you might be a little reluctant to talk to me, so I guess I'll be the one doing the talking," she finally says. "You'll never guess where I saw your boyfriend last night."

As the coffee drips into my cup, I roll my eyes. Great. She saw him go into the courthouse to meet his probation officer. Thankfully, unless she saw him *inside* the courthouse, it's unlikely that she knows why he was actually there.

"Oh, I know where he was last night," I assure her without turning around. "But thanks for your concern."

"Wow. I wouldn't be okay with my partner visiting a prostitute, but damn, if that's how you guys do things, I guess that's all you," she says sarcastically.

It's a good thing I'm not holding a cup of hot liquid yet, because that causes me to spin around.

"Why the fuck would you think he was visiting a prostitute at the courthouse?" I hiss, trying not to yell. And hoping like hell she's not spreading that whopper around.

"The courthouse? Who said anything about a courthouse?" she asks. "No, no. I saw him go into the house of a known prostitute in National City yesterday."

"You're such a liar, Avery," I spit at her. "Even if he was in National City for some reason, how in the hell would you even know this person was a prostitute?" Though my mind is already scrambling for an explanation. Maybe that's where his parole officer lives? Though I toss that out quickly. Surely he'd have to check in at an official location. And why would a parole officer be a suspected prostitute?

"I'm staying there with my aunt," she responds before my brain can make any sense of this. "A car parked in front of her house yesterday around five. Your boyfriend got out and went down the road, into a house on the other side of the street. The woman who lives there has been a prostitute for years. Everyone in the neighborhood knows it. He clearly parked far enough away so his car wouldn't be associated with that house, and he was in there for a couple of hours too. She must be something if he —"

Before I know it's even happening, my hand cracks sharply across Avery's face. I should be horrified that I slapped her. I should be worried about getting fired. But right now, I'm red-hot raging mad.

"How *dare* you," I seethe, seeing right through her. "You can't have him, and you don't want me to either, so you make up this bullshit? You're just as bad as Lacey. You're going to ruin his life if you go around telling people these lies, Avery."

She steps closer, her cheek flaming red and swollen.

"He told you he was going to the courthouse, did he?" she whispers, putting it together. "Well, maybe next time he's supposed to be 'at the courthouse,' you should follow him. Then you'll see that I'm *not lying.*"

I laugh in her face. "You're delusional. Even if he is going to someone's house, I'm supposed to, what, go up to her once he's gone and accuse her of being a prostitute? Yeah, that'll go real well. I don't know what game you're trying to play, but it's not going to work."

Avery stares at me. "Look. We were friends once, Becca, so I'm going to try to forget all the shit that's been going down between us lately for just a minute. You barely know this guy. And I'm telling you the truth. If it were me, I'd want to know. So I'll tell you what. I won't breathe a word of this to anyone. Then you have all the space you need to figure out that I'm being honest. And that, while it did make me happy to think it might ruin your fun because you've been such a bitch to me lately, I'm *not* Lacey."

"*I've* been a bitch? You went after Vincent when you knew I liked him," I snap.

"But it made you do something about it, didn't it?" she insists.

I can't help the laugh that escapes me. "Don't even try to pretend that's why you did it. If you want to avoid the Lacey comparisons, maybe try not sounding like such a lunatic," I reply. "And about that. Did Lacey finally fuck you over too? Because last I checked you were her happy little lap dog."

Avery's nostrils flare and her eyes narrow. "I did my best to give her the benefit of the doubt. She was my friend. I don't just turn my back on friends without my own proof," she responds, her voice laced with accusation.

"Are you saying that's what I did? Because that's fucking rich," I retort. "Unlike you, I don't need solid proof that someone is no good. Actions speak pretty clearly for themselves."

Her sinister smile returns. "Oh, you mean, like visiting a hooker? Yeah, that speaks loud and clear," she replies matter-of-factly. "My break is up, and your coffee is getting cold. Good luck with your boyfriend. You're going to need it."

With that, she turns and leaves.

When I return to the nurses' station, still furious and with a lukewarm cup of coffee, I find a slip of paper on my chair. On it is an address in National City. I crumple it in my fist furiously, but before I can make my way to the garbage can, Dr. MacDougall comes around the corner. So instead, I shove it in my pocket and slide into my seat, pretending like I'd been working all along. He stops to have a conversation with Dr. Franklin, and by the time they're done I've managed to actually get back to working. It takes all of my focus to keep going to the end of the day without punching someone or something, but somehow I manage.

CHAPTER 15

Avoiding Vincent on Thursday evening is easy enough. It's not like we hang out every night.

While I don't necessarily believe Avery, it's a hard thing to just shake off. And a hard subject to broach with a guy you've been dating for only a few weeks. Especially when there are things you still don't know about him. Things he doesn't want to share yet. Things you hope have nothing to do with prostitutes.

As I sit at the nurses' station desk on Friday afternoon, with happy hour looming, I know I'm not going to be able to pretend like Avery didn't just drop the hooker bomb.

"Hey," a soft voice says, cutting into my thoughts. I look up to find Jules, with her arms resting serenely on the countertop, her auburn hair pulled back into a sleek ponytail, her hazel eyes examining me with concern. "You okay?"

I give her my best attempt at a smile. "Nothing a little booze won't fix," I reply flippantly.

She tilts her head, clearly seeing right through my bullshit. As usual.

"Then let's go," she replies, pulling the band out of her ponytail and letting her long hair go free.

"We've still got a half hour," I gripe. "And how do you look like a fucking hair model at the end of the day," I point up at my crazy bun, "while I look like I have an octopus trying to escape out of the top of my head?"

Jules laughs as she rubs her scalp. "If it helps, I *feel* like I have an octopus trying to escape out of the top of my head," she assures me. "And you know I have the power to dismiss you early. So, what do you say? We'll go ahead of the crowd. I'll buy you a drink. And you can tell me what's on your mind. We haven't gotten to talk just you and me in a while, Becca. Please?"

With a sigh, I look back at the computer screen, realizing I wasn't about to get anything done anyway, so I shut it off.

"Don't have to ask me twice," I say with a forced smile, rising to grab my purse. "But when I take my hair down, no laughing when it doesn't go like a Pantene commercial."

Jules presses her lips together and makes a crossing motion with her fingers over her heart. "Deal."

With a smirk, I let my bun loose, sending curls poofing everywhere. As crazy as it must look, it feels damn good. And it's one of my favorite things about the end of a workday.

"You want to change?" she asks as we head down the hall, knowing scrubs aren't my preferred look outside of the hospital.

I shake my head. "Just get me to the liquor," I joke.

She shoots me a worried glance that I choose to ignore. I'm not opening this can of worms within earshot of anyone we work with.

* * *

"That's … that's …" Jules sputters.

I polish off the martini in front of me, waiting for her to finish her sentence. She doesn't, but I get what she means. It's a lot.

"Yep," I agree.

"Do you believe her?" she asks.

"Do I believe Avery that my … whatever the hell he is went to see a prostitute?" I shake my head, looking grimly down into my empty glass. "I don't want to. But how do I just ignore that kind of information?"

Jules lays a hand over one of mine, and I look up.

"I hate to put this so bluntly, but you either trust him or you don't," she points out.

"Then I guess I don't," I reply with a shrug.

"Okay, weird question," Jules hedges. I gesture for her to continue. "Is it him you don't trust? Or men?"

I let out a sharp laugh. "Well, don't you just get right to it?" I smile, spinning the empty glass in my hands while I consider that. "Men."

"You want to trust him."

I look up through tears. "Yes," I admit. "I do. But I grew up with a mother and father who only kept their hands off each other long enough to fight, not giving a shit if their kids heard or saw any or all of it, and four brothers who talked loudly and proudly about each of the many 'sluts' they banged. Respect and trust weren't exactly the norm at the Dillon house, especially coming from the men."

"So you think all men are like your father and brothers?" she presses.

I huff a laugh. "Not at first. But the more I dated, the more it seemed that way. Until him."

Jules smiles sadly. "It's always 'until,' my dear. Until you value yourself. Until you find someone who values you. Until you stop letting your past dictate your future," she says.

"Speaking from experience, are we?" I ask sarcastically. Then immediately regret it. "I'm sorry, Jules, I didn't mean it."

She leans back in her chair, crossing her long, slim legs. "No, that's fair," she allows. "I don't have the best track record with men, and at some point I just stopped trying. But I've seen how you've changed since you've been into this guy. I thought it was a good thing, but some of the things you've told me tonight make me wonder. Though that doesn't mean it still can't be."

"Why'd you think it was a good thing?" I ask curiously.

"Well, the rotating door of hookups stopped," she responds drily. "I always figured that'd be the sign you found The One."

That gets a chuckle out of me. "Honestly, I was over it before him."

"So you were already ready for the next thing. But I know you — you don't settle for just anyone. Which means there's something between you and this guy," she says. "Do you think it's worth trying to make it work?"

"I want it to. But I don't even know how to have those kinds of conversations with a dude," I admit. "I'm terrified, Jules. That I'm going to scare him off. Or worse, that it's true." I slump my head onto the table, then abruptly spring back up at the stickiness. "Okay, that was a bad idea." I grab a napkin, rubbing furiously at my forehead while Jules laughs.

"Well, news flash, kiddo," she replies. "Nobody really knows how to have those kinds of conversations. They're always hard, and they're always awkward as hell. If you care enough about being in a relationship with him, and he with you, you guys will get through it. If not, it wasn't meant to be."

"Ya think?" I ask hopefully, starting to realize for the first time that I do want to talk to Vincent about it. I've just never been in a position like this. Never wanted to talk through things. Never had anything to talk through.

"I don't think, I know," she replies firmly. "But I do have one question."

I raise an eyebrow. "Okay ..."

"Is there a reason you haven't told Sasha any of this?" she asks softly.

I scrunch my face up. "Honestly? Because I don't think she'd really understand," I admit. "I mean, I know she's got my back. But this is new territory for me, and I just felt like ... I don't know, it might make it worse?"

"Yeah, she is kind of in her little Cal bubble," Jules says. "I'm happy for her, but I know what you mean. Although ... maybe you should go talk to your mom."

I blanch at the suggestion.

"Where the hell did that come from?" I ask sharply. Jules knows about the love-hate relationship I have with my family, and my mother in particular. I love her, don't get me wrong, but my dad isn't the only one she fights with constantly. She and I have gone at it something fierce many times over the years. At some point I decided it just wasn't worth dealing with it to try to have a close relationship with her.

"Hear me out," she pleads. "You have this perception of your family that's affected your relationships with men. But have you ever talked to her about it as an adult?"

I shake my head. "You know that woman and I are like match and kindling."

"Maybe. But she might have insights that surprise you. She is your mother, after all. And I can't help feeling like she may have more of a role in your mistrust of men than you think." Jules purses her lips after she says that, like she's worried she just crossed a line.

I narrow my eyes, not sure I like where she's going. "What, exactly, do you mean by that?" I ask tersely.

Jules takes a deep breath, and I know she's about to go there. "I mean, maybe you're also afraid that you're like your mother. That you're going to end up picking someone like your father," she says. "From the sound of it, you and Vincent have gone through quite a bit of drama already. Maybe you're just as afraid of it working out."

My stomach clenches, and I feel a scowl pull at my face. But I don't know if it's because I agree or disagree.

Scratch that.

"Fuck, I hadn't even considered that," I admit. "And because it pisses me off ... you might not be wrong."

Jules shoots me an apologetic look. "I know," she says, and we both laugh a little. "But I know you pretty well, babe. And I've never seen you be afraid of anything for very long. You've got this."

I swallow hard and nod. She's right. I'm a grab-life-by-the-balls kind of girl. I've got this.

"Thanks, Jules," I reply with a sigh.

"More booze?" she asks with a small smile.

"More booze," I agree.

We both get refills and Jules spends the rest of the time until our coworkers show up catching me up on hospital politics and a few bits of gossip I'd somehow missed. All hail the original Gossip Queen. But then, really, I'm backing off that whole scene, and Jules has always had her ear to the ground, what with being so involved and having worked in most parts of the hospital. If I'd ever had an older sister, I imagine she'd have been a lot like Jules. If nothing else, I'm grateful in this moment that I have good friends.

The boost I got from our conversation was necessary to act normally once Harper, Mason, and Vincent show up together, joining me, Jules, Sasha, Cal, Zoe, and Ethan.

Thankfully, once Vincent slides into the booth next to me, it's not like there's time or space for private conversation. But the small touches he uses to keep anchored to me are more comforting than I thought they'd be. Like reassurance that he's real, that's he's with me. And I know that's just as big for him as it is for me.

At some point, Ethan actually manages to engage Vincent in real conversation across the table, and it gives me an excuse to watch him. Well, stare at him, if I'm being honest.

His dark hair is messy from a long workday. His leather jacket drapes over the booth behind him, allowing the white V-neck tee he's wearing to show off the tattoos winding up his chest and down his upper arms. He seems relaxed and at ease, even though conversation isn't usually his thing. And always heartbreakingly gorgeous. And mine. I hope.

He finishes a sentence and catches me staring out of the corner of his eye. His lips tug up into a small smile, and his eyes meet mine. Usually, when he looks at me like that, I can see the desire in his eyes. But this time they're warm and relaxed. The normalcy of it all is like a punch in the gut, because I know I'm going to have to blow apart this sweet spot we've managed to find. But not tonight.

Tonight, I let him take me home.

As soon as we're inside, his fingers lace into mine, pulling me gently into his embrace.

"You were quiet tonight," he murmurs, looking seriously down into my eyes.

"Guess we switched roles," I tease.

He smiles so wide it crinkles the corners of his eyes. "I wouldn't go that far."

"Are you making fun of how much I usually talk?" I reply sassily.

"I wouldn't say 'making fun,'" he hedges with a mischievous smile.

I give him a look back, daring him to say more, but he just laughs. Smart man.

"It was a long week. Guess I'm just tired," I finally reply. It's true, though it's not the reason why I was so quiet.

Vincent advances with me in his arms, causing me to walk backward down the hall to my bedroom.

"I've got just the thing for that," he replies, pushing me through the bedroom door and onto the bed.

"Mmmm, now we're talking," I reply, licking my lips and looking up at him.

"Strip," he demands, tossing his jacket on the chair in the corner and kicking his shoes off.

When that's all he does, I shoot him a disappointed look. "You first."

He walks to the edge of the bed, staring down at me impassively.

"Guess I'm going to have to do it for you, then."

He leans down and removes the scrubs top, then the camisole I'm wearing under it. My scrubs bottoms go next, leaving me in just a bra and panties. But the infuriating bastard is still wearing far too much clothing.

"Lay on your stomach," he directs.

I raise an eyebrow at him while I scoot back and flip over, silently just glad that he didn't push further on why I'm not so much with the talking. I'm happy to fill the silence with sex and have him be none the wiser until I know how I want to handle this. And I try like hell not to think about whether or not he's actually been fucking a hooker while I wait, facedown and mostly naked.

The bed creaks as his weight is added, and I feel him crawling over me until he's settled over my backside, his knees on either side of me. I'm about to look back and ask him what in the holy hell he's doing when his hands land on my shoulders, gently kneading the sore muscles in circles.

"Ohhhh," I groan. "That feels *so* good." I tuck my face back into my arms, giving him better access to my neck.

Strong thumbs slide firmly over the nape of my neck, swirling down my spine. His hands work symmetrically, undoing the knots along my shoulder blades, skimming firmly down my arms then sides, undoing the tension in my lower back. After a good fifteen minutes, he finally slides further back, his hands continuing down my hips, then over my backside.

"Damn, you've got the most gorgeous ass," he murmurs.

I turn my head to look back at him with a smile, feeling much more relaxed. "Glad you're a fan of the big booty," I joke.

"You have no idea," he says, planting his hands firmly on the backs of my knees. In one, swift movement, he pushes them toward the head of the bed, raising my ass in the air.

I squeal in surprise. Before I can protest, he pulls my panties down and spreads my legs open, so I'm exposed to him. His fingers slip between my thighs, and when they dip in my folds, he shakes his head and curses. Like he's surprised that a gorgeous man rubbing me would make me wet. I let out a sigh of pleasure and sink into the mattress.

I'm not surprised this time when his hot, wet mouth meets my skin. He kisses a trail up my thigh, his tongue reaching for my clit. I grind unapologetically into his face, eager for it. He firmly licks in circles until I'm shaking, then pulls away.

I look back, planning on asking for more, only to see him shirtless, removing his pants. When his gorgeous cock springs free, I have no more words. His eye catches mine as he fists himself, stroking up his length. I nod, silently asking for it, and he climbs behind me, wasting no time as he sinks into me.

We both groan at the perfect, delicious fit. But damn, I need more. I buck my hips, encouraging him to start moving. And he does, sparing nothing as he takes me roughly. The harder he goes, the more helpless I become as my orgasm swirls and churns inside me. I'm practically one with the mattress when I finally come, moaning loudly into the comforter.

He waits until I've relaxed to pull out, rolling me onto my back. Because I sure as hell can't do it myself. I'm exhausted. Emotionally, and now physically, from how hard I've just come. But the sight of him over me, pulling my panties off completely, still hard and ready to take me again gives me a second wind. I open my legs in a silent plea.

Like a magnet, he's back between my legs as if he belongs there, like it took effort for him to *not* be there. And when he slides back in, it feels so fucking good, so fucking right. Like we were made to do this, just with each other.

As he works over me, the things I'm feeling as he fucks me … it's beyond intense, on every level. And I don't want to name it. Not now. Not while it all feels so …

"Oh, damn," I cry as he leans fully into me, his skin meeting mine, his cock pushing deeper than ever.

"God, yes," he groans in my ear.

We work together, and in moments we're both coming, loudly, insanely, in crazy bursts of white-hot fire burning through our skin. Everywhere he's touching me is on fire with pleasure, until I crash back to earth with him still on top of me.

He strokes my hair away from my face, kissing me gently. His tenderness undoes me, and I feel like I want to cry because I realize on a visceral level that I don't want Avery's claims to be true. I want him to be the man I hope he is. The man who I …

I avoid looking in his eyes, knowing the emotion will just completely shatter me. Because no matter how much I've tried not to think it, especially now, he fucking owns me. Body, mind, and heart. I don't know when it happened or how. And I know it's probably just about the worst place to be in this exact moment. But it doesn't matter now.

Because I know without a doubt that I'm in love with Vincent DeMarco.

CHAPTER 16

The reality of my feelings for Vincent hits me like a ton of bricks, and I realize Jules is right. So much about my past is messing me up right now. And before I can unpack Avery's accusation and what it means for our relationship, I need to get my own head straight.

So here I am, standing on the porch of the house I grew up in. About to open Pandora's fucking box. Vincent wanted to come with me, to meet my family, but I deflected. I need to be here alone if I'm going to get the answers I'm looking for, not bringing him in deeper into my life.

I must have been standing here lost in thought longer than I realized, because I haven't even knocked when the door swings open. Isabel Feliciano Rodríguez Dillon stares back at me, leaning against the doorframe. It's like looking thirty years into my future: Her dark curls have but a few streaks of grey. Her skin is still smooth. She's a bit rounder in the midsection than when I was a little girl, but her face, her posture, have every bit as much attitude as ever. There was never any question in my mind where I got it.

"I didn't believe you'd actually show up," my mother says in her still-noticeable Puerto Rican accent. Considering she's been here nearly forty years, that's saying something.

"What, a girl can't just come home to visit her family?" I snark back, pushing past her into the house.

I can practically feel her eyes roll behind me as she slams the door shut.

"On a Saturday evening?" she calls after me as I make my way into the living room. "Let's just say it raises some questions."

"Dad home?" I ask, dodging her attempt at getting me to spill the beans right away.

"He and Chris are finishing taking down a tree in the backyard," she says as I settle onto the old gray couch.

"Didn't this couch used to be blue?" I ask. "Wait … Chris? He's back from New York? When did that happen?" The youngest of my older brothers at just over four years older than me, Chris is a photojournalist who, last I knew, was living in New York City.

"That was a different couch, and yes," she replies, settling down near me. "He's staying with us until he finds a place."

My eyebrows pop up. "So he's *back* back?"

"So it would seem," she replies, crossing her short legs under her. "And I guess I'm glad to hear we aren't the only ones you don't keep in touch with."

"Hey, I call at least once a month," I protest.

My mother shoots me a sharp look. "And say next to nothing," she replies. She shakes her head. "So are you going to tell me what's going on? You're not pregnant, are you?"

I snort a laugh. "No, Mom, I'm not pregnant," I reply impatiently.

She gives me an expectant look, and I sigh.

"Look, I know I haven't come around a lot lately. And I'm sorry. I've just been busy with work and —"

"Boys?" she guesses.

I fight the urge to snap at her.

"Yes, fine, boys," I admit.

"Mhm. Tell me about him," she replies with a knowing smile.

"What makes you think there's a particular 'him'?" I ask, my walls still firmly up. As much as I came here to talk about exactly this, there's no undoing a lifelong pattern. And I'm not in the habit of having deep talks with my mother. This is going to be difficult, at best.

My mother opens her mouth, no doubt to give a snarky response, but she's cut off by Dad and Chris entering through the back door.

"Izzy?" Dad calls.

My mother levels a look at me before rising to meet my dad in the kitchen. I follow her through the open doorway between the two spaces to find Dad and Chris rummaging through the fridge and cupboards.

"Sean, what are you doing? Get your grubby paws out of there," Mom snaps at him.

Dad straightens up with a grin, and I get a good look at what she's talking about. They're both covered in dirt from head to toe. Chris gives me a little wave behind Dad's back.

"We were thirsty," my dad says defensively.

Chris cocks his head toward the attached dining room, and I follow him while Mom and Dad continue to argue.

"Home, sweet home," I mutter as I sink into a chair at the table across from Chris. He kicks his sweaty, socked feet up on the chair next to him. "Better not let Mom see you do that."

He gives me a cocky smirk. "Nice to see you too, Sis."

I stick my tongue out at him, and it's like we're kids all over again. We both laugh.

"So what happened to New York?" I ask.

He runs a hand tiredly through his dark wavy hair. Like all of my brothers, he looks just like Dad — thick, beautiful hair wholly unlike the wiry and crazy locks Mom and I have, light amber-brown eyes, and skin fair enough to pass for purely European. On top of being pretty easy on the eyes, they all have Dad's charm too. Well, when they want to; otherwise they're usually just assholes. But then, I'm their annoying little sister, so I get more than my share of that sort of thing.

"It was going great until I slept with my boss," he admits.

My brows pull together. "Guy or girl?" I ask. Last I'd heard, he worked for a guy who was starting his own travel magazine, and I didn't think he swung that way. Not that I'd care if he did.

"*She* was a woman," he corrects me with a hard glare. "One of the editors at the Times."

I hold my hands up. "Hey, whatever, it's all good. How come you didn't tell me you were back?"

Mom bursts angrily into the dining area, slamming a glass of lemonade in front of each of us before storming back into the kitchen.

Chris's eyes follow her out as he chugs the drink. "I only got in a couple days ago. And, you know, dealing with Mom and Dad has taken all of my energy."

I snort. "Seriously. It's no wonder I have no clue what a healthy relationship looks like."

Chris's eyes land on mine. "Boy trouble?" he asks slyly.

"Why do you all presume that the only reason I'm here is because of a boy?" I ask angrily.

"Ooh, hit a nerve," Chris says, his grin widening. I forget how much my brothers are like sharks. A little blood in the water and it turns into a feeding frenzy. "Come on, Beck, seriously. You okay? Mom says you don't come around anymore, yet here you are. Something must be up."

I heave a sigh and drop my head on the table dramatically. "Fine, yes, it's a boy."

"So? Do I need to go kick someone's ass? Or is it something else? Need advice?" he asks.

I lift my head and give him a surprised look. "You'd kick someone's ass for me?"

"If that's what you wanted. I've got to make up for being a shitty brother all these years somehow," he replies. He points at my untouched lemonade. "You gonna drink that?"

I roll my eyes and slide it across the table to him.

"You're not a shitty brother," I allow. "Though you weren't the best relationship role model either. Not that that's your fault."

He stops halfway through my drink. "How was I not the best relationship role model? You were like, what, twelve when I moved out?"

"I was fourteen," I correct him. "To be fair, it wasn't just you. Josh and Justin were bad too. Though none of you hold a candle to Ryan."

Chris rolls his eyes and snorts. "You were a kid. I'm surprised you even remember any of that."

I try not to look hurt. "I was old enough," I reply. "And you guys ... well, you weren't exactly shy about graphically describing your exploits with all the skanks you dated."

He gives me the most confused look I've ever seen on his face. "I honestly don't remember it that way at all," he says slowly. "I didn't even kiss a girl until I was eighteen, Beck. Not that that's really any of your business."

My jaw drops. "Then … wait … no," I stutter. "Seriously, Chris, I distinctly remember this. There was this one time, you were talking about Sarah, the girl you took to junior prom, and how she —"

He holds up a hand. "Gave me a blow job in the limo? Yeah, that didn't happen." His ears turn red and he looks behind me, presumably to make sure Mom and Dad aren't within earshot.

"Look, you were young. And yes, there were things said that probably sounded pretty bad. But we were teenage boys, Beck. We talked a lot of shit. And I'm sure we said some not nice things. Do you know why?"

I shake my head, totally bewildered. Chris rubs his dirty hands over his face, then finishes off the lemonade before continuing.

"It may surprise you to know that Ryan was the only one who really got any action when we were growing up. The rest of us … well, I guess we were just trying to live up to him. And Dad. They were both so vocal about … enjoying women. I think we thought we had to be the same way. It was all just talk, though. Stupid, immature, and almost entirely fabricated to impress other people."

"But the way you talked about those women —"

"Was totally and utterly disrespectful," he agrees. "I know. I guess I didn't know that you were paying attention to all that macho bullshit. You might be right — if that's what you heard and took as bible, you really *don't* have any idea of what a healthy relationship looks like."

"That almost sounds like you're agreeing that Mom and Dad aren't exactly role models in that area either," I point out.

He laughs. "I think that's obvious. They've always been nuts. But, you know, we're adults now. Our relationships are our problems. Just because our parents aren't exactly the paragon of a functional marriage doesn't mean we can't figure out our own shit."

"Doesn't it, though?" I push. "Because I'm finding it kind of difficult to know how to do this whole relationship thing."

Chris's eyebrows shoot to his hairline. "Holy shit, are you really in an actual relationship? My sister? Wow," he murmurs.

I cross my arms over my chest defensively. "I'm trying to be," I say. "Not that you bitches made this any easier."

He laughs. My older brother, one of the men I grew up with, someone I looked to as an example, *laughs* at my struggles.

"Becca, you are more headstrong than all of us put together. Don't pretend like you haven't always done things exactly the way you wanted to," he tells me, swirling the ice in his now-empty glass.

"That may be true, but you guys really messed me up. I feel like I have no idea what respect looks like to 'normal' people," I insist.

Chris shakes his head. "You put a lot of stock into things you heard," he replies. "We were stupid teenagers. We would never say those kinds of things about women now. It's not exactly like you saw any of us in real relationships."

"Except you just screwed your boss and ended up back here, tail between your legs," I reply.

He looks at me levelly. "Wow, well, I think I'm going to go take a shower now. Before I yell at my little sister for making assumptions about things she knows nothing about." He rises, anger clearly written all over his face.

"I'm sorry, Chris," I say. "I'm just having a hard time. And I'm trying to understand how I got here."

He considers me for a moment before sitting back down.

"Kate and I dated off and on for the better part of a year. I asked her to be my girlfriend, to really give it a shot. I was in love with her," he explains quietly.

"Oh, Chris," I breathe.

He waves a hand. "I don't need pity," he grumbles. "It's not the first time I've been in love, and it won't be the last. But it's never easy, Becca. It's always a risk. And Mom and Dad are proof that somehow even the most dysfunctional relationships can work, if it's with the right person. The way they are? It's weird, yeah. But it is what it is, and somehow it works for them. There is no one model for a perfect relationship. It's just loving someone enough to get up every day and decide to be with that person. Despite all the weirdness. Or maybe because of it, I don't know. That's it."

Dad chooses that moment to enter the dining room, freshly showered and holding a glass of lemonade. But I can't help noticing that his shirt buttons are done up all wrong. When Mom follows him in a moment later, her clothes are slightly disheveled and her hair is damp at the ends.

I shake my head and cover my face. Chris bursts out laughing at my reaction.

"What did we miss?" Dad asks, settling into the chair at the head of the table.

I peek through my fingers to see the most fake innocent expression ever on his face, and it sends me into gales of laughter as well. Chris and I laugh until we're crying, while our parents stare at us like we're nuts.

"Well, this is fun," Mom eventually says. "Are you staying for dinner?" Her question is directed at me, so I compose myself enough to respond.

Wiping at the tears of laughter, I nod. "Yeah, I think I'd like that, thanks, Mom."

She gives me a small smile and a quizzical look before patting my shoulder and rising.

"I'll go get started, then. If you still wanted to chat, you can come help," she offers.

"I think I'm good," I say, giving Chris a smile. "But I'll help anyway."

Dad gives me a bewildered look as I follow Mom into the kitchen, while Chris smirks. And while I end up keeping the conversation with my mother light, telling her only general things about Vincent and me, I feel like I got what I came for.

CHAPTER 17

After the visit to my parents' house, I spend a lot of time thinking about what Chris said. About what Avery said. About what I want to do about it all.

I decide pretty quickly that Jules was right: I was afraid of becoming my mother. Well, having a relationship like my mother's and father's, because I'm so much like my mom. But what Chris said makes a lot of sense. You find something that works for you. It doesn't matter what it looks like to everyone else.

I thought I'd been in love once. It was when I was eighteen. I'd been on a few dates with a guy over the course of a few weeks. We talked a lot on the phone too, even though we only managed to meet up those few times. That should've been my first clue.

He was about ten years older than me, and I found him not only attractive but fascinating. He'd traveled to exotic places, dined at the best restaurants, moved in social circles I could only dream of. But it turned out I was one of many women, or girls, as it were, that he was seeing. And by "seeing," I mean "fucking." I wasn't a woman then, despite what I thought. But now, at twenty-six, I feel like I'm *really* in love for the first time.

And the fact that there are things about Vincent that I don't know give me pause and make me feel like I made a bad decision. Until I realized it wasn't a decision at all — I didn't decide to fall in love with him, I just did. Lord knows I'm impulsive, but I also don't get serious. And in all honesty, if I could've chosen who to get serious about — with my head — it would *not* have been Vincent DeMarco.

I knew from the start he had "bad boy" written all over him. But that's just a label. And you fall for a person, not a type.

He's surprised me on many levels. But I can't discount my concerns. And that Avery's story might not just be a story. Though that doesn't mean there isn't more to it.

While I consider all of this, I put off seeing Vincent. But by Tuesday, when he texts again asking to hang out, I've decided the time has come to just talk to him about it. Otherwise, it's going to haunt me, make me question myself, make me act in ways I don't want to. I may have dated around, but I don't play games. And I'm into this way too deep to screw around.

Thankfully, Sasha is busy with her own relationship, preparing for her last finals, and finishing her degree. Jules is once again all wrapped up in hospital business. And Harper is busy with Mason, not that we're as close anyway. So nobody pushes me about how things are going, why I'm so quiet all of a sudden and all that.

Even so, I'm a bundle of nerves on Tuesday night as I wait for Vincent to show up at my place. I'd asked him to come here rather than going out so we could talk privately. Assuming I can keep it from turning into a sex-fest, which is what I'm sure he was expecting with that sort of invitation. Normally, he'd be right.

When he knocks, I open the door, immediately proven right. He's wearing a tight black tee that hugs his muscled frame, with low-slung, fitted jeans that show off his thick thighs and, I'm sure, his gorgeous ass. Oozing sex appeal, he smolders in a way that's practically irresistible before he even says a word.

"Hey," I say, trying to sound casual but barely squeaking out the word.

A sly smirk appears on his face, like he thinks I've been struck dumb by his hotness. Again, normally he'd be right.

"Hey, yourself," he replies. "So, you gonna let me in, or what?"

I realize I've been standing fully in the doorway, blocking his entry, so I step back.

"Of course, yeah, come in," I say, feeling a blush creep up my neck. Seriously? I do not embarrass easily. This is going to be harder than I thought.

I close the door and follow him to the couch. He sinks into his usual spot in the corner, but I don't settle in his lap like I usually would. Instead, I sit down next to him, facing him with my leg tucked under me.

"I need to ask you something," I say plainly.

He sits up a little, a look of concern flitting over his features before he quickly smooths his face back to a neutral expression.

"Sure, of course, what's up?" He's trying to sound cool, casual. But I can tell he's just as nervous as I am.

I take a deep breath. "Were you in National City last Wednesday after work?" I ask.

Whatever he was expecting, it clearly wasn't that based on the look of surprise on his face.

"Wow. Um. Yes … yes, I was," he replies slowly. "Why?"

Well, he didn't deny it. So that means at least the first part of Avery's story is true. Shit.

"I thought you had to check in with your parole officer?"

"I did. And then I went to visit a friend," he says simply, with no further explanation.

My brows pull together. "You made it sound like checking in was going to take longer. Since, you know, you said you couldn't make it to have dinner with Sasha and Cal. But you could go hang out at a friend's house for a couple of hours?"

His whole body stiffens. "How do you even know where I was, and for how long? What the hell is going on here, Becca?" His immediate defensiveness makes my stomach drop. People are only defensive when they have something to defend.

"Someone told me they saw you."

"Yeah? Who?" he asks.

"It doesn't matter. Is your 'friend' a prostitute?" I ask plainly.

He scoffs. "Is that was your source told you?" he returns in an accusatory tone. "That I was cheating on you with a prostitute?"

I consider that for a moment. "Cheating would imply we're exclusive. Which we've never actually agreed to be," I allow. "But yeah, basically, that's what they said."

"I don't know what kind of guy you think I am," he replies coldly, "but I don't cheat. Whether we've agreed to be exclusive or not, I haven't fucked anyone else. And I don't *ever* pay for sex. But what pisses me off the most is that you felt the need to even ask me that."

"I didn't ask you if you paid for or fucked a prostitute," I reply hotly. "I asked if the person you were visiting was also a prostitute.

There's a difference." I don't miss that he said he hasn't *fucked* anyone else. Not that he hasn't dated anyone else.

"Please. I can read between the lines," he retorts.

"You know what I love about this conversation? That you didn't actually deny that the person you visited is a prostitute," I point out. "Or that you're not dating them or something."

He rises from the couch. "I don't need to sit here and listen to this. You either trust me, or you don't."

Sick of hearing that phrase, even though it wasn't from him before, I stand up to face him, hands on my hips. "Are you telling me if someone saw me go into some pimp's house or something, you wouldn't want to know what was going on?"

"Gigolo," he corrects. "A male prostitute is a gigolo. And no, I would trust you if you told me nothing was going on."

"Wow. *Someone* seems to know a lot about prostitutes," I snap. Even though I know I shouldn't have said it, right now I don't care. "And trusting that nothing was going on and wanting to know why I was there in the first place aren't the same thing. All I asked is where you were and who you were with."

"That. That right there is what I don't need. Someone who wants to know where I am and who I'm with at all times. You don't trust me. Message received. I think we're done here," he says.

"Seriously? You blow me and my friends off to go hang out with someone you didn't even tell me about, and I'm not allowed to ask questions about that?" I press. "If that's over the line, then yes, I think we're done here." I cross my arms over my chest and glare up at him.

He rubs the heels of his hands into his eyes before dropping them back to his sides and looking at me imploringly.

"Okay, fine, I get why you'd have questions," he finally allows. "But do you trust that I'm not dating, fucking, or whatever with this person? That I just don't want to include you in every detail of my life all the time?" The pain on his face cuts through me like a knife.

"I do," I say. "I trust that. But that explanation doesn't make me feel any better, because now I'm worried that we're not on the same page. Because if there are parts of your life you want to keep me out of, maybe this isn't that serious to you."

"Says the woman who didn't want me to have dinner at her parents' house on Saturday," he replies.

"I ..." Well, fuck. He's not wrong, but it's not for the reasons he thinks. "I do want you to meet my parents, there were just some things I had to take care of." He stares at me pointedly. "Yeah, okay, I get it."

"Do you?" he asks in earnest. "Because this is serious to me. I wouldn't be with you if it weren't, and I thought you knew that. But you gotta give it time. I can't give everything all at once. Believe me, I wish I could."

His explanation tugs at something inside of me. Well, several somethings. On one hand, he's absolutely right, and I knew all of that on some level. On the other hand, I can't help feeling like there's still something off about all of this. All of his deflecting and defensiveness just doesn't sit well. There's more to this story, and it feels important somehow.

But I remember what Chris said about a relationship being a choice. And my heart's made the choice for me. If I don't try to see it through, I'll always regret it.

"Okay," I say softly, my defensive stance melting.

He blanches. "Okay?"

I look up at him. "Yes. Okay. Can we stop fighting now and have makeup sex?"

He looks down at me, a muscle in his jaw ticking. His hands reach up to cup my face, and he steps toward me so our bodies are touching.

"You mean so much to me, Becca, you have no idea," he says, his forehead dipping to meet mine. His lips follow, sliding over my mouth in earnest.

I reach up, wrapping my arms around his neck as I open to him. Needing his kiss, his touch, to erase the feelings of unease that linger.

What I don't do is say the words he just said back to him. Because it's too close to "I love you." Something I want to say. But I couldn't bear not to hear it back. Not right now. Instead, I stick to what I know. I let him slowly undress me in my living room, while I slowly undress him. I let him ease me onto the couch. I let him inside me. When I come, when we come together, it feels like surrendering on every level.

CHAPTER 18

At the beginning of the day Wednesday, Vincent's words ring through my head, and something still just doesn't sit right with me. Unfortunately, the more I think about it, the more my sense of unease grows. By the end of the day, I'm a nervous wreck.

After work, I sit in my car, rocking back and forth, my mind flipping through everything we'd said to each other. When it occurs to me, I never asked if he planned to visit the friend again tonight. Yet somehow, I assumed he would. Why did I assume that?

I search my memory for any clue or reason and come up empty. Just because he checks in with the parole office every Wednesday doesn't mean he goes to that person's house every Wednesday. But I can't ignore the gut feeling that I'm right, that he's going there again today, even after our argument, and that that's why I'm so worked up. It also occurs to me that I don't need to take Avery's suggestion of following him. She gave me the address. I can simply go there. If he never shows, nothing lost. And if he does … well, I could ruin his trust forever. But I could also learn what he's hiding.

Unfortunately, I'm a risk-taker through and through. Especially if it puts me in a place of power. And knowledge is power. *That.* That is why I feel so off — I feel powerless not knowing. My impulsiveness gets the better of me, and I pull the piece of paper I'd crumpled into my pocket and rediscovered later out of my purse. The fact that I even kept it tells me I was always going to do this at some point. I know it's a stupid move. But clearly, on some level I always knew I'd use the information.

It's not a long drive, but every second, every inch, feels like eternity. When I finally spot the house, I drive by, getting a good look at the plain, one-story blue rambler with chain-link fencing.

There's an old Ford Focus in the driveway and a few toys scattered in the yard. I circle the block and find a spot to park down the street that's close enough to see the house but far enough to escape notice.

After sitting in the car for ten minutes, a sharp rap on my window nearly scares me to death. I look up to find Avery, arms crossed, somehow looking both annoyed and intrigued.

I roll down the window.

"Goddamn, Avery, you nearly made me shit my pants," I chastise her.

"I see you took my advice," she says smugly. "But this is where he parks, and if he's here at the same time as last week, it'll be any minute now. Go down to the other side of the street if you don't want lover boy to see you. I'll be inside," she points at the nondescript gray house behind her, "with popcorn." Giving me another superior look, she turns and leaves without waiting for a response.

I don't hesitate, doing exactly as she suggested, even though now I feel even dirtier for this whole operation. Knowing Avery is going to witness whatever goes down is almost enough to make me abort the whole thing. Almost.

But I don't get time to second guess myself. Vincent pulls up mere moments after I've settled in my new spot. Fuck. I *knew* it.

I watch him get out of his car, look around, and walk up to the front door. It opens, but I don't get a look at the person inside before he walks in.

He's been in there a good half an hour before I start to wonder what my plan was going to be. Spoiler alert: I didn't have one.

Do I go up to the house while he's there and try to look inside? Too creepy, and someone might call the cops if I look like I'm prowling around.

Do I just go up and knock on the door? That idea has merit. If the person he's visiting answers, I might be able to learn something just by seeing them. But if he saw me ... I decide I'd rather avoid that. So my best bet, really, is to approach the house after he's gone. Maybe pretend to be selling something.

Or I could find my sanity and just go home right now. Because I'm fairly certain I've lost my damn mind.

Unfortunately, Vincent comes out a few minutes later, gets in his car, and leaves. After being there for not quite forty-five minutes. Enough time to … well, to do a lot of things. My stomach turns, and before I can find my senses, I'm out of the damn car and headed for the house. I hope Avery enjoys the show.

As I walk, I concoct a quick story in my head starring the church I'd passed on my way in. Here goes nothing.

I don't notice any signs of security as I approach. The gate is unlocked, there's no doorbell camera or anything else that I can see. That's good, at least.

I knock, and it doesn't take long for the door to open. An attractive older woman who looks to be in her forties answers the door. She's got dyed platinum blond hair and wears a fitted, leopard-print pantsuit that looks expensive on her svelte frame. If she's a hooker, she's a classy one.

"Hi," I greet her with a huge, fake smile. "I'm with St. Mary's Catholic Church, and we're looking for donations of clothing or household goods for our first rummage sale of the summer. Do you have anything you'd like to give?"

I want to smack myself. What in god's name am I doing?

The woman eyes me up and down. "I go to St. Mary's, and I don't remember them saying anything about a rummage sale," she replies suspiciously.

My heart pounds in my chest.

"Oh, it's something that the singles groups are doing," I reply, trying not to sound caught out.

"What'd you say your name was?" she asks, still clearly not buying it.

My brain scrambles for a fake name, but I'm clearly not good at this because before I can stop myself, I reply, "I'm Becca." And I hold out my damn hand. *Becca, the complete moron.*

Her eyes widen a fraction. And I know I've been caught.

"You're —"

But before she can finish her sentence, a little boy around two years old toddles up and tugs at her pants. "Come play," he insists.

Then he turns toward me. And I'd know those features anywhere: Vincent's luscious dark hair, his deep, dark eyes, his brow line, his nose … this kid has them all, in the cutest, most angelic little package I've ever seen. And I can't help the gasp that escapes me.

I look back up at the woman in horror.

She looks down at the little boy. "Go play, sugar, I'll be right there, promise," she tells him sweetly.

I work to find my words. "I'm sorry, I didn't mean to bother you, I should —"

She reaches out and grabs my arm. "You shouldn't be here. It won't work out well for you." Her expression is inscrutable.

I want to say it already hasn't worked out well for me. Vincent has a child with this woman. Talk about huge secrets. What else don't I know? How far down does this rabbit hole go?

"I don't think you'll have to worry about that," I promise her, trying to hold back tears. Because I'm going to have to tell Vincent I was here. One way or another, this discovery is going to end our relationship.

I turn to head back down the walkway. Only to see Vincent himself, coming back up the sidewalk toward the gate holding a shopping bag. He freezes in place when he sees me. I stop, and the tears come pouring out, despite myself.

"Becca, what the fuck are you doing here?" His feet restart, and he pushes through the gate, stopping right in front of me.

I've never heard him sound so angry. And even though I know he has every right to be, I'm instantly equally furious.

"I had to know. And I'm glad I came. Now I see what you've been hiding. *Who* you've been hiding. How far does this go? Are you two married? Do you live here, just a happy little family? Is that why we never go to your place? How big of a joke am I to you, Vincent?" The words tumble out without any effort, any recollection of forming them.

"We can't talk about this here, Becca. Get out of here, now," Vincent replies harshly.

"Why, so you can get me alone, whisper your sweet nothings, make me buy your story?" I say back angrily. "Not gonna happen. I'm not buying what you're selling anymore, asshole."

"Fuck," I hear loudly from behind me. The older woman has appeared back in the doorway. "Georgie's off early and on the way home, Vincent. You both need to get out of here."

Vincent suddenly looks terrified.

"Oh, so you're *not* together?" I ask. "She's already married. I see. Yeah, wouldn't want the husband to come home and find her lover here. Figure out that their kid looks *exactly like you.*"

"You saw Elijah?" he gasps, eyes wide.

I close my eyes, tears trickling over my cheeks. Such a perfect name for that adorable little saint.

"Yes. But don't worry, I'd never do something against the best interest of that little boy," I promise. "Just do me a favor and lose my phone number, would you?"

As I walk past him and out of the gate, a small coupe pulls up in front of the house. The driver steps out, and it's not a jealous husband, just a young woman with long honey-blond hair. She looks at me, confused, then her eyes land on Vincent behind me.

The pure rage in her eyes is my first clue that something is seriously wrong.

CHAPTER 19

"What are you doing here, Vinnie, and who the fuck is this?" the girl snaps as she slings a beat-up purse over her shoulder. She looks to be in her late teens and is wearing a waitress uniform.

"I don't know, some chick," he says, sauntering up next to me and giving me a look like he's never seen me before, then turning his lazy gaze back to her. "And I think you know why I'm here, Georgette."

Georgette ... Georgie. Not the older woman's husband. Her ... daughter? I look between her and Vincent, realizing that I had it wrong. The older woman isn't Elijah's mother, this girl is.

"Becca, dear, I have those donations for you," a voice rings from behind me just as the pieces click into place in my mind. I turn to see the woman who'd answered the door walking down the path, holding a black garbage bag. She stops right in front of me and all but shoves it in my arms. "You tell Pastor Flynn I said hello, and I'll see you both at mass this Sunday." She gives me a tight smile that clearly says, *Now get the fuck out of here.*

But if she thinks it's that easy to get rid of me, she's sorely mistaken. Especially with "Vinnie" glaring daggers at me while his girlfriend isn't looking.

"Ma, what the hell?" Georgie snaps, grabbing the bags out of my arms. "You know I want to resell anything you used to donate. I need the money more than your stupid church. And what the fuck is he," she points at Vincent, "doing here? I told you he's not allowed to see Elijah."

Georgie's mom holds her hands up. "I don't know, that's between you two," she says airily, stepping back toward the porch. As she moves, her glance shoots back to me, still frozen in place on the sidewalk. "Becca, dear, you can run along now."

Georgie's head whips back to me and scans me up and down as her mother ducks back into the house. Fucking coward.

"You're wearing scrubs," she says acidly. "You're not here to see my mother. You're here with *him*, aren't you?" She gets up in my face, looking like she's about to push me.

"You need to back up off me right now," I say, hands flying to my hips.

Vincent steps between us, putting his back to me and pressing Georgie away. "Leave her alone, she's got nothing to do with this." His voice is filled with quiet menace, and a chill runs down my back.

The bitch *hisses* at him like a fucking cat. I freeze in place, the anger at her challenge totally replaced by fear of getting in the middle of this argument. I don't even try to sneak away, for fear of making it worse. Because clearly this bitch is cray-cray.

"This is the trash you're with now?" she screeches. I bristle at this bitch calling *me* trash but manage to keep my mouth shut. "And you think you can just bring her here *and* see Elijah behind my back? I warned you, Vinnie —"

"I didn't bring her here," he interrupts her angrily. "And he's my fucking kid too, Georgie. You can't make me stay away from him just because I don't want to be with you."

More pieces drop into place at his words. The reason for his sneaking around. For keeping secrets. He's not just a dad; he's a dad to a kid with a psycho bitch for a mom. A psycho bitch who clearly isn't about to let him go without a fight.

"Like hell I can't," she screams. "He's *mine*. I can do whatever I want. I told you, you leave, don't come back. We're a package deal. It's both of us, or neither. You know the deal."

"You can't *do* that, Georgie," he grinds out angrily.

I peek around Vincent's broad back and watch her step up to him, glowering.

"Watch me," she says. Then she turns and runs into the house.

Vincent whirls on me, looking more tortured than I've ever seen him.

"You couldn't just fucking trust me?" he barks at me. "You had to follow me here?"

"Apparently, I was one hundred percent right not to trust you," I point out. "Considering this massive part of your life you've been keeping from me." Deep down, I don't want to fight about this with him. I just want to run.

He crosses his arms over his broad chest. "You have no idea what you've started," he mutters, shaking his head. "You should get out of here while you can."

"*I've* started? She would've found you here whether I showed up or not," I scoff. "How the fuck is any of this my fault?" Like hell I'm going to take the blame for this. For *his* secrets. Even though, on some level, I get why he didn't tell me. But I don't want to think about that right now. All I know is the hurt I'm feeling.

He runs a hand through his hair, agitated, and opens his mouth to reply, but is cut off by the front door of the house bursting open. Georgie comes out, dragging a crying Elijah by one hand, a duffel bag in the other.

"Mommy, noooo," Elijah screams. His little wail breaks my heart in half. Something about the kid just gets me right in the chest.

"Shut up," she snaps at him, glaring daggers at Vincent and I as she storms past us. She throws the bag in the trunk, then puts Elijah in the car seat in the back while Vincent stares with wide eyes. My chest feels tight, and I fight the urge to stop her. As if sensing my tension, Vincent puts an arm up to hold me back.

"Where the fuck are you going?" he demands, finally finding his voice.

The petite blonde slams the door shut and saunters up to him.

"I'm leaving. With Elijah. Same deal, Vinnie," she says in a deceptively soft voice. "You can have it all," she bats her eyelashes up at him, "or nothing." She takes a step back and turns to open the driver's side door. "Last chance."

Georgie's mother appears next to me. "Don't do this," she pleads with her daughter.

Vincent takes a step toward the car so he stands between me and his ex, then looks back at me with regret in his eyes. Georgie stares at him expectantly.

It's the moment of truth. Will he go with her? This woman who clearly holds the key to a past I knew nothing about until today? A past I've been trying to pry out of him for as long as I've known him? Or will he choose to stay here, with me? A woman he's known a fraction of his child's life. A woman whose trust he's broken? I'm no genius, but I know what I'd do.

Vincent turns back to her, closing the distance between them. His hand slips under her chin, tipping her face up to look into his and, despite my anger, my hurt, and the betrayal I feel, my heart breaks seeing him touch her like that.

"I swore I'd always be there for our son," he says. It's quiet, but I can still hear every word. Hell, you could hear a fucking pin drop. It's like the world has held its breath in this moment. "But nothing's changed between us, Georgie, and you can't make me be with you so I can see my kid. And I'm not going to let you take him."

Just as the knot in my chest unravels the tiniest bit, the soft expression on her face melts into tight rage. With a sudden, swift movement, she knees him in the balls.

He doubles over, crying out in pain, and she takes the chance to get in the car, snapping the locks shut behind her. I roll my eyes. I could've told him she'd do that.

Georgie's mother unfreezes beside me, striding quickly down the walk to the car window, around a still-bent-over Vincent. She bangs a hand on Georgie's window.

"Stop this right now, young lady," she calls sternly.

Georgie flips her off and starts the car, just as Vincent manages to pull himself back up. Quickly, he skirts to the front of the car, putting his hands on the hood.

I watch in horror as they have a staring match standoff. The man I love, despite everything, and a crazy bitch behind the wheel of a two-ton-plus vehicle. With their child in the backseat. What insane, fucked-up parallel universe have I landed in?

In a move nobody expected, Georgie *backs out* of the spot down the street, and Vincent almost falls flat on his face. Georgie's mother and I gasp simultaneously. Georgie guns the engine, but Vincent barely has time to right himself, much less move, when the car shoots forward, gaining speed fast. He's not standing far from the curb, but the car swerves just enough to hit him as it goes past.

My heart stops as I watch his body fly over the hood of the car on the driver's side as she continues to accelerate forward, rolls off to the side, and lands in a heap on the street as she drives off.

Without a thought, I hurtle forward to him. I streak past Georgie's mom, who stands, stunned on the sidewalk.

"Call 911," I command as I make it to Vincent's prone form.

He lays on his back, unconscious. His jeans are torn, his legs obviously badly damaged as the left one is sitting at an odd angle, though I can't see anything more than a scrape. I scramble up to his head, moving to examine the back side, which is in contact with the pavement. I see a small pool of blood steadily growing larger.

A low moan from the sidewalk catches my attention. I look up at the panicking woman, who fumbles with her phone.

"Oh my god," another voice cries. Avery runs up from my other side, settling down next to me. "I saw everything. What can I do?"

I look at Georgie's' mom, who still hasn't managed to place the call.

"Call 911," I tell her. "I've got him."

Avery nods and quickly pulls out her phone and dials.

I sit down on the pavement behind Vincent's head and remove my scrubs top. Thankfully, I have a tank top on underneath. I carefully brace his head and neck and lift so I can scoot my knees under him. With his shoulders resting on my knees, I roll my shirt and hold it gently on the back of his head wound while I hold the weight of his head with my other hand to keep his head and neck straight and supported.

My eyes flick back up at Avery's voice, now clearly talking to a dispatcher.

"They want to know if he's breathing," she tells me.

I nod. "He's breathing but unconscious. Head trauma with bleeding, likely skull fracture, and possible spinal damage, as well as contusions and possible fractures to the lower extremities. I have his head and neck in a stable position, but we need an ambulance *now*."

I focus on my emergency training, breathing steadily as I maintain gentle pressure to contain the bleeding. If I press too hard, any fractured pieces of skull could penetrate, causing even more damage.

Don't think about that, Becca, I tell myself. *Breathe. Focus. Stay steady.*

Avery puts a hand on my shoulder, and it's strangely reassuring. I hear her relaying the information, continuing to talk to the person on the phone as we wait. I vaguely recall that Paradise Valley Hospital is probably three minutes away by ambulance. I'm trying to focus on that fact when Vincent's eyes flutter and open, and my heart skips.

"Hey," I say soothingly, relief flooding through me. If he's already conscious, there's hope that the head trauma isn't as bad as it could be. "I need you to stay perfectly still, okay? You were just hit, and an ambulance is on the way."

He blinks hard but doesn't respond.

"Blink again if you heard me, okay?" I ask.

He blinks.

"Tell her he's conscious and responsive," I call to Avery. I hear her relay the information and take a subtle breath before addressing Vincent again. "You're going to be okay, do you hear me?"

He blinks. I feel tears prick the backs of my eyes. I hear sirens in the distance. *Thank god.*

I can't help glancing up to look for the ambulance, and my eyes fall on Georgie's mother. Her hand is still clenched around her phone as she stares helplessly at the three of us. I try not to let anger take over. I still need to focus on keeping Vincent still. But damn, bitch couldn't — or wouldn't — even call for help. Who are these people and how did Vincent ever get involved with them?

Moments later, a police car appears down the road, followed by an ambulance.

"Avery," I say softly, my eyes flicking to hers.

She nods. "I'm here. What do you need?"

I glance over at Georgie's mom, who looks like she wants to run. "Make sure the cops know what happened, that they talk to her," I gesture with my head toward the shocked older woman, "and that her daughter has potentially illegally abducted the son she has with Vincent."

Avery's eyes go wide, and I suddenly hate that I have to trust her right now. But there's nothing more important than making sure Vincent and his son are both okay. There's a sentence I never thought I'd say.

I'm distracted from my concerns as the medics arrive, and I work with them to get Vincent into a neck brace, onto a stretcher, and hooked up to oxygen to minimize chances of further damage. Once they're loading him into the ambulance, I turn back to Avery, who is talking with one of the police officers.

I join them at the squad car and see Georgie's mom sitting there, though she's uncuffed.

"They're taking her in to give a statement," Avery explains quietly as the officer turns to talk to his partner.

"And you?" I ask.

"I'll give one too, but I can join you at the hospital first if you need someone there with you," she offers.

"Wow. Um. Thank you. That's … surprisingly nice of you," I admit. "But I'll be okay. Is there any way you can go with them and bring her to me when you're done? I'd like to have a little chat with her."

"I'll try. They're going to want a statement from you too."

I nod. "I know." One of the medics calls that they're ready to go. "I'll be at Paradise Valley. I can do it from there."

Avery reaches out and gives my hand a squeeze. "I'm so sorry about this, Becca. About everything, really. I didn't think anything like this would happen, I swear."

I give her a vague, tired smile. "Thanks, but it's not your fault." The medic calls out again. "Gotta go."

Without waiting for a response, I turn and bound toward the ambulance, hopping into the front seat while the other medic pulls the back door closed behind him. The driver gives me a sympathetic smile before flicking on the lights and sirens.

I lean back into the seat for the short ride, trying to breathe through the distress of the last minutes.

"You a nurse?" the driver asks, eyeing my scrubs.

"Medical assistant," I correct. "At Rutherford."

He nods. "Then you know your friend is going to be fine. Vitals looked good."

"How were his legs?" I ask. It's the one thing I didn't have time to check, what with making sure he didn't bleed out on the pavement.

"Left femur is definitely fractured. Contusions on both legs. Pelvis seemed stable, though," he replies succinctly.

I nod. "Good." All easily treated and healed. As long as the skull fracture isn't too bad, all things considered, it could have been much worse.

But for once, I don't say any of the million things that are on my mind. Because when I do, I'll have to think about the big, brown eyes of that little boy as his mother threw him into the back of that car. As much as I care about Vincent, the idea of something happening to his son because of all this … I shake myself, unwilling to *what if* myself into a panic attack. One thing at a time.

Thankfully, we arrive at the emergency room before I can think too hard, and I accompany them as they wheel Vincent in through the emergency doors. Once he's handed off to the ER team, though, I have no choice but to stay the reception area. I'm not family, and even if I were, right now the hospital staff need to do their jobs. I know that better than anyone.

Unfortunately, I don't even have enough information about him to fill out the forms. It's a huge slap-in-the-face realization how little I really know Vincent DeMarco.

Thirty agonizing minutes later, Avery arrives with a police officer … and Georgie's mother, who at least looks chagrined at this point.

I give my statement to the officer while Avery hangs on every word. I don't try to stop her. At this point she's at least earned the right to hear what I know. She did help at a critical moment, after all.

I thank her for helping, and she leaves with such little fanfare that I'm starting to think maybe she's not all bad. Not that I plan to be friends with her after all the shit she pulled. But it's enough to ratchet down the animosity that had been raging between us. So that's something.

I'm left in the waiting room, just me and Georgie's mother. I slink into a seat next to her.

"I hate to have to ask you this, but is there anyone else we should call? Vincent's dad? Does he have any other family here?" I ask.

She shakes her head. "He's got no one here besides me," she replies. "I don't know about his dad."

I sigh. The little I know tells me even if his dad cared, he's still in Queens, so there's not much he could do. And he and Vincent aren't exactly close, anyway. I decide against calling Mason for now, unsure of how much he knows about this situation. I don't want to do anything to make it even worse.

"So, what's your name?" I ask. She looks up at me with tired eyes. "Because I keep calling you 'Georgie's mom' in my head. Might be easier if I actually knew what to call you."

"Crystal," she offers quietly.

"Crystal," I repeat back. Seems more like a stripper name than a hooker name, but what do I know? "So the officer told me they haven't found Georgie and Elijah yet."

She presses her lips together and sighs. "I don't know where she is," she says defensively.

I give her a hard stare. The woman did allow Vincent to see his son against her daughter's wishes. But Georgie is still her daughter.

"Would you tell me if you did?" I ask.

The indignation in her eyes is real. "Absolutely," she insists. "Georgie can't take care of that little boy on her own. And no matter what you think of me, I love my grandson."

I gathered as much, since she was clearly trying to get rid of me before her daughter realized who I was. Or, who I was to Vincent, as it were.

"Wait, what do you mean, *can't*?" I ask.

Crystal gives me a reluctant glance. "Georgie has some mental health issues," she admits. "It's not her fault."

Well, that's one way to shut down questions, even though now I have a million more. I consider that for a minute before asking my next question.

"Why didn't you call 911 when I asked you to?" I ask, purposely switching the topic.

And also because, while I was waiting, I realized it might be because she's trying to protect her daughter, which clearly she is. Or it could also be because she's had enough run-ins with the law not to want to involve them. Either way, I'm curious.

"I wanted to," she says slowly. "I just … froze. The situation with Vincent … it's complicated."

I look at her in disgust. "So complicated that you wanted him to bleed out on the damn street?"

"No," she says forcefully. "I knew the police would come too. And that Georgie would try to use this against him again. I didn't want that for him. But I would've called if your friend hadn't."

"In the future, you should know that minutes count," I snap. "He could've died by the time you figured out your shit. Thank god Avery was there." Through my anger, her words sink in. "Wait, *again?*"

"The history between my daughter and your boyfriend is very long, and very complicated," she replies.

"Well, try to use short, simple sentences, and I might be able to keep up," I reply sarcastically.

She huffs a dry laugh. "You should really ask Vincent. It's his story to tell. But for my part, obviously, I thought he had a right to see his son. Georgie didn't agree, and it's caused … friction. Between her and I. Between her and Vincent. On top of everything else, my daughter is extremely stubborn. It's her best and worst quality."

A woman in scrubs appears through the double doors and approaches.

"You're here for Vincent DeMarco?" she asks.

We both rise and nod. "He's stable now," she tells us. "He has a broken leg, two broken ribs, and a minor skull fracture with no brain damage. He's going to be just fine. You can see him now if you'd like."

Crystal looks at me nervously. "I really shouldn't, I don't want to upset him," she hedges.

I glare at her. "He's going to have questions I may not be able to answer. You're coming with me," I insist.

She shrugs in acceptance, and we follow the nurse to a semiprivate room with an empty second bed. Vincent sits propped up in the other, his head and chest wrapped tightly in bandages, his left leg propped up in a fresh cast from hip to ankle.

I tap his IV bag with a small smile.

"Hope they're giving you some good drugs," I say by way of greeting.

He reaches out to squeeze my hand.

"You're pretty," he says.

I can't help laughing. "That's a big yes," I tease.

He smiles, but it doesn't reach his eyes. "I was kidding," he explains. "But yeah, I'm good." His eyes move to Crystal. "Where is she? Where's Elijah?"

Crystal shakes her head helplessly and doesn't respond.

"The police are looking for them," I supply. "Don't worry, Vincent, they'll find them. They're going to come talk to you soon."

He snorts. "The cops? Great, that's the last thing I need right now."

I furrow my brow before remembering he's on parole.

"You can't possibly be in any trouble because of this," I say.

He looks up at me, then looks at Crystal. "You want to tell her about the last time I got in trouble with the police?"

Crystal flushes beet red.

I look between them, confused.

"I'll tell them," she finally says. "I've let her get away with too much. I'm sorry, Vincent. I should've told them sooner."

"Told who what?" I ask, still puzzled.

Vincent snorts. "I wasn't even sure you really knew until just now," he admits, bitterness filling his words. "But I guess that answers that question."

Crystal settles on the bed next to him, squeezing his hand so hard her knuckles turn white. "There's more at stake for me than you know, but Elijah is more important."

"Someone want to fill me in here, or should I leave you two to have a moment?" I ask crossly. Even though I have no right to be the upset party right now.

Crystal rises from the bed and faces me. "I think Vincent can fill you in from here. I need to go amend my statement to the police," she replies. "Anything I can do to make what comes next … well, not as much of a shitshow. For Elijah."

"For Elijah," Vincent says pointedly.

She swallows hard and nods resolutely before leaving the room.

Vincent and I stare at each other silently.

"I'm sure you're tired," I finally say. "I can go. You don't owe me an explanation."

"I kind of do," he replies. "Sit." He pats the bed next to him. I stand there, battling between deathly curious and exhausted from the drama. "Please?"

I take a seat, careful not to hurt him.

"So. You're a dad. And your ex is —"

"Trying to kill me?" he supplies.

"This isn't the first time?" I ask, surprised.

"No, it is," he assures me. "I hear it's thanks to you that she didn't succeed."

I can't help rolling my eyes. "You weren't hurt *that* bad," I reply.

"Still. Thank you."

My cheeks warm. "You're welcome. So you gonna tell me about the last time you got in trouble with the cops? The full story this time."

"The full story," he promises.

"If you feel up to it," I hedge.

His dark eyes sweep over my face for a minute before he responds. "After what just happened, I think you deserve to know." He takes a slow, deep breath. "Crystal is an escort. Not a prostitute."

My eyebrows shoot up. "There's a difference?" I ask.

"Eh," he replies, and we both laugh. "Anyway, the guy who ran her agency also ran a construction business by day. He was the boss who called the cops on me. After I broke things off with Georgie the last time."

"The last time?"

"Yeah. The last time. Lord. Guess I need to go back further, huh?" I give him an encouraging look, and he squirms. "I met

Georgie at a party in Queens. She was visiting her cousin. We hooked up and I found out once she'd gone home, she was pregnant. And she'd lied about her age. Told me she was eighteen, but she was barely seventeen. Said if I didn't move out here to take care of her and the baby, her mom was going to have me arrested."

I scoff in disbelief. "Crystal? She's terrified of involving the cops. I can't see that happening."

"Yeah, that was a lie too. Georgie just wanted to get me out here. And once I was out here, she got me a job with her 'Uncle' Nate. The first time I broke up with her, he threatened to fire me if I didn't give it another shot with her. Between that and Elijah … well, I figured it couldn't hurt to give it another go."

"Let me guess," I interject. "That didn't work out because she's … how do I say this politely? Sanity-challenged?" He smirks at me … and more pieces click together. "So he set you up and had you arrested when you wouldn't stay with her."

"Bingo," he replies. "She still let me see Elijah for a while, and I always suspected Crystal knew about Nate setting me up, but I didn't ask. Didn't want to rock the boat."

"So what changed that?" I ask. "Georgie letting you see Elijah, I mean."

Vincent's expression darkens.

"After a while, I started seeing someone. When it got serious, I wanted to introduce her to Elijah. Georgie flipped out. I think she thought on some level that I'd come back to her. So it just totally set her off," he explains.

"Ah. So new girlfriend, no more Elijah. So you stopped having new girlfriends," I realize.

He shakes his head sadly. "I wish it were that easy. Georgie attacked Rachel. Then slit her tires for good measure. *Then* she cut me off from Elijah, telling me I'd only get to see him when I realized we were meant for each other."

The sorrow on his face rips through me. And I feel like a first-class ass for poking around for answers all this time. I can see how hard this whole situation has been on him and why I'd be the last person he'd want to tell.

"So … you didn't see things getting serious with me and thought it'd be safe, then?" I hazard. Even though that explanation makes me feel things I don't want to admit.

"God, no," he replies vehemently. "I tried, Becca. I tried not to fall for you. So fucking hard. But it was useless."

I look up into his eyes, shocked. Because it's like he's describing exactly how I felt. And now I know it wasn't just me. It reminds me how much I've come to care for him in the last month. And the last thing I want to do, even though I'm still pissed that he didn't tell me all of this sooner, is to make this harder for him.

"Me too," I admit. "But for that exact reason, I'm not going to make this more difficult for you. When they find her, I don't want to be the reason you can't see your son anymore. I'll stay away, Vincent, I promise."

"What if I don't want you to?" he asks huskily.

I close my eyes against the swell of emotion that rises in me at his words. I don't want to either. But this isn't about what I want. Hell, it's not even about what he wants.

"This isn't about that. It's about what's best for your son," I whisper. I open my eyes.

"You're right," he agrees. "But that doesn't mean …" He trails off with a frustrated sigh. "I guess we'll just have to see how it all plays out."

"Guess so. Because the most important thing right now is to find them, and —" I freeze midsentence as it hits me. "I think I know where they might be."

CHAPTER 20

It's nearly midnight when my phone rings.

"Did they find them?"

"Hello to you too." Vincent's deep voice has a hint of laughter, and I can't help hoping that's a good thing.

"I'm on the edge of my damn seat here, and visiting hours are over so I can't come strangle you for taunting me. Spit it out already."

"Yes. They found them. Georgie is in custody for attempted manslaughter, and Elijah is with Crystal," he replies. "I don't know why I didn't think to have them check Nate's place. You're a genius, Becca, and I owe you big time."

My whole body deflates with the relief of knowing Elijah is safe.

"You don't owe me anything. I'm just glad I was able to help."

"You did more than that. Crystal told the cops she knew Nate set me up for the theft charges, and apparently Georgie has already admitted it."

"She did what, now?" I ask incredulously. "Are you serious? Why would she do that?"

"She's not in her right mind," he replies. "They're going to have her evaluated. I think they think she's on drugs, but Georgie's just messed up, Becca. I've known that for a while now."

"Damn," I say. "Well, maybe she can get the help she needs then."

"I hope so," he murmurs. "But I should let you go. You have to work tomorrow, and you've already dealt with enough drama for one day."

"Oh, I'm not going in tomorrow," I respond smugly. "I'm going to be right by your side first thing. I had another idea."

"I'd try to pry it out of you, but it sounds like you plan on holding it over my head," he teases.

"Smart *and* sounding much better already," I reply. "I'll see you in the morning, Vincent."

* * *

When I walk into Vincent's hospital room, the happy look he gives me quickly melts into confusion when he sees my companion.

"Hey," he greets me warily.

"Hi," I reply brightly. "Vincent, this is Ms. Suarez. She's from Child Protective Services and will be working with the DA's office on Elijah's case."

Ms. Suarez steps forward and extends a hand to Vincent, who takes it with a bewildered look.

"I'm so sorry to hear about what happened, but it sounds like your prognosis is good," she offers.

"Yeah, thanks. I'll be released in a day or two, then out of the cast six to eight weeks after that," he agrees, still looking totally unnerved. He looks at me. "I'm sorry, why is she here?"

I chuckle.

"When I gave my statement last night, I asked what would happen to Elijah. They gave me a number to call to talk to the case worker assigned. Instead, I showed up at their offices this morning and had a little chat with Ms. Suarez," I reply.

"And I wanted to speak with you directly," she offers to Vincent. "After a quick review of the case, even without the confession of attempted manslaughter, your ex-wife's —"

"We were never married," Vincent interjects sharply.

Ms. Suarez blushes. "My apologies. *Ms. Johnson's* mental health evaluation will weigh heavily in the custody matters. Her mother's statement seems to imply she won't be found mentally sound to have sole custody of Elijah," she responds.

"So, what, Crystal will?" Vincent asks.

"Is that what you want?" she asks.

"Better her than Georgie," Vincent responds with a one-shouldered shrug.

Ms. Suarez glances at me, then looks back at Vincent.

"Are you saying you don't want custody of your son, Mr. DeMarco?" she asks pointedly.

Vincent's jaw drops. "No, I … I honestly never even thought it was an option," he admits.

"And why not?" Ms. Suarez asks.

"I have a criminal record," he replies, looking down into his hands.

"Except that the charges against Ms. Johnson will include conspiracy to frame-up," she responds. "And since she's already confessed to it, it's just a matter of process and time until that conviction is removed from your record. And I should point out that Mrs. Johnson, her mother, also has a criminal record for solicitation, albeit in the distant past."

I smother a smile. Escort, my ass.

"What are you saying?" Vincent asks, wide-eyed.

"I'm saying that, if things go the way it appears that they will, if you wanted it, you could have sole custody of your son. Or shared with Mrs. Johnson, if that was your wish," she says plainly.

"Are you serious?" he gasps.

Ms. Suarez and I both laugh.

"Quite," she assures him.

"I … I'm just …" he stutters. "Thank you. Yes, that's what I want. Please. Oh my god." He scrubs his hands over his face, clearly in disbelief.

Ms. Suarez rises and offers a business card, which he accepts. "Then I trust we'll be speaking again soon. I wish you a speedy recovery, Mr. DeMarco," she says with a smile.

"Thank you," he says again.

Ms. Suarez gives me a nod, and I wink back. With a chuckle, she slips out the door, leaving us alone. I look back at Vincent, who is staring down at the business card in his hands.

"You okay?" I ask softly.

He looks up, his eyes swimming with tears. "So beyond fucking okay," he admits before they spill over onto his cheeks.

It makes me tear up too, and I rush to wrap my arms gently around him. "I'm sorry you had to go through all this, but I'm so happy that you'll get the chance to really be Elijah's daddy."

He pulls back, palming my face in his hand. "Thanks to you."

I shake my head. "You would've gotten here eventually. Maybe even without this," I gently touch the bandage on his head, "if I weren't around."

He wraps his hand around my fingers, drawing them to his mouth. "I don't remember you running me over with a car," he murmurs. "In fact, I'm pretty sure you're the one that held me together afterward. You're still holding me together."

I grin. "So I guess this means I don't have to stay away after all?"

"You'd better not," he replies, with a mock menacing glare.

"Yeah? Think you can put up with me for a while longer?" I tease.

His eyes turn serious. "I think the question is, do you know what you're getting into? My life's about to change, Becca. I'm going to be responsible for another human being."

I nod. "I know. You're going to be great. And I'll be right there with you."

"Seriously?"

"Seriously."

"Why?"

I take a deep breath and put my hands on either side of his face. "Because I love you, dumbass."

Vincent laughs so hard he shakes, until he grabs his side. "Ow," he exclaims.

"Sorry," I reply with a guilty look, dropping my hands.

"I love you too, you know," he says so easily that I'm shocked into silence. He stares at me expectantly. "Did I just render Becca Dillon speechless?" He starts to laugh again, then thinks better of it as he holds a hand to his side, simmering down into a low chuckle.

"I'm … yeah, I didn't expect that," I admit.

"I didn't expect *you*," he says huskily, his eyes dark and intense. "I was trying to focus on my job. My kid. Staying off Georgie's radar. Then you blew apart my life." His gaze is so tender it tears through all my usual bullshit.

A blush heats my cheeks, and I can't find words. Embarrassed and speechless. This might be a first.

"I don't know what to say to that," I admit quietly, fidgeting with the hospital blanket covering his uninjured leg. "Except … maybe, I'm sorry."

His brows pull together. "For what?"

I look up at the ceiling and work my lips between my teeth for a moment, trying to put my thoughts together. When I look back down at him, the patience and love in his eyes hits me right in the gut.

"For not trusting you. I guess I just had this … this idea in the back of my head that you were a certain type of guy," I admit.

"Yeah, I get that a lot," he replies with a grim expression.

"You don't deserve it," I respond heatedly. "And I'm such a fucking hypocrite. At the same time I assumed you'd be an awful boyfriend, I still wanted you. I couldn't see past my own bullshit assumptions. And turns out, I've got a lot of them. Hot guys are all talk. Bad boys don't make good boyfriends." I pause, nerves welling in me. "Some girls you don't take home to mom."

Vincent's eyes cloud over. "That's what you think? You're not the kind of girl a guy would want to take home?" he asks, his voice thick with emotion.

I blink back tears. "On some level, yeah," I admit. "But I didn't even realize I thought that until I figured out that I'd put a label on you that I kept trying to make you live up to. Because that's exactly what I've been doing to myself. Trying to live up to my own reputation."

"I get it," he says, taking my hands in his. "Especially at Rutherford. Man, I've never heard people talk so much shit in my life. They sure had a lot to say about you. Even before we were going out."

"Oh, lordy," I groan. "I can only imagine. Is that why you were so standoffish with me at first?"

He considers that for a moment. "Yeah, probably," he admits. "So I guess we're both guilty of believing the hype." He brings one of my hands to his mouth and places a gentle kiss on my palm. "But that was before I knew you. You're nothing like all the shit they say, Becca. You're loyal, and fierce, and a fucking goddess. My fucking goddess. If my mom was still around, I know she'd love you. Because I do."

I close my eyes, but a tear slips out anyway. I wipe it away hastily, but he grabs my hand to stop me.

"Hey," he says softly. I open my eyes to look into his. "I see you. All of you. It's what made me fall for you. Don't ever forget that."

I lean in, unable to stop myself, capturing his lips. Just to feel his mouth against mine. The warmth and connection I have with him in this moment is indescribable.

"Thank you," I whisper after breaking the kiss.

"Anytime, beautiful," he whispers back, then pulls his head farther away. He gives me a funny look. "This might be a weird time to ask … but was I hallucinating, or was Avery there last night?"

I chuckle. "Oh, you weren't hallucinating. She's the one who saw you at Crystal's last week. She's staying at her aunt's place down the block."

He groans and leans back into the stack of pillows behind him. "So I guess everyone at work already knows everything?"

I tilt my head. "I'm not so sure about that. I kind of think she'll keep her mouth shut."

"That'd be a first," he scoffs.

I snort. "True story," I agree. "Does it really matter, though? We've got each other now, bae. Doesn't matter what they say anyway."

He swipes his thumb over my cheek. "You're right. Nothing else matters."

I hear a soft knock on the door, and I pull back with a smile.

"Well, there is *one* other thing that matters," I say slyly.

Vincent raises an eyebrow.

"Come in," I call.

The door opens and Crystal peeks around it. I look down and see Elijah peering around her legs. His eyes go wide when they land on Vincent. I hear Vincent's breath catch behind me when he spots his son.

"Daddy's broken," Elijah gasps.

Crystal and I chuckle.

"I'm gonna be just fine, buddy," Vincent calls. "Come here."

Elijah looks up at Crystal, who nods in encouragement. I take a step back to give them room as Crystal follows him to the bed, helping him climb up next to Vincent. Elijah settles into the crook of his dad's arm on the uninjured side, resting his tiny hand on Vincent's broad chest.

My breath catches in my throat as Vincent plants a kiss on the little boy's head, squeezing him tightly into his body.

"I missed you, bud," he murmurs into Elijah's hair.

Elijah rolls his eyes and looks up at Vincent. "Daddy, I saw you yesterday," he huffs. "But Daddy … Mommy was naughty." He says the last bit in a fearful whisper.

"I know," Vincent assures him. "But it's going to be okay. It's all going to be okay from now on. I promise."

My heart breaks thinking of all the drama this poor kid has been through.

"I'm going to go and let you guys have some time together," I say softly.

Vincent looks up at me.

"Stay," he says quietly. "Please."

Crystal gives me a look. "If you plan on sticking around, you should go introduce yourself," she suggests.

"Really?" I ask quietly. "You don't think it's too much right now? I don't know anything about kids. I don't want to scare him."

"Kids are resilient. Trust me," she assures me. "I'll be in the waiting room if you need me." Before I can protest, she slips out.

I approach the bed warily.

"Bud, this is my friend Becca," Vincent says to him.

I stick my hand up for a high five, which Elijah promptly smacks with his own sticky little hand.

"'Sup, dude," I greet him.

"Hello," Elijah says. "Do you like *The Octonauts*?"

I shoot Vincent an amused glance. "TV show," he mouths.

"Well, I've never seen the show, so I don't know," I tell the bright-eyed little boy looking up at me curiously. I sit down next to him. "Why don't you tell me about them?"

It was clearly the right thing to say, as Elijah launches into a stream-of-consciousness info session on what is obviously his favorite show. When he requires me to parrot something back, I happily do so, just to hear his excited little voice. And to see the glint in Vincent's eyes watching us interact.

As scared as I was of this part, it's a lot easier than I thought it would be.

We don't visit for long when Crystal comes to collect Elijah to get home for an early lunch. Once they've gone, one look at Vincent tells me he could use some rest.

"I should go too," I tell him.

"Stay just a little longer," he pleads. Then he stares at me for a moment. "I can't lie. Seeing you two together … damn, Becca." He puts a hand to his heart, and he doesn't have to say anything else. I felt it too.

"He's a great kid, Vincent."

"Yeah, he is. But … it's a lot. I get that. I hope you can give it a chance, though," he says, vulnerability seeping out of him.

I sigh heavily. "Are you serious right now? He's like a little version of you. I couldn't look at that kid and not love him," I assure him. "The moment I saw him yesterday … god, I can't even with this." I wipe away tears. "Trust me, I'm not going anywhere."

"You have no fucking idea how happy I am to hear you say that," he admits. He gestures with both hands for me to come closer. I slide down next to him, folding into his uninjured side.

I look up into his eyes, more sure than ever. This is where I'm meant to be. As nuts as it seems that a little more than a month ago he was just a guy I was screwing around with. And now I can't imagine life without him.

As he looks down into my eyes, I can tell he feels the same way.

"Are we crazy?" I ask him.

"I'm crazy about you," he replies with a smirk. "And I'm so glad you know everything now. I wanted to tell you, I swear. I just didn't know how. I didn't want anything bad to happen."

I nod. "I get it. I think we're both in new territory here. But there's nobody else I'd be here with."

His dark eyes burn into mine, his mouth reaching down. I meet him with my lips, stroking mine gently against his. Keeping it light, even though it's a struggle.

He finally pulls back. "Me neither," he agrees. His eyes start to drift closed. "Becca?"

I look up again to see his head tilted toward me, his eyes closed.

"Hmmm?" I ask softly, knowing he's probably already half asleep.

"Stay," he says on a soft breath that turns into a snore.

I contain a laugh, pulling the blanket around us. I look up into his gorgeous face, an unmistakable ache in my chest.

I lean up and place a soft kiss on his cheek.

"Always," I whisper. And it feels true. Because I've never cared about anyone the way I care about him. Never loved like this. Never felt like such a fucking sap. Sasha is going to make so much fun of me. And she's going to be so damn happy.

I'm so damn happy. Because I'm pretty sure I've found the love of my life. And like hell I'm going anywhere.

YOU *Can't* BUY LOVE

CHAPTER 1

"Do you think it's too soon to propose?"

I stop scanning the crowd of graduates in their caps and gowns waiting for the ceremony to start and slowly turn toward Cal. When his blue eyes meet mine, I can't tell if he's joking or not. He's British, so he always has a small, polite smile on his stupidly handsome face.

"Yes," I say bluntly. I shake my head slightly in annoyance and sigh.

He looks forward again, pensively staring at the stage for a moment, until he says, "I meant, is it too soon for me to propose marriage to Sasha, just to be clear."

I snort. "I knew exactly what you meant," I assure him. "So I presume that was British for, 'But why is it too soon, Jules?'"

Cal presses his lips together, trying to suppress the smile that says that's precisely what he wanted to say.

"Well, now you mention it ..." he replies.

"Where do I even begin?" I murmur, more to myself than him. "For starters, Sasha is graduating with her master's in nursing today. And I *know* you wouldn't want to take the attention off that achievement. So today is out."

"I didn't mean —"

I hold up a hand to stop him, which is immensely satisfying as it's something I could never do while we're at work together. He is still more or less one of my supervisors, after all.

"Oh, I'm just getting started," I respond. "Now that she qualifies to become a nurse practitioner, she's going to have to deal with hospital administration to get promoted. And I think we both know *that's* not going to be a walk in the park, even without being engaged to one of the doctors in our unit."

His brows pull together, and he runs a hand through his thick, dark hair. "I hadn't thought about that," he allows.

I raise an eyebrow at his uncharacteristic lack of forethought. "So I presume this idea just popped into your head then?" I ask. "Though you've only been dating, what, four months? Which, by the way, is pretty much why yes, it's way too soon."

Cal blushes, and I have to chuckle. For being a doctor and such a firm presence at Rutherford Hospital since he started five months ago, you'd think he'd be a little smarter about keeping his relationship with one of his nurses under wraps, even if it's not technically against the rules. Not asking his head nurse practitioner, while in a public place mind you, if he should propose.

"You're right," he agrees. "It was a silly idea."

I lay a hand gently on his arm. "Sasha is like family to me," I remind him. "So really, all I care about is whether you really understand what proposing means. If you're ready to stick with her. You know, till death do you part and all. Because if you hurt her, I don't care if you're pretty much one of my bosses, I will have to kill you."

He looks me seriously in the eye. "She's it, Jules. I promise."

My heart melts. I resist reassuring him that they're clearly meant to be and that I know Sasha feels the same way. Because she hasn't outright said it, but we've worked together and been close friends for the better part of a decade. I can just tell.

"Then you have my blessing," I reply.

"To do what?"

I jump in surprise at the voice suddenly coming from my other side. I whirl to see Becca, grinning like she knows exactly how much she just scared the crap out of me.

"About time you showed up," I chastise her, ignoring her question and gesturing to the stage, where an older man in black robes is standing at the podium and tapping the microphone. "They're just about to start."

Becca flips her mane of chocolate curls over her shoulder, hands on hips. All sass, as usual.

"The party never starts without me," she says with a wink, sinking into the chair next to me. As she takes her seat, I notice for the first time her boyfriend is with her. Great, I'm literally surrounded by happy couples.

Not that I don't like Vincent. Becca is as volatile as Sasha is steady. I couldn't have two more different best friends, yet somehow they've both found men who suit them perfectly. Vincent is laid-back enough to deal with Becca's outrageous personality, but still exudes a strength that she bows to. It's actually fascinating to watch, because lord knows as her supervisor I could use a few tips on how to keep her in line.

As the ceremony begins and the speeches drone on, watching Cal watch for Sasha while Becca and Vincent make googly-eyes at each other makes me wonder if I'll ever find someone who suits me perfectly. But it was all I could do to get time off on a Saturday to make it to a huge milestone in one of my closest friend's lives. Anything besides that or someone dying, and there's no way I'd be able to get away from work. That all of us somehow managed it is nothing short of a miracle. Anyway, with that kind of schedule, dating is pretty much off the table.

I shouldn't complain. I do love my job, despite recent struggles with the way the hospital is run that have made it less enjoyable than it once was. Though understaffed hospitals and overworked medical professionals aren't exactly uncommon. And this life was my choice.

That's my mantra: This choice was mine. There are a lot of things you can't control with any job. But I get to help people, get them out of pain, out of fear, and hopefully living better lives.

It's why I asked to be in the cardiac unit over emergency, intensive care, or even maternity. I've worked all over the hospital, and cardiac is one of the few units where you often see the same patients regularly, get to know them, and get to really understand your impact on their lives.

Bringing myself back to the moment, I watch Sasha take the stage finally to accept her diploma. Her dark blond hair is pulled into a conservative ponytail, her grin wide and infectious as her eyes nervously scan the crowd, probably searching for Cal. It occurs to me that my closest friends, who started as just coworkers, have impacted *my* life just as much as we impact our patients'.

How would I make it through each day without these strong, supportive women? Let's be honest — I probably wouldn't.

So, while I'm happy that they're both coming into full lives of career success, love, and all that … well, I can't help noticing that I'm standing still. Possibly even going backward as the jerks in charge of my job continue to test the limits of my patience and hamper my ability to give the best care possible. I can feel it changing me, tearing at the shreds of my sanity.

I shake myself, focusing back on the moment once more as the ceremony wraps up and we rise to find Sasha and shower her with the love and pride she deserves.

* * *

When I get back to my small, quiet apartment that night, I settle onto the still practically brand-new couch. Even though I've had it for years, I'm not exactly here enough to lounge around on it. I mostly stumble home after a workday that's twelve hours at best, sometimes stretching to as many as sixteen, after which I bolt down dinner — assuming cheese and deli meat on crackers with half a bottle of wine counts as a meal — then fall asleep fully clothed on top of my bed with the TV on in the background.

It's a glamorous life I lead. Thankfully, this evening I'm spared my usual crap dinner, as we'd all gone out after the ceremony for a real meal. But without the physical exertion I'd have had throughout the day at work, my relatively calm outing has left me wide awake. And with far too much time to think. A dangerous situation for a single thirty-four-year-old woman who is becoming increasingly unhappy with her career, her love life — or lack thereof — and … well, life in general. I haven't even had time to admit that to myself until this moment.

I rise restlessly, stalking into the bathroom. A long, hot shower can fix just about anything. I turn on the tap and examine my face in the mirror as the water heats. My dark red hair is getting ridiculously long, trailing almost down to my backside. Which is saying something, given that I'm five-foot-ten. My naturally thin frame is leaning toward undernourished from long hours, hard work, and little food. I've never been one to remember to eat regularly, and it's taking its toll. The dark circles under my eyes, despite my attempts at hiding them with makeup, pretty much underscore that I'm desperately in need of more than five or six hours of sleep a night, some downtime, and probably a whole lot of other crap that falls under "self-care." As a medical professional, you'd think I'd take my own advice and look after my health. But I've always been better at helping others do that.

I turn my back on my reflection and get in the shower. The heat instantly soothes me, and I stand under the scalding stream until I physically can't take it anymore.

Once I'm out and dried off, I don't even dress, simply flopping down on the bed in my robe. Life finally catches up with me, and my mind goes blissfully blank as I drift to sleep.

* * *

"Sundays are for rest and fun, Jules. You don't have to come in here *every* week on your only day off," Katie scolds me as I tidy the common area of my parents' nursing home.

"Don't start," I warn her. "You know I'd come in to see Mom and Dad anyway."

Katie's big brown eyes give me a pitying look, and she doesn't even have to say it. I know they don't recognize me, but it doesn't matter. They're still my parents, and it comforts me to see them, to be part of their lives, even if it doesn't change anything.

I avoid talking about it, continuing to fold blankets, arrange magazines, or whatever the hell else will keep my hands and mind busy.

"You seem especially restless today," she remarks.

"Is there anything you don't notice?" I turn to her and cross my arms over my chest.

She gives me a patient smile. "We've been friends a long time," she reminds me. "Are things at the hospital that bad? Or is it something else?"

I watch my parents at the table in the corner while I consider how to answer her question. It still amazes me how, even though they don't know each other, much less their own daughter, they still somehow always need to be in each other's spheres. My heart aches at the thought of a love so deep that, on some level, it persists even through the ravages of their respective diseases.

"You know the Rutherford Group," I murmur distractedly. In fact, Katie was a nurse at my hospital before going into elderly care. It's how we met, all those years ago. "Always focused on expansion. It's just been an annoyance in the past as far as funding goes, but it's changed things too much now. Taken too much from the hospital. I just don't get why they don't care more about that."

"Maybe they don't know?" Katie suggests, continuing to count pills to go with the lunches we'll serve shortly.

I look up and catch her eye. "I know what you're trying to say, and there's no way in hell I'm going around my bosses to tell them. I'm already in enough trouble with MacDougall for speaking my mind at last quarter's budget meeting as it is."

"Suit yourself," she replies.

Damn Katie and her gentle nudges. She's right, really. Someone needs to say something.

"So what happens to Mom and Dad," I say, my voice thick with emotion as I gesture angrily at my parents, "when I lose my job for fighting that battle? Who's going to pay for their care?"

Katie looks up evenly at me. "Now, Jules, it's not me you're really mad at, is it?"

I snort. Katie is almost like a mother to me, and it's hard not to resent her honesty sometimes. Especially when I'm not ready to hear it, much less do something about it.

"No, I'm not," I finally agree.

"So who? Dr. MacDougall is the chief of cardiac. As self-important as he's always been, he's just a puppet of hospital administration. You know that," she chides.

"I know," I admit. "Unfortunately, he's as far up the food chain as I'm allowed to go without endangering my job. But believe me, I've been tempted to drive straight to Warren Rutherford's office and give him a piece of my mind."

Katie's eyebrows jump. "Surely, you realize that going directly to the president and CEO of the Rutherford Group is overkill. There must be someone between Malcolm MacDougall and Warren Rutherford who can do something."

I shrug. "If I'm going to risk my ass, might as well go straight to the top. Besides, it's his name on the fucking hospital. He should know what kind of reputation he really has among people who aren't paid to kiss his ass."

She laughs. "Except you are paid to kiss his ass, indirectly, as it were," she points out.

I shake my head. "Oh, Katie, you know me better than that. I grew up with nothing. Money means shit to me. There's no amount of it you could pay me to kiss anyone's ass, *especially* not Warren Rutherford."

Her aged lips pucker. "You're lucky everyone here but me is senile and won't repeat that to anyone who matters. Be careful, okay? We can always figure out a way to take care of your parents, but I'd hate to see you tank your career."

"It's all talk," I assure her. "You know I'm only blowing off steam. I'll keep going, same as I always have. Taking it up the ass with a smile on my face."

Katie gives me a mischievous smile. "You say that like taking it up the ass is —"

I throw my hands over my ears. "Gah! Don't even go there," I say, squeezing my eyes shut. "My fault, I should know better than to say things like that around you."

Mother figure or not, Katie has always been *way* too comfortable talking about sex. Had she worked at Rutherford at the same time as Becca, I imagine they'd have been thick as thieves. And I'm no shrinking violet but, in my opinion, some things should stay private.

I peel open an eye to see that Katie has walked off, chuckling to herself. I shake my head and walk to the kitchen to start on lunch. As much as I hate talking about Rutherford, budgets, and their fucked-up politics, I'm just glad Katie didn't get on me about dating again. I've got enough crap to worry about without the pressure to add a man to the mix. Lord knows they usually cause more problems than they solve.

CHAPTER 2

"Damn, Sash, back at work at six a.m. on a Monday morning already. Isn't there, like, a honeymoon for graduates?" Becca asks, tapping her chin thoughtfully.

Sasha rolls her eyes as she puts her purse in a drawer, and my eyes shoot sharply to Becca, wondering if Cal said something to her about proposing too. I sure hope not. He, of all people, should know what a gossip she is and that his chances of keeping it under wraps would be zero once she knew. I may be tied into the gossip loop to keep tabs, but Becca nearly lives for it.

Thankfully, Becca doesn't return my look, so I'm fairly certain it was just an offhand comment.

"Honestly, Becks, if there were, do you really think I'd take one anyway?" Sasha shoots back.

"True story, my too-serious sister-from-another-mister," Becca replies with a wink.

"God, you're all perky again now that you're getting laid regularly," Sasha grumbles.

The three of us snap to attention as Cal turns the corner.

"Good morning, Dr. Thompson," we say in unison.

"Good morning, ladies," he replies, winking at us as he passes. Well, probably winking at Sasha. But I'll take it. It's the most male attention I'm bound to get this week, save elderly patients who can't keep their wrinkled paws to themselves. Though that's lessened since Cal joined and helped put a stop to the backlash for reporting those kinds of things.

A lot has changed since he started working here, really. Aside from curbing patient sexual harassment toward the staff, he's also convinced hospital administration to upgrade a few key pieces of medical equipment that were hopelessly ancient technology. Unfortunately, it was only a few, and we're still drastically behind across the board. And the expenditures made us even shorter on funds for staffing. Two steps forward, ten steps back.

"All right, ladies, time for the morning staff meeting," I say, throwing as much pep into my words as I can.

"Oh, boy," Becca grumbles sarcastically as she rises to join me.

I ignore her and march us into the conference room. MacDougall trails in behind us, clearing his voice pointedly to quiet the assembled crowd.

He goes through his usual lectures before reminding us that this Thursday is the Rutherford Group's annual charity event and that anyone who wants to attend can coordinate to have their shifts covered if necessary. It takes everything I have not to snort disdainfully.

Seriously, it's just an excuse for San Diego's elite to suck up to one another, schmooze, and have free booze, all in the name of whatever pet cause they've picked this time around. Nobody but the chiefs and directors ever attend. Why would we? We're the little people, we mean nothing to them. They'd probably mistake us for the serving staff or something anyway.

Finally, the meeting is over, and we can actually start getting real work done. Except, as I go to leave, MacDougall catches my arm.

"Ms. Magnusson, I'd like a word," he says quietly.

I suppress an eyeroll. Even when he was just another doctor, MacDougall always called me "Ms. Magnusson." Not "Nurse Magnusson" or "Julianna" like all the other doctors do. Just another way he's always treated me differently. I swear, the old bastard has it out for me.

"What can I do for you, Dr. MacDougall?" I ask as pleasantly as I possibly can.

"I'm afraid my wife is having surgery this Thursday and I'll need to be available to her that evening. I'd like you to go to the gala in my stead."

My jaw drops. "Surely one of the doctors should cover instead?" I ask, already knowing he'll consider that "talking back."

"Given your recent criticisms of leadership, I think it would be a good opportunity for you to observe their capacity for generosity," he says. "And the importance of our role in the greater cause for advancing medicine."

I fight to keep the sneer off my face. As if whatever fakery was put on at this fancy party would stop me from remembering all the ways in which our "leadership" is screwing us right now. No, that's not what this is. He knows how much I hate this kind of bullshit. This isn't an opportunity. It's punishment for embarrassing him in front of the budget committee, plain and simple. I take a slow, deep breath and remind myself: *You chose this job. You can deal with these assholes for one night.*

"Well, sir, I suppose if you think I'm the best person to represent our department, then I'd be delighted," I reply sweetly.

He quirks an eyebrow. "Excellent," he says. "See that you stay the whole evening and do try to make a good impression on behalf of the staff here. I'll arrange for your shift on Friday to be covered accordingly. And, Ms. Magnusson?" I raise an eyebrow to acknowledge him. "I expect you to show all of our administrators the respect they're due, as well as Mr. Rutherford and his guests."

Now both my eyebrows shoot up. Warren Rutherford will actually be there. I guess I hadn't thought about that part. Well, this presents a potential opportunity, indeed. A very risky opportunity. But still, one to consider. And hey, either way, I get Friday off. I can't remember the last time that happened.

"Of course," I agree curtly.

With a contemplative look, MacDougall nods and takes his leave. And all I can think is, *Oh, I'll show them the respect they're due, all right.*

* * *

"I can't wear that," I scoff as Becca holds up the daring red dress. The thick silk, strapless mermaid-style gown has an extreme sweetheart neckline and is far more overtly sexy than anything I've ever worn. That's not even my main objection, though. Red? With my hair? She's nuts.

"Trust me," she insists. I give her a deeply skeptical look, at which she rolls her eyes and thrusts the dress in my direction. "At least try it on."

I grimace but take it from her and lay it over the dresses I'd selected. And, not for the first or last time, I wish Sasha didn't have to work late tonight. I have no doubt she'd help me pick a dress I was actually comfortable in.

Just to needle Becca, I try on a conservative cream-colored ballgown first. As I stand in the changing room, I have to admit I'm not that excited by it. But it definitely screams "rich and snobby," so I figure it's probably appropriate. I open the door and step into the wide seating area, complete with pedestal and three-paneled mirror.

Becca's face instantly sours. "You look like a fuddy-duddy," she says.

I laugh. "That's kind of the point. Blend in with all the other fuddy-duddies."

She shakes her head and pushes me up on the pedestal so I can fully appreciate the disaster that is this dress.

"You look shapeless. And boring. You're gorgeous, Jules. Why would you want to hide that under all this damn fabric?"

I roll my eyes. "Fine, I agree, this dress sucks. I'll go try on the other one I picked."

"Nononononono," she objects, wagging a finger at me. "Red dress next."

"Fine, whatever gets this done fastest," I agree, lifting the giant skirt. I still almost trip getting off the platform. If it wasn't already out, it would be now. I can totally see myself falling down a set of stairs in this behemoth.

Once back in the dressing room, I shed the dress, unceremoniously piling it in the corner, then I slip into the red dress.

Before I even look in the mirror, the soft fabric against my skin feels like heaven. A rich person's heaven. It's beyond luxurious feeling. So when I turn toward the mirror, I'm already a little sad knowing it's going to look horrible against my auburn locks.

Except it doesn't. The bright red somehow perfectly complements my hair color *and* skin tone. And holy hell, is it sexy. The plunging sweetheart neckline fits perfectly around my chest, shaping me in a way that puts the girls where they used to be ten years ago. It's a lot of cleavage, but I've never felt more beautiful.

I open the door, now expecting the fabric that's fitted snugly against my outer thighs and knees to make walking practically impossible.

Except it doesn't. It has just enough give to make walking feel like being caressed every time I take a step.

My eyes are wide when Becca notices me. She jumps up, clapping her hands.

"Yasss, girl," she calls. "Damn, you look hot."

She grabs me, practically shoving me up onto the platform. She fusses around me, flaring the base of the dress. Then, she wrangles a salesperson to get some shoes that match, so we can get the full effect.

I'm silent as she works, carefully smoothing my hair over my shoulder so it cascades down one side in the front. I dip my head forward so it falls over my eye, giving myself a sultry look. Somehow my hazel eyes look greener now. I seriously look like a model in a fashion magazine. This dress is miraculous.

Becca catches my eye in the mirror, smirking.

"See. Told you. Tell me you don't love this dress."

"I don't love this dress," I deadpan.

She pulls a skeptical face.

"I want to *live in it*," I breathe, doing an impatient little dance.

"Girl, if I looked like that in something, I'd want to live in it too," she responds. "Just promise me you'll at least use this dress to get a little ass."

My mouth pops open. "Becca!" I gasp.

"What? You can't tell me it hasn't been a long time. And if you can't get some looking like *that*, well ..." She shrugs.

I roll my eyes. "As if I'd be interested in any of the billionaire playboys who will be there. They're witless morons with too much money, too few manners, and a yen for a photo-op so they can show off the fact that they can give away millions left and right. Please."

"Fine, then a cute waiter or something. I'm just sayin', you never know," she says. "But you are getting this dress, yes?"

I take a deep breath and look at my reflection. "Yes," I sigh.

Becca grins. "That's my girl," she says with a wink. "And if nothing else, you can knock Warren Rutherford dead before, you know, ripping him a new one."

That gets a laugh out of me. "Eh. I'll only be ripping him a new one in my dreams. But I like where your head's at," I reply.

"We'll see," she murmurs. "Personally, I can't think of anyone better to put the old bastard in his place. He'll never know what hit him."

As I stare at myself in the mirror, I think about that. This dress makes me feel bold, that's for sure. Let's just hope it doesn't encourage me to do anything stupid.

CHAPTER 3

"I'm sorry, can you repeat that?" I ask, stopping in my tracks. So abruptly, apparently, that Sasha keeps walking a few steps before she realizes I'm no longer next to her.

She turns back to me, stepping close so she can keep her voice down. "They said I can have the job but not the promotion," she repeats.

My brows scrunch together. "What does that mean?" I ask. But almost as soon as the words are out of my mouth, it clicks into place. They want Sasha to do all the work without the title or pay. I gasp at their audacity. "*No.* They wouldn't."

"Would and did," she grumbles. "I don't know what to do, Jules. They're hiring NPs right now at UCSD Medical for nearly twenty thousand more a year than I'm making."

I shake my head slowly. "This is insane. They know we need another ARNP in the unit. Sarah and I are working ourselves to death trying to cover everything."

She shrugs sadly. "Clearly, they're happy to let you keep doing that. Or let me get away if I don't like their offer."

My eyes meet hers. "You're not really thinking of leaving, are you?" I ask. But then I feel like a selfish ass. "Of course you are, I'm sorry. I understand. You need to do what's best for you. But my god, how can they do this to you after all your years here?"

"Things have changed here," Sasha points out. "To be honest, between the way things are now and being with Cal, it might be for the best if I leave anyway."

"I thought you loved it here?" I can't help trying to convince her to stay. It'd be like losing a family member if she left. Even though I know we'd still see each other outside of work. It would just be one more thing that made this place less bearable.

"In some ways, I do," she agrees. "But come on, Jules. I know neither of us are the type to complain, but …" She looks around to make sure nobody is listening, then lowers her voice. "Shit's bad."

I have to laugh at that. "True."

Unfortunately, I have an appointment, so we part ways, unable to talk more about it. But the whole thing just sits poorly with me all morning.

So, after lunch, I do something I know is probably stupid and go see MacDougall in his office. It goes about as well as I expect, and it's a complete waste of breath to attempt to convince him that we *need* another official nurse practitioner for scheduling reasons, that Sasha has invested eight years at Rutherford and deserves it, that they're going to lose her if they don't step up. It's all for naught, and we're both annoyed with each other by the time I leave his office nearly an hour later.

When I leave that afternoon, early so I can get ready for the gala, I'm not so convinced I'll be able to keep my mouth shut if I run into Warren Rutherford. Or, you know, if I seek him out for the sole purpose of letting him know exactly what I think of his expansion strategy and its impacts on the hospital that started it all. Because if Sasha goes … well, it's the first proverbial rat fleeing the sinking ship. And maybe I should take the hint.

* * *

Dressed to the nines with a pair of slender silver heels and a black clutch to complement the stunning gown Becca chose, my hair is sleek and curled, my makeup dramatic and sexy. I've never felt so confident.

But, in the back of the Uber I called to take me to the gala, I also decide that tonight isn't the time or place to make my stand. I just need to endure this punishment and not get myself in any more trouble. Mouthing off isn't going to help. I doubt I'll be able to get anywhere near Warren Rutherford anyway, though even if I could, why would he listen? He wouldn't. So no point in risking my job for nothing.

When I arrive at the swanky marina-front hotel around seven, it's still fully light out and pleasantly warm. Thankfully, the strapless, figure-hugging dress also seems to breathe well, because I feel cool and dry under its silky fabric.

I rearrange my hair back over one shoulder so it cascades down my front. I stare up at the impressive awning over the hotel's entrance, including giant, domed chandeliers already lighting the expensively tiled pathway. I roll my eyes at the opulence as well-dressed people stream by me, getting it out of my system.

With a resigned sigh, I make my way inside to be greeted by a stunning glass- and wood-paneled wall. Six huge panels tile across the center, a gorgeous fragmented purple and blue wave cresting across its width. I don't realize I'm blocking traffic with my gawking until I'm elbowed sharply, waking me up to the fact that I'm standing in the middle of the entrance.

With a deep blush, I watch those in formal wear splitting off to the sides and disappearing into archways on either side of the hotel's front desk. As I follow, I note signs directing attendees of the Rutherford Group's annual gala to the Grand Hall. I descend stairs under one of the archways, and the first thing I notice is huge, dark, wood-paneled doors that open into a gigantic ballroom in front of me. I'm too busy trying to take everything in to notice the podiums on either side of the ballroom entrance.

"Name on your ticket, ma'am?" the attendant at the podium to my right asks. I look over to see a woman in a navy hotel uniform smiling politely at me.

I feel myself blush again as I backtrack a step or two.

"I'm so sorry. It's Julianna Magnusson," I offer. "I'm attending in Dr. Malcom MacDougall's place."

A few taps on a tablet later, and she offers me a plastic square something like a credit card, with a number printed on it and a chip embedded in the corner.

"Here you are, Ms. Magnusson," she says. "You may use this to bid on any of the silent auction items inside. Cocktails are being served here and also in the Seaport Foyer upstairs. You'll use your card to attend the banquet in the Seaport Ballroom in an hour and to be admitted to the concert in the Harbor Ballroom, also on the second floor, later this evening."

My eyebrows shoot up as I thank her and take the card, slipping it into my clutch. This whole affair is even fancier than I thought.

It must've cost a fortune. But then, judging by the fat cats happily crowding the auction items lined on tables against the walls, I imagine it's going to pay off quite nicely. Plenty of other partygoers gather at small, standing-only tables scattered around the center of the room as waiters with trays of drinks and appetizers make their rounds.

As I move forward I notice that just past the entrance, in the center of the room, is a large sign on a golden stand declaring that all proceeds from the evening will go to the Alzheimer's Foundation of America. All the air goes out of my lungs and my eyes fill with tears. I know MacDougall couldn't have known that that's what slowly took my father from me over the past decade, but it makes me hate him all the more. How can I watch these people, who can buy the best of everything, including medical care, have a party under the guise of helping people like my father, who were helpless physically and financially against the ravages of this disease?

I know I should be happy that they're raising money for Alzheimer's research. But looking around at the people laughing, drinking, and socializing, it all feels so wrong. This. This is why I never come to these things. Do any of these people really even care?

As a waiter with a tray full of tall flutes of sparkling wine passes in front of me, I deftly snatch one and gulp half of it in one go. I know MacDougall said "the whole evening," but if I can manage to at least survive through dinner and speeches, I figure that's enough. You know, in case there's a pop quiz. Though even that could be another two hours or more. Either way, after that I'm out of here. Until then, booze.

I finish my drink and swap my empty for another full glass before I approach one end of the silent auction spread, intending to at least work my way around the room to see what ridiculous, over-the-top prizes are being offered. And I'm not far off. There's the normal stuff like gift baskets of luxury spa products and chocolate, amusement park vacation packages, and service gift cards for photographers, masseurs, and catering. The kinds of things that local businesses pitch in to support a good cause and attract new customers. But there's also a private concert by a big-name pop artist, a week's vacation in a villa in Tuscany including airfare and a private driver and translator, and a private yacht party for up to three hundred people. Yeesh. Rich people. I bet those last ones all come directly from Warren Rutherford and friends.

But when I come across a four-hour sunset hot air balloon ride experience up the coast, I can't help it. I stop, a pang of longing shooting through me. Riding in a hot air balloon has been on my bucket list as long as I can remember. I've looked into it, but even if I could get the time off work, the cheapest one I've found is the better part of a thousand dollars, and I really can't justify that.

I take a deep drink of the champagne in my hand. With a glass and a half of liquid courage bubbling in my veins, and wearing a dress that makes me feel like I can do anything … well, I can't help myself from tapping the small machine next to the description with my card and entering a modest bid. When in Rome and all. And maybe I'll get extra points with MacDougall for actually participating.

"Good choice," says a voice next to me.

I look up, and my head swims a little at the motion from the effects of the alcohol. That's what I get for being a hundred and twenty pounds and downing it so fast on an empty stomach.

But if I thought that was dizzying, it's nothing compared to the man fixing me with the most gorgeous smile I've ever seen. On an equally gorgeous face framed by well-styled medium brown hair, with deep-set light brown eyes that remind me of golden honey. His full lips are parted ever so slightly as his eyes slide down my body, sending shivers up my spine.

"Thanks," I manage as my eyes travel over his well-tailored classic black tux. Even in heels, he's just a bit taller than me, with broad shoulders and a strong build. My tummy flip-flops. I tell myself it's the alcohol. Or I try to tell myself that. But being a little tipsy … well, I don't want to listen.

He extends a hand. "I'm Noah," he offers.

"Julianna," I reply, slipping my hand in his. Instead of shaking it, he raises it to his lips, placing a kiss on the back. And I swear, I've never understood what the word "swoon" really meant in a romantic sense until this moment.

"That's a beautiful name," he replies.

I don't even care how cheesy his line is, every deep, spine-tingling word out of his mouth fans the flames of my attraction to him.

"You can call me Jules," I counter.

He cocks an eyebrow and gives me a devilish smile as he lets go of my hand. "Duly noted. Sorry, I don't have a nickname. It's just Noah." His grin widens.

"It's a good name," I reply with a shy smile. God, I'm such an idiot.

He laughs. "Thanks. So, why the balloon ride?" he asks, gesturing around. "Of all the things on offer."

Another partygoer approaches, forcing me to step aside to let them access the machine. Putting me closer to the handsome and alluring man in front of me.

I look up at him, having to remind myself to breathe. Though that just reinforces his effect on me as I get a whiff of his intoxicating, expensive-smelling cologne. I clear my throat, trying to shake it off.

"I've always wanted to ride in a hot air balloon," I reply with a simple shrug.

"Ah, so you've never been before?"

I shake my head lightly, indicating I haven't. "Plus, you know, it's for a good cause and all."

His expression turns pensive. "Yes, yes it is," he murmurs. He looks up again, catching my eye. "So what do you do, Julianna?"

Hearing him purposefully use my full name sends another set of shivers running through me. Both because he intentionally ignored my direction, and because it sounds *so* good coming out of his mouth.

"I work at Rutherford Hospital," I admit.

He grins so wide, I notice a dimple in his left cheek. Could this man get any hotter?

"Let me guess. You're a nurse," he replies.

I put my hands on my hips. "Why, because I'm a woman?" I shoot back. "I could be a doctor for all you know."

He presses his lips together for a moment, clearly trying to suppress a smile. "No, because I know all the doctors at

Rutherford," he explains. "I work for the Rutherford Group in operations. We liaise with hospital administration."

I raise an eyebrow. And I'm briefly tempted to find out if this guy has any pull. But then I remember, I'm playing nice tonight and *not* putting myself in a position to get fired.

"I see," I say shortly.

He studies my face for a moment, and I wonder what he's trying to read there.

"Let's not talk about work," he finally replies, as if he can tell going down that path would lead to nothing good. "Tell me more about *you*."

I take another nervous gulp of champagne, emptying my glass this time. "What would you like to know?"

Noah flags down a waiter and gestures for my glass. I hand it over but wave off a refill. Best to wait until dinner, when I've got something in my stomach to help slow the drunkenness.

"Well, let's start with where you're from. Are you a San Diego native?" he asks, taking a glass of champagne for himself and leading me to one of the tables so we're out of the way.

"Born and bred," I admit. "You?"

"Same," he replies.

He proceeds to question me about everything — age, though not directly, whether I have siblings, my favorite foods, hobbies, those sorts of topics. And I quiz him right back. The more we talk, the less I feel like tonight is punishment. Among other things, I find out he's forty, a never-married and self-professed workaholic, has an older brother and a younger sister, and likes skiing, when he can get away for it. And that every word out of his mouth makes me like him more. But that might be the obvious chemistry floating between us as we share coy looks and smiles. I haven't flirted in so long, it almost feels like it shouldn't come this easily. But then, he's so easy to talk to. And so, so dreamy.

Unfortunately, we're interrupted about twenty minutes later when a nervous-looking young man in his mid-twenties approaches and gets Noah's attention, telling him something discreetly in his ear.

He turns back to me with an apologetic look. "I'm so sorry, but I need to step away to take care of something work related," Noah says.

I can't help my look of surprise. "So much for not talking about work tonight," I tease. "It's fine, though, really. It was lovely chatting with you."

He lifts my hand, placing another kiss on the back. "And I enjoyed chatting with you. I'll look for you later at the banquet, Julianna."

And with a confident wink that sets loose a cadre of butterflies in my stomach, he's gone.

I try not to look like a lost puppy once I'm on my own again. To avoid just that, I decide to find my way upstairs to see if there are more interesting cocktail options in the Seaport Foyer.

I'm not disappointed, on several counts, as not even a few minutes later, a Manhattan in hand, I'm heading onto a beautiful terrace just off the foyer that overlooks the marina. The sun is just starting to sink toward the horizon, and I don't think it's a coincidence that dinner was timed with sunset. It's absolutely stunning, showcasing all the best things about San Diego as the boats dip lazily in water that sparkles with all the colors of the clear sky.

But surprisingly few other partygoers are on the balcony. Not that I mind. It means I get to watching the changing colors above me without pressure, without having to schmooze, all while fulfilling my requirement to be physically present.

At nearly eight, I decide I'll stay to watch the sunset before going in, even if it makes me late. It's just too gorgeous to pass up.

"Beautiful, isn't it?"

Wondering how I already know his voice so well, I turn with a smile to see Noah settling his arms on the balcony next to me.

"How'd you find me?" I ask.

He straightens up and gives my dress an obvious once over. "You're hard to miss."

I let my hair shift into my face. I'm both flattered and a little shy again all of a sudden.

I feel his hand slip under my chin, lifting my face to look up into his.

"You can try to hide behind that gorgeous mane," he says, running his thumb along my jaw, "but red dress or not, you were born to stand out, Julianna."

"We should get inside," I mumble. My eyes dart to the glass doors behind us, to the crowds of people filing into the ballroom. "Dinner is starting."

He considers me for a moment, not moving an inch.

"Meet me after. Right here."

"You're awfully bossy," I remark, my lips curling into a smile despite myself.

"Are you saying you don't want to?" he teases, his hand sliding from my face, down my shoulder, over my arm to hold my hand in his.

I give his hand a small squeeze before withdrawing, frankly overwhelmed by how drawn to this man I am. I'm not used to noticing men or being attracted to them, much less actually wanting to act on it.

"I'm not sure yet," I reply.

He tips his head back and laughs. "Oh, I think you are. But you're not a risk-taker, are you?" His heated gaze is borderline cocky as he watches me. "I'll be here at ten. I hope you are too." But something about his tone is so sure that I can tell he thinks I will be, which is underscored when he doesn't say another word before walking back into the foyer. I lose sight of him quickly as he slips into the crowd.

While I watch the sun fully set, even I don't know what I'll do. Because this second meeting had a different tenor to it. His invitation was laced with the promise of something I haven't allowed myself in a very long time.

Too long, I decide. It's time to make Becca proud. Not that that's the measure by which I live my life. But I've been hardworking, single-minded, and overly cautious for so long. And sometimes it's good to do something you'd never normally do. Or someone, in this case.

With a catlike grin, I turn and head in for dinner.

I scan my card as I enter to receive my seating assignment, and discover I'm sharing a table with the Rutherford Hospital chiefs, all of whom I know rather well. So dinner is a much more comfortable affair than anticipated, especially knowing many of them secretly side with me over MacDougall and aren't really thrilled about being here with the glitterati either.

The food is divine, of course, though I nearly choke on it when the head of maternity jokes that it better be for a thousand dollars a plate. So when the speeches start a few minutes later, I'm already back in a place of appalled disgust at the opulent show of wealth and arrogance that surrounds this whole event.

The first speaker is from the Alzheimer's Foundation, which I actually enjoy. Hearing that this event might actually do some good makes me just slightly less grumpy. But when that's followed by a speech by Warren Rutherford himself, touting the Rutherford Group's stellar reputation, state-of-the-art hospitals, and vast resources that must be used to advance medical solutions and not just fix medical problems … I swear to the Almighty, it takes every ounce of strength I have not to call him out on the spot.

I actually even think about what I'll say. But I realize three things: First, being near the entrance of the room, with the stage on the opposite side of the cavernous space, there's no way I'd even be heard. Second, I'd just be humiliating myself in front of people who almost certainly couldn't care less about anything I had to say. And finally, that even if I did somehow manage to form an intelligent argument that could be heard all the way across the room, the spectacle of it all would almost surely get me immediately escorted from the premises. Which would almost certainly get back to hospital administration and end with me being fired or, at the very least, disciplined.

No, if I want to give Warren Rutherford a piece of my mind, it needs to be up close and personal. I down my fifth glass of alcohol, in the form of an expensive cabernet sauvignon. A potent one, as the longer he goes on, the more I drink, and the more convinced I am that I have to speak to him.

So when he descends the stage to a round of polite applause, I watch him return to his table on the right of the stage as waiters start to make the rounds with desserts and coffee. So I know exactly where I need to go.

I stand up, make some excuse about needing to stretch my legs, and start walking along the back wall to approach his table from the side. No need to make more of a scene than necessary.

I stumble more than once, and someplace in my drunken mind I realize I'm in no shape to have this conversation. But it's like something has taken over my body and I'm being propelled toward him. Though even the same part that knows approaching him in this fashion is a mistake wants to see this done on some level. And I know I'm not going to chicken out now. I'm going to tell Warren Rutherford exactly what I think of his little speech.

CHAPTER 4

I've nearly made it. Thirty feet more and I'll be face to face with the head honcho. The president and CEO of the Rutherford Group. The man whose name is on the hospital I've worked at for sixteen years. The hospital that's now so poorly run it's a joke. One I'm about to let him in on, since he seems to be under the impression that it's a paragon of advanced medicine and a jewel in the crown of his empire.

As I pass the table just before his, I'm grabbed hard around the wrist as someone rises from a seat next to me and stops me short of my goal.

"Where do you think you're going looking like hell's fury?" a familiar voice murmurs in my ear.

I spin around, attempting to take my arm back, but am pulled gently but firmly toward the speaker. Noah comes into focus as I look up into his face and read a warning there.

"Let me go," I insist as quietly as I can.

Noah pulls his head back, wrinkling his nose. "You've been drinking. Quite a lot, by the smell of it. I'm not letting you go anywhere until you tell me where exactly it is you're planning on going and to what end." His tone is firm and brooks no argument, not that I exactly want to have one here. We're already getting a few looks from the people at his table. I wouldn't so much mind, but better to save that for the real show.

I jut out my chin defiantly. "Let's just say I need to correct a few bits of misinformation in Mr. Rutherford's speech," I reply, trying my best not to sound drunk and failing miserably.

And Noah *rolls his eyes*.

"Come with me," he demands, abruptly sliding his arm around my waist and leading me forward. It's practically impossible to resist. He's very strong and very right — I'm a little too inebriated to control myself.

So I'm not able to get away as he leads me through a door in the right wall, sharply around a corner, and into an office just behind the ballroom. Closing the door, he finally lets me go.

"What are you doing?" I demand nervously as he faces me with his back to the door.

"Keeping you from embarrassing yourself," he says bluntly, arching an eyebrow.

"I'm not that drunk," I protest, even though it's taking everything I've got not to slur my words. "And you don't even know what I was going to say."

His eyebrow climbs higher. "First, yes, you are," he replies. "Second, you forget that I work for the man. I know what he's like, Julianna, and it doesn't matter what you were going to say. You're an employee at one of his hospitals, and he doesn't like being challenged by his subordinates. Especially not in public. And your current state just makes that all the worse. Your cause was lost before you even started. So, you're welcome."

"Well, I must not be totally smashed, because that actually made sense," I grumble, sinking defeatedly onto a hard settee next to the door.

He sits down calmly next to me. "Does it even matter what he said? All that matters is they just raised millions of dollars for a good cause. Was it really worth ruining your career to correct him?"

I look up at his beautiful face, suddenly completely self-conscious of what a mess I must be.

"Someone needs to," I whisper as my eyes fill with tears. "Because it's not about the speech. Well, not just about the speech. If he really thinks Rutherford Hospital is state-of-the-art …" I shake my head. "I've thought about going to see him before tonight. He should know what it's really like. Not just for the employees, but for the patients."

Noah tips his head to the side. "Their numbers always look good, or so I've been told," he says slowly. "Why don't you tell me?"

"What good will it do?" I ask, running my hands distractedly over the soft fabric of my skirt.

"Maybe it'll make you feel better to get it off your chest," he suggests, leaning back and slinging an arm behind me.

I give him a wary look, not convinced. But what the hell — what do I have to lose? I'm certainly not going to lose my job for telling Noah. So I take a deep breath. And I let it all out. About how we've been understaffed for years. That our equipment hasn't been updated to the point that even broken machines haven't been replaced, much less functioning ones swapped out for ones that are faster, more accurate, and simply vastly superior technologically. All in the name of the almighty budget.

Which was great until they hired Cal. I leave out that I know exactly how big his signing bonus was. But I don't leave out that they hired him right before denying the other medical staff raises for the second year in a row. Or that Sasha, a loyal employee of nearly a decade, was denied a promotion to a position we need filled to keep up with demand, to avoid employee burnout, and to relieve the doctors of unnecessary work. All for, in the grand scheme of things, a mere pittance over what she currently makes.

By the time I'm done, I do feel better. And, at the same time, so much worse. Because if nobody outside of our hospital — well, besides Noah — hears about it and does something, it'll impact so much more than just my job. Because it's undeniable at this point. The hospital won't survive if something doesn't change.

"Well, if that's all true, I understand why you felt the need to correct him," Noah finally says drily after I've finished.

"Of course it's true. Why would I lie?" I reply tiredly.

He lays a hand over mine, stroking the back gently with his thumb.

"You sound more clearheaded now," he says gently. "Do you feel better?"

I take a deep breath and straighten up, letting my hair fall back over my shoulders. "I do. Thank you for listening." I give him a stern look. "Are you going to let me leave now?"

A slow smile spreads across his face. "If I let you leave, do you promise to stay away from Warren Rutherford?"

"The urge has passed," I assure him. "Though I think it's just about the time I was supposed to meet someone on the terrace."

"Ah. Yes," he agrees, checking his watch. "A bit after, actually. So our distinguished leader has probably left the building anyway." I don't miss the sarcasm in his voice. He rises, offering me a hand.

I stand, slipping my hand in his, trying to shrug off lingering anger. And feeling a little too sober for comfort.

"You look like you could use a distraction," Noah murmurs, looking into my eyes.

I look away for a moment, a swell of emotion churning through me. "Very much," I reply.

I feel his hand on my cheek, and I look back up into his eyes. From the desire on his face, I already know what his next words will be.

"I have a room upstairs."

And there it is. My insides clench at the implied invitation. And even though I'd already decided earlier that I would accept, I find myself unable to voice my response. So I simply nod.

His eyes harden and his hand closes around mine firmly. He leads me out of the room and to the elevators by the stairs in the main foyer. We ride quietly, hand in hand, up nearly twenty floors before it stops. His silent, steady presence is calming, and I follow him gladly down a long hall until he pulls a keycard out and opens one of the doors at the end.

We enter into a roomy suite, with a small, elegant seating area that connects to the sleeping quarters. The giant, fluffy bed at the back of the room looks like it popped right out of a fancy brochure.

I feel almost glamorous as he lets my hand go and turns to survey me. I may be exhausted, but I know what he sees as he takes me in. A woman in an expensive dress. Made up to look like the kind of woman I'm sure he's used to bedding. And I see a gorgeous man in an expensive suit who looks like he's going to devour me bodily before the night is over.

Normally he's everything I'd hate in a man. Clearly well-off. And though he's obviously intelligent, he's also bossy and more than a little arrogant. Not undeservedly so. But right now, I don't care. I'm happy to let him take charge. Because I need to let go. I need to not think.

I watch as he undoes his bow tie, letting it hang as he unbuttons his shirt, revealing hard pecs and a set of abs worthy of his gorgeous face.

I lick my lips in anticipation as he stalks toward me, slipping a hand into my hair and grabbing me by the back of the neck.

"You're beautiful, Julianna," he murmurs, his hand sliding behind me to find my zipper. He stares into my eyes as he gives a sharp tug. I feel the dress fall away, the cool air in the room sending goosebumps across my exposed back, stomach, and legs. It's an interesting contrast to the heat building between my legs as his hand trails down my back, coming to rest on the top of my thong.

I step into him, resting a hand on his chest, offering my mouth to him. I can't remember ever wanting to be kissed so badly. Ever being set on fire by so little contact.

He grips the hair at the base of my neck, tilting my head back. A small gasp escapes me as his mouth descends upon my neck, and I feel his tongue swirling up, to my jaw, his lips feathering across my cheek before meeting mine.

His hot mouth is hard and demanding, and I yield without thought. Our bodies meet, the solid plane of his chest pressed against my breasts as his tongue slips into my mouth. All the sensations are almost too much, and I'm dizzy with desire already.

Noah's mouth becomes more insistent upon mine, and suddenly his hands slip under my backside, lifting me to him. I wrap my legs around his waist as he turns and carries me to the bed, expertly mounting it on his knees and moving up to lay me on the pillows.

He undoes my bra, pulling away from my mouth so he can remove it. After it's been tossed to the floor, he pulls his own shirt and jacket off, throwing them after it. I rear up on my elbows, grab his belt, and quickly undo it, popping the button of his pants open before sliding the zipper down.

But I'm too impatient to wait any longer. I reach into his underwear, grasping, stroking, desperate to ready him. He watches patiently, the only sign of his enjoyment the tensing of his abs as I run a thumb over the moist tip of his cock. I pull it out, and the mere sight of it has me twitching in anticipation. But he's still not quite ready for that. Since he's too far over me for me to sit up, I use my other hand to pull his hips closer to my mouth.

"God, yes," he breathes, understanding what I want. He leans a hand against the giant headboard behind me and tilts forward so he's angled down, his expanding cock just over my face. With a grin, I open to him, giving a few sharp licks and sucks until I surrender.

He takes the cue, thrusting into my throat, his head tipping back with the pleasure of fucking my mouth. I encase him with my lips, enjoying the feel of him sliding over my tongue, getting harder on each thrust, until he's filled me to the point of gagging. I give him a few more seconds before pressing on his hip.

Obligingly, he backs off, swinging his body over me and standing next to the bed to pull off his trousers and underwear. The sight of his hard cock curling toward his abs has me soaking wet for him. I reach out and grab him, stroking as I stare him down.

"I need this," I beg.

He inhales sharply, grabbing my hand. "Careful what you ask for," he warns.

I prop myself up again, pleading with my eyes.

I can see him considering something, but after a few seconds he fishes a condom out of a bag I hadn't noticed in the open closet behind him. When he turns back to me, it's rolled down his length, and I lie back, practically vibrating with need.

He climbs over me. "I wanted the first round to go a little slower," he admits, prying my legs open and settling between them. "But you're just too damn sexy." He runs a hand between my thighs and groans.

"Obviously, I think you're pretty damn sexy too," I tease back, fully aware of how slippery wet I am for him.

"You haven't seen anything yet," he murmurs, pulling me toward him and lifting one of my legs as he fists himself. "But right now, I think we both need me to fuck you senseless, Julianna."

I arch off the bed at his husky, dirty promise. And before my back meets the mattress again, he's plunged into me so forcefully that my entire body clenches around him and a long moan escapes me.

He doesn't stop, though, and immediately starts fucking me so hard that I forget everything but him. And his cock. And his hands, which are caressing me everywhere he can reach as he takes me. It's sensory overload, and I fucking love it. My orgasm builds so quickly that I don't even have time to warn him before I'm screaming and clenching around him. But not even that stops him.

He continues to fuck another orgasm out of me a few minutes later with a well-timed caress of my clit. I throw my arms over my face, unable to look at how sexy he is without feeling like I'm going to come apart at the seams. Never has a man taken me with such confidence. Never has my body responded to someone so voraciously. Never have I wanted to be owned the way he's owning me right now. But it feels out-of-this-world amazing.

Not even knowing it was possible, I'm aghast as he speeds up even more. I move my arms back down so I can watch him, the sweat sheening off his toned chest as his breathing accelerates. My legs start to twitch as a third orgasm builds under his intensity. I work my clit on my own this time, riding the wave of his efforts as I find my high. As I explode in body-melting bliss, I know he finds his release when he throws back his head and thrusts so forcefully into me I swear I'll be feeling it for the next week. In the best damn way possible.

He slumps forward while he catches his breath, then holds the condom in place as he pulls out. Once he's discarded it, he sinks onto the bed next to me, panting.

"I can't move," I say.

I feel his chuckle rumble through our touching arms.

"Good," he sighs. "Me neither."

After a few minutes of silent thought, I realize something out loud before I can stop myself. "I just had more orgasms in the last twenty minutes than I've had in the last two years."

He rolls onto his side, propping his head up on his hand.

"How's that even possible?" he asks curiously, with surprisingly little judgment.

"I'm sorry, were the cobwebs down there not a good warning?" I joke, rolling toward him.

He wrinkles his nose and shakes his head. "I think I know what the problem is. You have no idea how stunning you are, do you?"

I narrow my eyes at him. I'm not going to give this guy a hard time about being superficial. Not now. There's no point.

"My looks are beside the point," I explain. "I've just had too much on my plate for … any of that."

"There's never too much on your plate for orgasms," he replies seriously.

I slide toward him, running a finger down his chest. "Well, tonight I have nothing on my plate *but* orgasms," I say softly, looking up at him from under my eyelashes, trying to steer this away from my lack of a sex life these past couple of years.

Unsurprisingly, he takes the bait, smiling widely as he leans in and places a firm kiss on my lips.

"Perfect. What do you say we see how many we can manage?" With a wicked grin, he presses me onto my back, sliding down my body, trailing kisses all the way down to the still slick and now very sensitive warmth between my legs.

His tongue flattens against my sex, lapping at me until I'm aching and moaning once more. He goes at it like he means it, and it's not long before I'm coming from just his tongue. And he doesn't stop, slipping a finger into my pussy as I ride down the wave. I didn't expect it, and I buck my hips, a stream of curses flying from my lips. Still, he persists, stroking me until I settle into the sensation, then bringing me to orgasm again slowly with just his hand as he watches me.

"Five," he murmurs, kissing back up my belly, breasts, and neck. He slides out of bed and I catch sight of his cock, which is now hard again, and I pulsate with anticipation, knowing what he's out of bed to do.

Sure enough, he slips on another condom, and comes back to me. He helps me up, then turns me around, kneeling behind me and sliding in even though I'm tight and tender. But once he starts moving, it's only pleasure.

He pauses to gather my long hair in his hand.

"Your hair is fucking amazing, Julianna," he growls as he wraps it around his fist and uses it to pull me back onto his cock.

"Your dick is amazing, Noah," I growl back at him uncharacteristically. "Don't stop."

With a slam, he shows me that he clearly had no plans to. He pulls at my hair again until I have to lean back, and his cock presses down into my G-spot. I cry out and he wraps his other hand around my breast, working my nipple as he keeps me pulled taut with his hand and my hair and fucks me like an animal, hard and fast, from behind. Just when I think I can't take anymore, he switches it up, his hips pressed tightly against my backside, tilting so he rubs me inside until I'm building to a peak that has my whole body shaking.

"Let it out, baby," he urges through gritted teeth.

As if it was what I was waiting for, his command sends my orgasm tearing through me, triggering his as well.

This time when we sink down to the bed, sleep follows. Because you can't have six orgasms and not expect to need a nap.

CHAPTER 5

Orgasms seven and eight happened after we'd had a few hours of sleep in the form of Noah going down on me again before another session of mind-blowing sex. Then number nine when we woke again around six o'clock this morning with slower, off-the-charts sensual sex. Now, at nearly seven o'clock, I'm finishing a quick rinse in the shower while Noah accepts room service breakfast.

I come back into the room naked because, well, all I have to wear is a lacy underwear set and a fancy dress. And oddly, I don't feel self-conscious being naked around him at all. Normally, I'm hyper-aware of my flaws with a man, but with Noah, even naked I feel gorgeous. Must be the effect of all the orgasms.

Breakfast has been set at the coffee table in the seating area, so I join Noah, who is sitting on the couch in his briefs munching on a piece of toast. His eyebrows jump when he sees me.

"Are you really going to eat breakfast naked?" he asks, though I can tell he hopes the answer is yes.

"Are you really wearing tighty-whities?" I tease, settling in the chair across the coffee table from him.

"Are you really complaining about seeing me in underwear?" he parries back with a cocky grin.

I roll my eyes. Of course he knows how good he looks in them.

"I can go put on a robe if it makes you uncomfortable," I reply airily.

"Don't you dare," he says in a commanding tone. Normally, that kind of bossiness would be a total turnoff, but coming from him it's … sexy. Damn him. "Eat. I need to be at work by nine, and I'd like to make it a round ten orgasms before that."

"You must be a supervisor or a director or something," I state.

He leans back, polishing off his toast. "Why do you say that?"

I raise an eyebrow as I pick up a banana and peel it. "Because you're clearly used to telling people what to do."

"I think informing someone that they're going to have another orgasm is a little different than telling people in an office what you expect of them," he says slowly.

I note he didn't deny that he's in some sort of position of authority. But he has that air about him, so he doesn't really need to confirm what's already obvious. Either way, I'm happy to let him think he has control. It's not going to matter in a couple of hours anyway. Still, I eat the whole banana, licking it suggestively as I do.

Noah shakes his head and laughs but waits for me to finish without saying anything.

"Enjoy the show?" I tease him.

"You're a little rebel, aren't you?" he murmurs back huskily. "Thinking you're so clever with that talented tongue of yours."

I shrug blithely in answer. Internally, I'm shocked by myself. How have I become this seductress? It's equally terrifying and exciting.

He rubs his thumb over his bottom lip, and I swear the expression on his face alone has me wet again. Even though I'm so sore, I still want him. I forgot what it was like, to want someone like this. Not that I think I've ever wanted someone quite so much.

Noah lifts his backside off the couch and slides his underwear off. His semi-hard cock bounces free, but he stops it with a hand, stroking himself up and down. I make to rise from the chair but he gives me a stern look.

"Sit down," he says, somehow making it sound both like a polite request and a command.

Either way, something in his tone makes me do it without thought.

"Good girl," he purrs. "Now put your legs up on the arms of the chair."

I look at him in disbelief.

"Just trust me, Julianna," he insists.

Still skeptical, I do as he asks, spreading my legs open for him. He eye-fucks my pussy from across the small space, and I feel my nipples harden as I watch him continue to stroke himself while he looks at me.

"Now, since you've obviously been neglecting masturbation, I'm going to give you a little instruction," he explains. "I'm going to tell you where and how to touch yourself, and you're going to do it. Understand?"

I inhale sharply, both totally turned on and instantly anxious. But I nod anyway, more interested to see how this plays out than I'd have thought I'd be.

He proceeds to issue various commands that have me touching my chest, my breasts, my stomach, between my legs. He asks me how each touch feels while he continues to work himself, breathing harder as I breathe harder. Stroking faster as I stroke faster. Until he's helped me find a way to stroke my clit — in hard swipes from right to left — that, in combination with all the touches that built me up, sends tremors through my entire body.

I don't know if he's really helped me unlock self-stimulation that actually does it for me like none ever has, or if watching him while he watches me is what's doing it for me. Either way, within about fifteen minutes, my tenth orgasm crashes through me as Noah erupts across from me. The sight of his cum squirting onto his hard stomach sends me careening back to my peak before I crash down, shaking and riding the intense pleasure still thrumming in my veins.

He tips his head back, resting it on the back of the couch as his erection recedes.

When the shaking finally subsides, I climb slowly out of the chair and move around the room, gathering my clothes and getting dressed while he watches me silently. Eventually, Noah heads into the bathroom to clean up. I guess that means it's time to get back to reality.

I slip the dress on, up over my hips, and hold it to my front. I pad into the bathroom as Noah finishes wiping himself with a towel and turn my back to him.

"Zip me up?" I ask softly.

With a small smile, he does, then turns me to face him. He strokes a hand down my cheek.

"I'm going to give you my phone number. Call me if you want to," he says.

I raise an eyebrow. "You're not going to ask for mine?" I ask. Then it occurs to me. "Ah. I see. You already have a girlfriend." After the words are out of my mouth, I hope to god it's not a wife.

But he laughs. "No, the only relationship I'm in is with my job," he assures me. "But I have a feeling if I asked for your phone number you'd either say no or give me a fake one."

A guilty look crosses my face before I can stop it, and he smirks at me as if to say, *See? I was right.*

What I don't say is that even if he gives me his number, I still won't call him. This was fun, but let's face it: It's not like I have the time or inclination to get into anything with him anyway. But regardless, I let him scribble those ten little digits down on a piece of hotel stationery, slipping it into my clutch before I put my heels back on.

"Thanks for stopping me from doing something stupid last night," I say as we stand at the door. "And, you know, for the rest." I can't help the grin that settles on my lips. It was a night to remember, that's for sure. And it's probably going to have to tide me over for a while. Though hopefully not another two years. Hell, maybe I *will* call him someday if I need another night stuffed full of orgasms to keep me going.

He steps into me, cupping my cheek in his hand. He kisses me with his usual abruptness, crushing his lips to mine in such a seductive way that I almost regret leaving. But he's not for me, I remind myself. Maybe nobody is.

"I hope to hear from you soon, Julianna," he murmurs.

"Goodbye, Noah."

And with that, I slip out the door without looking back.

CHAPTER 6

"I don't know whether to be impressed or worried," Sasha admits after I've confessed everything over a late lunch on Sunday.

I chuckle. "Let's just chalk it up to drunken insanity," I joke, pushing the mostly uneaten food around my plate. "Seriously, I must've been crazy. I don't do that. Ever. And definitely not with a guy like him."

Sasha tilts her head and looks at me in that analytical way of hers. "Well, it's hard to know what he's really like, but no, I don't think I've ever known you to have a one-night stand," she agrees.

"Well, my dear, it's not the first time," I admit, ignoring the bit about what Noah is or isn't like. It's moot. "But then, that was a very long time ago, when I was young and frivolous. This felt anything but frivolous. I think it just needed to happen, if nothing else to distract me from the whole Warren Rutherford almost-mess."

"Oh, crap, speaking of almost-messes, I forgot to tell you," Sasha says, setting her water glass down with wide eyes. "MacDougall announced at yesterday's staff meeting that someone from the Rutherford Group is going to be joining the hospital administration team tomorrow to oversee some 'organizational restructuring.'" She does air quotes around the last two words.

"Noooo," I groan, sinking my face into my hands. "Not more budget bullshit!"

Sasha reaches over and strokes my arm reassuringly.

"So you'd heard about this? Are they really coming in to get rid of people?" she asks.

I drop my hands. "No, I hadn't heard, but I'm not surprised. Mrs. Knowles was promoted to director of the hospital, and she was the loudest proponent of budget cuts at last quarter's meeting,"

I grumble. I spread my hands out in defeat. "Guess that means she's getting her way."

"But why bring someone in from the Rutherford Group?" Sasha asks thoughtfully. "They haven't needed to do that before when letting people go. And lord knows there's been plenty of firings this past year."

"When staff-to-patient ratios dip below a certain level, they need approval," I explain. "Though I've never heard of them actually coming to the hospital to work with administration." I light up with a sudden thought. "Oooh, maybe they're going to fire one of the subdirectors or department chiefs. God, I hope it's MacDougall."

"I can't remember them ever having to do that, though," Sasha replies with a frown.

"Me neither," I agree. "But then, things have changed a lot. And not for the better. Because cardiac is already running understaffed. We simply can't afford to lose more people and keep up with our load."

"Preaching to the choir, sister," Sasha replies drily. "Now. Can I ask if you're going to tell Becca about your little fling? Since you clearly didn't invite her for brunch."

"I think you know I'm not," I admit, feeling a little guilty. I polish off my orange juice to hide my blush. While I may not be as private a person as Sasha is, which is why I know she'll understand, this is just something I don't want broadcasted. But I know it'll hurt Becca's feelings if she finds out and I didn't tell her. "At least, not right now. I love her, but she can't keep her mouth shut to save her life. And I don't really want it getting back to MacDougall that I turned his punishment into a sex-fest."

"If it helps, I think he's going to be a little distracted kissing Warren Rutherford's son's ass this week," Sasha says with a smirk.

My eyebrows jump. "Is *that* who's joining the admin staff? James Rutherford?" I ask.

"If that's Warren Rutherford's son, then yes, that's the rumor," she says.

Our waiter appears, dropping off the check and asking if everything was okay as he clears our plates. With our assurances that it was great, even though my food was barely half-eaten, he smiles and leaves us to return to our conversation.

"Well, he's director of finance for the Rutherford Group, so that makes sense in a way, I guess," I say thoughtfully. "But wow. That kind of seems like using a bazooka as a flyswatter."

"I didn't even realize his son worked with him until I heard that on Friday. Do you know anything about him?" she asks.

I fill out the tip and sign the receipt as I try to recall the little I've heard about him. Setting the black holder aside, I lean my elbows on the table.

"Just that he's a massive playboy," I say. "He's in the local society pages a lot for all the events he goes to. The women he dates. But I haven't heard much about him professionally."

"Is he hot?" Sasha asks bluntly, and I have to laugh.

"You're the last person I'd thought would care about that," I tease her.

Sasha rolls her eyes. "*I* don't care, but I know Becca is going to. Just trying to mentally prepare for nonstop comments if he is," she explains.

"Yeah, I thought that would die down now that she's with Vincent, but she still seems to be as vocal about good-looking guys as ever," I muse. *But then, who doesn't love a little eye candy, I suppose*, I think to myself. "Yes, he's pretty hot. Same features as his father, but you know, younger. I think he's in his early forties. Black hair. Blue eyes. Rich as sin. So of course women love him, though probably not as much as he loves himself. Lord help me, I hope I can keep my mouth shut while he's around."

"Message received, you despise entitled rich boys," she replies with a laugh. "I'm sorry, Jules. I hope this doesn't make things even harder on you at work. But I'm here, okay? You can vent to me whenever you need to."

"Be careful," I warn hear teasingly. "I might make you live to regret that offer."

She laughs and we wrap up our lunch, each heading our separate ways. I spend the rest of the day with my parents at the nursing home, thanking god it's the one Sunday a month Katie takes off. Because I know she'd suss out my little affair in an instant.

Even without the pressure of her presence, my head isn't in what I'm doing. I'm mentally checked out as I flip between wondering what shitstorm I'll be walking into at work tomorrow and flashes of my time with Noah. By the end of the day, I'm so over having all this time to think and just ready to deal with whatever comes next. Best to start getting it over with.

* * *

At our staff meeting first thing on Monday, we're told that there will be two mandatory attendance meetings this morning, one each for half of the hospital staff, to introduce everyone to our new addition, let us know more about the plan going forward, and to answer questions.

So, with little more than an hour's notice, MacDougall leaves it to me to divide our rota between the two meetings. He doesn't even ask about the gala, so clearly he's already distracted by this new development.

With Becca's help, we're able to rebalance our morning appointments to split the team evenly enough to manage. Since we don't accept walk-ins and there's nearly always a cancellation or two, I'm confident we'll be okay. It's been longer than I can remember — a decade or more — since our last all-staff mandatory meeting. Here's hoping they grant leniency if any of the emergency or maternity docs need to bow out, because it's not like we can turn those patients away or tell them to wait. But with the way things have been around here lately, I do wonder if there would be consequences. That's how bad things have gotten, and how out of line with reality administration's expectations are.

Still, just before eight o'clock, I head to the meeting, leaving Sasha in charge of the nurses' station. I purposely go by myself, as I know I'm going to have a hard enough time containing myself. No need for my bad attitude to rub off on anyone else.

I make my way to the sublevel, using the stairs, even though they come out on the cafeteria side. It means there's nobody else using them, and I have another minute or two to brace myself.

As I walk the long hall past the cafeteria to the auditorium, people are streaming out of the elevator and the south stairs toward the meeting room.

I see a few familiar faces but keep my greetings to a terse smile and a nod. I'm in no mood for banter. Thankfully, once I'm inside, the huge theater-style room is already almost full, so I'm able to take a seat near the back without being noticed. Not that in a room of more than two hundred people anyone's going to pay attention to me.

I can see Mrs. Knowles and her assistant, Lisa, preparing things on the small stage. I crane my neck, looking for the chiefs. I catch MacDougall's balding head in the front row, seated next to the maternity chief. There are a few others in their row, but I don't recognize any of them well enough to identify them from behind, fifty feet away.

With a shake of my head, I cross my arms and lean back in my seat, ready to hear exactly what James Rutherford is going to say before I decide whether or not I'll go totally off the deep end.

At eight on the nose, Lisa calls us to order and the chatter dies down.

"Thank you all for coming," Mrs. Knowles says from center stage, clearing her throat. It echoes through the microphone pinned to her shirt. "I'm going to get straight to it as I know you all have very important things to be doing." She pauses like she's expecting applause or something. What, does she want a fucking cookie for recognizing we have more important things to do right now? I barely contain my eye roll. Thankfully, she continues even without a reaction. "As your department chiefs informed you this past Friday, we will have the privilege of hosting a distinguished member of the Rutherford Group, who will be here to assist us in a hospital-wide organizational restructure. Our role as Rutherford's staff will be to fully support this effort to make our hospital run more efficiently and more smoothly." I nearly scoff out loud. *And by "efficiently," you mean "with fewer people,"* I think. "So, without further ado, I'll hand this over to our newest team member to introduce himself."

She looks pointedly at someone in the front row, who rises and climbs the stage. I'm too busy trying not to laugh at her use of the phrase "team member" to notice the person doesn't look like the pictures I've seen of James Rutherford until they turn around.

My heart drops into my shoes as he takes the microphone and pins it to the black suit jacket that's perfectly tailored over his broad shoulders, his full lips pulled down in concentration, his perfectly styled brown hair and gorgeous face unmistakable.

Noah.

But … no. What in the ever-loving-fuck is he doing here? I'm too stunned to do much but try to pick my jaw up off the floor as he looks up and smiles widely at the crowd.

"You're probably wondering why Mrs. Knowles didn't fully introduce me," he begins. "I wanted the chance to tell you a bit about myself. I've been the director of operations at the Rutherford Group for almost eight years now, working with our hospitals for another five before that. I specialize in organizational structuring, and since Rutherford Hospital is of particular importance to our group, I wanted to oversee this project myself. Now, there's no need to worry. I'm here to help. I want to make this hospital the absolute best it can be. And it's something I have years of success with, so please know you're in good hands." He winks at the crowd, and more than a few female titters ring through the room. His charm and commanding presence are palpable even from here, but rather than reassuring me, all I can feel is ice running through my veins. He spreads his hands invitingly. "Now, I wanted you to know *me* before I told you my name. So you know I've got what it takes to help, and that I'm here for the right reasons."

The pieces click together in my mind. And there's only one reason he'd be going about it this way.

"You're Noah *Rutherford*," I blurt out loudly.

Eyes the color of golden honey meet mine, and his smile falters for a fraction of a second as I see the recognition in his expression. But he's obviously well practiced at this, because his mask is back on in an instant.

"Yes, that's right," he agrees, as his eyes hold mine for a moment longer before they turn back to the rest of the crowd. And I feel like I've been punched in the gut. "But you can all call me Noah. I'm not here because I'm a Rutherford. I'm here because what you do is important, and I want to make sure we do everything in our power to support you. With that said, I look forward to meeting each and every one of you and addressing any concerns over the coming weeks. So I'll allow your chiefs to fill you in on the plan as it evolves, but for now I'm happy to answer any questions you might have."

I can't take it for another moment. Before I know what I'm doing, I'm on my feet and leaving the room. I don't even look back to see if he notices or cares. I can feel my anger rising, and I don't want to tempt fate.

I burst into the hallway, stomping all the way to the stairs, then fly up them in a rage. As I round the corner to a surprised Sasha, I simply shake my head in an attempt to discourage any questions. Unfortunately, Becca is also at the desk, and doesn't seem to notice, or doesn't care, about my obvious mood.

"That was over fast," she says, turning in her chair as I pace the floor behind her. "Well?"

"Well, what?" I snap.

Sasha raises her brows.

"Damn, girl," Becca says. "What's got your panties in a twist?"

I stop pacing and cross my arms over my chest. "Our new administrator isn't *James* Rutherford," I say pointedly to Sasha. "It's *Noah* Rutherford." I give her a meaningful look.

She looks askance at Becca, then back at me. "*The* Noah?" she asks quietly, her tone laced with concern.

I nod curtly, then scrub my hands over my face. I drop them to find Becca looking between Sasha and me.

"Okay, what's going on?" she asks sharply. "Why is he *The* Noah?"

Sasha looks to me desperately.

"I … met him at the gala. He stopped me from giving Warren Rutherford a piece of my mind after I'd had too much to drink. What he didn't tell me was that he was his son," I explain, giving her as much of the truth as I'm willing to right now. "I didn't even know Warren Rutherford had two sons." I press my lips together, trying to master myself.

"So?" Becca asks with a shrug.

I sigh and roll my eyes. "I vented to him. Told him everything I wanted to say to his father. I never would've done that if I knew who he was. Because clearly it made him want to take a closer look at the hospital."

"That's … not a good thing?" Becca hazards.

I throw my hands in the air. "Not if he's going to start firing people," I shout. A passing orderly shoots me a look. I lower my voice. "I'm sorry. I'm just pissed off."

Becca examines me for a minute, arms crossed over her chest. "There's something else going on here. I can count the number of times I've seen you visibly pissed off on one hand. Did this guy do something else to make you think …" She trails off and her eyes go wide as I see the moment the logical conclusion pops into her head. "Oh, Jules. Tell me it's true."

I freeze.

"It *is*," she hisses.

"Please, don't say a word. Especially not now, Becca," I reply harshly. "I can't take any more right now."

Becca mimes zipping her lips, locking them, and throwing away the key. Sasha taps her foot in thought.

"I am going to need details at some point though," Becca whispers. I shoot her a death glare. "I didn't mean now. Sorry." She mimes the zip and lock again, and it softens me just a little as I smile and huff a laugh through my anger.

"You know," Sasha interjects abruptly. "I'm kind of with Becca. Maybe it is a good thing. Maybe he really heard you."

I shake my head. "The guy's as arrogant as they come. And clearly not honest. He spouted all the usual corporate bullshit that spells layoffs. I've seen it enough times to know the deal, ladies. I'm sorry to say it, but it's just the truth."

"Well, shit," Becca says blandly. "This just got a whole lot less fun."

"You're telling me," I murmur, looking down into my hands and blinking tears out of my eyes. I can feel them watching me, and I'm back to pissed off in a heartbeat. I look up and shoot them death glares. "Well? Don't you two have things to be doing?" The sharpness of my tone sends them both scurrying about their business. And I do my best to focus on mine and forget Noah Rutherford even exists.

Noah *Rutherford*. How could I not ask his last name? How could I not realize? Stupid doesn't even begin to cover how I'm feeling. Like a complete and utter moron is closer to home. But also, totally terrified of whatever happens next.

CHAPTER 7

I spend the rest of the day waiting for Noah to appear around every corner I turn, in every common area I pass through. By nearly three o'clock I'm seriously considering feigning illness so I can go home and hide. Unfortunately, that's not a long-term solution. Nor does it stop Lisa from finding me as I'm about to head in to see a patient.

"Hey, Jules," she greets me as she approaches the counter.

"Hey, Lisa," I reply, rising from my chair. "I'd ask how you've been, but I imagine you've got your hands full at the moment." I give her a sympathetic smile.

"You have no idea," she agrees with a heavy sigh that puffs out her chubby cheeks as she brushes her wavy brown hair out of her face.

"Well, I'd love to hear more about it, but I have an appointment to get to. Was there something you needed?" I ask pointedly.

"Oh, right, sorry," she replies, blushing. "Mr. Rutherford would like to see you in his office at the end of your shift. He's two doors down from Betty."

I raise an eyebrow. First, because I know for a fact Mrs. Knowles would be furious if she heard Lisa use her first name. Second, is he seriously summoning me to his office? He really is an arrogant jerk if he feels the need to rub this in my face.

I briefly contemplate having her tell him to go stuff it but nix the thought just as quickly. Might as well clear the air now and let him know exactly what I think of his omitting his last name when he seduced me.

"I see," I reply tersely. "I'll see him around six then."

Lisa nods, but I don't wait for any further response. I turn and head to meet my patient, trying to shove my boiling rage deep down. I can't let this affect my job.

Except it already has. And I have a feeling it's not going to get a lot better from here.

* * *

I stand at his office door for a full five minutes, staring at the muted-orange slab while taking deep breaths. I don't know if I'm more nervous or angry. Knocking seems like a bad idea. But so does leaving. Knocking it is. I rap hard three times, and my pulse kicks up about fifteen notches.

"Come in," he calls.

Great, he can't even be bothered to get up and answer his damn door. With a sigh, I turn the knob and enter. He doesn't look up. Sat behind a hospital-issue gray metal desk, his eyes are fixed on the laptop in front of him, the sleeves of his white button-front shirt rolled up to his elbows, displaying his toned forearms. Memories try to push their way to the surface of the last time I saw him using those forearms, but I shove them back and focus.

"You wanted to see me, *Mr. Rutherford?*" I say with more than a little sarcasm, standing in front of his desk and folding my arms over my chest.

That gets his attention. His light brown eyes dart up with a look of disapproval. He closes the lid of his laptop and gestures to the chair next to me.

"Have a seat," he instructs, rising from his chair. As I sit down, I watch him rise and round the desk, closing the door to his office. My stomach flips with nerves, and I can't tear my eyes from him as he returns to his seat. He leans back, resting one arm on the armrest and crossing his legs while he considers me. "You didn't call."

I let out a dry laugh. "No, I didn't. Is that a first for you?" I shoot back.

"You're pissed. I get it. You have every right to be." He looks so damn calm it riles me even further.

I tap my finger on the metal armrest of the chair, willing myself not to rise to any bait he dangles. I decide on the spot that there's no use asking why he didn't tell me his last name. Or what he planned to do with the things I told him. He's clearly untrustworthy, so whatever bullshit he comes up with just doesn't matter. What does matter is what he plans to do next.

"Is there something work-related you wanted to talk to me about? Because otherwise, I don't think there's anything for us to discuss," I respond.

"I hope you understand that I couldn't let what you told me pass, Julianna," he says firmly.

"Well, *Mr. Rutherford*," I say pointedly. "While I can understand why you felt the need to take action, I do hope you'll fully consider *everything* I said before making too many cuts."

I can practically see his defenses rise as he uncrosses his legs and sits up straight in his chair. "I'm here to fully assess the operating needs and personnel of this establishment, *Ms. Magnusson*," he snaps back, "and I'll do whatever I deem necessary to bring things in line with the Rutherford Group's plans for this hospital."

I snort. "That's not what you said in your pretty little speech this morning," I point out. "But then, I shouldn't be surprised. Bossy, arrogant, *and* you talk out of both sides of your mouth. I should've known you were a Rutherford from the start."

His nostrils flare and he leans forward. "I'm here because I'm good at what I do. And clearly this place needs to be taken in hand if employees would rather whine about their jobs than go through the proper channels to see things improved."

A shot of adrenaline courses through me, but I control myself. Though my voice shakes as I reply, "You have no idea who I am, how hard I've worked to do exactly that, and to look after my nurses and patients all at the same time. This place needs someone who cares about the staff. Who considers how much of ourselves we put into our jobs. It doesn't need someone coming in and making decisions about who stays and who goes neither knowing nor caring about what's been really happening, and who is really at fault for the current situation. Maybe if you pulled your head out of your privileged, know-it-all ass, you'd realize that the problem *started* with your almighty 'proper channels.'"

By the time I'm done, I'm shaking with anger, but I hold his gaze, unwilling to show weakness. And unable to believe that I spent an entire night with this man. Which just further proves that one-night stands are a very, very bad idea.

He leans forward onto his arms, fixing me with a dangerously stoic expression. "I called you in here hoping we could agree to move forward amicably. But let me make one thing clear," he says, carefully enunciating each word. "If you ever speak to me like that again, you'll be fired on the spot. If employees have been allowed to talk like that to their superiors, then I think I may have had exactly the right idea of what's been going on here. So if you can't show respect, learn to hold your tongue."

"I see, much like your father, you don't like to be challenged by your subordinates," I reply before I can stop myself. "I show respect where it's earned, Mr. Rutherford." I rise from my chair, knowing I need to leave before I push it too far, if I haven't already. I give him one last look, sadness overtaking me for just a moment, wondering where the man who made me feel like a goddess is. Or if it was all just an act. A lie.

I turn to leave.

He doesn't stop me.

CHAPTER 8

I don't say a word to anyone. Not even Sasha, even though I know she'd be sympathetic. I just feel like talking about Noah and this whole mess would breathe more life and energy into it. So instead, I carry on as usual, ensuring the cardiac unit runs as smoothly as it can, putting that first. It means, at least, that there's too much to take care of to spend any time being angry at Noah Rutherford. Or time to wonder what curveball he's about to throw the hospital, or me, next.

The rumor mill is in full swing, wondering the exact same thing, so I know if so much as a pin drops out of place in the hospital, I'll hear before its echo has vanished. Though there's plenty of talk about the hot new addition to the administration staff. *That* I ignore as much as humanly possible.

The week continues eerily quietly. On Wednesday, MacDougall asks me to provide a full inventory, staff rota, our appointment schedule for the next three months, and our patient statistics for the last year. I barely bite back a snappy question about when exactly I'm supposed to do all that with everything else on my plate. I know exactly where the request is coming from, and I don't want to give our new overlord any reason to come looking for me or be dissatisfied with our unit in any way. If we're really lucky, maybe we'll come out of this relatively unscathed.

It's a lot to hope, I know.

I manage to get it all together by the end of the week, though MacDougall still grumbles about how long it took. And again, I somehow hold my tongue, not wanting to point out that *he's* our chief and he should really already have all that data or be able to easily assemble it on his own. But he's long "delegated" any real responsibility out. As far as I know, he spends his days seeing only his favorite patients and playing games on the ancient desktop computer in his office.

At nearing seventy with vision and hearing issues that would prevent him from performing surgeries — not that he was ever a particularly great surgeon anyway — it's only his grasp of politics and his in with the current administration that has kept him from being forced into retirement. But given how entrenched he is, I have no illusions about getting rid of him. They'll let me go long before they get rid of Malcolm MacDougall. Doctors of his experience and stature come with legend and tenure that outstrips even the most hardworking of the nursing staff.

On some level, I get it. A well-trained doctor is difficult to replace. But so is someone who actually gives a shit about the hospital.

I'm so irritated that I even skip the Friday evening team happy hour at our usual bar a couple of blocks away from the hospital. It's all happy couples now anyway, save me and a few others. One of those "others" being Ethan Malone, a nurse in our unit, who has always followed me around like a lost puppy. Well, me and several others on a rotating basis. But now with Sasha, Becca, and Harper all taken, I'm fearful of becoming his sole focus.

He's adorable in a little brother kind of way, though he's actually about my age. But with everyone pairing off, I feel his stares more now. And I can't even think about drinking alcohol anymore around a guy without being reminded of my last booze-soaked mistake of a night. Not that I'm in any way attracted to Ethan. Not like I am to Noah. *Was, Jules, was*, I firmly remind myself. Ugh.

I don't have time to consider what a bad place I'm in mentally before I head to the nursing home on Sunday morning. Katie is going to have a field day once she finds out what's happened in the last ten days.

But as soon as I walk in, she approaches me with a concerned look that freezes me in my tracks.

"What's wrong?" I ask, not bothering with pleasantries.

She lays a hand on my arm and stands close. "Your father's had some changes the last few days," she says quietly. "His trouble swallowing caused him to choke on Friday. He definitely got something down his windpipe and has been coughing since."

I internalize a sigh. "Any sign of fever?" I ask grimly.

She shakes her head. "Not yet. We'll get him scanned first thing on Monday in any case."

"Okay," I say softly. "Thanks for letting me know."

We stare at each other somberly. We both know this could lead to a lung infection. Which would almost certainly lead to pneumonia, given that he's eighty and has been battling this disease for so long. He's already having trouble getting proper nourishment with his swallowing issues. Complications like this are all too common at this stage, unfortunately. He's been lucky, really, to manage as well as he has for so long. It's been more than a decade, and his neurological decline has been steady, so we knew one of his symptoms would lead to more serious problems at some point.

Still, Katie gives me a lot of space, and I spend more time with Dad than usual, observing him and trying to keep him hydrated and comfortable.

As we're cleaning up from lunch, Katie smiles softly.

"Why don't we talk about something else?" she offers. "How are things at the hospital?"

I level an impatient look at her. "That's not exactly an improvement in the conversation," I respond drily.

She chuckles tolerantly. "Well, I'd ask you about your love life instead, if you had one, but we both know that's ..." She trails off as she takes in my expression and what I can feel is the extreme blush that's covered my face. A knowing smile creeps across her face. "Oh, ho ho. Well. I guess we *do* have other things to talk about, eh?"

"Is there any chance we could just not?" I grumble, turning to finish putting the dishes away.

"You pick. Hospital or love life. We can talk about whichever you want," she replies airily.

"Unfortunately, it's kind of the same conversation," I finally reply with a sigh, turning back toward her as I toss the drying towel on the counter. I throw it a little too forcefully, as it ricochets off, flying over the countertop and into the main area.

"Well, this ought to be good," she replies as she retrieves the towel. She places it gently on the counter and leans against the sink, staring at me expectantly.

I hold my breath, the pressure to spill my guts building until it's like a dam waiting to burst. Because I need to tell someone. To complain to someone.

"MacDougall made me go the annual charity gala last week, and I ended up sleeping with Warren Rutherford's son," I blurt out. "Except I didn't know it was him. He stopped me from drunkenly confronting his father, then I told him everything I hated about the hospital and how it's run before going back to his hotel room that night. Then Monday morning he shows up at the hospital, apparently to 'restructure,' and now I'm not sure if I'm more scared or angry. It's just a mess, Katie. I've made a bad situation worse, and I have no idea what to do now."

Her brow furrows. "James or Noah?" she asks.

"Huh?" I ask, totally taken aback by her response.

She shakes her head, picking up the tray full of medication she'd prepared earlier and gesturing for me to follow her.

"Which one of his sons?" she repeats. "James? Or Noah?"

I shake my head. "How did you even know he has two sons? And their names? *I* didn't even know that. And what difference does it make which one? I just gave my career a good, hard shove over a cliff."

Katie chuckles and ignores me as we enter the first room and she sees to her patient. On our way out, she gives me a smug smile.

"You forget," she says. "I worked there, all those years ago, when it was just Rutherford Hospital. No Rutherford Group, nothing to distract Warren Rutherford from pouring his heart and soul into his first hospital. Those boys lived in those halls once they were old enough to do real work, and I got to know them both quite well. And while certain things change as we age, our basic personalities stay quite the same from babe to ..." We enter my mom's room and she gestures at my mother's grimace on our entrance. She's always hated taking medicine. "Well, old age. As you can see."

I gently help ease Mom's anxiety by rubbing her back and humming the "Spoonful of Sugar" song from *Mary Poppins* that she'd sing to me every time she made me take medicine as a child. And though I know she can't consciously remember since her dementia took most of her memories not long ago, it still soothes her. Proving Katie's point. On some level, we are always who we are deep down, our experiences and feelings somehow coded into us even when we can't recall them anymore.

I blink tears from my eyes as we leave the room.

"Noah," I reply softly.

"I thought it might be," she replies. "James was vain, even as a teenager. I imagine he's even worse now. Hard to see you going for someone like that."

"And Noah? He's arrogant, a bully, and a liar. Hard to think I went for someone like that. Even if it was only one night," I grumble.

She gives me a questioning look as we enter the next room. "That sounds nothing like the young man I remember," she says, handing a small paper medication cup to the waiting elderly patient. "He was honest to a fault. And very serious. A little too serious, if you ask me."

"Good thing I didn't," I reply snarkily, helping the resident with their water as Katie takes the empty cup back.

"Except you said you have no idea what to do now," she points out. "But if you're done with your little pity party, I'll tell you what I think you should do."

I put my hands on my hips. "Okay, Yoda, what do I do now?" I gripe.

"Noah Rutherford was always very self-contained and hardworking. He worked best alone, calling the shots. He could walk into a unit, take stock, then have the place in order top to tails within weeks. No fanfare, no talk — he'd work quietly behind the scenes with the people who could actually get things done while James schmoozed and talked up a storm with everyone else. He never said as much, but I could tell it got on his last nerve."

"So what does that have to do with me?" I ask.

"If you want to avoid career suicide, you need to figure out what Noah's trying to do and help him do it," she says plainly. "Because right now, he's seen you drunk and whiny, and you need to show him that's not what you're about. Otherwise, when he cleans house, you'll be on the list of things that go."

I squirm, uncomfortable with that level of honest and direct statement of fact. She's right. The night we met wasn't my finest hour.

"That didn't seem to bother him when he decided he wanted to see a lot of other things about me," I grouse.

"Sounds like neither of you were thinking entirely with your heads that night," she points out. "But if he's still the person I knew, he's not going to do things that are against the best interest of the hospital."

"Except he said he was going to do what was in the best interest of the *Rutherford Group*," I reply, "not the hospital. What if he makes things worse?"

"You say that like it's not in the Rutherford Group's best interest to improve things at the hospital," she insists. "I find it hard to believe that'd be the case. So think of it this way: What if he makes things better? Does it matter how he goes about doing that?"

"Yes," I insist, my brain spinning through all the horrible things he could do in the name of improvement.

"Why? Because you know what's best and he doesn't?" she asks, raising a brow. "You're more like him than you know. You have to be the one calling the shots all the time or you're not happy." She shakes her head and continues down the hall. But I'm left standing there, mouth open.

I accused him of needing to earn my respect. But she's right; that's a two-way street. I've done nothing to earn *his* respect. I've whined, I've jumped into bed with a man I hardly knew, then I blew my lid and acted like a bitch in his office. Granted, not without cause, but if I didn't know me, I wouldn't have much respect for me either.

Fuck it all, Katie is right.

I'm going to have to make nice with the arrogant asshole who may or may not be out to destroy everything I've worked for.

CHAPTER 9

I return to work on Monday morning with renewed determination to take the high road and prove to Noah Rutherford that I'm not just a whiny employee. And hopefully to get in his good graces enough to be let in on whatever he has planned, so I can either prepare for it or jump ship before it's too late. I hope to hell it's not the latter.

At the morning meeting, MacDougall informs us all that Noah will be in our unit this afternoon to take a tour, meet everyone, and ask a few questions. I try to quash my nerves, but the tension must be obvious, since as soon as we're back at the nurses' station, Becca and Sasha both pounce.

"Okay, we've been leaving you alone on this, but I can feel your anxiety right now, girl," Becca says as quietly as she can, her eyes darting both ways down the hall.

Sasha nods in agreement, reaching out to gently squeeze my hand. "What can we do?" she asks softly.

I huff a dry laugh. "You girls are sweet, but I'll be fine. I'm sure I'll barely even have to see him, much less talk to him." They both give me skeptical looks. "*Really*. I appreciate the concern, though."

Suddenly, MacDougall materializes around the corner, causing us all to bolt upright and look like we were working all along.

"Ah, Ms. Magnusson. Good. I thought I should inform you that you'll be conducting Mr. Rutherford's tour this afternoon," he says, pompously staring down his old, crooked nose at me. "He'll be by at one o'clock."

Now my eyebrows shoot up, my chill totally gone. "I'm sorry, what?" I all but screech. I feel Sasha squeeze my hand hard, snapping me back to the reality of the situation. "I mean, of course, sir. Will you be joining us?"

"You can just bring him to my office when you're done with the formalities," he responds. "I'll take it from there."

And without waiting for a response, or even thanking me, he walks away. I have to take three deep breaths before I'm not seeing red.

"We'll take care of the schedule," Becca assures me.

"And I can ask Cal to do the tour with you," Sasha offers. "He's a great buffer."

I look between the both of them gratefully.

"Thank you," I say, breathing out a sigh. "But I'm sure Cal has more important things to do than hold my hand. Besides, I've been more or less doing a good part of MacDougall's job for years, might as well do this too."

"This is different," Becca says quietly. "We have to put up with a lot of bullshit around here, but you don't have to do this alone just to prove you can, Jules."

"Actually, I think I do," I reply.

Sasha squints at me. "For Noah Rutherford, or for yourself?" she asks insightfully.

I give her a dim smile. "Both."

* * *

At a quarter to one, I'm trying to distract myself with paperwork when someone clears their throat. My eyes snap up to the counter. Noah. Of course he's early.

I take a deep breath, click save, lock my screen, and shut off my monitor.

"Mr. Rutherford," I greet him formally, rising and rounding the desk to meet him. "Welcome to the cardiac unit."

I try not to notice how handsome he looks in the plain tan slacks and navy button-front shirt he's wearing that, once again, has the sleeves rolled up to the elbow. And his shirt is again so well-tailored that it fits snugly against the muscles of his biceps and chest. Good lord.

"Nurse Magnusson," he replies with a polite nod. But his confused, darting glance betrays his cool tone. "Will Dr. MacDougall be joining us?"

I slip my hands into my pockets, willing myself not to laugh at his obvious discomfort. This might be more fun than I thought.

"I'll be conducting your tour before you meet with him," I reply. "Is there anything particular you'd like to start with, or shall I just show you around?"

"Is there a reason he asked a nurse to conduct the tour rather than doing it himself?" Noah asks testily.

"Nurse practitioner," I correct him. "And I'm afraid you'll have to ask him that yourself. If you'd like, I can take you to his office straight away instead?"

He considers me for a moment before giving a small shake of his head. "Lead the way," he says. His expression is unreadable, but I don't let it faze me.

With a well-practiced fake smile, I do just as he asked. I show him everything. The exam rooms, the observation rooms, the surgical areas. Storage, supplies, sterilization areas, equipment trolleys, the whole shebang. I walk him through our patient numbers, our typical staffing rotations, our interdepartmental transfers, everything. Well, almost everything — I skip the breakroom since that seems like a bit much.

We manage to snag a few minutes each with Dr. Carson, our senior cardiologist, and Cal, and Noah asks them each the same generic questions before continuing on our way.

He meets most of the nursing staff, all of the MAs, and a handful of orderlies who are shared with other departments.

After more than an hour of walking the entire unit while talking endlessly, with few questions from him, we finally circle back to the nurses' station. Becca sits at the desk, quiet as a mouse, but I know her ears are wide open.

"So that's everything I can think of," I tell him. "Did you have any further questions for me on our numbers or anything else we covered?"

Noah looks a little overwhelmed.

"Not at the moment," he admits. "Everything seems to line up with the reports I was given."

I snort. "It should, since I made those," I reply.

That gets an eyebrow raise. "When is the other ARNP scheduled again?" he asks.

"Nurse Marcus works night shift and Sunday," I respond. "She should be here around six. I think the only other staff member you didn't meet is Dr. Franklin, and he's on medical leave for knee surgery until next week. I think that covers everyone."

"Almost. What's Dr. MacDougall's patient load like?" he asks.

Becca coughs behind me and I purse my lips. "Well, he's our next, and last, stop," I reply. "I'm sure he'd be happy to discuss that with you."

Noah huffs a small laugh. "I'm asking you, Nurse Magnusson."

I rub my lips together, trying to figure out how to say this without putting myself in danger.

"Dr. MacDougall typically serves in a more administrative capacity," I reply hesitantly. "As such, he only sees established patients."

Noah nods slowly. And I'm pretty sure he understands exactly what's going on.

"Do you have any other questions for me?" I ask, itching to get this over with.

"No," he says. "But I will say, I've had a fair few conversations with the other chiefs and doctors in the hospital. Your name came up quite often."

I bite back a laugh. "Yes, well, I've worked here for sixteen years, in almost every part of the hospital," I reply with an affected shrug.

"Huh," he grunts. "Yes, well, that might explain things, as it usually came up when I asked who had the most knowledge of how things *really* work around here."

I try not to look smug. I really do. I'm not sure if I'm successful or not, because he just stares at me for a minute.

"Like I said, I've worked here a long time. And I do my best to listen to the people I work with to understand what's going on. I'm often involved in resolving interdepartmental issues."

"Seems like a lot of talk doesn't filter up the proper channels," he replies.

I hear Becca huff softly behind me, but Noah makes no sign that he heard her, so I try to pretend like it didn't happen and hope she doesn't do it again.

"Oh, it does," I assure him. "At the proper times. For example, we discussed many of those issues at our quarterly budget meetings last month."

That gets a startled look from him. "You went to *budget meetings*?" he asks incredulously.

"Well, I'm on the budget committee, so yes," I reply, folding my arms over my chest defensively.

"I wasn't aware nurses ..." He trails off at my steely glare. "My apologies. I wasn't aware that *nurse practitioners* were typically involved in budgeting."

Oooh, I got *his apologies*. I'm sure that doesn't happen often.

"Each department has a chief and one or two other representatives, based on department size, who are acquainted with the department's needs to properly represent that unit's interests," I say with a shrug. "Dr. Franklin hates dealing with financial matters and Dr. Thompson is too new to have a full understanding of everything. And Sarah — sorry, Nurse Marcus, prefers to keep her night hours, so she's not able to attend the meetings. So it's me and Dr. Carson. Is there an issue with that?"

"No, no issue at all," he murmurs, his eyes scanning my face. "I think I'm ready to speak with Dr. MacDougall now."

"Then right this way," I reply, gesturing to the corner left of the nurses' station. As he walks around it and out of sight, Becca holds up a hand as I pass. Suppressing a smirk, I reach out and high-five her as I walk by. Take *that*, Noah Rutherford.

* * *

I'm with a patient later that afternoon when there's a knock on the door. I excuse myself and step out to find Sasha twisting her fingers anxiously in the hall.

"Mr. Rutherford wants to see you in his office," she says softly. "He called just now and didn't say when, so I thought it best to let you know immediately."

I shake my head. Here I thought he was starting to understand.

"If he calls back, I'm with a patient. I'll go up once I'm done, but you'll have to get Becca to have Dr. Carson or Cal cover my four p.m."

"I can take over now, if you'd like?" she offers.

I fold my arms over my chest and give her a stern look. "You're not doing ARNP duty unless you're *paid* to do ARNP duty," I respond. "But thank you."

With a weak smile and a nod, Sasha walks away, leaving me to return to my patient.

As I wrap it up, I can't help wondering if Dr. MacDougall said something to Noah that prompted this. I shake myself, trying to focus on the task at hand, instead of the sea of what-ifs.

It's not long before I'm heading up to Noah's office anyway, braced for whatever's coming.

His door is open when I arrive, but I still knock politely, hovering in the doorway.

"Come in," he calls without looking up. "And close the door behind you."

Oh. Fuck.

I swallow hard and do as he asks, sinking meekly into the chair across from him. He finishes whatever he was writing on the tablet in front of him, then throws the pen down, leaning back in his chair and crossing his legs.

"I owe you an apology," he says frankly, threading his fingers together in his lap.

I snort and say, "Several, by my count." Then immediately wish I could crawl in a hole and die.

But he doesn't get angry. In fact, he tips his head back and laughs. And damned if the sound, the absence of sternness from his expression, doesn't remind me of the Noah I met that first night. My insides tighten in a way that's totally contrary to the moment.

"Yes, probably," he admits, clearly amused.

I spread my hands. "What for?" I ask, trying to cover my gaucheness.

"For doubting you. I've reviewed your reports and, after speaking with nearly everyone in the hospital, everything you said to me at the gala was spot-on. Technology and staffing both have serious deficiencies."

Our eyes meet, and there's something more in his expression than an apology. It's the first time he's mentioned that night since our initial meeting here in his office. And something about the reference has injected a tension into the room that wasn't there a minute ago.

"I told you I wasn't as drunk as you thought I was," I murmur, not breaking eye contact.

He leans forward. "Yes, you were." His expression is intense. Intense like … a flash of his face while he was inside of me crosses my mind, and I inhale sharply. I've been so careful not to think about it since he showed up, but that one slipped through my defenses.

"Okay, maybe right at that moment I was. But not …" I stop, blushing, realizing that whatever I was about to say would be completely inappropriate. That everything I'm thinking is completely inappropriate. And suddenly, I remember Katie's advice. Taking a deep breath, I get my head back on straight. "But that's not the point. I'm glad to hear you understand the issues we're facing. What can I do to help?"

His lips pull into a small smile as his eyes roam over my face. Like he's remembering what I looked like while he fucked me too. I squirm uncomfortably in my chair, hoping I can regain some semblance of self-control.

"You can help me figure out how we get the employees to speak up more," he eventually replies.

And just like that, reality crashes in like a bucket of ice water.

"I'm sorry, did you not hear me earlier when I said they already are? Maybe you should be asking how we get leadership to listen. But that might be a touch too ironic."

Damn my mouth. I clamp it shut as I watch him assess me. Differently this time. Colder.

Not that I blame him. Why can't I control myself around him? I'm not one to pick fights, but I can't seem to help myself around him for some reason.

"Complaining to one another, and random strangers," he looks at me pointedly, "doesn't count. I'm talking about approaching their supervisors directly — privately — to report issues or concerns. Not broadcasting them to the grapevine and hoping that leadership will magically be able to separate fact from gossip. That can't be coming through one person, no matter how qualified she is. Each employee needs to be able to own their own voice or there's no knowing how much of a problem something really is."

"Uh, except by using your eyeballs, maybe?" I retort, totally ignoring his sort-of compliment. "You literally *just* said you've looked into things and came to the same conclusions I did. Why does it take loads of people complaining before the chiefs or directors act on something? Shouldn't *they* be the ones proactively looking for ways to make things run better around here?"

"They do have some responsibility, yes," he admits. "But they have many others that prevent them from being everywhere all at once. And I understand why they wouldn't rely on one squeaky wheel to be their only source of knowing when action needs to be taken."

I snort. "You mean I've worn out my welcome with MacDougall, so he doesn't believe me anymore."

"He does think you exaggerate, yes," Noah admits.

I throw my hands in the air. "Fine. Then maybe start directing leadership to stop punishing people who report issues. I'm the only one who does because I know they won't fire me. Or, at least, I care more about fixing things than being fired."

His brow furrows. "Punishing in what way?"

Oh, fuck. I know I've stuck my foot in my mouth now. Because no matter how I answer this, I'm screwed. If I backpedal, I prove MacDougall's point that I'm exaggerating. If I tell the truth, I'm speaking negatively about my bosses without any way to prove that I'm being honest. And clearly Noah Rutherford is all about proof.

How do I convince him that they've fired people for less? That they often fire people simply to replace them with friends, or children of friends, or people who are willing to kiss their asses? That nobody wants to give them any excuse to get rid of anyone who isn't indispensable? How can a man like Noah Rutherford understand any of that when he's likely only in the position he's in because of his name, even if he is good at what he does?

Instead of asking all these questions out loud, I sit silently, giving him a pleading look. Asking without words that he not make me voice these things.

I've never felt so powerless as his eyes demand answers. But I have none to give.

"You're not going to tell me, are you?" he finally murmurs.

I shake my head, looking down into my lap. A few tears fall onto my hands, and it makes me angry. Angry that I've shown vulnerability in front of this man. This man who I was so happy to be vulnerable with not so very long ago. But that was when I had no idea who he was or what he was capable of.

With a sigh, he rises, opening his office door. I stand at the clear dismissal, not meeting his gaze. Too upset to acknowledge his power in this moment.

"I can't help if you don't talk to me," he says as I pass him.

I freeze, but I don't turn around.

"Sometimes being a leader means helping people who are too afraid to use their voices," I say, my own voice strained.

"Julianna," he breathes softly.

And I turn and catch his eye before I can stop myself. My fragility in this moment is reflected in his eyes. I can see that he's struggling. That he doesn't know what to do. But I have a feeling it's about more than what we'd been discussing. And I don't know what to do about *that* either.

He steps toward me, raising his hand to brush a tear from my cheek. I don't flinch or make any move to stop him. It feels too good to remember what it's like when he touches me. Even if it's just a small touch. A single moment.

"I see how much you care about this place," he says, looking down into my eyes. "You can trust me, I swear. I'm not trying to make this harder on you."

"How can I trust you when you didn't believe me in the first place?" I point out.

"Because trust, like respect, is earned," he replies firmly. "And for what it's worth, you've earned both from me."

My lips part and my eyes close.

"But you haven't earned mine," I whisper.

I reopen my eyes and look up at him. I knew there would be hurt in his eyes, but I wasn't prepared for what that would make me feel. That I feel for him at all. This is all so ... messy.

"I will," he promises.

I feel his hand slide around mine, then he lifts it to his lips. He places a kiss on the back of my hand, transporting me back to the moment we met. A moment filled with hope. But this time I don't swoon. Because I know exactly who he is now. And though hope still blooms somewhere inside me that this whole situation will work out for the best, I can't see it ever working out with him. No matter what my traitorous heart says.

CHAPTER 10

"I still don't know why being a Rutherford counts against him," Sasha insists as she twirls her martini glass on the small bar table. Even though it's a Tuesday night, the place was still too packed to snag a booth. "Shouldn't that mean he cares *more* about the hospital?"

I shake my head. "I wish that were true," I reply. "But if it were, why would things be the way they are now?"

"I'm with Sash," Becca pipes up. "Dude may be a daddy's boy, but they can't afford the bad press if they start tearin' shit up."

"Except every employee has signed NDAs, so how would anyone ever know?" I point out. Granted, those are supposed to be for patient confidentiality, but it extends to all hospital business.

"Pfff," Becca scoffs. "Please. I could drive Vincent's truck through the loopholes in that thing."

"Vincent lets you drive his truck?" Sasha asks curiously.

Becca shrugs and I wave a hand. "You're both missing the point. Just because he's a Rutherford doesn't mean he's going to make things better. The Rutherford Group is all about the bottom line. Sure, it may have started to help people, but they've long since focused more on profitability and appearance."

"Well, they clearly don't pay attention to staff complaints," Sasha agrees drily. She raises her glass. "Here's hoping we're not all looking for jobs by the time this is all over."

"I'll drink to that," I say, lifting my highball glass to meet hers.

"Hell, I'll drink to anything," Becca jokes, her pint glass meeting ours.

We all take a drink, then Becca sets hers down and rubs her hands together.

"So, are you planning on jumping back into bed with Moneybags?" Becca asks with a lascivious grin.

"Nope, nope, nopety, nope, nope, nope," I chant. "I hadn't planned on it even *before* I found out who he was when he started working at our hospital."

"Awww, come on. Just because he's a jerk doesn't mean you can't hit that again," Becca whines. "That man is fucking *hot*."

"Becca, you think every man is fucking hot," Sasha points out.

Becca wrinkles her nose and sticks her tongue out at Sasha. "Do not. How many times did I turn Mark down?"

Sasha tilts her head. "Twenty-five? Thirty? I lost count."

"Precisely," Becca says matter-of-factly. "So don't go pretending like I don't have standards. Or that Noah Rutherford isn't delicious in those tight-as-hell shirts. Damn, that boy's got some muscles."

I choke on the sip of alcohol I'd just taken. Well. Guess I'm not the only one who appreciates Noah's workwear.

"Look," I hedge. "I'm not saying he's not attractive. Or that that night wasn't … well, it was phenomenal. Record-breaking." Becca raises an eyebrow, and I hold up a hand. "But I've learned my lesson about dating at work. And even if I didn't, he's exactly not my type."

Becca looks insulted, and I know what's coming.

"First of all," she says, snapping a finger up, to count or for emphasis, I'm not sure which, "dating at work has turned out pretty damn well for us," she gestures between her and Sasha, "and second of all, girl, please. Rich and handsome isn't your type? But mostly … I'ma need to know exactly what records we're talking about here." She leans forward on her arms, eagerly awaiting my response.

I roll my eyes so hard it hurts a little.

"First of all, you don't *need* to know anything about that night," I mimic her, shutting that down real quick. "Second of all, *no*, entitled rich boys just don't do it for me." Such a lie. Well, in this case anyway. Because Noah very much did it for me. Ten times. "But mostly, I'm just past that phase where I'm open to risking my career for a man. No offense to either of you, but you both are fully aware of how badly that can blow up in your face."

"Well, you're not wrong," Sasha agrees hesitantly. "But we know you pretty well, Jules. And it feels less like you're not open to this because of who he is and more because, well, you've kind of just given up on the whole dating thing." She shrinks back into herself and shoots Becca a look, clearly begging for support now that the words are out of her mouth.

I open my mouth to protest, but Becca beats me to the punch.

"Don't even think about disagreeing with that," she says sharply. "You were severely dick-deficient for way too long. Try to deny it."

I purse my lips together, nostrils flaring. She knows I can't.

"That's right," she says smugly, crossing her arms over her chest. "So don't even pretend like you didn't enjoy it. Or that regular access to the D wouldn't vastly improve your life."

Sasha blushes bright red and hides behind her drink.

I shake my head, knowing it's impossible to argue with Becca.

"I'll take that under advisement. Can we talk about something else now?" I beg.

Becca happily launches into a story about Vincent and some cute thing he did last weekend, and I gratefully down the rest of my drink while she does, muttering encouraging noises and agreements here and there. Once she's exhausted, Sasha manages to catch us up on her life. And it feels nice to listen to them, to not think about my own crap. At least for one night.

* * *

The next afternoon I get a most unexpected voicemail on my cellphone telling me I've won the hot air balloon ride I bid on at the gala. Certain they must be mistaken, I call the number to correct them, only to be told that it was the annual "gimme" prize — the one auction item that *everyone* will win that year. Apparently it's a secret item that is different at every gala to try to get people to bid on multiple items in hopes of snagging the freebie. Who knew? I'm given an email address to contact the person who runs the rides.

And for the first time this week, I'm actually smiling as I compose and send an email. Though I'm also hoping I'll be able to manage to get it scheduled around work, a bit nervous that the sunset part of the "sunset hot air balloon experience" is toward the *end* of the ride. Which would mean the ride would start in the late afternoon. A near impossibility with my job. But nothing ventured, nothing gained.

To my utmost surprise, by the end of the day I've learned the person running it has an opening for Sunday. Saturday is the Fourth of July, and apparently the Sunday booking didn't realize they'd made it for the wrong day, thinking they'd get to see fireworks. Their stupidity is my gain, and I agree to meet at five o'clock, beyond excited. Also a first for the week.

* * *

On Thursday my high takes an abrupt cliff dive when, as I'm handing things off to Sarah that evening, MacDougall calls her into his office.

With a sick feeling in my stomach, I decide to hang around and wait to hear what he wanted. Sarah comes back not fifteen minutes later looking grim-faced.

I wait expectantly as her eyes follow one of the orderlies around the corner before she says anything.

"They're letting Caroline go," she tells me in a low voice.

"*No*," I gasp. "You're already short nurses on second shift. What the hell?"

She rolls her eyes as she pulls together a stack of files. "Apparently, we don't have enough patients to require more than one nurse."

I throw my hands up. "Like that's all you guys do. Who is going to handle sterilization, stocking, and setup?"

Sarah sighs deeply. "Zoe and I will get it done, don't worry," she assures me in an uncharacteristically snappish tone.

"Hey," I say, laying a hand on her arm. "I hope you know that's not how I meant it."

"I know," she agrees. "I'm just shaken up. The way he was talking … I don't know, Jules. I wouldn't be surprised if they get rid of me next."

My blood turns to ice. "Why would you think that?"

She glances both ways down the hall. "When I met Mr. Rutherford night before last, he asked if I thought we needed a full staff for second shift. If there needed to be *anyone* besides an on-call doc."

"But you told him about all the other functions you guys perform, though, right?"

"Of course I did," she scoffs. "He didn't seem convinced you guys couldn't handle that as part of first shift."

A boiling anger bubbles in my gut. "Then maybe he needs a little more convincing," I say heatedly.

"Don't do anything rash, Jules," Sarah says, a warning in her voice.

I give her a look. "Why, because if I get fired, then you have to work the day shift?"

She grins. "Can't get anything by you. Seriously though, I don't want you to put yourself in the crosshairs, okay?"

"You know me. I can't make any promises."

She gives me a concerned look. "Yeah, that's what I'm afraid of."

"Whelp, I'm done for the day. See you for morning handoff?"

"Mhm. See you tomorrow," she grumbles, heading to put away the stack of files she collected.

As soon as she's gone, I head for the elevator. Time to give Mr. Moneybags, as Becca so aptly named him, a little dose of reality.

While I ride up in the elevator, I pull my ponytail loose. A sigh escapes me. It's a small dose of relief before I step into the lion's den. Hopefully he hasn't left for the day already. Though something tells me he'll still be here.

I find out quickly that I'm right, as I approach his open office door and see him on his cellphone, pacing the back wall of the small room. He runs a hand through his hair, clearly agitated as he talks business gibberish with the person on the other end.

I stop in his doorway, leaning against the frame as I watch him. It's more hypnotic than I'd like it to be, watching his muscles ripple under his shirt, his honey-colored eyes lit up and intense.

Then they land on me and my stomach does that damn flip-flop thing. Traitor. I wave meekly and he quickly ends his call.

"Julianna," he says, sounding half like a greeting, half like he's surprised to see me. He gestures at the chair across from his desk as he retakes his seat. "What brings you here?"

I approach, standing next to the chair, but not sitting.

"I think you know. How am I supposed to trust you, respect you, when you don't even bother to give me a heads up before firing one of my nurses?" I ask pointedly, my tone laced with as much disgust as I can manage.

"I wasn't aware I needed your approval," he responds sharply.

"You seriously didn't think I'd be a little unhappy with that?"

"Unfortunately I'm not here to make you happy, *Nurse Magnusson*," he replies.

My eyebrows shoot up. So that's how he wants to play it.

"We're really back here, huh?" I ask, shaking my head. "Fine. In case it wasn't obvious, second shift doesn't just sit around and twiddle their thumbs. We don't have the staff to manage their duties as part of first shift. I can give you whatever data you need to substantiate that. But I'd like you to reconsider letting Caroline go."

He's silent for a moment. Hopefully reconsidering. But when he rises from his chair and comes around the desk, leaning on its edge so he's right next to me and at my level, I have no idea what to do. His nearness is unsettling on several levels, and I can see darker amber flecks in his honeyed eyes. I swallow hard, suddenly unable to speak.

"What if I told you that letting her go is part of a bigger plan that I can't share yet?" he ventures.

"Short-term pain for long-term gain? That's what you want to sell me?" I ask, crossing my arms.

He grins, and it sends my tummy flipping again. Damn him.

"Yes, something like that," he admits.

"Except that would require me to trust you," I point out. "Which I don't yet."

He raises an eyebrow. "You said 'yet,'" he replies, sounding a bit shocked. "That's progress, Nurse Magnusson." This time when he says my name, it doesn't sound like an admonishment. It sounds ridiculously sexy. And I suddenly feel like the temperature in the room has jumped a good ten degrees.

"You're not going to flirt your way out of this," I insist. But even I note that I don't sound particularly convincing.

"No?" he muses, his eyes searching mine. He rises, towering over me. He's taller than I remember, but then, the last time we were this close, I was wearing heels. "I guess you'll just have to wait until I can prove it to you, then."

"What does that mean?" I ask warily.

"It means, if you can't trust me, at least give me some time," he replies.

"But you're still going to let Caroline go."

"Yes, I'm still going to let her go."

I narrow my eyes at him. I can't honestly say Caroline was our most productive nurse, and if I'd had to pick someone to go, it probably would've been her.

"Fine," I reply tersely. "But don't be too long about it."

I turn to leave, but he catches me by the elbow. I look back up into his eyes, which are now so filled with intensity it takes my breath away.

"Don't look at me like that," I whisper. But I can't move, pinned in place by his gaze.

"Then don't come in here with your hair down," he whispers back. He reaches up and runs his hand down the locks tumbling over my shoulder and along my arm. Shivers race up and down my spine.

"Noah ..." But even I have no idea what I was going to say.

"Why didn't you call?" he murmurs.

"Why does it matter?"

"I don't know. It just does."

I pull back. "I'm sure you'll get over it. As it is, if it wasn't off the table before, it certainly is now."

"It doesn't have to be," he replies.

"Yes, it does."

"Why?" he insists.

"Why won't you let this go?" I retort. "I'm sure there are a million other women who would happily hop into bed with you." It comes out angrier than I intend, but I don't like him putting me in this position.

But Noah looks sincerely offended. "I'm not my brother, I don't sleep with just anyone," he says.

"Just employees who can't say no?"

"You can say no. You do say no. Quite often, actually," he points out.

"I'll keep saying it until you listen. But it's not fair for you to keep asking, given your position. You must realize that," I throw back at him.

"You're right," he admits, leaning back against the edge of the desk and giving me a little breathing space. "It's not fair. But then, you're not exactly being fair either. You were fine sleeping with me when you didn't know my last name."

"That wasn't usual for me either," I respond. "Believe me."

"I do. It was special. This," he gestures between us, "is something. You're not the least bit curious if it's more than good sex?"

"No," I lie. And I have to stop myself from correcting him that it was *great* sex.

He laughs. "Damn, you're stubborn."

"Yep. So you might as well give up now."

He pushes up off the desk, looking down at me. "Is that what you want? For me to give up?"

I throw my hands up. "I've only been saying it this whole time," I reply in exasperation. "But I guess you weren't listening."

"Oh, I heard you, loud and clear. But the thing about reading a person is not just listening to their words," he replies, his eyes fixed intently on mine. "It's also their body language. How fast they're breathing." He pauses pointedly, and the bastard is right. I'm practically panting. "The blush of their cheeks." Fuck him, he's right again, and it only makes me blush harder. "Sometimes our bodies betray us, Julianna."

I clench my jaw against the surge of desire welling in me. He's not wrong. If he pushed just a little harder, we'd be fucking on the desk in no time at all. And I'd be loving every minute of it. Until it was over, anyway. After which I'd be kicking myself for more or less sleeping with the enemy. It was different when I didn't know that that's who he was.

But he backs off, stepping away and going to his side of the desk. He puts his hands on the back of his desk chair, and we stare at each other for a minute. I'd break the silence, but I have no clue what to say. For once.

"I don't mean to push," he finally says. "But I'm not going anywhere. And you'll see. Just give me more time, and you'll understand."

I shake my head, snapping myself out of the trance he's had me in. He doesn't know me at all. He doesn't know where I come from, what my life is like. Someone like him could never understand my world. So while I am obviously still very attracted to him, no amount of time can change our fundamental differences.

But hopefully, if nothing else, whatever he's got planned for the cardiac unit, and Rutherford Hospital, will start to make sense. And maybe it'll even all be okay. Then I can get back to my life, sans Noah Rutherford.

CHAPTER 11

I spend Sunday morning at the nursing home, trying not to worry about my father's now raging lung infection that isn't responding well to antibiotics. Aspiration pneumonia looms in his future, and I know I'm just going to work myself into hysterics if I think too much about it. Or about my mother's increasingly frail frame. Their respective degenerative diseases are eating away at the strong, loving people I once knew.

And my finances, for that matter. But I try not to discuss any of that while I'm there, with Katie or otherwise. All I can do is what's in my power and let go of the rest. It's certainly a constant battle when I'm not at work, when I'm not so busy there's no time to think.

But as I head out of the city a half hour ahead of my scheduled hot air balloon tour, the excitement overrides it all, and the only thing I can think about is soaring among the clouds, feeling free for once in my life.

I follow the directions I was given to an address along the coast, just west of the Del Mar Fairgrounds. Driving down the road toward my destination, I can already spot a striped red-and-white domed top that must be the hot air balloon. Excitement unfurls in my stomach. And maybe a bit of nerves too.

I pull into a driveway with a heavy iron gate that sits open and drive down the narrow road. It ends in a large, circular parking lot with a large storage shed on the south side. I park just inside the circle, on the easternmost edge. A vast field surrounds me as I step out of the car.

The only other vehicle there is a Range Rover, parked on the westernmost side of the circle. Beyond that, I can see the balloon. I let out a snort, realizing I should have known that one of Mr. Rutherford's rich friends owned the balloon and donated rides for all their stuck-up jerk friends. In fact, I bet they own this whole parcel of land. Prime freaking waterfront real estate just outside of San Diego proper for their luxurious little hobby.

Lord, I hope I'm not about to spend three hours with the most pretentious asshat on the planet. With a sigh, I resign myself to whatever I'll have to endure to do this. Because like hell I'm passing up this opportunity.

Equal parts guarded and eager, I approach. But as I get closer, I don't see *anyone.* Just the large, high-sided woven brown square basket that looks like it could comfortably hold six people, and the massive balloon hovering over it. Thick ropes clearly bolted into the ground are attached to pegs on the corners of the basket, holding it to the earth.

I stand about twenty feet away, unsure of what to do, realizing I never got a name or a phone number for the ride operator.

"Hello?" I call out nervously.

A man pops up from inside the basket, holding a wrench in his hand. Well, that explains that. A loud noise above him startles me, drawing my attention up to the mechanism in the balloon's opening that is now spewing fire, presumably to keep the balloon properly inflated.

When my eyes drift back down, the man has moved toward me. And if I was startled a second ago, now I'm just shocked. And pissed off.

"What the fuck are *you* doing here?" I snap as Noah approaches.

He grins, rubbing his hands on a dirty rag as he takes in my fitted jeans and green T-shirt.

"She's mine," he replies, gesturing toward the balloon. "And it's nice to see you too, Julianna."

I cross my arms over my chest. "I should've known," I grumble, shaking my head. "Any particular reason you didn't bother mentioning that you *owned* the damn hot air balloon trip I was bidding on?" I scoff internally, adding it to the list of things he conveniently forgot to tell me that night.

He tucks the rag in his back pocket, stopping in front of me. "I don't usually start conversations with, 'Hi, I'm Noah Rutherford. Would you like to take a ride in my hot air balloon?'" he replies.

I raise an eyebrow, willing myself not to laugh at him mocking himself. "Really? It seems like that's exactly the kind of thing that would impress the kind of woman you'd want to be with," I retort.

"Oh, ye of little faith," he says with a smile, shaking his head. "Does that mean you're not interested in going up?"

My throat constricts at the idea of not going.

"Can you really fly this thing?" I ask, not even sure if I really want to be trapped with him. Because he looks so casual in his old, faded jeans and white tee. So happy. So *hot*. I'm only human, after all, but I don't want to be tricked into falling for his charms. Into forgetting what he's done, and may still do.

"Yes. I'm licensed, insured, and have been doing this for the better part of twenty years, Julianna. You have nothing to worry about."

He sounds and looks so confident that it's difficult *not* to believe him. About this, at least. And I realize I want to believe him. Maybe it's just because this is one of the things I've wanted to do for a long time, but what the hell. Which makes me realize something.

"You didn't make this the 'gimme' prize after the fact just so you could get me alone, did you?" I ask suspiciously.

Noah tips his head back and laughs. "No, but that would've been pretty smooth, wouldn't it?" he teases.

I glare at him, unconvinced. "Or incredibly presumptuous and creepy."

I hear the rumble of a vehicle behind me and turn to see a large truck pulling a trailer parking next to the Range Rover. Two men jump out, bringing a couple of bags with them as they approach.

"Julianna, this is my ground crew," Noah explains as the men join us. "John," he gestures to the older of the two, "and Robbie." Both have the same dark hair, eyes, and complexion. I suspect they are father and son.

They greet me politely, and the three of them confer over whatever it is they brought back, making some adjustments and doing their thing. Not long later, Noah comes back to me.

"She's ready. So what'll it be, Julianna? I promise I won't bite," he teases, hands on hips, a challenging smile on his full lips.

I lift my chin. "I'm not scared of you, Noah," I reply firmly. The words have more meaning than I intended them to. Though on second thought, that might not have been an accident.

But his smile widens regardless. "That's my girl," he replies. "Come on."

I don't even have time to react to his words before he's pulling me by the hand toward the basket. John takes a moment to give me a few simple instructions — basic stuff like don't lean over the basket in the air, don't touch anything, and stay out of Noah's way if there's an emergency. As he talks, Noah climbs into the basket. Then it's my turn.

I mount the stepladder and let Noah help me ease down into the basket. Even just holding his hand in that small moment sends my stomach flip-flopping.

And before I know it, the ropes are untied, and the burner, as it's aptly named, is firing the air in the balloon up so we're lifting gently into the sky. There's little time for talk as Noah finishes communicating with the ground crew and navigates us over the treetops. As we rise, more of the land and ocean around us becomes visible, and my excitement spills over.

Suddenly, I understand the temptation to lean over the side, but I resist. It's not like I can't see everything anyway. Little is obscured by the four ropes tying the basket to the balloon, and I barely feel the slow drift as we rise. It's almost like being in a tall building. Well, unless you look down. I try that once and only once before keeping my eyes trained on the horizon, which seems endless.

Tears fill my eyes and I feel Noah next to me. I look up to find him smiling down at me.

"Beautiful, isn't it?" he asks softly.

I nod, unable to form words. In the late afternoon sunshine, the clear skies are gorgeous, the views of the water, the downtown skyline in the distance, and all of the other visible landmarks beyond stunning. It's even better than I thought it would be. Floating through the air like we're celestial beings, separate from everything below us while we look down on it as if it's all part of a diorama. It's surreal.

After a few minutes of staring in awe, I look back up at Noah.

"I see the draw," I admit. "It's a beautiful escape, Noah, thank you."

If I had endless amounts of cash, I'd probably own one of these too. But that part I don't admit out loud.

Noah lifts a camera I hadn't noticed he was holding, silently asking permission. I nod and put on my best impression of a smile as he takes a few pictures of me and the views around us. When he lowers the camera, he looks at me carefully.

"What are you escaping from?" he asks simply.

I snort. "What are *you* escaping from?" I return, unwilling to be the first to offer anything personal.

He gives an understanding smile that doesn't reach his eyes.

"Is it weird that I use something my family's privilege gave me to escape *being* a Rutherford, if only for a little while?" he muses.

"That's not weird," I admit, for the first time considering that Noah didn't choose to be who he is. "Why work for your dad, then, if that's something you need to escape from?"

"Oh, it's not work that's the problem," he clarifies. "If it were, I would've done what my little sister did and gotten into something totally unrelated to the family business. No, I actually love the job. It's the name. Sometimes it opens doors, but most of the time it just puts people's guards up." He looks at me pointedly.

"Well, I'm sure the doors it opens are worth the ones it closes," I reply drily, looking away.

"True," he replies thoughtfully. "It did help me raise millions for Alzheimer's research. Thanks to generous donations like yours."

I look back at him in shock, and he winks at me.

"*You* picked the Alzheimer's Foundation of America?" I gasp.

"I did. Is there a problem with that?" he asks with a frown.

"No, I just … why?"

In stark opposition to his usual confidence, he shifts uncomfortably. "My nan," he finally says by way of explanation, looking away. "It was the least I could do, after everything she did for me."

My heart breaks for him. He chose it because he knows what it's like to watch someone he loves suffer from it. I reach out and take his hand.

"Hey," I say, getting him to meet my eyes. "I understand how powerless you feel. But I'm impressed that you used the power you have to do something about it."

"Do you?" he asks, looking so forlorn I want to wrap him in my arms.

I close my eyes and sigh. "I do. My father has it too."

Before I can even open my eyes again, he's pulled me into his arms. I think about resisting for a moment, but it just feels too good. I lean into him, and he rests his chin on the top of my head.

"How's he doing?" Noah murmurs.

"Not good. He's eighty and has had it for about ten years. He's got a lung infection now, and I'm afraid he's not going to be able to fight it much longer." I stop, unable to say anything else without losing composure. I take a deep breath to steady myself before pulling away.

As I pull back, his hand sweeps down my arm, then squeezes my palm gently.

"I'm so sorry, Julianna, I had no idea," he replies.

I shrug, withdrawing my hand. "Wouldn't be so bad if my mother didn't start suffering from dementia a few years back too," I respond. "Seeing both of them like this … it's rough. So I understand is all. How's your nan?"

Noah looks at me with pity written all over his face, and it cuts through me, self-consciousness crawling across my skin.

"She had other issues that were more pressing," he finally replies, thankfully not offering any words of sympathy for my family's situation, "but the hardest part was watching her go through it all without the ability to remember what was happening to her. It made everything so much worse. She passed away a few years ago, though, so her fight is over. But I'll do everything in my power to help others avoid going through that. To avoid having to watch loved ones go through it."

The heaviness of his declaration, of the thoughts I usually keep at bay with busyness, it all sits like a boulder on my chest, making it difficult to breathe. I turn away, needing to focus on my surroundings, the beauty that we're floating through.

"Shouldn't you be steering or something?" I ask abruptly.

I feel Noah's heat behind me. His smell invades my senses. It simultaneously makes me angry and … well, other things I'm not ready to admit to.

"The wind has us, Julianna. I'm just here to make sure you stay safe," he says quietly. "There's still a bit until sunset. Are you hungry?"

I blink away tears I hadn't realized were there and turn to him with a forced smile.

"Sure, what have you got?"

He unearths a picnic basket that had been tucked into the corner. It's filled with champagne, crackers, cheese, and cookies. Not exactly a well-rounded dinner, but it's all delicious and indulgent, so I can hardly complain.

While we eat, he tells me about his little sister and her career as an artist. How angry that made his dad, and how much his nan used to laugh over it all. It makes me ache with memories of my parents when we would all laugh and joke and … well, love.

Watching Noah talk about his family is also very revealing. He loves them all, clearly, but is obviously often at odds with his father. It makes me wonder why he chose to work so closely with him. Surely, given his education, experience, and name, he could work anywhere. But I don't ask. I already feel like I'm softening toward him too much. I don't want to dig that hole deeper. Because after this is over, he still has my career, and the careers of everyone I care about, in his hands. Hands I'm still not entirely sure I can trust.

As it is, the sunset almost does me in. While we drift back to earth, the glowing orb dips below the horizon, lacing oranges and pinks into the dimming sky, then deepening to purples as the ground gets closer and closer.

While we're still hovering over the treetops, and after Noah has radioed his ground crew, I feel his eyes on me. I look up and give him a smile.

"This was better than anything I could've imagined," I assure him. "Thank you."

"You deserve it," he says huskily, drawing a little too close for comfort. His hands come to my shoulders, and I swallow hard. "And so much more."

I make to pull back, but his fingers hold me firmly in place. He studies my face for a moment, and I have to force myself to breathe. And to not give in to the sultry look he's giving me. I stay as still as possible. But then, I think to myself, *He's not a T-rex, Jules — staying still isn't going to make it so he can't see you.* And laughter bubbles out of me.

"What's so funny?" he asks, his lips pulling up into a smile.

I shake my head and press my lips together, thankful that I managed to disrupt the moment. I pull out of his embrace. "Nothing, just a silly thought. So how do you land a hot air balloon?"

Taking the hint, he steps back.

"Well, see, that's the thing," he says. "The hot air balloon kind of lands you." He gives me a wink and picks up his radio. He either doesn't see or chooses to ignore the nervous look I shoot him.

But as it happens, there was nothing to worry about. Despite seeming awfully close to some trees, we land pretty cleanly in a grassy area. It's not long before the truck appears, with the Range Rover on its tail. John climbs out of the truck, Robbie out of the Range Rover. They work to help Noah secure the basket.

Noah climbs out first, then helps me out. Robbie hands Noah his keys.

"They'll handle the teardown," Noah assures me. "I'll drive you back to your car."

I guess I hadn't thought too much about the fact that hot air balloons don't land where they took off, or that that meant after several hours of being together in the balloon we'd need to spend more time alone in a car. Without the majestic views to distract us.

But I don't have much choice, so I go with him, trying not to notice how ridiculously luxurious the leather interior is. Or how good he looks leaned back in his seat, one arm draped casually over the steering wheel. I stay silent, not trusting myself to engage further after the forced intimacy of the evening.

When we finally pull up to the original meeting spot, next to my car, Noah cuts the engine and looks at me.

"I hope you enjoyed yourself," he says.

"I did, thank you," I reply simply.

"Good. And I hate to end this evening on a sour note, but I want you to hear this from me. Since last time didn't go so well."

My heart jumps into my throat. "You're firing someone else," I realize. God, I'm so stupid. Of course he is. Of course he was playing nice all evening, building up my trust for exactly this moment. I steel myself, wiping my expression blank, not wanting to give him the satisfaction of any kind of response. "All right then. Who?"

He shakes his head and splays his hands out.

"It's not one person, Julianna. We're going to be letting go somewhere around a quarter of the hospital's staff," he admits.

My heart starts hammering in my ears as blind rage threatens to overtake me. It takes every ounce of self-control that I possess not to let it out.

"If you're trying to get me to trust you, tricking me into a hot air balloon ride with you, then ending it by telling me you're going to be firing a bunch of my friends isn't exactly the way to go about it," I finally say tightly.

The look he gives me is filled with fire and fury.

"You bid on the damn prize," he replies hotly. "I didn't trick you into anything. And yes, it's shit luck that this happened at the same time, but would you rather have found out with everyone else at work tomorrow? Because I thought hearing it from me, honestly and beforehand, would show you that I'm not trying to blindside you."

I throw up my hands. "I meant for you to take what I've said into consideration. To trust me. To involve me in these kinds of things. Not just give me the heads up when you're about to drop the ax. What difference does it make? There's nothing I can do about it now."

He slams a hand on the steering wheel in an uncharacteristic display of anger. "Dammit, I did listen to you. But in the end, it's not totally up to me. This was just decided Friday, so it's not like I had a lot of time to tell you. And if I'm being totally honest, you're not even meant to know."

"Great, so, what, I'm supposed to be thankful you told me anyway? Even though it's completely what the hospital *doesn't* need and there's nothing I can do about it? Thanks for keeping me in the loop," I shoot back in disgust.

He glares daggers at me, making me even angrier. "Did it ever occur to you that you may not know *everything*? That you may not be the best person to decide what the hospital does and doesn't need?" he retorts.

"It doesn't matter now," I mumble. "I should get home. Sounds like I'm going to need to be well-rested to deal with the shitstorm tomorrow." I make to get out of the car, but he grabs my arm.

"Julianna, wait, I don't want to leave things like this," he pleads.

I pull my arm away and climb out of the car. "There's nothing to leave. This is the way things are, Noah," I shoot back over my shoulder. I slam the door behind me, climbing into my car and getting the hell out of there before he can stop me.

I angrily replay the whole scene over and over on the drive home. By the time I climb into bed, I'm far too pissed off to sleep. So I toss and turn for hours, knowing that my lack of sleep is going to make this so much worse. Not that all the sleep in the world will change what's about to happen.

CHAPTER 12

Monday is every bit as hard as I thought it would be. I'm an absolute mess: exhausted, angry, and surly in a way that I never am. I'm usually the positive one in tough times, the one to assure everyone else that everything will be okay, that we'll make it work, figure it out.

But when MacDougall announces that some of the staff will be let go in the coming days, despite everyone's clear panic, I don't have it in me to put on a brave face and reassure them. How can I when I know exactly how deep they plan to cut our already overworked staff?

I shut out even Sasha when she asks what I know, unwilling to talk about Noah Rutherford. Even *thinking* his name makes me angry.

But on Tuesday, when they let the first ten percent go, I realize I have only myself to blame for bringing attention to the hospital. I'm the one who told Noah about the problems here that made him want to look closer.

This round we only lost Harper. Becca, Sasha, and everyone else are understandably heartbroken. She was the last non-doctor hired, though, so I'm not surprised. And I'm also heartbroken, but in a totally different way. The disappointment I feel is all with myself. And in knowing there's nothing I can do to stop this.

Though midweek, I wonder if there is.

Tail between my legs, I go to Noah's office, thinking I might be able to make a case to keep the rest. Maybe I can get him to listen.

But he won't even see me.

And that's when the anger starts again.

I'm storming toward MacDougall's office to give him a piece of my mind instead when a voice stops me.

"Whoa there, Jules," comes Cal's lilting British accent.

I whirl on the spot to face him peeking out of his office door. He holds up his hands in an obvious "I come in peace" gesture, but it doesn't make me any less pissed off.

"What?" I snap.

"Given the look on your face and the direction you're heading, I think maybe you and I should have a little chat before you do something ill advised," he suggests gently.

"What good would that do?" I huff, crossing my arms over my chest.

His eyebrows shoot up. "Well, probably a whole hell of a lot more good than having a go at the chief of the cardiac unit," he replies patiently.

I furrow my brow and frown. The man has a point.

"Fine," I reply, following him into his office.

He sits back in his chair, and I slump into the one in front of his desk.

"So, care to tell me what has you in a strop?" he asks.

"Oh, I don't know, maybe the fact that they've just fired a bunch of people and are about to fire more even though we're stretched thin as it is?" I snap.

"Mmm," he hums. "Are you sure that's what's really bothering you?" He gives me a knowing look. And it hits me.

"Sasha *told you*?" I say accusatorily.

His brows pull together. "I'm afraid I don't know what you're referring to," he replies, and I don't hear any dishonesty in his words. "I was speaking of the fact that you've been walking around in a mood ever since Noah Rutherford joined us a couple of weeks ago. So I presumed you had some sort of previous issue with him that's really fueling all this rage."

I snort. "You could say that."

He raises an eyebrow. "So this isn't really just about the firings, is it?" he prompts.

I fold my arms over my chest. "No, I suppose not."

"What's it about, then, Jules? You're always so levelheaded. I've never seen you like this, and I find it rather disconcerting. Please, tell me, I'd like to be able to help if I can," he prompts gently.

I heave a deep sigh and rub my eyes. "I met Noah Rutherford at the charity gala last month. Except, I didn't know who he was, and I ..." I chew on my lip self-consciously, not sure how to put this. "I may have shared my concerns about the hospital with him."

Cal steeples his fingers under his nose and thinks about that for a moment. Then his crystal-clear blue eyes look up to meet mine.

"You think this is all your fault," he deduces.

"Yes," I breathe. "No. I don't know. Maybe. If I hadn't said anything, he wouldn't be here. So yeah, I guess, in a way, I think this is my fault. For a while I thought he might listen to me and really understand where the problems are coming from. But it seems I was wrong." I shake my head, the anger seeping out of me as despair takes over.

Cal leans forward, placing his elbows on his desk and spearing me with a hard look.

"I hate to break it to you, but if this is anyone's fault, it's mine," he replies.

"You've only been here six months, how is any of this your fault?" I ask tiredly.

He blows out a breath and leans back in his chair. "The thing is, you've worked at Rutherford Hospital your entire career, am I correct?" he asks.

I tilt my head, unsure of where he's going with his question. "I had a job at one other hospital before Rutherford, but it was less than a year. So basically, yes."

"Through my training and career I've now worked at ..." he pauses, squinting as if he's trying to do the mental math. "Eight different hospitals in the last ten years. So I've got quite a lot more to compare it to than you do." The arrogant edge to his tone makes me bristle, but he's usually got a point when he gets like this, so I let him continue. "At every single one of those hospitals, the nurses always say they're understaffed and overworked. Do you know why?"

I roll my eyes. "Because it's a universal problem that hospital administrators don't understand how much nurses actually do?" I scoff.

Cal huffs an unamused chuckle. "No, Jules. I know it feels like that. But it's because you do a damn hard job. And shorter shifts and more people aren't going to change that. Your shifts aren't designed for your comfort, they're designed to keep the hospital running smoothly for the patients. That's not to say there aren't times when we are, in fact, understaffed, because good medical personnel are hard to come by. And I'm afraid much of Rutherford's staff isn't up to standard, which is contributing to your feeling that we're unable to handle everything that needs doing."

"You told your bosses all of this, didn't you?" I gasp. *That's why they're letting people go.*"

"Julianna," he says with a caution in his voice. "I think we both need to stop thinking about this situation as if one person is responsible. Yours was the voice that raised the red flag. Mine was another voice that added to the picture. Hell, even Dr. MacDougall is a small player in everything that's happening. There is a hospital full of opinions, piles of data, and all of the Rutherford Group's staff and experience behind the actions that are being taken here. So your anger is for naught. It's difficult, I know. Change always is. But nothing you can say to MacDougall will help. In fact, all it's likely to do is land you in hot water."

I look up at the ceiling and blink back tears.

"God, Cal, I hate it when you have a point," I say, my voice thick with emotion. Once I've mastered myself, I look back down at him.

"I know," he replies with a wink. "Feel better now?"

I shake my head. "Not really. But you're right, mouthing off to MacDougall is just going to make things worse. Thanks for talking me off the ledge."

"Anytime," he replies, rising from his desk. "Now, I'm sure I'm supposed to be somewhere right now."

I smile. "Yeah, probably me too."

He pats me genially on the back and we both go about our business. But I wasn't lying. I really don't feel better, because I've realized my only options seem to be to just deal with it … or leave. And somehow I still can't help feeling like Noah is the problem here. That he's still talking out both sides of his mouth by trying to keep me happy yet still enact all the harsh changes that are being handed down. Because it can't be both.

* * *

The week marches on despite everything, but when Becca comes back from her lunch break on Friday, she looks like she's going to be sick.

"You okay, Becks?" Sasha asks quietly, jumping up and rubbing her back gently.

Becca fixes her with a sad look and shakes her head. I set down the patient file I'd just retrieved for my next appointment and round the nurses' station counter.

"Hey, what happened?" I ask.

Becca looks up at me with tears in her eyes, and my stomach drops. I can't remember ever seeing Becca cry. She's such a tough cookie, and usually a master at hiding her more vulnerable moments.

"They just fired Vincent," she whispers.

"No!" Sasha and I both exclaim at the same time.

"Those bastards," Sasha adds.

"I'm so sorry," I say.

"He didn't deserve it. He's been through too damn much," Becca snaps, angrily wiping at her eyes.

"It's not going to mess up anything for him, is it?" Sasha asks, knowing Vincent is still dealing with the legal fallout of what he and Becca went through with his ex last month.

"No, he's got time to figure something out before it becomes a problem," she assures us. "He's just been so … happy. This really hit him hard."

I pull her into a hug. "It's tough seeing the people you care about upset," I respond, even though I'm talking about me and her. But it applies to us all at the moment, really.

Becca gives me a squeeze then lets me go. "Yeah. I know we'll get through it. It just sucks is all. Thanks for listening, bitches," she says.

We all laugh a little. Trust Becca to lighten the mood, even when she's the one who's upset.

"You know we're always here for you," I tell her.

She nods.

"Except right now, you're supposed to be in exam six," Sasha points out with a small smile.

"Okay, fine, except right this exact second," I agree with a chuckle. "You gonna be okay?"

"Yeah, I'm fine, Jules, thanks," Becca assures me.

As I walk away, I can hear Sasha continuing to console and commiserate with Becca. And the day's not over yet. I know there will probably be at least one person to go from our unit too. So I can't help the feeling of dread that sticks with me as I go about my duties.

The afternoon flies by and, before I know it, Sarah shows up as I'm returning an EKG machine to the supply closet.

"Holy crap, is it already five-thirty?" I ask as I close the closet door and return to the nurses' station.

"Yep. How'd it go today? Who got the ax?" Sarah asks bluntly.

I shake my head. "Becca's boyfriend over in intensive care. Randi up in maternity. Nobody from cardiac," I reply. I open my mouth to continue the list, but as if I cursed it, MacDougall comes down the hall looking stern.

"Nurse Marcus, I'd like a word with you in my office, please," he says in a condescending tone.

Eyes wide, I look at her in horror. She shakes her head, clearly already having realized we weren't out of the woods yet.

As I go about finishing my end-of-shift rounds, my stomach is all in knots. Thankfully, when I return to the nurses' station right at six, Sarah is already back, though looking grim.

"They're killing second shift and going to an on-call model," she says before I can ask. "I've been offered a position in oncology. Zoe will move back to day shift."

"Well, shit. That's definitely going to make things tough around here. Though it could've been worse. At least they didn't fire anyone, right?" I prompt.

She shrugs but stays silent. As she makes for the supply cabinets behind the desk, something about her posture, her attitude, doesn't sit right with me.

"What else happened?" I press.

She turns and looks me squarely in the eye. "Sasha will be promoted to ARNP in my stead. She'll train under you."

My insides jump a little with happiness. *Finally*, they're going to promote Sasha. But I give Sarah a funny look. "And that's a bad thing because ...?"

"Because I wasn't even given the option to stay in cardiac and have Sasha move. It just doesn't seem fair. This whole thing stinks of favoritism," she seethes.

"Well, technically, Sasha's worked here longer than you," I point out. "Granted, not in an ARNP role, but still."

Boy, was that the wrong thing to say. I can practically feel Sarah's anger as she abruptly turns her back to me and fishes around in the cabinets.

"That's not how seniority works around here, and you know it," she snaps. She turns back toward me with an armload of empty bins. "But then, I'm not fucking Noah Rutherford, so I guess I don't get a say in any of these decisions."

My jaw drops and her eyes narrow.

"Don't even deny it, Jules. Of all people, I never thought *you* would stab me in the back," she says hotly.

"I ... who did you ..." I stutter, unable to get out a coherent sentence. But she doesn't give me a chance, storming past me.

"I don't want to hear it. Just go. Your shift is over anyway."

And then she's gone. I stand there, completely flabbergasted. Sasha and Becca are the only ones who know, and I trust them both. Even Becca, despite her gossipy tendencies, because she's practically like a sister to me, and I know she'd never betray my confidence. So the only way Sarah could know is if the information didn't come from me, Sasha, or Becca.

Noah. Noah told someone here.

And now the rumor mill knows.

Fury rips through me. After all he's done, all he's doing, adding this to the pile tips me over the edge. I'm over taking this bullshit from him. I don't care if he fires me on the spot, he's going to hear exactly what I think of all the changes he's handing down. Hell, even better if he does. Then at least he won't have completely ruined my reputation. Because he's already ruining where I work and the lives of people I care about.

I know the bastard is still here, and it's time to let him have it.

CHAPTER 13

It takes all of my strength not to bang on Noah's office door like I'm trying to break it down. Even though I feel like doing exactly that, which causes me to knock a little more forcefully than I'd intended.

When the door swings open in my face, I jump back in surprise. Noah looks equally surprised — and unhappy — to see me, though he recovers quickly.

"Come in and sit," he barks, stepping back.

I enter and he closes the door behind me, but rather than sit down, I whirl on him.

"Don't *ever* come banging on my door like that," he snaps, beating me to the punch. "Now *sit down*."

"I'm done taking orders from you," I retort. "How *could you*, Noah? Better yet, *why*? Does it make you feel like a big man for everyone to know you've fucked me? That if you can conquer Julianna Magnusson, everyone else should suck your cock too?"

A look of shock passes over his face before it's replaced by anger. "I haven't told a soul," he swears. "Is that why you came in here flying off the handle?"

"Oh, you haven't even begun to see me fly off the fucking handle," I promise in a low voice. "If you didn't tell anyone, who did then? And even if you deny that, you can't deny that you promoted Sasha at Sarah's expense. How do you think that made me look?"

He advances on me, causing me to take steps backward. "I can't do what you ask, you're angry," he seethes. "I try to do something else you asked for instead and you're angry. What do you want from me, Julianna?"

As the back of my legs hit the desk, he stops advancing. But now I'm pinned, and it doesn't help my anger any.

"Why does the rumor mill know we slept together?" I insist, ignoring his other statements.

"I don't know," he insists tightly. "Does it even matter?"

I look up into his eyes, their normal honeyed brown shade a hard amber.

"It matters to me. When this is all over, you'll go back to your ivory tower. But I'll still have to deal with the reputation of having fucked Noah Rutherford in exchange for … well, anything they feel like chalking up to me being your plaything. You may be untouchable, but *I'm not*. None of this would have ever happened if you'd just told me who you were."

I choke on a sob. And it makes me realize what I'm experiencing is so much worse than anger. There's emotion here. Feelings. Ones I don't want to have right now.

His expression softens, and it makes it even worse. He reaches up and cups my cheek in his hand. "You've never been a plaything to me," he says on a sigh. "And I honestly don't know how they found out. But I can't undo that. And I wouldn't, in a million years, undo our night together either."

He eyes my lips like a starved man, and my insides tighten. I close my eyes, and I'm torn between my logical brain, screaming all its anger, all its objections that he's the enemy, and the memories that his smell and his closeness evoke, causing a physical response I'm having trouble controlling.

His thumb brushes over my bottom lip. "This week has been rough for me too. And I've wanted to come to you a million times," he admits. "But I didn't want to push you away either. Seems like that was inevitable, though. But fuck if I wish it weren't."

I open my eyes and look up into his. And all logic flies out the window. All I want is his lips. I *need* his lips. His hands. His body. I hate that I do. But right now, I want to wipe away everything. Forget everything. And the only time I can remember being able to do that was with him inside me.

It stirs so many emotions. Anger comes back to the forefront. One minute I want to rage at him, to make him pay for the hurt he's had a hand in causing. The next I want him to take it all off my mind with his body. How thin the line between love and hate is.

I put a hand to his chest as the lust battles with my anger.

Then I hear someone walking down the hall just outside his office door. And it brings me fully back to my senses.

It's time to put a stop to whatever this moment might have been. Because it won't undo any of the hurt. Not really.

"It's not just what you're doing, it's also who you are," I explain. "So yes, it was inevitable."

He takes a step back, letting out a breath. He looks so defeated, so tired, that I know he wasn't lying about this being hard on him too.

I equally care and don't.

In any case, I'm too exhausted for any of this now that the fight has gone out of me.

"For what it's worth, I'm sorry," he says quietly. "I never wanted to hurt you. I'm not sure what I can do about the rumor mill, but I will see what I can do to make things right with Nurse Marcus. That may mean your friend will be moved to another department, though."

I nod my understanding, knowing he's not the kind of man who apologizes easily. It adds to my confusion, to the ball of emotions swirling inside me.

"Thank you."

I don't dare look at him. I simply slip past him, heading for the door.

"Julianna?" he calls after me.

I stop, hand on the doorknob, and chance a look back. He has his hands shoved in his pockets, his expression defeated.

"I can't change who I am. So if it's that much of an issue ..." He shakes his head. "Well, I guess I'll have to accept that that's where you're at."

"Good," I say tightly, even though his words still hurt. "I guess we can both move on now."

His jaw tightens. "If that's what you want."

I nod. "That's what I want."

After that, I don't give him the chance to make this harder, and I leave.

I beat myself up the whole way home. For what, I'm not sure. I'm so confused and I don't know what to think.

Well, I know one thing. Things aren't going to get any easier at Rutherford Hospital in the near future. So now might be a good time to explore my options.

Time to dust off my résumé.

* * *

"Seriously? You're just going to switch jobs? Just like that?" Katie's expression is skeptical.

I don't blame her. Even I'm having a hard time wrapping my head around it.

"Not 'just like that,'" I reply, using my fingers as air quotes. "But I don't think it would be a bad idea to have an out."

Katie shakes her head. "If you say so, but it sounds an awful lot like running from your problems to me," she responds.

"Even after working there all this time, spending years building up a reputation of trust and integrity, one stupid rumor and they all think I'm whoring myself out for my friends," I point out, shaking my head. "And who knows what else the Rutherfords have planned for us. Seriously, Katie, I'd be an idiot not to be thinking about a Plan B."

"You're not an idiot, Jules. Not if you stay or if you go. And not even if you do secretly have the hots for Noah Rutherford," she replies airily.

I roll my eyes. Only Katie can see right through me. "Fine, I have … urges when he's around. But I'm a grown woman. I'll manage."

"Well, I hope you do more than manage," she responds. "I hope you jump that —"

I put my hands over my ears. "Lalalalala," I sing. I see Katie's mouth close into a smirk, so I drop my hands. "Subject change, please."

"Oh, good, because I have news," she says.

"That you waited until now to mention?" I ask incredulously.

She waves a hand dismissively. "You needed to vent. Anyway. You remember that drug trial for Alzheimer's patients with lung infections?"

"Yeah, the one we tried to get him in the first time this happened," I recall, my face falling. Dad's lungs keep getting worse, though they haven't officially declared it aspiration pneumonia yet. "Why?"

"Well, he's in," she says simply.

My mouth pops open. "Really? Did we reapply?"

Katie shrugs. "I guess they kept his file open, since they have access to his status in the system. Any which way, they said they had an opening for him now."

"Oh, thank god," I say, breathing a sigh of relief. "When can they start him?"

The drug in question has had a high success rate of not only eliminating infection but also improving lung functionality afterward. It will mean less suffering overall and less risk going forward.

Katie grins. "I gave him his first dose yesterday. He gets another after lunch today. Shall we?" She gestures to the kitchen, and I happily follow. As we work, she fills me in on the details of the program. Not only are they providing the drug for free, but they'll also be paying for all of his medical expenses. So all I need to pay now is the room and board for keeping him in the home. Which, frankly, was the cheapest part of this whole arrangement, so it's an unexpected and very pleasant surprise. Finally, some good news.

* * *

Unfortunately, when I return to work on Monday, my gossip spidey-senses start tingling immediately. Something in the air just feels off. I stop at the help desk to find Melinda, the morning shift receptionist, practically vibrating out of her seat with excitement.

"Morning, Jules," she chirps.

"Hey, Melinda, nice weekend?" I ask, knowing she needs the small talk to warm up.

"Oh, it was great," she gushes. "Hal and I went out on the boat with some friends. How about you?"

"My dad got into a drug trial for his lung infection, so things are looking up, thanks," I reply with a forced smile. I just wanted to shake her and ask her to spill it already.

"That's wonderful, I'm so happy to hear that," she replies. "So have you heard yet?"

Fucking finally.

"Heard what?" I ask innocently.

She giggles. "You know that sexy Mr. Rutherford who's been here the last few weeks?" she whispers loudly. Why she bothers, I don't know, because you could still hear her all the way up in neurology on the top floor with that tone. And there's no way in hell she didn't hear the rumor about me and Noah, so I'm pretty sure she already knows that I'm well aware of him, to say the least.

"What about him?" I ask, playing along, eyes wide in feigned excitement.

"There are pictures of him all over the gossip sites this morning," she says. "With a *movie star*."

My eyebrows jump, and I'm not pretending to be interested now.

"Show me," I demand sharply, ever the masochist.

Melinda happily taps away at her computer and turns the screen toward me. Sure enough, there's Noah. In all his gorgeous glory, wearing a charcoal suit, headed into one of the nicest restaurants in town with the gorgeous blond Piper Black, a young, popular film actress who's so hot right now even I've heard of her. She clings happily to Noah's arm, positively oozing sex appeal in a tight black dress that leaves absolutely nothing to the imagination.

My stomach turns, the carafe of coffee I called breakfast threatening to make a reappearance.

And I realize suddenly that Melinda is watching me. Or watching my reaction, as it were. Shit. She definitely knew. Still, I manage a feeble smile.

"Was that over the weekend?" I ask quietly.

She nods. "Saturday night," she confirms.

"Well, isn't that something?" I murmur. Guess he moved on pretty damn fast. Clearly, our night together didn't mean that much. Though he was probably only acting like it did so he could get a replay in his office. I suddenly feel like I'm going to be ill again.

Melinda gives me a feline grin, clearly noting and enjoying my discomfort.

"Guess he's more like his brother than we knew," she comments with an affected shrug.

I force a small laugh, but it sounds pathetic even to me.

"Guess so. Anyway, best be getting to it. Have a great day, Melinda," I reply.

"You too," she calls to my retreating back.

A shot of disgust rolls through me. Because Piper Black is exactly the kind of woman I'd imagine someone like Noah with. I was an idiot for thinking I could ever hold the interest of a man like him. Which is fine, because I didn't want to anyway … right?

The rest of the day is awkward as ass. Even Sasha and Becca give me a wide berth, believing me to be the woman scorned. I don't say anything to anyone about any of it. I'm not breathing life into any of this gossip. I just want it all to be over.

By the end of the week, the rumor mill has decided I'm the victim in this situation. Just another woman used up by another philandering Rutherford playboy. It should be a welcome turn of events, but the whole thing has just made me sick to my stomach.

So when a private cardiologist's office contacts me on Thursday for a Sunday interview, I happily accept. It was the one job in a sea of listings where I actually knew someone who'd worked there and could recommend me. I was starting to worry the job market was too cutthroat right now, so the in saved me. Because it's time to start lining up Plan B, since things sure as hell aren't getting any better around here.

CHAPTER 14

The job interview with Dr. Foster, the private cardiologist, goes well. So well, in fact, that he tells me on the spot that he's ready to extend me an offer whenever I'm ready to leave Rutherford Hospital, assuming that's in the next few weeks.

I should feel better having solidified my Plan B. But all I feel is more pressure to make a decision.

But Wednesday brings a development that firmly shoves me over the edge.

Becca gets called into MacDougall's office at the end of the day. She returns not five minutes later, pale and shaking.

"I've been fired," she says plainly.

Sasha and I both stare in shocked silence.

"You've … been fired?" Sasha asks haltingly.

Becca nods, gathering her things from behind the desk while blinking back tears.

"For what?" I demand.

Becca shrugs. "Part of the cutbacks. What else?" she says. She's keeping her words short, but I can tell how upset she is.

I grab the purse out of her hands and set it on the desk.

"Come with me," I direct, grabbing her by the elbow and marching down the hall to MacDougall's office.

I rap my knuckles on the door but don't wait for an answer, since I can see the old bastard is sitting at his desk, probably having gone back to playing solitaire or something.

"Dr. MacDougall, a word?" I ask sharply as I pull Becca inside.

He looks up with disdain. "I thought I might have to endure some theatrics from you, Ms. Magnusson."

My hackles rise, but I don't let him provoke me.

"Can you clarify what Ms. Dillon just told me, please?"

With a theatrical sigh, he folds his arms on the desk in front of him.

"As part of our cutbacks, we've unfortunately had to make the difficult decision to let Ms. Dillon go, effective immediately. If that's unclear, I can use smaller words," he says.

My eyes narrow. The old fucker is *trying* to provoke me. And something smells seriously fishy here.

"I was under the impression that all of the cutbacks had happened the week before last. Nobody else in the hospital was let go today. Why Becca?"

Becca shifts uncomfortably next to me.

"I'm afraid all of that is above your pay grade, so run along and do your job. You wouldn't want to be next, would you?"

I pull my head back and my eyebrows shoot up.

"Was that a *threat?*" I ask sharply.

"Consider it a warning for speaking out of turn," he replies just as harshly. "That kind of insubordination will no longer be tolerated here, and if you don't like it, you'll have to take it up with the Rutherford Group."

"This came from Noah Rutherford?" I clarify.

"As did all the cutbacks, Ms. Magnusson, but that's neither here nor there. Please see yourself out."

I march back to the nurses' station; this time Becca has to race to keep up with me. Sasha looks up in surprise at our abrupt return.

"I take it that didn't go well?" Sasha squeaks.

I shake my head furiously. I look Becca squarely in the eye.

"Go home. I'm going to go have a little talk with Noah Rutherford. Something stinks about all of this, and I'm not taking it lying down. Not this time," I say.

"Jules, please, don't," Becca replies. "I don't want you to put yourself on the line for me. I can find something else. I will find something else. Vincent's already gotten hired on at UCSD Medical. I bet I can too. I'm just … it was just a surprise, that's all. Please, please, please, don't jeopardize your career for me."

I huff. "Oh, Becca, you know me better than that. I already have another job lined up. Don't you worry about me either. But neither of us are going down without a fight."

Sasha looks between us nervously.

"What can I do?" she asks.

"Hold down the fort," I instruct her. "I'll be upstairs."

"Text me later?" Becca asks, looking at us both.

Sasha nods, but I'm too distracted to respond, already formulating what I'm going to say to the bastard in my mind. He hasn't talked to me all week. I thought it was because of how tense things have been between us, but now I'm thinking it might also have been because he was about to do something I didn't like. Since last time he did tell me and that blew up in his face.

He's right about one thing, anyway. He definitely can't win with me.

Becca heads out as I go upstairs. I wring my fingers together anxiously, itching to let it all out.

Once on his floor, I practically race down the hall to his office. The door is open and I enter without knocking. As soon as he looks up, I can tell he knows he's in for it. He rises, going around me to close the door.

He turns, sliding his hands in his pockets, clearly waiting for me to speak first.

I size him up, deciding what I want to say. And I realize I don't want Becca to have to come back to contend with these asshats. And I don't want to keep dealing with this bullshit either.

"Since Dr. MacDougall just made it clear that my particular brand of feedback is no longer welcome here, I'm submitting my resignation to you directly, effective immediately," I say. And fuck if it doesn't feel good. Like a weight is lifted from my chest that I no longer have to play this game of cat and mouse.

Noah's mouth turns down in a frown. "May I ask why?"

"Does it matter?" I snap back, crossing my arms over my chest.

With a sigh, Noah saunters back to his desk chair, sinking into it. "You're an asset to this hospital. I'd like a chance to convince you to stay," he replies.

"Not a chance in hell," I retort. "It was one thing when I thought you were sincerely trying to help, that your hands were tied. But when you turn around and go behind my back to have my friends fired, that's my limit. I'm done. I'm over all these games and all this bullshit. I. Quit." I'm practically giddy with the freedom those words bring. "Have a nice life, Noah."

I turn around and leave. I hear him calling after me, but I don't care. About any of it. Not anymore. Stick a fork in me, I'm done.

I head back downstairs.

Sasha looks up once more as I approach.

"I just quit," I inform her.

Her jaw drops and I laugh.

"Are you serious?" she gasps.

"One hundred percent," I assure. "Don't worry, hon. Best decision I ever made."

"But … I …" Sasha stutters, clearly at a loss.

I grab her by the shoulders. "You're going to be just fine, I promise. They'll bring Sarah in for day shift. They'll have to now. She'll help you learn the ropes. And you know we'll see each other plenty. Now, I'm going to get out of here. It'll ruin my dramatic exit if I have to explain myself too much." I give her a wink.

"Well, you seem happy," she finally admits, pulling me into a hug. "Talk later?"

"You bet," I assure her, grabbing my purse. "See you later, my dear."

"Bye, Jules," she says sadly.

But nothing can ruin my high right now. I waltz out of that place with a swagger in my step. I feel like I've finally taken control back. Now I'm going to celebrate with a relaxing bubble bath and some champagne. Hell, I may even wait until next week to start with the private cardiologist's office. Goodness knows I've earned a little break.

Unfortunately, the only break I get is the time it takes me to stop at the grocery store for a celebratory bottle of wine on the drive home. When I get to my place, Noah is sitting on my goddamn front porch. He rises when he sees me approaching.

"Boy, you really don't know when to quit, do you?" I say to him, not even commenting on his complete lack of boundaries in looking up my address.

"Guess I don't," he replies. "But then, seems like you know all about quitting. Care to teach me?" It'd sound playful but for his aggressive demeanor.

"Nope. I'm good. Now, can you please move out of the way? I need to celebrate my new freedom," I snap. He's being a real buzzkill, and I'm already over this conversation.

"First, tell me who was fired," he insists.

I pull a face. "You're not seriously pretending like you don't know," I scoff.

"I'm not in the habit of asking questions to which I already know the answer," he insists testily.

"Are you screwing with me right now?" I ask, seriously confused. "Because Dr. MacDougall explicitly said it was at your direction that Becca was let go."

Noah's jaw tightens. "Then I'll be having a word with Dr. MacDougall, because it *wasn't*."

I look at him skeptically. Dr. MacDougall is a lot of things, but I've never suspected him of lying. Then again, Noah is also a lot of things, but I'm coming to learn he's not the lying type either. The serious-omitter-of-highly-relevant-information type. But liar? No, he's too *principled* for that.

"Whatever, I have to pee, can you please get out of my way?" I demand.

He levels a look at me, but steps aside. I unlock the door and go in, determined to shut the door in his face. But he puts his damn foot on the threshold, stopping me.

"Ugh, whatever, I'll deal with you in a minute," I snap. I really do have to go. One of the worst things about being a nurse is never getting enough downtime to use the bathroom. It's a long-ago learned habit to hold it until I get home. But any longer and I'm risking a bladder infection. So I just leave the stubborn bastard there and drop the wine bottle on the kitchen counter on my way to the bathroom.

After I've done my business, I kick my shoes off in my room and pull my hair out of its ponytail before heading back to the living room.

Unsurprisingly, Noah is still there, sitting on my damn couch.

"And apparently you can't take a hint either," I remark drily as I head into the kitchen. I grab the bottle of wine and a single wine glass. I bring it back to the living room and sit on the couch next to him, since there's nowhere else to sit, and pour myself a glass of wine.

"What, you're not even going to offer me some?" he asks. And the sourpuss has finally faded into a teasing smirk.

"Nope," I confirm. "I don't offer beverages to uninvited visitors. So what's it going to take to get rid of you?" I take a deep drink of the wine. The liquid is heaven in a glass, and I immediately feel myself relaxing.

"If I promise to talk to Dr. MacDougall about Becca, will you rescind your resignation?" he asks.

"Hmmm, let me think about that," I reply. I take a sip of wine. "Nope." I flash him a grin and take another drink.

"Are you really that happy to get away from me?" he asks, leaning back into the couch.

"God, yes," I admit. "Won't you be glad to not have to worry about pissing me off anymore? Aren't you as exhausted as I am?"

"My main goal is the health of the hospital. My feelings don't matter. And even though I know this has been hard for you, *you're* good for the hospital, Julianna," he persists. "So I'm going to do whatever it takes to get you back."

I drain my glass and set it on the coffee table. I give him a challenging look, but he doesn't comment on my drinking. Smart man.

"First, just talking to him isn't enough. If you can't guarantee that Becca will get her job back, you're wasting my time," I reply.

He raises an eyebrow. "Well, before I can do that, I'm going to need to know why he fired her, so I can't really guarantee anything."

"Except I already told you he said it's because you told him to," I say, exasperated.

"I believe that's what he told you, but management can't always share the real reasons they do things, you know," he insists. "For legal or personal reasons. Who knows. But I can't make any promises without the full story."

"So, you want me to come back on the off chance you *might* unfire her? No thanks."

"What about your job? Your career? Aren't you worried about finding work?" he asks.

"Nope, already have another gig lined up. Any other questions?" I ask with a grin.

That shocks him, and I want to laugh.

"I'll make it worth your while, I promise," he insists.

"I want a ten percent raise," I reply, pouring myself another glass of wine.

"Five," he counters.

"Seven."

"Done."

"I'm still not convinced."

And Noah *laughs*. "This. This is why you have to come back. Who else is going to keep me on my toes?" he asks.

I huff a dry laugh. I should've known. He likes it when we argue. Damn, that explains a lot.

"I'm sure Piper Black is more than capable of keeping you on your toes," I reply drily.

He pulls a face like I'm crazy.

"I'm sorry, were you not photographed on a date with her recently? Did I imagine that picture? Or maybe it was Photoshopped," I say sarcastically.

"Oh, I went out with her," he assures me. "But it was only to take the heat off of you."

"Pffff," I scoff. "Please. I'm not stupid enough to believe that."

"Well, believe it or don't, but please slow down on the wine," he says.

I raise an eyebrow. "Now why on earth would I do that?"

He leans toward me. "Because it's been too damn long since I fucked you, Julianna, and I'd prefer you were completely sober this time."

My whole body clenches at his words. "What makes you think I'm going to hop into bed with you?" I ask shakily. Then, without thinking, I set down my wine glass on the coffee table.

"Who said anything about bed?" he murmurs, his eyes dropping to my lips. It's the only momentary warning I get before he kisses me.

It's different than the first time. Just as hungry, but slower and deeper. Like he's giving me the chance to keep a clear head and stop it if I want.

Part of me wants to stop him. But another part of me remembers what it's like when I don't. I hesitate long enough to where he presses me back on the couch, laying on top of me so that I can feel every inch of his hard body against me. It definitely doesn't help me want to stop.

Still, I break my mouth from his. "We shouldn't," I protest.

He pulls his head back enough so I can look into his eyes.

"We should've, and much sooner," he insists. He leans up, running his hands down my chest. "You have no idea how difficult it's been to resist doing this." He pinches my nipples through my scrubs top and I arch into him. "Or this." His hand drops between my legs, stroking me through the fabric. I can't help the moan that tumbles from my lips.

He takes it as permission, pulling at my bottoms until I'm bared to him. Now his hand wanders, unhindered, to the slickness that's waiting.

"Goddamn," he groans. And without warning, he slips two fingers into me, causing me to gasp and writhe beneath him. There goes any thought of stopping him. Any desire to. "Tell me what you want, Julianna."

"I don't want to think," I reply automatically. "I don't want to be able to think."

With a smirk, he places a thumb on my lips. I suck it hard until he pops it out of my mouth. Then he reaches under my shirt, yanking back my bra cup and swirling his wet thumb around my nipple. I feel it harden under his touch, and the sensation heightens the pleasure he's giving me between my thighs. And it definitely keeps me from thinking about anything but the mind-numbing bliss that I can feel unfurling in my core.

"You're beautiful," he murmurs as he speeds up his assault and pinches my nipple between his thumbs. "Tell me you only come for me."

My breathing hitches. "Only for you."

"Good, baby," he says silkily, pressing his thumb into my clit as he rubs my G-spot inside. "Come now for me, Julianna. I want you to clench that gorgeous pussy of yours around me." As he's speaking, my orgasm floods through me and I do just that. He pumps slower as I unclench, now blissfully blank and happy.

Maybe he's right. Maybe we should've been doing this all along. Life is much simpler when you can't think too hard about anything because oxytocin is flooding through your veins.

I close my eyes as his hand stills and withdraws, allowing myself to float in nothingness, my body humming and warm. I hear a zipper being undone. A foil packet being ripped. My body throbs in anticipation.

Strong hands grab my hips, and I open my eyes in time to watch as he flips me onto my stomach, lifting my ass in the air and angling it toward the front of the couch.

"Ohhh, yes," I groan. "Please, give it to me."

"Fuck, Julianna, I could come just from hearing you ask me for it," Noah groans. I feel the tip of his cock pressing at my entrance. He works it up and down, spreading my wetness, teasing me.

"Please, Noah," I beg again.

"Please what?"

I bury my face in the couch and let out a growl of frustration. "Fuck me, dammit. Now," I demand.

His hands clench on my hips, and he buries his cock in me so hard it forces my head into the cushions. Yes. This. This is what I needed. He slams into me mercilessly and my body soars, every nerve ending alight with pleasure. I'm so steeped in bliss that the only sign of my actual orgasm is the spasming of my walls around Noah's cock. I hear him groan as he finds his own release. When he pulls out, I slump back down to the couch feeling like someone has removed my bones.

I hear Noah walk away. A toilet flushes. A sink runs. Then I hear him return.

"If you keep laying there like that, I'm going to have to do something about it." His deep voice cuts into my cloud of serenity.

I crack an eye open to see him smirking down at me. "Mmm. Like what?" I ask.

He grins and scoops me up with lightning reflexes, carrying me into my bedroom and depositing me carefully on the bed. He kisses me on the mouth, his tongue sweeping against mine briefly before kissing his way down my center, servicing each nipple on his way through the fabric of my top, then moving between my legs. He flattens his tongue against my sex, running it slowly over the whole length of my core a few times before using the tip to tease my clit.

My hips start working without my permission, grinding against his face. Any descent I'd had from my high abruptly vanishes as I'm vaulted back into the clouds, my mind foggy with lust.

I feel Noah's tongue leave me, only to be replaced by the gentle pressure of his finger.

"Tell me you missed this," he demands.

I lift my head to meet his eyes. "I missed you," I admit in a whisper. "Even though you were right there."

"I know exactly how you feel," he assures me, then proceeds to fingerfuck a fourth orgasm out of me before sliding up to mold himself against my jellylike body.

We lay in silence for a while until the fog starts to clear. Though I'm still much less in my head than usual. It's nice. Being with him this way is nice.

"Why couldn't we have more of this and less of being at each other's throats?" I muse out loud. "That would be nice."

"You're the one who didn't call," he reminds me. "I was ready to keep doing this from day one." He gives me a smirk, but I can tell he really means it.

"Yes, well, I think you still like the fighting," I reply.

He laughs, nodding his agreement. "You get all passionate. It's hard not to want to bend you over my desk and fuck you when you're all riled up like that," he responds.

"Yes, well, at least we're well-suited in the bedroom," I reply, finally starting to really come back down to earth. And realizing that we're back to exactly where we started.

"And we're not outside the bedroom?" he asks.

"What does it matter?" I ask rhetorically, rising from the bed. I remove my scrubs top, undershirt, and bra all in one motion so I'm completely naked. "I'm going to take a shower. Want to join me?"

"As tempting as that offer is, I actually need to go back to work," he grumbles. "And don't think for one minute that we're done with this conversation."

"You're not done," I say, "but I am. Enjoy the rest of your day, Noah."

"Does that mean you'll be back to work tomorrow?" he presses, rising from the bed and putting himself in front of me.

"Seven percent raise and you do everything in your power to bring Becca back on?" I ask, pressing my naked body against him. His pupils dilate and his mouth opens. I suppress a triumphant smile.

"That's the deal," he agrees. "Now stop trying to get me to fuck you again."

I let my grin loose. "Oh, Noah," I reply. "If I was trying to get you to fuck me again, you'd know it." I wink and saunter into the bathroom, pleased as punch that my inner confident sex goddess seems to have re-emerged. "Lock the door on your way out."

I turn on the shower and let the steam fill the bathroom. Just as I step into the shower, I hear the front door shut. Jules one, Noah zero. Or actually, Jules four, Noah one. But I'll take it anyway.

CHAPTER 15

I go back to work the next morning, much to Sasha's surprise. I promise to tell her later, when we're not at work. I definitely don't want to restart the rumors about Noah and me.

Becca is likewise back at work by lunchtime. She doesn't say a word, simply high-fiving me on the way in. That's Becca.

MacDougall is furious. We normally don't see much of him, but he spends the day hovering and huffing and asking all kinds of nosy questions.

Part of me is smug at my victory. The other part of me wonders what the hell he's up to and if I'm going to regret my power play.

Early that afternoon I get paged to the nurses' station while I'm cleaning up after a procedure. When I get back to the desk, Becca hands me my cellphone.

"It's been buzzing constantly," she says. "The number isn't in your phone book, but I didn't want to turn it off in case it was an emergency."

"Thanks," I reply, going to put it in my pocket, but before I can manage to, it buzzes again.

"Hello?" I answer.

"Hey, beautiful," Noah's voice says over the line.

"Are you seriously calling me while I'm at work?" I ask with a laugh.

"I'm seriously calling you while you're at work. I didn't want to wait too long to ask you to go to dinner with me tomorrow night."

"Can't. We always do team happy hour Friday evenings." Which I may or may not actually attend, but I don't tell him that. Best to keep him on his toes. Especially since he apparently likes that.

"Hmm. Saturday then?"

I hesitate, knowing going on a real date with him is an awful idea. But the guy did just get my friend unfired and secured me a huge raise.

"Fine."

"I'll pick you up at seven," he replies, and I can hear the smile in his voice. I hate myself for it, but it makes me smile too.

"I'll see you then," I agree.

"Not if I see you first," he teases.

I roll my eyes and hang up, handing it back to Becca. "You can put it back in the locker," I tell her.

She looks at me expectantly. "Well?"

"Not here," I say in a low voice. But I give her a wink. "Tell you later."

She waggles her eyebrows and grins. "I'ma hold you to that, boo."

I round the corner to go back to the exam room and finish up, but I run smack into MacDougall.

"Ms. Magnusson, please come with me," he says curtly.

I look at him in bewilderment. "Why?"

And by the irritation on his face, I half expect him to bellow "Insubordination!" then and there. Thankfully, he doesn't. He simply turns and stalks away, pretending I didn't ask. So I follow. Sure that nothing good will come of it, but also sure I don't really have much of a choice.

He heads into his office, seating himself in his chair and gesturing for me to sit. I perch on the edge, bracing myself.

He opens a drawer and grabs what appears to be some sort of form. He spends a few minutes filling it in while I sit in confused silence. Finally, he turns it toward me and slides it across the desk with a pen.

"This is a conduct warning that will be added to your file. Please read it and sign at the bottom," he directs haughtily.

I suppress an eye roll and look down at the form, scanning the few lines he'd filled in under my name, employee number, and the date and time.

"I'm being written up for personal use of a cellphone while at work?" I ask, aghast. "Are you kidding me?"

"I'm not 'kidding you,' Ms. Magnusson. I witnessed it myself. Sign the form."

"I want to see the rule that says I'm not allowed to do that," I insist. "Because I've never heard of it."

"Really?" he scoffs. "Because there are signs all over the hospital, Ms. Magnusson. Let's not play these games."

The irony. Oh, the irony.

"Those signs *request* that *patients* not use their cellphones while in the hospital. They do not *forbid* the *employees* from using them," I point out. "We all put our cellphones in a locker to minimize the potential for equipment interference. But emergencies happen, so sometimes we need to answer our phones."

I realize I'm wasting my breath, but I can't not fight this totally bogus write-up.

"Yes, well, I might be willing to overlook such a case, but your call was *clearly* personal in nature," he replies with a sniff.

"I had no control over the nature of the call, and I kept it brief. Are you seriously writing me up for this? Because I'm not an idiot. I know that repeated warnings can give you grounds on which to fire me."

He looks startled for a moment before he composes himself, and I know I just hit the nail on the head. He's been hanging around looking for reasons to write me up so he could fire me. Or maybe Becca. More likely both of us, in punishment for going around him. I should've known.

"Then perhaps you shouldn't have violated the policies *you* signed when you started working here," he responds.

That makes me laugh out loud. I can't help it. "You realize when I started working here I was eighteen years old? Do you remember if we had a cellphone policy on the books in 2003? Because I sure as hell don't. I want to see where I signed agreeing to that before I'll sign this write-up," I insist.

"You'll sign this right now or you'll be written up for noncompliance as well," he replies, going purple in the face. "And with two on the books, I'll be well within my rights to submit your termination paperwork."

I raise my eyebrows. "And I'm well within my rights to request that we involve administration at this point, as I feel I'm being threatened into signing something I don't think is valid," I respond. I rise from the chair. "Shall we?"

MacDougall sits there, sputtering for a bit before he purses his lips. "I don't think that will be necessary."

"Oh, I think it is," I insist, snatching the paper from the desktop before he can retrieve and destroy it. "I can go on my own, if you prefer not to join me."

"I … that is to say …" he stammers. "I'm too busy for that sort of thing at the moment. Get back to work." He turns purposefully toward his computer, ignoring me with all of his might.

I take the write-up with me, chuckling on my way back to the nurses' station. Becca looks up curiously at my amusement.

"What?" she asks.

I jerk my head toward the door. "Take a walk with me and I'll tell you."

She raises an eyebrow but joins me. As soon as we're off the unit, I tell her what happened and warn her that he clearly has it out for me, and probably her too.

"Damn, so are we headed to administration next?" she asks.

I wave a hand, folding the piece of paper into my breast pocket. "Of course not. Not unless he forces my hand, anyway. But I will document this in an email and send it to myself. Just in case. But I wanted to warn you first so you didn't fall into any of his traps."

Becca blows out a breath. "Geez, well, this is going to be fun," she says sarcastically as we make our way back to cardiac.

I pat her on the back as we get to the desk. "Don't worry, it won't last forever. I have a plan."

"Oooh, I like the sound of this," she replies gleefully. "What can I do to help?"

I give her a wink. "Just be you, babe. Just be you. And let me know if anything happens, okay?"

She gives me a salute. "You got it, boss." She looks at me funny for a second. "You know, you seem different."

"I feel different," I admit. "I think having a fallback plan, being able to quit if I want to, gave me a new perspective. It's liberating."

"Well, whatever put that smile on your face, I'm all for it," she responds. "For a second I thought you might be gettin' some. But ya know, the whole liberated woman thing is cool too."

That gets a laugh out of me. "Can I tell you a secret, Becks?" She leans in with an eager look, and I drop my voice so even if you were standing ten feet away you wouldn't be able to hear. "It might be a little of both."

Becca's eyes go wide and she doesn't respond out loud, simply holding up a hand for a high five and doing a little dance on the spot. With a chuckle, I high-five her, then we both go about our business.

When I have a lull later that afternoon, I go see a couple of old friends in different parts of the hospital.

I hit up Ben Ferris in billing first, having known him almost the whole time I've been at Rutherford. I even introduced him to his now-wife. So when I ask him to compare MacDougall's appointment charts with insurance claims and patient invoices for the last year, he doesn't bat an eyelash, and I know he'll keep his mouth shut.

Same for Tara Scopes in what's basically the human resources area of hospital administration; we've been good friends for more than a decade, and she happily agrees to quietly research MacDougall's history of employee write-ups.

I leave work at the end of the day finally feeling like I'm regaining some modicum of control over the chaos that has become my life. And hoping like hell it's not all about to blow up in my face.

CHAPTER 16

I'm sifting through patient files on Friday afternoon when Sasha approaches the nurses' station with an air of urgency that immediately puts me on high alert.

"I was just called into MacDougall's office," she hisses to Becca and me before we can say a word. "They're moving me to the cardiovascular intensive care unit."

"What the hell?" Becca asks angrily, but I hold up a hand.

"And they're moving Sarah to day shift here, yes?" I ask Sasha.

She looks at me, bewildered. "Yes, how'd you know that?"

I shake my head, not wanting to get into it here. "Later. They're promoting you to ARNP though, right?"

Sasha nods. "And supposedly giving me a raise, but the ICU chief will go over all that with me on Monday," she agrees.

"Wait … so what's the problem with this?" Becca asks, confused.

"I … guess there's not one? I was just worried it would upset you guys," Sasha admits.

"Well, I mean, it'll suck not getting to talk as much as we normally do, but you'll just be right down the hall," Becca replies with a shrug. "And you know, more money for you, so yay."

"You don't look very 'yay,'" I point out drily. "But I have to get into exam eleven, so you can tell me why at happy hour."

"Aw, hell yes, you're coming?" Becca asks, looking significantly more chipper.

I chuckle. "Wouldn't miss it," I reply with a wink. "See you ladies there?"

"See you there," they say in unison.

* * *

It's nearly seven by the time I make it to our usual happy hour spot a few blocks from the hospital, and as soon as I'm inside I can hear the lot of them loudly chatting and laughing from the booth they occupy across the room. And seeing as the place is pretty packed, that's saying something.

I make my way over, hoping that means everyone is starting to feel better about their lives and their jobs, after everything that's been going down.

As I approach, I note that it's more or less the usual crowd: Sasha and Cal on one side, Becca and Mark at the back, and Zoe and Ethan opposite Sasha and Cal. It's almost like three happy couples, except Zoe and Ethan are just friends, and Mark only wishes he were with Becca. Hopefully, now that Vincent's working across town and not able to join happy hour anymore, that won't give Mark any ideas. Not that Becca can't take care of herself.

In any case, they all greet me as I approach, and Sasha slides over to let me sit next to her. I give her a squeeze around the shoulder and congratulate her on her promotion, realizing I hadn't done that earlier.

We talk a bit about the switch, then as soon as I'm sure nobody else is paying attention, I give her the highlights of my conversation with Noah about shuffling her and Sarah, apologizing for not mentioning it sooner. It's hard to remember what I have and haven't told people these days. The drama has been very real and pretty overwhelming.

Thankfully, Sasha's not one to hold grudges or pay much attention to what other people say or do anyway. And I know not working with Cal will take some of the pressure off keeping their relationship under wraps. So it all worked out in the end.

I don't miss the looks Ethan shoots me through a couple of rounds of drinks. Unfortunately, after my second beer, I get up to use the ladies room only to find that Zoe has gone home to her wife, leaving Ethan's side of the booth conspicuously empty. As much as I'd like to avoid his advances, I'd also rather not make it look like I'm scared of him by insisting on sitting next to Sasha anyway.

So I resignedly slide into the booth next to him, giving him a small, forced smile.

"So, what'd I miss?" I ask, trying to engage the whole table so as to avoid solo talk with Ethan.

"You'll never guess who came in while you were gone," Mark says with quiet excitement, pointing at the bar.

I turn, already suspecting who I'm going to see. Yep. Noah. Accepting a beer from the bartender. Thankfully, his back is to us and he's across the room. I turn back, wishing the sight away. What the hell is he doing here?

"What the hell is he doing here?" Becca whispers angrily, voicing my thought verbatim.

I shrug, trying to play it off. "Obviously, the same thing we are," I reply. "It *is* the closest bar to the hospital, after all."

Sasha gives me an *Are you okay?* look that I choose to ignore.

"Dude, we should invite him over," Mark says obliviously. "Maybe he'll buy us all beers. That's what rich guys do, right?"

I arch an eyebrow. "You obviously don't know Noah Rutherford," I grumble.

And like he heard, Noah turns and our eyes meet across the room.

I'm spellbound, staring at him, not daring to breathe. Hoping nobody notices that I can't take my eyes off him.

But I needn't worry, as in mere moments he looks away. Like he barely recognized me. Like he doesn't know or care about me.

I should be happy about that, but I find myself annoyed anyway. That he's here. That he's for some reason acting like I don't matter. I don't even care if it's to spare me having to explain what's going on between us to my friends. For some reason, I just can't shake the slight.

"You okay, Jules?" Ethan asks quietly from next to me, putting his hand on my thigh.

I look down at the hand and then back up at him. My, he's bold today. I reach down and give his hand a squeeze, subtly moving it to the seat between us.

"Great, thanks," I assure him. "How are you doing, Ethan?"

He grins widely at the perceived encouragement. "Much better now you're back," he says. I sigh internally.

Unfortunately, everyone else at the table has moved to individual conversations too, and I'm forced to make small talk with Ethan for a while. He keeps touching me in little ways — mostly on my hand, arm, and shoulder — and looking dreamily into my eyes.

I wish I wanted someone like Ethan. Someone who was sweet, steady, and eager to please. He's everything Noah isn't. Yet somehow, here I am, bored to tears and unable to stop thinking about Noah Rutherford.

Thankfully, once our glasses start running low again, and it's so busy our waitress hasn't been by in a while, the guys decide to go get us another round, leaving Sasha, Becca, and I at the table together.

"I think I'm going to bail before the guys get back," I say, faking a yawn. "Becca, I trust you can handle the extra beer?"

She cracks a smirk. "Oh, I sure can, but let's call a spade a spade here. Which one are you running from: Noah or Ethan?"

I shake my head and huff a dry laugh. "I don't know, both?"

Becca looks over my shoulder. "Whelp, you didn't run fast enough," she mutters.

I turn my head in time to find Noah closing in, looking grim-faced.

"Ladies," he greets us curtly. "Ms. Magnusson, may I have a word?"

Before I can even respond, he grasps me firmly by the elbow and steers me out of the booth. I only have time to give a bewildered look and gesture of *WTF* toward Sasha and Becca before he's pulled me through the crowd to the hall that leads to the restrooms.

He pulls me past both the men's and women's rooms, to the gender-neutral stall at the very back. It's only once he's pulled me inside and closed and locked the door behind him that it's quiet enough to protest.

"What the hell, Noah?" I growl up at him.

He grabs me by the shoulders in answer, turning me away from him and planting my hands on the flower-papered wall. He presses himself behind me, his fingers finding their way to my breasts, his breath hot on my ear. No kissing. No caressing. Only raw need that borders on anger.

"Don't talk," he commands.

I open my mouth to protest when one of his hands drops down the front of my pants, roughly grabbing my sex, stroking between my lower lips. My back arches and no words of dissent escape me, only a throaty moan. It's so sudden, but it feels so damn good.

"I'm going to fuck you right here, baby," he promises gruffly in my ear, both of his hands dropping to my waistband and sharply tugging my scrubs bottoms to my ankles. An instant later I hear a zipper, then the rip of foil, then his hard cock on my backside. I hate it, but I'm so turned on, already soaking wet and wanting him inside me.

So when he sinks deep into me, I greedily tilt to accept him, using the leverage of my arms on the wall to get him all the way in.

His hands grasp my hips an instant before he starts a punishing rhythm. My core tightens around every hard thrust, the pleasure ripping through me. But in mere minutes, I feel him pick up speed, hear his breath hitch, then feel him pulsate inside me as he groans out his orgasm. He gives one final, mighty thrust, burying himself completely in me. His front joins to my back, his arms encircling me so we're fully connected.

"You're mine, Julianna," he utters in my ear. "Nobody else's. Do you hear me?"

"I'm not a possession," I say, panting. I shuffle to work his cock out of me, and he grabs the condom to stop his cum from spilling all over.

I turn to face him, putting my back against the wall.

"Is that what this is about? Marking your territory?" I ask angrily.

"I saw that guy you were sitting with. He doesn't get to touch you like that anymore," Noah says, tying off the condom, tossing it in the trash, and pulling up his pants.

I make to pull mine up, but he stops me.

"And you don't get to tell me what to do," I snap.

"I'm not done yet," he growls, dropping into a squat, his tongue finding its way between my legs. His fingers follow, sinking deep into me while he laps at the wetness he made between my thighs.

"Fuck," I gasp, grabbing him hard by the hair. My first thought was to pull him away from me, to rail at him that he doesn't get to tell me who I spend time with, who touches me, but I find myself angrily pressing him into me harder, opening my knees, relishing in the pleasure he's giving me.

His wicked tongue scrapes across my clit as his fingers pump furiously over the spot inside. An orgasm builds so fast and furiously that I don't have time to think about how fucked up this is before I'm choking back screams from my orgasm.

He pulls away and I slump back, catching my breath as he wipes his face and washes his hands.

Once I'm collected enough, I stand up and fix my clothes, then turn to him.

"I can't do this, Noah," I spit at him as he throws the paper towel in the garbage can and faces me. "One minute you're on my side, saying all the right things, acting like a good guy. The next you're an arrogant, entitled, possessive asshole. This isn't going to work. I can't date you."

"Oh, really? Your mood swings seem plenty capable of keeping up with me," he retorts.

My hands fly to my hips. "Fine, we're both all over the goddamn map with each other," I allow. "But that's my point. This isn't me. This isn't what I want."

Someone bangs on the door.

"Occupied," Noah snarls loudly. Then he turns back to me. "Then let's get off this damn rollercoaster. Together."

I shake my head. Why does this all have to be so complicated? "I'm not the one who tried to fuck you into submission. Goodbye, Noah."

I let myself out to run smack into a very confused-looking guy who clearly was waiting for the larger, private bathroom. I can't even imagine what the look will be on his face when Noah comes out next, and I don't care. I walk straight out of the damn bar without looking back.

CHAPTER 17

"I can't handle this anymore, Becks," I groan first thing Monday morning. "If I have to keep working in the same hospital as that man, I'm going to lose my shit."

Becca rolls her eyes. "Girl, I've got the market cornered on overly dramatic, and you're putting even me to shame. Chillax. I mean, seriously, you don't even have to see him almost ever, and I'm sure all this shit will be done at some point."

I shake my head. "He's like a disturbance in the force," I insist. "Even when he's not right here, he's messing with my life. Like that whole rumor about us."

"Please," Becca scoffs. "Nobody's even talking about that anymore. And they wouldn't have been talking about it in the first place if you guys weren't stupid enough to go up to his hotel room *together*. Note for next time, boo: He goes first, then you meet him there, nobody's the wiser."

I pull a confused face. "I'm sorry, do you know something I don't?" I ask. "Did someone see us?"

"Ohhhh, fuuuuuuck," Becca says, her eyes going wide. "I forgot to tell you, didn't I?"

I snap my head back. "Oh my god, yes, you did," I exclaim. She looks at me sheepishly. "Well? Spill it already!"

"All right, all right, yeesh," she replies theatrically. "The rumor mill may have passed down that the chief of emergency saw you two leaving the gala together. Hand in hand. And getting into an elevator to the bank of rooms over the ballroom area."

"And they went spreading that around? Holy fucking shit," I gasp.

"Ehhhh, I think it was more like they told one person, in confidence, who obviously couldn't keep their mouth shut," she allows, with the clear air of understanding as someone who has done exactly that more than once. "Either way, sounds like you guys weren't exactly discreet about it. And at least it wasn't Moneybags himself who couldn't keep his mouth shut."

"Oh, because that gets him off the hook for being a domineering bastard," I grumble.

"Jules. Darling. The price you pay for a man who gets you all worked up in bed is that sometimes he's gonna get you all worked up other places, and not always in a good way," she says patiently. "It just goes with the whole dynamic."

"Well, then you and Vincent must have off-the-charts amazing sex because you guys sure do bitch at each other in public enough," I tease.

She bobs her head on her neck. "You know it. And really. You must know it, because you and this guy are obviously at each other's throats. And I'm still waiting to hear how *hot* that must mean things are between the sheets." She purses her lips and looks at me expectantly.

I heave a deep sigh. "It's like my birthday and Christmas and a Marvin Gaye song all wrapped up in one," I admit. "But that's not the point."

"Oh, I think that's *exactly* the point, darling," she replies, with laughter in her voice. "But I see you've got a ways to go before you realize that. It's all good. Take your time."

We're interrupted by Ben Ferris appearing around the corner with a sheaf of papers nestled in the crook of one arm.

"Ah, Jules," he greets me with a smile. "I have something I think you're going to like."

I hop out of my chair, gesturing for him to come around the corner.

"We have fifteen minutes until our morning meeting, so I'm all ears," I assure him.

Ben plunks the stack onto the desktop, pulling the top sheet off the pile.

"This is the summary report," he points at the rest, "and that is the backup." He points to a bold number at the bottom of the left column. "Bottom line? That's the total amount that should have been billed for all of our subject's patients in the last year between both patient responsibility and what insurance would actually cover." He points to a number in the right column just to the side of the first number that's almost three times as much. "That's how much was collected from both the patients and insurance combined."

My eyes grow wide and my heart leaps in my chest. "Were the patients overcharged or was the insurance overbilled?" I ask tersely.

"Both," he replies. "Including insurance billing charges for procedures there is no record of being performed."

I gasp. No. Fucking. Way. Holier-than-thou MacDougall has been committing billing and insurance fraud.

"Yes, big deal," he murmurs. He fishes a thumb drive from his pocket. "It's all on here too, and I've got it saved to one of my own. I'm required to report these findings, but if you had a plan to do so first, I can wait a day at most."

I look up at him and let out a sigh of relief. "I have one more thing to follow up on, then I'll take this straight to Noah Rutherford this morning," I assure him. "Thank you, Ben, I really owe you."

He smiles. "Honestly, you've done me a favor. I'll get major kudos for bringing this issue to light," he replies. "But you're welcome. And Trish says hi, by the way."

"Tell her hi back," I reply with a distracted smile, grabbing the sheaf of papers. With a wave, Ben disappears back down the hall, and I turn to Becca.

"Don't worry about the staff meeting, I'll cover for you," she assures me, clearly having paid attention to every word. "Go get it done, boo."

Suddenly, I'm giddy, and I can't help but unleash a grin. "I'm going to go see Tara before heading up to Noah's office."

Becca nods and salutes. "See you when I see you."

I nod, too preoccupied for much else, and head up to Noah's floor, since Tara's office is at the other end of his hall.

Unfortunately, when I get there, she doesn't have anything else incriminating. He's pretty much written up everyone at some point or another. Guess I shouldn't be that surprised. But I don't need anything more from her anyway. Not with what I got from Ben.

So I march straight to Noah's office. I knock with my free hand but don't get an answer. So I knock again, impatient to share this information with him. When I still get no response, I try the handle, and it pops right open.

Noah looks up at me from his desk, aghast, and clearly on a phone call.

"It's important," I mouth.

His nostrils flare and his eyes tighten, but he wraps up the call and gestures for me to enter.

"It damn well better be *very* important for you to interrupt me like that," he says in a threatening tone.

I drop the stack of papers on his desk, passing him the summary report. "Oh, I think you're going to want to look at this report as soon as possible," I assure him smugly. I let his eyes scan the paper for a minute. When his jaw drops, I know he's understood. "See, Dr. MacDougall made it very clear to me last week that he was going to do everything in his power to have me fired after deducing that I had something to do with getting Becca back. So rather than wait, I asked a couple of key people to help me look into his goings-on at the hospital a little further, concerned that he'd tried to pull something similarly shady in the past. But even I never dreamed he'd be involved in something this big."

Noah's eyes snap up to meet mine. "Do you mean to say others are involved?" he asks sharply.

I realize my phrasing did imply that. "No, I just meant that I didn't imagine him doing this sort of thing," I clarify.

"Nonetheless, that he could even get away with something like this merits further investigation as to how long it has been going on and how it's been overlooked," he says in a stern tone. Then he drops the paper on his desk and sinks back into his chair, rubbing his eyes. "Thank you for bringing it to my attention."

I stand there for a moment, trying not to feel like his reaction was slightly anticlimactic, or be annoyed by his curt dismissal, but after a minute I head for the door. Just before I leave, I decide to ask the question that's been bugging me all weekend.

"Noah?" He looks up. "Did you know I'd be at that bar on Friday?"

He drops his hands in his lap, looking completely worn out.

"No, Julianna. I didn't know you'd be at that bar on Friday."

His words sound truthful, but I hold his gaze for a moment longer, looking for any sign of deception. But I find none. It would be so much easier if I did. With a small nod, I turn and leave.

* * *

The week crawls by with a heavy sense of anticipation. But nothing happens. Nor for the week after. Every day that ticks by has me looking over my shoulder, wondering if MacDougall somehow was confronted, wormed his way out of trouble, and is about to rain hell down on me. So many times I almost go to Noah's office to ask. But I'm finally learning to ignore the fact that he's working in an office only a few floors over my head. So I let it be.

But two weeks to the day after I brought Noah the evidence on MacDougall, I arrive at my usual five-thirty in the morning start time to Dr. Carson waiting with Sarah at the nurses' station. And they're both just standing there. Dr. Carson looks grim, Sarah looks nervous.

"Morning, guys," I say hesitantly. "Any reason you're looking like doom and gloom this morning?"

"Jules," Dr. Carson greets me. "Now that you're here, let's all go have a chat in my office."

He ruffles a hand through his gray head of hair as he leads us down the hall and around the corner. But he doesn't turn into the last office on the left like I expect. No, he hooks a right into MacDougall's office. An office that, as I enter, I realize has been stripped bare but for the furniture.

"No," I gasp in disbelief. Even though I'd expected MacDougall would be fired. Hell, I'd *hoped* for it.

Dr. Carson settles himself in the chair behind the large, dark wood desk.

"I'm afraid so," he confirms.

Sarah and I sink into the chairs across from him.

"What happened?" Sarah asks, confused.

Dr. Carson gives me a loaded look. "Where to begin?" he muses. After a moment of thought, he resumes. "It will be announced this morning that four hospital officials have been replaced, and each job role in each unit has been given a new title and salary assignment to align with the new hospital budgets and staffing goals. It was always part of the overall reorganization plan to ask Dr. MacDougall to retire, but unfortunately evidence was brought to light that, upon deeper investigation, outed him, two other chiefs, and Mrs. Knowles as having collaborated to commit financial fraud against both our patients and the insurance companies. That last part is information not to be shared outside of this room."

We both gasp and nod. Not in my wildest dreams did I think this went as high as Mrs. Knowles.

"So you're our new chief," I deduce.

"That I am, Jules," he responds. "Though I suppose I could start calling you 'Ms. Magnusson' now." He gives me a wink to show he's joking.

I snort. "Jules is fine," I assure him drily.

"You said something about budgets and staffing goals?" Sarah points out.

"Ah, yes, that," he responds. "All of the chiefs, including the newly appointed ones, have been consulted over these last six weeks on patient volume, projected growth, and required staffing. After cutting what the Rutherford Group deemed to be individuals unfit to represent our organization, hiring to that staffing plan has been fully funded under new procedures to ensure candidates are both hired in a controlled and fair manner consistent with local, state, and federal regulations, as well as meet the job qualifications without bias."

Sarah and I share a meaningful look. Translation: no more hiring friends and friends of friends. No more hiring people just to get warm bodies in here. *Halle-freaking-lujah.*

"What about raises?" I press.

Dr. Carson smiles, obviously pleased with what he's about to share. "Oh, you're going to like this part," he responds. "Based on the newly defined job roles and target salaries, all hospital personnel's salaries will be adjusted accordingly — only upward, mind you — to put them at the appropriate salary based on their performances for those years they would've gotten raises. Plus, there will be an extra boost if needed to put everyone's compensation on par with industry standards. In some cases we're not talking about a lot of money, but it will counteract much of the disparity in pay across functions and encourage those who are still here to stay onboard long term. At least, I think that's the hope."

"Well, it sure won't hurt," Sarah snarks. She's always been particularly bitter, not having been granted the overnight shift pay differential the hospital offered back when she started. Not that she'll get that anyway, but it sounds like we'll all receive sizeable raises.

I wonder briefly if I'll get less since I already negotiated a pretty hefty hike out of Noah. And as soon as I remember him, a thought pops into my mind.

"Who will replace Mrs. Knowles?" I ask abruptly.

"For the time being, Noah Rutherford," Dr. Carson responds, confirming my suspicion. "But I believe the long-term plan is to identify candidates from within Rutherford Hospital or one of the other hospitals in the Rutherford Group family to fill that role."

"I see," I respond softly, looking down into my hands. I can feel tears pricking the backs of my eyes, and I blink them away, unsure of why I'm so emotional. Then again, all these changes are huge. Maybe being emotional about it isn't such a strange reaction.

"Any other questions?" Dr. Carson prompts.

"Not at the moment," Sarah responds carefully.

I shake my head.

"All right then, ladies. Let's go get this show on the road," he replies, rising.

I take a deep breath and follow. Glad for once to have news that's going to make things better.

CHAPTER 18

The mood throughout the hospital borders on party-like the whole week. I've seriously never seen everyone this happy to work here, this excited about changes being made. It's the feeling I've been trying to get back for *years*, and I want to cry with happiness.

On Thursday, however, I'm jolted back to reality when Lisa passes along that Noah wants to see me in his office at the end of my shift. Instead of worrying about butting heads with him, I purposefully decide to take it as an opportunity to thank him. It's the least I can do as, in the end, he really did deliver.

But it's also hard not to be nervous about why he wants to see me. Still, I power through, and work is still busy enough to keep me from thinking too hard about anything else

The end of my shift is upon me before I know it, and I stand once again at Noah's office door. You think I'd be used to it by now. With a snort at my own inner snark, I lift my hand and knock.

The familiar call of, "Come in," follows. I take a deep breath and open the door to the usual scene. Noah, handsome as ever, busy at his desk in a fitted gray dress shirt rolled to the elbows and black slacks. And when his honeyed eyes meet mine, it's every bit as jarring as it always is.

"You wanted to see me?" I ask, standing behind one of the chairs in front of his desk.

He looks at me, then looks at the chair, then looks back at me. But he wisely doesn't say a word. I suppress a smile at his lack of ordering me to sit down for once.

"I wanted to tell you I was able to match your mother with a program that will cover almost all of her care," he explains, picking up a few pieces of paper and handing them to me. "Since you have health care power of attorney, you'll need to be the one to authorize it. Just call the number circled there and reference the program listed beneath it."

I take the papers, absolutely stunned.

"I … wow, Noah …" I look down at the sheet, and sure enough the details listed seem to match my mother's situation. It also says the program is invitation only, so clearly I have Noah's influence to thank for this opportunity. In any case, between this program and the Alzheimer's drug trial my dad is in, I'll be paying less than a quarter of what I'd previously paid out of pocket.

And that's when it hits me. I look back up at him sharply. "You got my dad into that Alzheimer's trial too, didn't you?"

Noah freezes, and I know it's true.

"Yes," he admits. "I did." He looks at me, clearly wary of what's about to come.

"Why?" I demand.

He looks at me with … pity? No, that's not it. Something else I can't quite place.

"Can't you just be happy that I helped? Does it matter why?" he asks.

"Oh, now I really want to know," I insist. "What are you hiding, Noah?"

He takes a deep breath and stands to close the door. Seems like we have a lot of closed-door conversations. Ones that usually leave me pissed off. I brace myself for whatever he's about to say when he turns back to me.

He stands, not a half dozen feet away, staring at me with a vulnerability that's heartrending.

"Because I love you, Julianna," he admits. "And I'm doing everything I know how to make you mine."

I'm shocked into silence. No, "shocked" is an understatement. There are no words for what I feel right now.

My throat constricts.

War erupts inside me.

He's lying. He can't love me, I've been such a jerk to him. He's light years out of my league. I'm not the kind of woman someone like him would be with. So … why would he lie? Is he trying to manipulate me? To god only knows what end. Knowing how deluded with power and out of touch with reality people like him are, it's not out of the question.

Or worse, he's telling the truth. Maybe he thinks he loves me, but it's just because I've refused him? He's certainly a man who isn't used to being told no. The thrill of the chase and all. Forbidden fruit. Yes, that's it. This is another power trip. And he thinks he can get what he wants by buying me off. And once he's gotten it, he'll cast me aside when it's no longer fun.

I clench my fists at my sides, knowing I just can't take the chance either way. I've been hurt by men with far less power over me than him. Love is a gamble that rarely pays off under the best of circumstances. And I can't afford the risk.

"You can't buy love, Noah," I finally say, my voice thick with emotion. "Especially not mine."

"I haven't bought anything," he insists, frustration clear in his tone.

I open my eyes and laugh.

"Yes, you have," I respond. "You've bartered your influence, your name, to get things other people can't. And while I appreciate what you've done for my parents, the fact that your privilege got those things won't make me love you. Though I'll forever be in your debt."

I swallow hard and shake my head. The idea of being indebted to someone like him is hard to stomach. But even I'm not so stubborn as to look a gift horse in the mouth. Knowing my parents will be cared for in their last, difficult years, no matter what happens to me, isn't something I can walk away from.

"I should go," I murmur. "Thank you." I lift the papers. "For this. And for everything else. For what it's worth, you've earned my trust." Limited to anything but my heart, though it may be. But I don't say that part.

Noah steps forward, dangerously close, looking down at me. "But not your respect," he deduces.

I can't look him in the eye. Because there's a war raging inside me.

"It's hard to respect someone who won't leave you to make your own choices without trying to influence them," I explain. "I need space, Noah."

"I'm afraid to give it to you," he admits, his eyes glistening. He looks away and sniffs deeply, but when he looks back at me, he's fully composed. "Besides, you're stuck with me until we find a new hospital director, I'm afraid."

A tightness spreads through my chest at that thought. At the idea that he may pop up at any moment, pressuring me with his affections, his expectations. I weigh that against the thought of leaving. And I know which hurts less right now.

"Then I think it may be time for me to move on," I reply, sadness lacing my voice. "You have things well in hand here. I trust it'll all be fine without me now."

Noah's features tighten, and he studies my face for what feels like an age.

"Don't quit just yet. Give me a day. Let me see what I can do."

My brows pull together in confusion. "I'm not sure what good that will do. But okay, fine. One day."

Noah steps backward and turns to the door, holding it open for me.

"Thank you again," I say awkwardly. "For … everything."

"It was my pleasure," he replies with a small smile.

I nod but don't say anything else, simply walking out. Though really, there's nothing simple about it.

* * *

I wake up in that black part of night that feels timeless, panting and sweating. The dream that woke me still fully vivid in my mind. Well, memory, I should say.

Sheila's mom pulls up at the curb to my house, and I can't get out of the car fast enough.

"It'll be okay, Jules, you'll see," Sheila calls after me. "I'm sure something else happened at the dance after we left, and by Monday nobody will remember anything Heather and her stupid friends said."

I wave dismissively, not even bothering with a response as I stomp up the walkway into the house.

The front door flies open under my angry shove, and my mother comes running out of the kitchen, drying her hands on a dish towel.

"Heavens, Julianna, you scared me," she chides. "What's going on?"

Her eyes run over my angry face, clenched fists, and disheveled tulle nightmare of a dress. Just hours ago I was fawning over it. Now, it's a mess from being angrily picked at on the car ride home.

"Bobby Cordero asked me to dance," I snap.

She raises an eyebrow. "And that's a bad thing? Am I missing something?" she asks, throwing the towel she's holding over her shoulder. "I thought you had a crush on him."

I fold my arms across my chest. "Crushes are for little girls, Mom," I scoff.

She tries to hide her amused smile, but it just makes me angrier. Or maybe it's because she just stands there, waiting for an explanation. Or maybe it's because I do like him.

I sigh heavily and roll my eyes. "He only asked me because Heather Adams wouldn't dance with him," I explain.

"So? What does that matter? Didn't you want to dance with him?" she asks.

This time my hands go to my hips. "I don't want to be his second choice. That's embarrassing, Mom," I sass back.

"How do you even know that's why he wanted to dance with you? Surely he didn't say that?" she asks pointedly.

"Because I did dance with him," I say, tears of humiliation running down my face. "Then Heather told me after that he only danced with me because she said no."

"Ah, I see. So what happened then?"

I bite my lip and shake my head, tears continuing to spill down my face. My mom steps forward and wraps her arms around me.

"Come on, baby girl," she says gently. "You can tell me. Let it out."

I push against her, angrier still at being called a baby.

"If you must know," I snap, "he was standing right there, and he didn't say anything. *He just turned all red and left. Then Heather and all her friends started laughing at me. It was so embarrassing, Mom."*

She looks at me with sympathy written all over her face. "That does sound pretty awful. I'm so sorry, Julianna. Why don't you go get changed and I'll make you some cocoa?"

I sniff deeply, considering rejecting her offer, just to dish out some of the rejection I'm feeling. But cocoa sounds too good to resist. So I nod and go clean up.

Not long later, I'm sitting at the kitchen table in my PJs sipping the warm, sweet drink gratefully when my mom slides into the chair next to me with her own mug. She places a hand on my arm.

"I know you probably don't want to hear this right now, but as awful as Heather was, and as cowardly as it was for Bobby to leave, that doesn't mean she was right. Maybe he did want to dance with you. And maybe he only left because he was embarrassed by her too."

I look up and give her the stink eye.

"Doesn't matter," I grumble. "I'm still going to be a laughingstock at school on Monday."

"Oh, I think it does matter," she argues. "Maybe if you give Bobby a chance to explain you two can band together to show everyone Heather was wrong and just being a bully."

"But what if she was right?" I point out. "I'd rather just keep my head down and let it all blow over."

"Finding out the truth isn't worth it?" she asks. "You'd rather make an assumption and live with it than be open to the possibility that you could get what you want, Heathers of the world be damned?"

"Going up against her and all of her friends isn't worth it. Even if she's wrong, she'd make my life hell for turning the tables on her. I'm just going to focus on school like I always do."

My mom retracts her hands and sighs. "Someday, my darling young woman, you're going to learn that things are always more complicated than they seem, and taking the harder path can lead to things you've always hoped for but were too scared to go after."

I roll my eyes at her again. Parents have no idea how vicious seventh-grade girls can be.

"Easy to say when you're not the one who has to deal with it," I grumble. I finish off my cocoa and rise from the table. "Night, Mom."

Mom rises and puts a hand on my arm, stopping me. "I'm serious, Julianna. I know how focused you can be, and how quick you are to shut out things that you can't control. But some of the best things in life are the things we need to believe in enough to fight for. Just don't forget that, okay?"

"Yeah, whatever, Mom."

She shakes her head and releases me.

My twelve-year-old self left then, but in my mind now, I hold the picture of my mother close to my heart. The way she used to be. Loving, patient, and always there to guide me. But it's funny, in all these years she's been mentally absent, I haven't allowed myself to remember her like that.

I wonder what she'd say now. Maybe that's exactly what the dream was about. I haven't revisited that particular memory possibly since we had that conversation. But clearly my unconscious brain showed it to me for a reason. It's not rocket science.

I can't control Noah. Not his feelings, not whatever he is or isn't doing. Not what's going on at the hospital. And I get that in a way I'm rejecting him for whatever his reasons are because of all those unknowns, because it's too hard to trust that it'll actually work out. But it's all I know how to do, and it feels like taking back some of the control I've lost. Because choosing him would be a huge leap of faith that he's not exactly what I thought him to be from the start. Even his own actions have been a mixed bag this whole time, and there's enough bad that's come with the good to believe that, despite what I think are good intentions, his interest would lead to anything but heartache. And when there's more doubt than not, life has taught me that it's just not worth the chance.

Unfortunately, my conscious dismissal doesn't easily override my subconscious' nagging, and it takes a good long while, and a lot of tossing and turning, before I'm able to get back to sleep.

* * *

I return to work the next morning, and everyone is as chipper as they have been lately. But on top of my crappy night of unwelcome memories and even crappier sleep, the luster has totally worn off for me.

However, nothing could have prepared me for Dr. Carson's announcement at our morning staff tag-up that, going forward, James Rutherford will be acting as chief hospital director until a replacement is found. Questions shoot around the room as to whether he'll change anything that's already been put in place, but we're reassured he's merely acting as proxy for Noah, who has been called back to the Rutherford Group to handle other emergent issues.

Emergent issues, my ass.

Becca tries all morning to pull me into a conversation about how I'm feeling. But, in all honesty, I'm not sure how to feel. On the one hand, clearly Noah is giving me the space that I asked for. On the other, I wonder if it's just another ploy to manipulate me. Mostly, I hate even thinking about it all.

Becca finally goes to lunch, and I'm enjoying some blissfully quiet and rare time alone at the nurses' station when the last person I expected to see today shows up at the counter.

"Mr. Rutherford," I exclaim, hopping up nervously. "What can I do for you?"

James Rutherford's blue eyes scan me up and down in a way I'm not entirely comfortable with. He's shorter than I thought, and looks even less like his brother than I'd imagined. And while he's still a very good-looking guy, I definitely get a slimy vibe from his mannerisms and the little sneer that looks like it sits permanently on his face.

"You must be Julianna Magnusson," he says in a silky voice.

"That's me," I reply, still confused as to why he's here.

He extends a hand, which I reach over the counter to shake while I make a mental note to bathe in sanitizer tonight.

"I just wanted to meet you," he explains. "Noah said if I can trust anyone here, it's you."

I raise an eyebrow. So. Noah talked to him about me. And naturally, the playboy that he is, James Rutherford wanted to see what all the fuss was about.

"I see," I reply crisply, crossing my arms over my chest. "Well, I'm happy to help in a professional capacity in any way I can." I try not to stress "professional" too hard. "Is there something specific you had in mind, or ..." I trail off, letting the question hang in the air.

"Not at the moment, no," he replies. "But I'll be starting to interview current staff members to see if any are suitable to fill the director's role. I may ask you for your opinion, if that's all right with you?"

I wave a hand, palm up in agreement. "Absolutely, I'd be happy to," I assure him. "Does that mean you won't be interviewing external candidates?"

"That depends," he says with a smirk. "I'd hoped to promote from within so this didn't drag out. Hell, I'd wanted to sell this place off to the highest bidder weeks ago. But now I'm starting to think I might like it around here." His smirk turns toward leering, and I try not to shudder.

And then part of what he said sinks in.

"Wait, I'm sorry, did you say the Rutherford Group had planned to sell this hospital? That's not still a possibility, is it?" I ask, trying not to look as sick as I feel. After everything we've gone through, knowing that was ever a possibility and still might be ... *Calm your tits, Jules.* I take a subtle deep breath, trying not to think myself into a panic attack.

"That was on the table, yes, but don't worry," he replies. "I'm not sure exactly why, but for once my little brother and I didn't see eye to eye. He was dead set on turning things around here. You all should be worshipping the ground he walks on. He stood up to the whole board for this place until he got his way. God knows why, since UCSD Medical offered a fortune to make it their next surgical center. So see that you tell all your little friends not to waste this opportunity, eh?"

My throat tightens. I don't know if it's from knowing that Noah was really going to bat for us the whole time or from James's threat. Either way, the full truth of it hits me. I was so wrong on so many levels. Noah and I may have been at each other's throats constantly, but he was always on my side. On the hospital's side. I've doubted him this whole time for no reason.

Well ... for my own fucked-up reasons. Even my subconscious was trying to tell me to get out of my own way, to let this man in, that he isn't who I thought he was. One offhand comment from James Rutherford and my entire self-delusion that Noah is some sort of master manipulator is shattered. I know I probably only believed it out of self-protection, but still. I'm an idiot.

Meeting James's eyes, I nod mutely, knowing I can't say any of the things going through my head right now.

"Good," he croons. "Well, Miss Magnusson, it was an absolute *pleasure* to meet you. I'll be seeing you again very soon." He winks at me, and I give him the nicest smile I can muster, but I'm sure I still look a little put off. There might not be much hiding how skeezy I find him.

He seems unfazed, though, and responding is totally unnecessary as he heads out of the unit before I can even form a thought.

I slump into my chair and let my head fall to the desk. I squeeze my eyes shut against the tears threatening at the backs of my eyes as I start to realize almost everything bad I thought about Noah may have had more to do with my own bullshit.

"Whatcha doin'?" Becca's chipper voice breaks through my little pity party.

My head snaps up to find her coming around the counter and giving me a weird look.

I shake my head and bite my lip, still not sure if I can trust myself to talk. Becca instantly gets that something must have happened because she sets her purse down on the spot and rushes to wrap her arms around me.

"Oh, boo, you okay? Tell me what happened," she urges, stroking my back gently.

For some reason, it makes me laugh. She looks at me like I've lost my marbles, and it makes me laugh even harder. Because I have lost my marbles. I chased off the perfect guy because I couldn't see past the labels I'd put on him. On us.

"Okay, Jules, you're starting to freak me out here," she cautions, pulling back.

I shake my head and wipe my eyes.

"Sorry," I say, finally finding my voice. "I've just been a complete fucking idiot, that's all."

Becca arches an eyebrow and puts her hands on her hips.

"I will not have you talking about one of my favorite people that way," she reprimands me.

"You're sweet," I say drily. And then I proceed to tell her about my conversation with James. And how everyone was right — I thought I knew everything. But what I didn't know was that Noah was never the enemy, and what a complete fool I feel like.

"You're right," she says after I've finished. "You're a complete fucking idiot."

I swat at her playfully. "You're not supposed to agree with me," I tease.

She rolls her eyes hard. "Girl, I call it like I see it. You mistook chemistry for animosity. Sounds like you two can't be in a room without getting each other all worked up. And if you don't let it out between the sheets, what did you expect to happen? Honestly. You're usually way smarter than this, Jules," she admonishes.

I cover my eyes with my hands. "Goooooodddd, I hate it when you're right," I moan. I drop my hands. "What do I do, Becks? The man declared his love for me, and I shat all over it. I don't think there's any coming back from that."

Becca blanches. "He did what, now?"

My eyes widen. "I … may have forgotten to tell you about that part," I admit sheepishly.

"Well?" she demands, smacking a hand on the desk.

"You know, we probably have patients to see or something —"

"The short version, then," she insists.

I heave a deep sigh. I summarize it for her as best I can, feeling stupider and stupider with each sentence. "So yeah, he basically told me he loved me, got my parents' care paid for, and then I told him he was trying to buy me off. Then, come to find out, he's been going against his family to try to save this hospital, probably only because I wanted him to. So, you're right. I'm a complete fucking idiot."

"Good. So you realize he was probably doing all that *because* he loves you, right? Not to get you to love him?" she pushes.

I press my lips together. It's all too much truth to handle at once.

"Stop being right," I holler at her.

We both crack up laughing.

"Yeah, okay, I'll leave you alone now," she agrees. "But I trust you're not going to just let this go, yeah?"

"Yeah," I agree with a smile. "And I think I know just what I need to do to fix it."

CHAPTER 19

I send Noah a text message and coordinate a meeting at the office he'd been using upstairs just after my shift. Thankfully, he doesn't ask many questions, probably assuming I'm going to give him a hard time for switching things up with his brother without any warning.

I finish a little early and use the staff showers to clean up and change into a set of street clothes I keep in my locker for emergencies. I pull out my hairband and let my auburn waves tumble down my back. I'd rather be fresh and prepared for our conversation, rather than smelling like hospital and wearing rumpled scrubs. It's just a simple pair of jeans and a purple V-neck tee, but it's cute enough to give me the confidence I'm going to need.

Still, when I head upstairs close to six-thirty, I'm nervous as all hell. It doesn't help that when I approach the door, I can hear two voices inside. It only takes a moment to realize that James and Noah are both in there. While I can't hear what they're saying, the conversation sounds heated.

I hover a few feet from the door, unsure of whether I should approach. I'm spared deciding when the door flies open and James comes stomping out.

He gives me a curt nod but says nothing as he passes. With wide eyes, I carefully approach the now-open door. I peer in and Noah is pacing, running his hands through his hair, when he catches sight of me. He abruptly stops and smooths his rumpled sky-blue dress shirt.

"Come in, Julianna," he says, sounding tired.

I slip inside, gently closing the door behind me. When I turn back, Noah is seated behind the desk, an eyebrow cocked at the door.

"We need to talk," I say by way of explanation.

He presses his lips together, gesturing to the chair across the desk from him. He looks ridiculously stressed out.

I slink into the chair without protest, folding my hands together in my lap nervously.

"I hope I wasn't the cause of any friction between you and your brother," I say quietly.

Noah leans forward on those gorgeous forearms of his, shaking his head. "Not really. There's always been friction between James and me."

"Except, you disagreed with him because of me, didn't you?" I press. "About keeping Rutherford Hospital?"

He looks up in shock. "He wasn't supposed to tell you that. But yes, more or less. I didn't do it to buy your —"

I hold a hand up. "I know," I interject. "I know, Noah. You did so much without ever being asked. I doubted you from the start, and I was wrong. There was just so much tension, and things were already difficult here." I shake my head, stopping myself. "I didn't ask you here to make excuses."

"So why did you ask me here?"

I look up into his eyes. "To apologize. I'm sorry, Noah. I'm sorry I made this harder on you. I'm sorry I didn't trust you. But most of all, I'm sorry I believed you would ever try to buy my love."

He pushes out a dramatic sigh and leans back in his chair. "Thank you for saying that," he replies. Then he looks back up to meet my gaze. "From the moment you told me your story in that office outside of that ballroom, all I've wanted to do was help you. And that both intrigued me and totally freaked me out. Because that's not usually how I operate." He pauses, his eyes glassy. "I tried to ignore it. I decided in that moment to let it be, that it was just because I was so fucking attracted to you. But I couldn't get it out of my head after that. I couldn't get *you* out of my head." He huffs a breath out of his nose. "And now I sound like a total stalker."

A small laugh bubbles out of me. "Better a stalker than an idiot," I say. "Because that's exactly what I've been. I'm so stupid. I was totally blinded by my own biases. You may be Warren

Rutherford's son, but you're also so much more than that. You're fair. And kind. And so generous." I look up at the ceiling, blinking away my tears. "I'm so sorry, Noah. Truly. So, so sorry. I was so very wrong about you."

I hear the rustle of fabric, but I don't trust myself to look. To not cry. I feel him approach, settling next to me.

"Look at me, Julianna," he says, his voice soft but commanding. And as always, I can't resist it, and my eyes meet his as he's knelt next to me. His large, strong hands wrap around mine and he lifts them to his mouth, placing a gentle kiss there. "Everything I did was to make things better for you, easier. Whether you knew it or not. Hell, whether you *ever* knew it or not. It took me weeks to admit how fucking in love with you I was from that very first night. And if my money is what's keeping us apart, I'd give up every goddamn penny if it meant getting to be with you. I've never cared about the money. Not like I care about you."

My eyes fill with tears. "But I was so awful to you, Noah," I whisper. I close my eyes and shake my head. "How could you love me? All I did was make things harder."

I feel his hand cup my cheek, and I open my eyes to see him smiling. "Your feistiness is what drew me to you. And if you haven't realized it yet, we Rutherfords do love a good argument. And I'd rather argue with you than be alone with my piles of money."

I sniff and laugh. "You don't really have piles of money laying around, do you?" I ask skeptically.

He laughs. "No, I don't," he admits. "I was making a point. But I like that you felt the need to bust my chops anyway."

I chew on my lips to suppress my smile. "Does that mean you'll come back to work here?" I ask.

He gives me a surprised look. "If you want me to, yes, I can," he replies. "But if it's all the same, I'd rather not." A hurt look flits across my face, but he shakes his head, stopping my reaction in its tracks. "It's tough, being here, not touching you. That's all."

"I know how you feel," I admit. "It used to make me so angry that I found you so attractive."

"Really?" he says in a teasing tone. "Because you hid it so well."

I wrinkle my nose and shake my head at him. "Laugh it up, chuckles," I tease back, rising from my chair. "If this is how you're going to treat me, I'll just be going then." I turn to make for the door. As I hoped, he grabs my wrist, turning me back toward him.

"Oh, no, you don't," he growls, pulling me into his arms. He looks down into my eyes, his warm, honeyed irises trained on my face. "Tell me we can give this a shot."

I press my palms against his hard chest. "On one condition," I reply.

"I'm listening."

A feline grin splits my face. "I want you to take me on your desk. Right now."

His pupils dilate, but he doesn't move an inch. "Well, shit," he huffs. "Do you now?"

I smile beatifically up at him, wrapping my arms around his neck.

"I do," I confirm. "Because you have my trust Noah, and my respect." I pause, emotions rising in me that I've forbidden myself for so long. "And my love."

His hands tighten on my waist.

"Say it again," he begs, closing his eyes.

I bite into my bottom lip and smile, rising on my toes until my mouth hovers near his.

"I love you, Noah Rutherford," I whisper.

His lips crash against mine, his strong arms wrapping around me until I'm pressed tight against his chest as his tongue teases at my lips. I open to him, and our mouths dance for a moment before he breaks away, spinning me around in his arms.

His lips caress my neck as his hands work my breasts. His fingers trail down my stomach and to the button on my jeans. He pulls back slightly, his eyes locked on mine.

"Make no mistake," he says clearly. "I'm going to take you home after we're done here and we're going to set another orgasm record. But right now, I'm going to bend you over this desk and fuck you like I've been dreaming about for weeks."

I arch at his words. "God, yes, please," I moan. I grab one of his hands with mine, using it to stroke me through my jeans.

He nips roughly at my neck as he goes back to undoing my buttons, then with a rough tug he's got my jeans and panties pulled down to my thighs. A few scoots forward and my legs hit the desk. I lean forward obligingly, putting my bare ass on display for him. I thought I'd be self-conscious getting down and dirty at work, but it's *thrilling*. And so much more of a turn-on than I ever thought it would be.

He runs a hand down my backside, then between my legs. The noise he makes when he feels how wet I am just makes me more so. And the sound of his zipper lowering nearly sends me over the edge.

I look back to find him fisting his cock and looking at me from under hooded eyelids.

"Just so you know," he says, "this has already blown the fantasy out of the water. You're fucking perfect, Julianna." He rubs his bare cock between my legs, asking for permission. I nod eagerly, already knowing we're both safe. He eases the tip in, and I gasp. Much to my dismay, that makes him pull back out. "You're going to have to be quiet, baby." I nod and whimper, and an instant later he rewards me by burying himself swiftly to the hilt.

I have to choke back my moan, closing my eyes and pressing my forehead into the desktop to cope with how fucking good it feels. How much I missed having him inside of me.

"You okay?" he asks quietly and tenderly.

I look back at him. "So good," I breathe softly. "Don't stop."

His eyes darken and he swings his hips, expertly pounding me with just the right amount of force to fuck me hard yet somehow keep from moving the furniture or making any noise but the low sound of skin on skin. It's beyond erotic, and each thrust sends me soaring.

I reach back, needing to touch him, needing to hold onto him to withstand the pleasure without screaming my head off. His hand reaches out and grips mine. What I didn't realize was that would give him more leverage to fuck me harder.

"Oh, god," I moan a little louder than I intended. I bite into my lip. "I'm gonna come."

His only answer is to fuck me even harder, which sends me spiraling over the edge. I somehow manage to come silently, and it just makes the orgasm that much more intense. My body is so tight, my sex squeezing down so hard, that I feel, rather than hear, Noah join me in his own orgasm.

I slump face first onto the desk as I catch my breath.

Noah's hands caress my hips and he leans forward, placing a kiss on my lower back where my shirt has ridden up.

"I'm going to pull out now," he warns.

I take a deep breath, then nod. When he slips out, I lean up and shimmy quickly back into my pants, knowing I can change as soon as I'm home. Which will hopefully be very, very soon. Likewise, he zips up, righting his clothing and hair as much as possible.

"That was …" I trail off, having no words for exactly how fantastic that was.

He pulls me back into his arms. "Just the beginning," he murmurs, looking down into my eyes.

"My place?" I ask breathily.

"I'll race you there," he teases.

I give him an assessing look, not sure if he's serious. But probably best we leave separately anyway. So with the quickest of pecks on the lips, I snatch my purse off the chair and hightail it out of the room. His laughter follows me down the hall.

* * *

Much later that night, after several more rounds of mind-blowing sex, Noah lies next to me in my bed, running his fingers lazily through my hair.

"Did you mean it?" I ask, running my own fingers along his taut abdomen.

"Mean what?" he asks sounding happy and tired.

I prop myself up to look into his eyes.

"That you'd give it all up," I remind him.

"The money?" he asks, to which I nod. He scoots up on the pillow. "Of course. I can donate it to the Alzheimer's Foundation. I can always make more. It's just money."

"You don't have to, not really," I finally reply. "I guess I just have a hard time wrapping my head around both having that much money and being so willing to part with it."

Noah considers that for a minute. "We had very different upbringings," he allows. "But it really is just money. And you're right, it can't buy love. But it *can* help you do some amazing things for the people you love. While it's not everything, I enjoy being able to do those kinds of things." He looks down at me. "Everyone has different resources at their disposal. Some people have a talent for making money. Some a talent for healing." He gives me a meaningful smile. "I might as well use my talent to do good in this world. Money, like everything, is just a tool. It's not inherently good or bad. It's how you use it that defines you."

"Wow," I whisper. "That's ... well, I can't argue with that."

Noah chuckles. "How about this? How about you help me make sure I'm using my money to help people instead of being a stuck-up rich guy who blows it on cars and vacation houses and other stuff that doesn't really matter."

I smile up at him. "On one condition."

"You and your conditions," he grumbles in a teasing tone. "Go on."

"You keep the hot air balloon," I reply.

That gets a full-throated laugh from him. "Absolutely," he agrees. "Though I'd argue that the hot air balloon definitely helped me knock your socks off. So worth every penny in my book."

I roll my eyes and smack him playfully. "I'd argue, but you're not wrong. Though I was kind of thinking we could use it for therapy? Because it's such a spectacular experience, yet so chill and it doesn't have to last very long. It might be the perfect thing for some of the patients at my parents' nursing home. Something like that could go a long way toward improving the lives of people who are sick, lonely, and scared."

Noah's expression softens, and he flips me over onto my back, holding himself over me on his forearms.

"You're amazing," he murmurs, looking down at me. "I love you, Julianna."

I look up at him, unable to believe that we're here, finally. Getting over my own stupid notions of what someone like him should be like was the best thing I ever did.

"I love you too, Noah," I admit.

His mouth reaches down for mine, his lips tenderly caressing me. After a moment, he pushes off of me, climbing off the bed and pulling his briefs on.

I roll onto my side with a frown. "You're staying, right?" I ask, suddenly self-conscious.

He looks back at me and grins. "I'm just going to get a glass of water. Want one?"

I let out a sigh of relief, not sure where my sudden bout of nerves came from. "Yes, please," I reply.

He gives me a funny look, then comes back to the bed, leaning over and kissing me deeply.

"Don't worry," he assures me, looking intently into my eyes. "Now that I've got you, I'm not going anywhere. So you'd better get used to having me around."

I can't help the grin that spreads across my face.

"Promise?" I ask, batting my eyelashes at him.

He runs a thumb over my cheek. "I promise," he replies with a wink. "And you can take *that* to the bank."

I tip my head back and laugh. "Are you always this cheesy?" I tease.

He straightens up and smirks down at me. "Only for you, baby. Only for you."

As he walks away, chuckling, I sink back into the bed, happier than I can ever remember being. More in love than I can ever remember being. More hopeful than I can ever remember being.

As different as we are, I have to admit to myself that we just work. That Becca was right — there's a tension between us that's like a thread pulling us together. Fighting against it just hurt us both. But giving in to it? Nothing has ever felt this right.

I wasn't wrong; you can't buy love. But you also can't help who you fall in love with. You just have to be able to let yourself see them for who they really are, not just who you see them as. It's hard, getting past your own perceptions, past the hurts that scar you along the way. But I think that's the real lesson in life: being willing to revisit your assumptions before they keep you from living happily ever after.

Will I live happily ever after with Noah? It's early days, but I can see it happening. At least now I know I'm not standing in the way of my own happiness. And that feels pretty fucking amazing.

Bonus
MATERIAL

EPILOGUE — CALEB

Six weeks later…

When I first saw her, I knew she was special. In fact, it was right here, eleven years ago, that my eyes landed on the woman I am going to spend the rest of my life with. She just doesn't know it yet. Well, at least not officially.

I'm positive it was this exact hangar on a very similar day at the first Miramar Air Show I attended all those years ago. Same balmy weather, same sidewalks chockablock with people, same beautiful blue skies. And I'm holding hands with the same beautiful woman I merely glimpsed through the crowd all those years ago. I stop when I realize it, Sasha's hand tugging at mine as she continues forward.

When she feels the pull, her beautiful brown eyes look back at me inquisitively.

"Whatcha doin?" she asks teasingly as our friends get a few paces ahead before realizing we've stopped.

I can't help the grin that settles on my face.

"You don't know?" I reply, glancing over at Jules. I flick an eyebrow up and down in her direction and watch her press her lips together trying not to smile. She knows what's coming. She's probably wondered what took me so long. But the longer I thought about how to do this, the more obvious the answer became, so I had to wait until exactly this moment.

Sasha looks at me, totally confused, and it makes me laugh. I drop to one knee, still holding her hand and drawing her close. She gasps when she figures out what I'm about to do, her other hand covering her mouth as tears well in her eyes. Onlookers begin to stop and watch, realizing it too.

I take a deep breath. Can't go to pieces now, and definitely not with Vincent and Noah and the rest of San Diego watching.

"This is where I first saw you," I explain. "I never forgot that day, or what I felt for the gorgeous girl I spotted through the crowd. It's exactly what I felt when our paths crossed again just eight short months ago. And I know it's fast, but in some ways I feel like I've known you forever, Sasha. I love you more than I have words for. You're amazing, and every day with you since I pulled my head out of my ass to believe in you — in us — has been a gift. One I don't intend to waste."

I look down, using my free hand to fish around in my pocket.

"Get it, Cal!" Becca cheers from behind Sasha. The crowd gives an appreciative holler, and Sasha laughs through the tears that have started to slip down her cheeks.

Ring now in hand, I offer it up as I say my final piece.

"If you'll let me, I will spend every day of the rest of our lives making sure you know how much you mean to me. Will you do me the incredible honor of becoming my wife?" And even I have to blink hard against the tears forming.

I can feel the crowd holding its breath as Sasha grins down at me, her hand now fisted under her chin. And even though I'm pretty sure I know what her answer will be, I'm suddenly uncharacteristically nervous as bloody hell.

She says something so quietly that nobody can hear, not even me.

"You're going to have to speak up, love," I tease.

She puts her hand over her mouth again and laughs. Then she nods her head. I'm up before she has a chance to try to speak again, gathering her in my arms.

"Yes?" Even though I expected it, hoped for it, was dying for it, I have to be sure.

"Yes!" she exclaims loudly, throwing her arms around my neck.

The crowd goes bonkers, yelling and cheering. But all I see is her. Our lips connect, and it's wet from her tears and sloppy from our laughter, and it's fucking perfect.

I pull back before we can give the people around us too much of a show and offer her the ring, a princess-cut diamond on a platinum band. Classic, flawless, and beautiful, just like her.

She offers her left hand, and I slide it on her ring finger. Her eyes go wide as she looks at it.

"Oh, Cal, it's *gorgeous*," she murmurs just loud enough for me to hear.

"Let me see, let me see," Becca calls impatiently, trotting up next to us and grabbing Sasha's hand.

I let her slip out of my arms as Jules joins them and they all fawn over the ring. Vincent steps up to my left and Noah to my right as the onlookers go back to their business.

"That's a big fucking ring, man," Vincent notes as the girls gush and giggle.

"Yes, and quite the show," Noah adds drily. "Way to set the bar, bro."

"Sorry, guys," I say with a chuckle and a shrug. "But look how happy she is."

Sasha's eyes flick up to meet mine, as if she heard me. Which would be impossible, as nobody could hear anything over Becca right now. But we're connected like that, and I hold her gaze for a moment.

"I love you," she mouths at me.

"I love you too," I mouth back.

"You guys are disgustingly adorable," Becca pipes in, noticing our little exchange. "Now, when's the wedding?" She pops her hands on her hips and looks at us expectantly.

"Oh, boy," Vincent huffs, grabbing Becca by the hand and hauling her back toward the exhibit we were headed to. "Here we go."

EPILOGUE — VINCENT

Nine months later…

When I first saw her, I knew she was trouble. Thankfully, Becca's particular brand of trouble has just kept me on my toes for this past year. Not like the kind of trouble getting custody of my son from my batshit-crazy ex was.

Fortunately, that's all over, and these days Becca's rabble-rousing mostly includes teaming up with my kid to pull pranks on me. Gotta say I kind of dig it.

But fuck if seeing her dressed up as a bridesmaid at her best friend's wedding isn't a whole new level of trouble. The tight red number looks like it was painted on every delicious curve of her body. I swear it makes her boobs look even bigger, if it's possible for a dress to do that.

"You in that dress is giving me all kinds of ideas," I murmur in her ear as we wait for the bride and groom to enter the reception hall. I lean away and sling an arm on the back of her chair.

She smirks at me, my feisty little hellion. "Please tell me you're not going to propose at my best friend's wedding," she replies with an eye roll.

I shake my head and smile. "Baby, when I ask you to marry me, you sure as hell aren't going to see it coming." She looks at me incredulously, and I give her a calm wink in return. I lean in so my mouth is next to her ear again. "Guess I'll have to say it in a way you'll understand: Just say when, and I'll find someplace private to f —"

"What can I get everyone to drink?" The voice behind me nearly makes me jump out of my chair. I lean back and look at the waiter who has appeared behind us. I can't help it, I glare at the bastard for interrupting what was going to be some damn good dirty talk. Guess I'll have to make her squirm later instead.

"We'll have champagne," Noah responds from across the table. Jules gives him an adoring little look. I hold back a laugh. Dude's got balls to order for her, but clearly she digs it. Becca would have mine in a vice if I did that.

"I'll just have water," Becca tells the waiter.

I briefly consider asking for a beer but decide against it. While the wedding is a small, informal event, that seems a little too casual even to me.

"Champagne's cool," I say with a shrug.

When I look back, Jules is giving Becca a weird look, and Becca is glaring daggers back at her friend.

"Did I miss something?" I ask, wondering if I'm going to have to step in the middle of a bitch fight. Weddings always bring this shit out in girls.

"Water?" Jules asks.

Becca shakes her head firmly. "Not gonna do this here, Jules," she says, and I know that warning in her voice. It's one I would heed immediately. And while Jules seems to defer to Noah, I know firsthand she's not about to do that with Becca.

"Come on, Becca. You know Noah and I are leaving for a few weeks after this too. You can't just tell me?" Jules looks at Becca like a sad puppy, and I'm more confused than ever.

"Guess I don't have to," Becca responds sarcastically. "But I'm sure as fuck not stealing the thunder on Sasha's big day."

Noah raises an eyebrow but says nothing. Does dude know something I don't?

"What's going on, baby?" I murmur so just she can hear.

"Nothing," Becca snaps, refusing to look at me.

Well, shit. This all went to hell in a handbasket quickly. I look at Jules helplessly.

"He doesn't know?" Jules asks archly.

Becca shakes her head, now clearly fighting tears.

Heads turn, but not toward us. Sasha's dad stands up near the entrance.

"All right, everyone, it's time to welcome the bride and groom," he calls.

I look at Becca. "Come on, talk to me," I say quietly, hoping with everyone distracted she'll tell me what's going on.

She shakes her head resolutely. For some reason, this whole thing is making me very uneasy. She's never been one to hold back, so whatever it is must be bad.

"Let's all welcome Dr. and Mrs. Caleb Thompson," he calls. The doors open, and a very happy-looking bride and groom enter to a round of applause and cheers from the small crowd.

"Becca, you're freaking me out here," I whisper. "Please, just tell me what's wrong."

Becca whirls on me as Sasha and Cal pass our table to get to the small one just beyond us set up for only them.

"I'm pregnant, Vincent, that's what's wrong," Becca snaps loudly.

Silence falls. And I swear every fucking person in the room is looking at us. But my brain stops and all I can think of is those two words. *I'm. Pregnant.*

Becca turns on Jules. "Happy now?" she demands.

"Oh my god," Sasha gasps, rushing over to our table.

"Well, this'll be a reception to remember," Cal jokes from behind her.

Jules is apologizing to Becca, but the sound fades out around me.

My ears buzz.

My vision swims.

"Vincent?" Becca's voice cuts through my shock. I blink up at her, and she's looking at Jules while angrily gesturing at me. "Great, Jules. You made me break Vincent."

"I'm not broken," I speak up hoarsely. "You're pregnant?"

Becca's eyes meet mine. I see fear there.

"Yes," she whispers. Then she clears her throat and looks at her friend. "I'm sorry, Sasha, I didn't meant to ruin your day. And, baby," she looks back at me, "I'm so sorry, I didn't mean for you to find out like this."

I've never seen her this worried, and it melts the shock right out of me.

"I'm gonna be a dad again," I say in awe. Then I jump up, grinning, and pull her into my arms. "Holy shit, I'm gonna be a dad again!" I can't contain myself.

The first time this happened I was too young to be happy about it. Everything was too fucked up. But this? This is fucking incredible. The woman I love, the woman I'm pretty sure is it for me, she's going to be the mother of my goddamn child.

"You're … okay with this?" she asks, pushing me back to look at my face.

I put my hands on her cheeks. "Are you fucking kidding me? We're having a fucking baby," I say intently. I drop my hands from her face and turn to our friends, now raising my hands over my head. Seriously, can't fucking control myself. "We're having a baby!"

Everyone laughs, and the clapping and cheering starts again. While the girls hug, Cal's the first to get to me. He doesn't even bother with the formal-British-dude handshake like usual, pulling me into a backslapping hug. Which, go figure, I happily return. Cloud-fucking-nine is a weird place.

"Congratulations," he says, clearly in no way bothered. But I still feel bad.

"Sorry to fuck up your day, man," I apologize. But I can't stop fucking grinning, so I'm sure I don't look that sorry.

He pulls back and laughs while Noah reaches out for a fist bump. There's a first.

"It's fine, really, I'm happy for you," Cal assures me. Sasha slides up next to him, and he wraps an arm around her.

"*We're* happy for you," she corrects, looking like a goddamn angel in her puffy white dress.

"Thanks," I reply, still grinning like an idiot. It's when I feel Becca pull at my arm. I look down at her. Her eyes are shining with tears. Though I hope they're happy ones this time. Everyone around us goes back to the reception, and Becca and I settle close to each other in our chairs.

"I thought you'd be mad," she says. "I was trying to figure out how to tell you."

I pull her against me, kissing her hair as she buries her face in my chest. "You should know me better than that," I murmur. "You and Elijah are my whole fucking world. And we've got so much love to give this guy." I lay a hand on her stomach.

"Girl," she whispers. "It's a girl."

"Yeah?" I ask with a laugh.

She shrugs. "Feels like one anyway," she replies, then smiles wickedly. "Thanks for being okay with this. I love you so damn much."

I lean down and kiss her firmly on her beautiful mouth. "Not as much as I love you," I murmur. "Do we get to tell Elijah when we pick him up from your mom's?"

She grins up at me. "Ohhh, let's tell them all. My mom is seriously digging this grandma thing, and my brothers are all home for our parents' thirty-fifth anniversary party. They're going to be just as happy as you are," she responds gleefully.

I shake my head. "Nobody's as fucking happy as I am, baby," I say seriously. "You wanna get married?"

She slaps me on the chest. "Well, you were right, I didn't see that coming, but damn, dude, you're gonna have to do a little better than *that*," she snaps.

I roll my eyes and dig the ring out of my pocket. The one I've been carrying for weeks, waiting for the right time. I hold it up between us.

"I really wasn't planning on doing this here, but if you insist," I tease her. "Marry me, Becca. Please. Make me the happiest fucking man on the planet. I want to do this right. Even before I knew, that's what I wanted, I've just been waiting for the right moment. You're an incredible fucking mother to Elijah already, and knowing we're going to have a baby girl —" Emotion gets the better of me, and I have to stop. I shake myself, fighting back tears. I don't need my chops busted for the rest of my life. I'd say by Noah and Cal, but frankly Becca is way worse in that department. That thought makes me laugh, giving me back a bit of control. "We're already a family. Let's make it official. What do you say? Be my forever girl?" I flex the ring between my fingers so the heart-shaped pink diamond catches the light.

"That is a pretty ring," she says with a smirk, then looking up at me from under her eyelashes. "And those were some very pretty words." She rests her chin on her palm, tilting her head and tapping her cheek as if in thought. "How about this: You *show* me whatever it was that you were going to say would happen in private before this whole shitshow started, then we have a deal."

I laugh and lean in. "You're telling me if I take you someplace and fuck you right now, then you'll agree to marry me?" Talk about a fucking win-win.

Her pupils dilate, and her tongue darts out to moisten her lips. I was already half-hard just saying it, but that sends me right over the edge.

"I'll meet you in the private bathroom by the kitchen in five minutes," she whispers. She stands up, excusing herself to use the ladies room.

I watch her go, laughing and shaking my head.

"What's so funny?" Jules asks curiously.

I laugh again, rising from the chair. "Nothing," I assure her. "I'll be back. I've gotta go seal the deal of a lifetime."

EPILOGUE — NOAH

When I first saw her, I knew she was everything I didn't know I needed. Like the missing piece of a puzzle I wasn't even aware I was putting together. I had everything, after all. I came from money, and I also had my own money. I had power. I had women. And plenty of all of it. At its best it was boring, save the few satisfying professional successes.

But Julianna Magnusson was a shot of fire in the darkness that set my world ablaze. One taste of her, and I was hooked in a way I never had been. A way that wouldn't let me rest until I had her. And the true test? She's owned me body and soul from the moment we met. Her passion for everything, her focus on what's important to her, made me remember what it's like to care.

These past two years have been a rollercoaster ride. I've been happier than I ever thought possible, only to spiral down into the depths of despair with her when her father passed away. We've seen one of her best friends get married and the other have a baby and an impending wedding herself. We've already agreed that the whole traditional marriage-and-kids route isn't for us, but I have no doubt that she's my forever.

What I haven't told her is that my father just laid down an ultimatum. One that will change both of our lives. I've gone slow with Julianna up until now. I know even letting her guard down to be with me was a lot to ask of her. Now I have to ask something else of her that's completely unfair.

At any other point in my life, with any other woman, this is the time I would've booked dinner at a pricey restaurant that ended with a gift of expensive jewelry and a night in bed that would never be forgotten. But Julianna isn't just any woman, and none of those things are going to impress her or distract her from the enormity of what I'm about to ask of her.

Instead, I spend all day Saturday shopping for and cooking her favorite meal, served with her favorite wine.

When I answer the door at eight, there she stands, gorgeous as ever in a simple pair of jeans and a T-shirt.

"Something smells good," she says by way of greeting.

I give her a small smile. "I cooked," I reply, stepping back to let her in.

"Well, that was sweet of you." She pauses to kiss me on her way by, and it's a welcome distraction. She hesitates, a hand on my chest. "You seem tense."

I raise an eyebrow. "Come in, let's have a drink and talk."

She raises an eyebrow right back, and I know she can tell something is up. Still, she lets me pour her a glass of wine and get seated on the couch next to her. The lasagna in the oven will keep, but apparently this conversation won't.

"My father called a family meeting today," I begin. "He wants to retire by the end of the year."

"And?"

"And … even though James is the eldest, he wants me to take over."

She sets her wine glass down on the coffee table, and I know I now have her attention.

"As in, you would be president of the Rutherford Group?" she asks, aghast. "That's … that's a lot, Noah. Wow." She goes quiet and pale as she takes it in. Exactly the reaction I was expecting. If I was the entitled rich boy she feared as director of operations, as president and CEO of the entire organization, well, that's a whole other level of power and influence.

"It is. So I turned it down." She looks up at me, gaping. "Actually, to be completely honest, I kind of quit."

Now, her eyes are practically bugging out of her head. "You quit?" she gasps. "Noah, I hope you didn't do that because of me."

I smile and shake my head. "Not like you're thinking," I reply with a small smile. "It's not want I want, Julianna. I want a life. With you. Running that company would take every bit of my time and energy."

"But you didn't have to quit. You could've just let James run the show, couldn't you?"

"I could've," I allow. "Except I had another opportunity come up this week. The group that owns the senior care facility your mother is in put out that they're looking for a buyer. Twelve facilities across San Diego County. I plan to put in an offer."

She waves her hands in front of her, signaling that this is all getting to be too much.

"Oh my god, Noah, that's insane," she finally replies. "Where do I even start with that?" She rubs her temples for a minute before looking up at me. "Where would you even get the kind of cash you'd need to do that?"

I shrug, leaning back into the couch. "I owned part of the Rutherford Group, which I'm selling to James. So, even if Dad doesn't want him to run the show, well, since he'll own a majority share, he kind of won't have a say. It'll be more than enough to cover taking over that operation."

"But … but … how?" she stutters. "I mean, isn't that going to be just as much work, if not more?"

I lean forward, looking deeply into her eyes. This is where I take a gamble. This is where I hope like hell she's willing to support me.

"Not if you help me run it," I say simply and seriously.

And she laughs. Not a small, ironic laugh. A full, body-shaking belly laugh that lasts a few minutes. Even my usually steely confidence slips a bit.

"Should I take that as a no?" I ask, unable to keep the snark out of my tone.

She bolts upright, eyes wide as she abruptly stops laughing. "Oh my god, you're serious?"

"Completely," I assure her. "When my father asked me to take over, I knew instantly it wasn't what I wanted. You've changed me, Julianna. Or maybe you've helped me be the man I've always wanted to be. Diseases and issues affecting the elderly have always been on my radar, they've always been my go-to for charitable events, volunteering, and press opportunities for the Rutherford Group. But they're more than that. This is what I want to do. You helped me realize that the privileges I have can make a difference. This is how I want to do it. But what I really want is to do it with you. We'd be unstoppable together, can't you see that?"

Her mouth settles into a little "o."

"Wow … I … I don't even know what to say to that, Noah," she admits. "That's huge. I mean … me? Really?"

I huff a laugh. "You don't see yourself, do you? You're highly educated, experienced, and have been instrumental in Rutherford Hospital's comeback to being one of the best hospitals in Southern California. Honestly, I think you're underutilized there at this point, and I wouldn't trust anyone else with the challenge."

"That might be the best compliment anyone has ever given me," she replies softly.

"Come here," I say, gesturing for her to scoot into me.

She does, and I can't help relishing the small ways she lets me be in charge. It shows me that she trusts me, and that's worth everything.

She folds herself into me, and I wrap my arm around her, staring down into her eyes.

"I know you're not a fan of big gestures or expensive things," I tell her. "But when this all came together, it felt like it was just for us. A project that combined our strengths toward something amazing. We'll be partners, in business and in life. But only if that's what you want."

She looks down, almost self-consciously.

"I guess I didn't think you thought of us that way," she mumbles.

My hackles rise, and I slip a finger under her chin, pulling her gaze up to meet mine.

"Then let me rectify that," I say firmly. "You are everything to me, Julianna, now and always. Nobody has ever challenged me or suited me better. I've never loved any woman as much as I love you. And neither of us may care about marriage or having our own children, but I want you by my side, every day, for the rest of my days. But I would do anything for you, so if you want something else, all you have to do is say the word."

Her eyes sparkle with tears as she looks up at me. And she's so heartbreakingly beautiful in this moment, I just want to touch her. But I refrain, letting her choose. Always letting her choose.

"I'm in," she finally says, a single tear finding its way out.

I wipe it away gently.

"For which part?" I ask.

She leans up and presses her lips gently to mine.

"All of it."

Something inside of me shifts, and her words sink deep into my heart.

"I'm going to take you to bed now," I murmur against her lips. "Because I love you too much right now to not be inside you."

She shudders beneath me. "What about dinner?"

I scoop her up and carry her toward my bedroom.

"Let it burn," I reply carelessly. "All that matters is you and me. And how much I fucking need you."

I settle her down onto my bed. She tugs at my shirt, pulling me toward her until our faces are close.

"Tell me you love me," she commands. But her stern tone is betrayed by her sly smile, and I know she's mocking how bossy I am in bed. The little minx.

"I love you," I reply without hesitation. "With everything I am. Now and always." I let my gaze go stern. "Now suck my cock and tell me you love me." And though I was going to pretend to be serious, even I'm not that domineering, and I can't help smiling after I say it.

She tips her head back and laughs. But her hands quickly unbutton and unzip me, stroking me until I'm hardening under her touch.

"I love sucking your cock, and I love you," she croons, licking up my shaft and flicking her tongue off the tip. "Now and always."

I reach down and tilt her face up to look at me.

"You own me, Julianna. Never doubt that. I'm yours. Completely, for as long as you want me."

She climbs up and wraps her arms around my neck. "I'll always want you, Noah. Never doubt *that*."

When our lips meet, I'm even more lost than I already was. I never could've imagined finding a woman who made me feel like I could do anything, like I could conquer the world. And we're going to do it together. Now and always.

THE END

A NOTE FROM THE AUTHOR

If you enjoyed this book, I would greatly appreciate if you would take a few moments to leave a review, even if it's just a sentence or two saying that you like the book and why. Reviews are valuable feedback that let both the author and other readers know that the book is an enjoyable read. When you leave a positive review it also lets the vendor know that the book is worth promoting, as the more reviews a book receives, the more they will recommend it to other readers. Regardless, thank you for reading this book, and for your support!

ACKNOWLEDGEMENTS

The end of another era, and there are so many thank yous that go along with it. To my husband, who supports me in every way imaginable. To my long-time friend and editor, Jenny, without whom I never would've published. To the indie author community, particularly Lindsey Powell, Eve Kasey, and Jacqueline Simon Gunn, all of whom, while also writing kick-ass romance novels themselves, find time to be amazing sources of support and encouragement to others. To the bookstagram community, who remind us every day of the beauty of reading and how it connects us all. And to all readers, even those who don't read my books, for an insatiable hunger for escape and wonder, without which an author's words would never be appreciated.

Coming December 3, 2020

LAST KISS UNDER THE MISTLETOE

CJ Roberts just wants to be a normal girl, have a normal job, normal friends, maybe even a normal boyfriend. Unfortunately, she's about as far from normal as it gets, because she can See the future. And like two sides of a coin, her twin brother, Matt, can See the past. Sounds like a neat party trick, right? Actually, it's frustrating and sometimes even dangerous. And if the past is any indicator, CJ can't do much to change what she Sees.

Drew Davies lives and breathes his job as a chef at one of the hottest restaurants in San Francisco. He's content to focus on his craft, and dating has always been on the back burner. That is, until he meets CJ. When sparks fly, things heat up quickly between them. It's an unexpected but welcome connection as the holidays approach.

But just as hope blooms, CJ has a vision that changes everything. She doesn't know how it will happen, but she knows Drew is going to die. Now she's left with a decision: Does she risk exposing herself to save Drew, or does she play it safe and let fate deal its hand? Secrecy has protected her until now, but can she really do nothing when the life of the man she's falling for hangs in the balance?

ABOUT THE AUTHOR

Melanie A. Smith is an award-winning and international best-selling author of steamy contemporary romance fiction. Originally from upstate New York, she spent most of her childhood in the San Francisco Bay Area before moving to Los Angeles for college. After that, she spent almost fifteen years in the Seattle Area, and now lives in the Dallas-Fort Worth area of Texas with her family.

A voracious reader and lifelong writer, Melanie's writing began at a young age with short stories and poetry. Having completed a bachelor of science in electrical engineering at the University of California, Los Angeles, and a master's in business administration at the University of Washington, her writing abilities were mainly utilized for technical documents as a lead engineer for the Boeing Company, where she worked for ten years.

After shifting careers to domestic engineering and property management in 2015, she eventually found a balance where she was able to return to writing fiction.

Melanie is also a Mensan and enjoys spending time with her family, cooking, and driving with the windows down and the stereo cranked up loud.

LINKS

For updates on my books, exclusives, giveaways, freebies, and more, sign up for my newsletter here:
https://mailchi.mp/melanieasmithauthor/signup

For exclusive swag, updates, giveaways, ARCs, and more, sign up my street team here:
https://mailchi.mp/melanieasmithauthor/romancereadersquad

Follow me on
Instagram: instagram.com/melanieasmithauthor
Facebook: http://fb.me/MelanieASmithAuthor
Twitter: https://twitter.com/MelASmithAuthor
Goodreads:
https://www.goodreads.com/author/show/18088778.Melanie_A_Smith
BookBub: https://www.bookbub.com/profile/melanie-a-smith

BOOKS BY MELANIE A. SMITH

The Safeguarded Heart Series
The Safeguarded Heart
All of Me
Never Forget
Her Dirty Secret (audiobook also available on Audible and iTunes)
Recipes from the Heart: A Companion to the Safeguarded Heart
Series
The Safeguarded Heart Complete Series: All Five Books Plus
Exclusive Bonus Material

Standalone Romance Novels
Everybody Lies
(audiobook also available on Audible and iTunes)
Last Kiss Under the Mistletoe (Coming December 2020)

Life Lessons: A series that can be read as standalones
Never Date a Doctor
Bad Boys Don't Make Good Boyfriends
You Can't Buy Love
The Heart of Rutherford: Life Lessons Books 1 – 3